...y'know it's gotta be... We want to express our thanks, too, y'know."

The WORLD'S STRONGEST REARGUARD | Labyrinth Country's Novice Seeker

**Misaki**
JOB: GAMBLER
The kind of girl who acts before she thinks. She is good friends with Suzuna.

**Kyouka**
JOB: VALKYRIE
Arihito's boss in his former life.

**Melissa**
JOB: DISSECTOR
An emotionless but highly skilled Dissector. Her mother is a demi-human.

**Madoka**
JOB: MERCHANT
A novice Merchant who assists new Seekers.

**Arihito**
JOB: REARGUARD
A former corporate
slave who is now in an
unidentified, all-powerful
support class.

**Theresia**
JOB: ROGUE
A demi-human girl
and former mercenary
who's grown attached
to Arihito.

**Elitia**
JOB: CURSED BLADE
A high-level Swords-
woman who teams up
with Arihito to save
her friend.

**Suzuna**
JOB: SHRINE MAIDEN
The daughter of a
Shinto priest. She was
reincarnated at the
same time as Arihito.

"I, Hidden God Ariadne, grant my devotee and his allies my protection!"

# The WORLD'S STRONGEST REARGUARD | Labyrinth Country's Novice Seeker

## 2

**Tôwa**

Illustration by **Huuka Kazabana**

Translation by Jordan Taylor
Cover art by Huuka Kazabana

SEKAI SAIKYO NO KOEI -MEIKYUKOKU NO SHINJIN TANSAKUSHA- Volume 2
©Tôwa, Huuka Kazabana 2018
First published in Japan in 2018 by KADOKAWA CORPORATION, Tokyo.
English translation rights arranged with KADOKAWA CORPORATION, Tokyo, through
TUTTLE-MORI AGENCY, INC., Tokyo.

English translation © 2020 by Yen Press, LLC

Yen On
150 West 30th Street, 19th Floor
New York, NY 10001

Visit us at yenpress.com
facebook.com/yenpress
twitter.com/yenpress
yenpress.tumblr.com
instagram.com/yenpress

First Yen On Edition: February 2020

Yen On is an imprint of Yen Press, LLC.
The Yen On name and logo are trademarks of Yen Press, LLC.

Library of Congress Cataloging-in-Publication Data
Names: Tôwa, author. | Kazabana, Huuka, illustrator. | Taylor, Jordan (Translator), translator.
Title: The world's strongest rearguard: labyrinth country's novice seeker / Tôwa ; illustration by
    Huuka Kazabana ; translation by Jordan Taylor.
Other titles: Sekai saikyo no koei: meikyukoku no shinjin tansakusha. English
Description: First Yen On edition. | New York, NY : Yen ON, 2019– |
Identifiers: LCCN 2019030466 | ISBN 9781975331542 (v. 1 ; trade paperback) |
    ISBN 9781975331566 (v. 2 ; trade paperback)
Subjects: CYAC: Fantasy. | Future life—Fiction.
Classification: LCC PZ7.1.T676 Wo 2019 | DDC [Fic]—dc23
LC record available at https://lccn.loc.gov/2019030466

ISBNs: 978-1-9753-3156-6 (paperback)
        978-1-9753-3157-3 (ebook)

10 9 8 7 6 5 4 3 2 1

LSC-C

Printed in the United States of America

# CONTENTS

# The Hidden God Awakens

Alone now that she'd teleported Arihito's party to the surface, Ariadne lowered her outstretched hand and wrapped her arms around her chest.

```
> ARIADNE activated TRANSFER TO SURFACE ⟶ ARIHITO'S
  party was teleported out of the labyrinth
```

The circuit-like pattern on her body glowed, and a "screen" appeared that displayed the current situation.

"Still functional... There must still be order in this world."

This order she spoke of was what allowed magic and skills to be used in the Labyrinth Country as well as in the labyrinths themselves.

Why were there entrances to labyrinths in the Labyrinth Country? Why were the dead of other worlds brought here? Ariadne couldn't remember how much time had passed since she'd been created, and she didn't have any memories that would give her the answers to those questions.

Such was the natural consequence of having been abandoned.

She was supposed to sleep forever in this room, deep below the earth where no one would ever visit, but then Arihito appeared with the key. It had been taken from her and tossed randomly into the labyrinth, but he had found the hidden stairs that led to her and brought with him the key in order to wake her.

"...For a human to do that..."

It was a miracle. She was vaguely aware of the concept based on the knowledge that all intelligent life shared.

Because she was now giving her protection to their party, she was able to learn from Arihito's license exactly how long she'd been asleep: 860 years. That's all the time that had passed since the construction of that miniscape, the place that contained all the labyrinths in which the Hidden Gods slept.

She hadn't been able to determine whether or not any of the other gods had been awakened. If Arihito and his party had already made a contract with another Hidden God, then...the door to this room would never have opened, and she would have remained asleep. The thought made Ariadne's chest twinge with a warmish, almost painful feeling. An emotion only those with limited lifespans should feel.

"Arihito... Steadfast rearguard. You who are endowed with such gifts..."

She had encountered Arihito's spirit when he placed the Activation Key in her. Unlike Ariadne, he wasn't lonely. But he'd lost his parents before he could even form a cohesive thought. He'd been scarred by the incident ever since, living with the regret that he hadn't been able to save them. He'd been witness to the cruelty of the world as a mere infant, sitting in the back seat of the car his father had been driving, his mother's arms still wrapped around him.

"…Is this…water…? Am I…?"

Ariadne noticed something running down her cheek and stopped it with her hand. She couldn't call the person who created her a "parent," but even though she kept trying to deny the similarities between her and Arihito's circumstances, she finally accepted that at the very core, they weren't really that different.

"If you intend to protect your companions from *behind*…then I will protect you from here."

The space around Ariadne warped to reveal a gigantic mechanical arm. She would use her remaining strength to protect Arihito and his party. She decided she wouldn't sleep until she heard his voice. After all, a god did not need to sleep.

# CHAPTER 1

# The Summit of District Eight

## Part I: The Caseworker's Shock

District Eight of the Labyrinth Country—the first district visited by those who had been newly reincarnated.

We had found our way to the hidden fourth floor in the beginner labyrinth, the Field of Dawn, and somehow managed to make it out without any serious injuries. We climbed up the long stairs that led from the first floor of the labyrinth back to town, noticing the moment we stepped out that the sun had moved significantly from where it had been when we entered. It was now evening. We crossed the square and headed westward to the Guild.

"Aaaah, I forgot how niiice fresh air is. The labyrinth is as bright and vast as it is out here, but it just feels different, you know," said Misaki happily with a big stretch. I still didn't know her full name. Her Gambler job had a lot of luck-based skills, and it was thanks to those skills of hers that we'd been able to find the hidden floor in the labyrinth in the first place.

"Mmm... Aaah, you're right; it really does feel nice," Igarashi agreed, extending her limbs, too. "Only the fourth floor really felt like a true *labyrinth*. It was definitely more claustrophobic." She was my manager in my previous life, where we worked at the same company, and now a member of the party with me as the leader. When we were first reincarnated, she'd been wearing a knit sweater and skirt, but now, her brown hair fell in soft waves around the Ladies' Armor she was wearing for her Valkyrie job. The armor was primarily white with a wide opening in the chest, which sort of stood out when she stretched. I had a hard time peeling my eyes away from her accentuated assets.

"Atobe, what're you staring at so intently?" she asked.

"Oh, uh, don't mind me. I was just thinking how glad I was we got out without getting hurt."

"I know… It's all thanks to you that we were able to defeat such a powerful monster," said Suzuna with a gentle smile. She was a childhood friend of Misaki's, and her job was Shrine Maiden. She looked like a traditional Japanese beauty with her straight, jet-black hair and rocked her special Labyrinth Country–version Shrine Maiden outfit.

We had encountered a Named Monster, so called because they had a set name, on the fourth floor of the labyrinth. It was a Giant Eagle-Headed Warrior, a very powerful enemy that could hit the entire party with multi-target attacks. We somehow managed to beat it because everyone worked so well together.

"……"

"You did a great job, Theresia. Thank you," I added. Theresia was a lizardman girl, a former mercenary who'd basically been my first companion here. She nodded readily when I expressed my gratitude, and the rest of the party smiled, too.

*Lizardman* was a misleading title; she wasn't some lizard-human hybrid. In fact, she really just looked like a girl in a lizard costume, except that she couldn't shed her equipment… That was one of the limitations of being a demi-human. Theresia's job was Rogue, and she served as the party's midguard, capable of both attack and evasion. She'd been helping me out ever since I first arrived here post-reincarnation.

"Arihito, are you sure you're okay? That last skill you used took a lot of magic, didn't it?" asked a concerned Elitia, a Swordswoman with a much higher level than the rest of the party. Certain circumstances, though, had led her to equip a cursed weapon, changing her job to Cursed Blade. She was a petite girl with golden hair separated into two pigtails, and she looked like she might have originally come from northern Europe. It made her look cute and sweet, but when it came to battle, she was our single most powerful attacker, capable of racking up huge amounts of damage.

Then there was me, the rearguard, a job that let me support these five girls from behind. After getting reincarnated, I had written *rearguard* down as my preferred job, and I was accepted just like that. I'm not sure if it was because I chose it, or if I was suited for it, but the job had helped my party climb the ranks faster than any other novice. The higher the rank, the better the quality of life, which meant that you didn't have to worry about your livelihood while you were also worrying about the risk of running into a strong monster out on an expedition.

"...Maybe this is just me, but when I'm up against an enemy with Arihito and he...calls out encouragement from behind, I feel really energized. You should keep that up," Elitia said to me.

"You're gonna make me blush if you keep saying stuff like that... But yeah, it's important to encourage one another." Calling out to my party members in battle was actually just my way of signaling that I was about to activate one of my skills, like Morale Support. But thinking about it, I guess I really did yell a lot during battle.

There wasn't a single monster in the labyrinths that you could let your guard down with. We needed to win every fight we found ourselves in and continue to seek without getting seriously injured—to achieve our goals.

For starters, we needed to turn Theresia back to her human form. She'd been resurrected as a demi-human after losing her life in the labyrinth.

Another was to make our way to the labyrinth in District Five, where Elitia's friend had been attacked and captured by monsters. We didn't know if her friend was dead or alive, but we were going to try and save her.

"Hee-hee, Arihito's kinda cute when he blushes. Don'cha think, Suzu?" asked Misaki.

"M-Misaki... That's not something I can just answer...," replied Suzuna.

"Looks like Atobe's not used to being complimented... Uh, I wonder if that's because I wasn't the kind of manager who praised my employees...," said Igarashi.

"N-no, that's not it. I think it's just part of my natural disposition."

Igarashi seemed a little apologetic at having remembered her time as my nightmarish manager. I had already moved on from it. I didn't know if she'd thought about how hard she had been on me in our previous life and was trying to change her ways, but ever since we were reincarnated and formed a party together, she'd been so nice to me that I could barely recognize her.

"......"

"...Th-thanks. You were complimenting me, weren't you?" I asked Theresia, who'd reached up and patted me gently on the head. She couldn't speak because she was a demi-human, but she could communicate in this manner... That said, I felt really awkward being pet by a girl who, based on her height, I could only guess was in her midteens.

We managed to make it to the Guild before they closed for the day. I waited until Louisa was done helping some other Seekers before she and I headed to the same special room where we'd talked yesterday. I told the girls they could do whatever they wanted while I reported, so they were outside the Guild hanging around until I finished. Apparently, it was the leader's job to report, but I guess we were just going to keep doing it like this regardless. I didn't mind at all either way; I found reporting to be one of the more enjoyable parts of seeking.

"Sorry, I might not smell the freshest. We just came back from the labyrinth," I said apologetically.

"What are you talking about? Sweat's proof of a Seeker's hard work, yes?" she replied cheerfully. I might be the type of guy who's easily swayed by women, but even if I weren't, I'd still turn to mush at a smile like hers.

"...L-Louisa, what are you doing?" I stammered as she came unexpectedly close to me. Maybe she was checking if I actually smelled since I was acting weird about it, but it was a little forward of her. Plus, I was flustered by how smoothly she'd managed to close the distance between us.

"Ha-ha... It's not enough to offend me, Mr. Atobe. You just smell like yourself." Louisa covered her mouth with her work folder and giggled. She wasn't acting like a caseworker; she seemed more like a good friend who felt comfortable letting her guard down around me.

*I get the impression that she isn't normally open with people, but she's obviously less guarded with me since we started working together... I have to be careful about how I act...*

"Would you mind excusing me for a moment? You can wait in the room while I go prepare some tea... Or perhaps would you like something stronger?" she asked.

"Uh... W-well, it's still light out... Would you share a drink with me, Louisa?"

"Would that be all right? Well, actually, a simple meal should be enough for me. It's bad for your health to drink every day." She seemed the type who'd like to drink every night if she could. Anyway, the Guild was pretty daring to serve alcohol to reporting Seekers.

"...I don't offer just anyone alcohol, by the way. Just for you, Mr. Atobe."

"O-oh. Ha-ha-ha..."

She'd probably get annoyed if I just said I wasn't sure what to make of that. I was pretty frustrated with myself for not being able to come up with a more tactful response.

I watched Louisa walk away to go prepare some tea, the soft material of her skirt clinging to her butt and emphasizing her curves. There was no safe place for me to look. The first day I met her, she'd struck me as so prim and proper, but my impression of her had changed quite a bit. I had to admit, I was happy to keep working hard to improve because it seemed like the better I did, the more she liked me.

I drank the iced herbal tea that Louisa brought and took a short rest before showing her my license. She pulled out her monocle, placed a hand on her chest, and took a deep breath before staring intently at the display.

"Let's take a look, then," she said.

```
◆Expedition Results◆
> Raided FIELD OF DAWN 3F: 40 points
> Raided uncharted territory in FIELD OF DAWN:
  Not evaluated
> ELITIA grew to level 9: 100 points
```

> Aʀɪʜɪᴛᴏ grew to level 4: 40 points

> Tʜᴇʀᴇsɪᴀ grew to level 4: 40 points

> Kʏᴏᴜᴋᴀ grew to level 3: 20 points

> Sᴜᴢᴜɴᴀ grew to level 3: 20 points

> Mɪsᴀᴋɪ grew to level 2: 10 points

> Defeated 8 Cᴏᴛᴛᴏɴ Bᴀʟʟs: 40 points

> Defeated 6 Pᴏɪsᴏɴ Sᴘᴇᴀʀ Bᴇᴇs: 48 points

> Defeated 12 Fᴀɴɢᴇᴅ Oʀᴄs: 120 points

> Defeated 7 Gᴀᴢᴇ Hᴏᴜɴᴅs: 140 points

> Defeated 1 Pʟᴀɴᴇ Eᴀᴛᴇʀ: 50 points

> Defeated 1 ★Gɪᴀɴᴛ Eᴀɢʟᴇ-Hᴇᴀᴅᴇᴅ Wᴀʀʀɪᴏʀ: Not evaluated

> Change in mutual trust with Tʜᴇʀᴇsɪᴀ: 100 points

> Kʏᴏᴜᴋᴀ's Trust Level increased: 50 points

> Sᴜᴢᴜɴᴀ's Trust Level increased: 50 points

> Eʟɪᴛɪᴀ's Trust Level increased: 50 points

> Change in mutual trust with Mɪsᴀᴋɪ: 100 points

> Awakened ???: Not evaluated

> Received ???'s protection: Not evaluated

Seeker Contribution: 1,018 points + unevaluated points

District Eight Career Contribution Ranking: 1


"……"

Louisa used her monocle to read the display, getting only to the second line, where she stopped and stared. It must've been the *uncharted territory* that got her... How should I jolt her out of this?

"…Louisa?"

"Eeeek?!" she shrieked and jumped in response, her chest jiggling so violently that it seemed about to pop out from her shirt's neckline. She was still shaken for a moment, but her face suddenly turned red—and she started fixing her hair, though there wasn't a single strand out of place, adjusted her shirt's neckline, and looked at me after clearing her throat.

"…I—I do apologize. I seem to have a breakdown every time I read your reports… You must be tired of it by now."

"Not at all… Even we were surprised ourselves. It seems like a lot of pieces just fell in place to make something entirely unexpected happen. Misaki's incredibly good luck played a large part."

"Ms. Misaki… She's the one who selected the Gambler job, correct? Her caseworker was originally one of my junior colleagues. Apparently, she desperately tried to write *badger gamer* as her job in the beginning. Quite unheard of for one so young."

It was the right decision to let Misaki join the party. If she hadn't met us, she most likely would have used her womanly wiles to make her way in the world. Having actually taken the time to speak with her, I'd learned that she was surprisingly innocent. She may look like a bit of a wild child, but deep down, Misaki was really quite earnest.

"Um… Mr. Atobe, are you…? Does a woman's age particularly bother you?"

"Age? No, I can't say I really care about that."

"…Oh, good."

"Hmm? Louisa, what did you just…?"

"I think I've found some motivation to work even harder," she chirped, ignoring my question… Her smile just then was perhaps the prettiest I'd seen on her since we met. But I couldn't just keep getting pulled off track like this.

I wondered if I could talk to her about the Hidden God we had found in the labyrinth. My license display showed we'd awakened *???*, so I would likely need to explain that to Louisa. Well, I'd just start from the top and work my way down. Louisa should understand if I could explain everything clearly.

"Louisa, about where it says *not evaluated*…"

"Yes, I was quite surprised myself… It's been a long time since I've seen that. It means that no person who achieved that particular result has ever returned to the Guild."

"Is that what it means? …Is it Guild policy for information regarding the discovery of uncharted territory to belong to the Guild as well as the Seeker?"

"No, anything discussed in this room will remain between you and me. Any report I make to the higher-ups in the Guild is only done with the Seeker's approval. The last thing the Guild wants is to ruin its relationship with excellent Seekers, so there is no policy that requires us to force information from a Seeker."

I guess, in other words, the Guild pretty much let Seekers do what they wanted, which I could sort of understand. The higher-ups couldn't coerce the Seekers to do something if they were actually weaker than the high-ranking Seekers. Still, my party was just getting started, so it wouldn't have been impossible for them to make us cough up the details to follow some regulation.

*So the reason they don't…must be, more than anything, that they want to encourage Seekers to gain experience and get stronger. But still…*

"…I know what you're thinking," said Louisa. "The current policy means the Guild will be unable to restrain the higher-ranking Seekers should they go out of control. Everyone has considered that possibility, which would lead to the disruption of order in the Labyrinth Country."

"But that hasn't happened. Does that mean every single high-ranked Seeker is hard-working and honest?"

"I wouldn't quite go that far. However, the more gifted Seekers who scale the ranks tend to prioritize exploring the labyrinths over influencing others. One reason for that is…the Secret Gods. I never would have thought you might come by one at such an early stage but find one you did—and even received their protection."

So Louisa did know about the Hidden Gods, but she didn't know that one had been sleeping on a concealed floor in the Field of Dawn. She likely didn't know the finer details surrounding the Hidden Gods, either. Her shock would make sense, assuming the Guild informed its employees about the gods' existence and nothing more.

"Mr. Atobe, I will tell you everything I know. The Founder of the Labyrinth Country created the teleportation gates to the various 'forgotten labyrinths' within the city's walls for seeking purposes. In other words, the country itself was established after the labyrinth entrances were gathered inside the city walls."

"...Why gather the labyrinths? Doesn't the fact that they were forgotten imply that they aren't of any value?"

"That's not the case. There are many mysteries regarding the labyrinths. Monsters and obstacles were put in place to prevent people discovering the treasures hidden deep within. Only the wisest and most powerful Seekers can unlock the secrets... However, there are many labyrinths where all those who have entered have died, and therefore, they've been abandoned. Even now, entrances to forgotten labyrinths are added under everyone's nose. And that can be attributed to people who still travel outside the city walls to continue to uphold the Founder's wishes, even though the Founder is no longer with us."

While they left exploring the labyrinth to the Seekers entirely, they continued to gather entrances...calling on the souls of the dead from other worlds, reincarnating them, and forcing them to become Seekers to seek in the labyrinths. If this "Founder" was capable of all that, then they likely had power rivaling the Hidden Gods, maybe even more. They might not be around anymore, but they definitely existed in the early days of the Labyrinth Country.

"I'm only relaying the message I got when I became an employee of the Guild, not from personal experience... This is more like an explanation you might find in a textbook," said Louisa.

"No, that's perfectly fine. These Secret Gods seem to have become an object of worship within the Labyrinth Country. Can you tell me why that is?"

"Because they are entities that provide protection to the Seekers. I have also heard that there is a certain amount of hostility between the gods themselves... But thankfully, there have been no fights between Seekers in District Eight because there are so few Seekers who have received that protection."

"In District Eight... Meaning there are fights in the higher districts between parties who have received protection from the Hidden Gods?"

"Unfortunately, yes. The Hidden Gods are deserving of our worship, but they are also sacred beings whose wrath you should not incur. In the event that two gods must fight, the Guild sanctions a location and intervenes if necessary. This is all to preserve the Labyrinth Country as it is."

I could just about imagine how fierce the battles between Hidden Gods could get based on Louisa's explanation. The country seemed to view the events as threats to the nation in the same way as accidents that might occur from someone attempting to open a treasure chest. Hopefully, we could avoid running into a god hostile to Ariadne, although I'd have to think of a way to prevent any actual combat from occurring if we did happen to encounter one.

"Now I understand that seeking out the gods is the greatest goal of a Seeker. Obviously, my abilities are limited, but I'll take extra caution in order to prevent anything terrible happening to the Labyrinth Country," I said.

"I'm grateful to hear you say that. I will do everything I can to gather more information on the topic from the Guild, as you request. The Guild receives a report whenever anyone who has a contract with a god is causing a disturbance, so I will be able to provide you with advance notice."

*She always works so hard to help me*, I thought. I imagined her opinions would hold more weight in the Guild as her reputation increased as well.

"Louisa, as our caseworker, does it also work in your favor if we continue to produce good results?"

"Y-yes... A caseworker receives a promotion if a party leader they are assigned to advances to a higher district."

"In that case, I'll have to make sure we keep working hard. I want to make sure you never regret being assigned to our party. I have to repay you for everything you've done for me."

"That makes me very happy to hear." Louisa smiled, her cheeks tinged pink. The lighting made her red lips look so supple and alluring...but I couldn't keep staring or my karma would go up.

"...I don't think your karma will go up now," she told me.

"Uh...?"

"N-never mind... It's nothing. I'm getting too ahead of myself... I'll exercise restraint tonight and just cook for myself at home. I'll never be able to face your party if I don't."

"Oh... Okay, I'll invite you some other time. Anyway, about this *not evaluated* part..."

"I will write a report about this section and investigate. I imagine your contribution points will be incredibly high after that, so it's likely you'll be able to move to District Seven without taking the test. How does that sound?"

No way I could turn down a free pass. Still, I was curious what the test entailed. I might be interested anyway, as long as it wasn't dangerous.

"I'm a little curious about what's on the test. Am I not allowed to know the contents unless I take it?" I asked.

"The test involves entering one of the labyrinths in District Eight and retrieving specific items or defeating monsters. The specified labyrinth changes each time the test is given, so unfortunately, I cannot tell you the specifics ahead of time…"

"No, that's all right. I'll have to discuss it with the party, but I think we might actually take it."

"Understood. Should you choose to take the test, it will be administered in two days. Please give me your final request to participate by the end of the day tomorrow."

I was curious how many contribution points I'd get for the four unevaluated items, but I was more focused on District Seven, since we'd be moving up there soon.

The next thing I needed to do was to go drop the things we collected off at the Dissection Center. I decided to ask the Carriers to take the things we sent to our storage unit to the Dissection Center for us, then meet everyone at our usual gathering point: the square in front of the Guild.

## Part II: Guard Dog

Once I finished my report to Louisa, I did my best to hold back my urge to see what new skills I could learn, instead deciding to wait until I got back home to take a good look. I didn't know how much information about my skills would spread if someone happened to sneak a peek while I was using my license and saw my skill list. Plus, I was starving; I wanted to meet back up with everyone and grab a bite to eat—but I saw some trouble going down as soon as I walked out of the Guild.

*Aren't those...Falma's kids and their silver hound...? Did they get caught up in some sort of trouble?*

"Your dumb mutt ran into me on purpose. How're you gonna make up for that?"

The speaker was a guy with shaved lines in his hair. He looked like the kind of thug you'd see covered in tattoos. Seemed he was trying to start something with the silver hound.

The huge dog with silvery fur was standing in front of the children, Eyck and Plum, and glaring back. No bystanders were trying to intervene and break things up—probably because the guy looked likely to blow up on anyone who did.

"Hey, hold up. I know these kids," I called out.

"Huh? Well, ain't that perfect. This stupid mutt got its damn hair on my leather shoes. You can pay for the damage... Three gold, and I'll forget the whole thing," he replied.

*Did he target the kids to try and shake them down for money? What a lowlife.*

He most likely decided the amount to demand when he saw me. Three gold wasn't an astronomical fee, and I guessed he could only be level 2 or maybe even 3. But I was just a rearguard; my role was to support allies. Personally, I didn't have much strength to speak of. I probably wouldn't come out unscathed from a one-on-one fight with someone near my level. There was also the problem of accruing karma; I couldn't imagine getting out of this without a fight.

"...Could I speak with the children for a moment?" I asked.

"Heh, you plannin' on squeezing some cash from these kids, too? Makes no difference to me how I get paid, but I'm a busy man. Make it quick," he replied.

I got the impression that your karma would go up if you made threats, but the man had played things well so that the silver hound had hit him first.

"Oh...! You came to our house that one time," said Eyck.

"Cion didn't run into anybody! That man was about to bump into Eyck, and Cion just—," started Plum.

"Shut up, you little snot! My license shows your mutt attacked me!" shouted the man.

"Eep...!"

My conscience wouldn't let me just walk away from an adult trying to pull a fast one on some children.

*But if we fight here in the middle of the street, my karma'll go up, and the guards will come and arrest me... How should I handle this?*

Cion, the silver hound, remained alert and was still staring at the man. I imagined he was probably stronger in a fight than a low-level Seeker, considering he was used to being the children's guard dog—that, and the fact he stood an impressive six feet tall.

"...Eyck, Plum. Think I could borrow Cion for a little bit?" I asked.

"Uh... L-lend? How do I...?" stammered Eyck.

"Um, o-okay... Eyck, look! The thing you got from Mommy!" said Plum as she reached into the back pocket of Eyck's shorts and pulled out a license. Cion and I hid the kids from view as Eyck pulled up the party list.

◆Current Status◆
> Cion was transferred to Arihito's party

*All right, that worked. I think we're ready.*

"...Hmm? What're you mumblin' about? Trying to get the dog to cover you? How pathetic," said the man. He also seemed to be a reincarnate like me, but he'd done nothing but make me dislike him, so I couldn't say I felt any kinship with him.

I needed to get him to come at us first... I wasn't very good at being openly mean, but I tried to choose my words to provoke him.

"Cion's done nothing wrong. Apologize to the kids, and I'll let it slide this time."

"You're actin' real high-and-mighty... I gave you a chance. Even if I attack that dog once, I won't get any karma for it. You know what that means?"

"So you're gonna hurt a dog? Even if the karma on your license doesn't go up, you think the people who see that are just going to let it go?" I said.

"Karma decides everything. You can't do nothin' to me just standin' there like an idiot!" The man pulled out a knife and went after Cion. Would karma even out if he tried to kill Cion, despite only being run into by him? As hard as it was to understand, he must've been planning to use Cion as an example to threaten us, since Cion was bound by karma and couldn't defend herself.

I put Eyck and Plum behind me, trying to reassure them, since they were both trembling.

"Don't worry, everything's gonna be all right. Cion isn't going to get hurt."

◆Current Status◆
> Arihito activated Defense Support 1 ⟶ Target:
                                                    Cion
> Jack's attack hit Cion
No damage

"Huh?!"

I could hear a cry of surprise as the man's knife bounced back before it touched Cion, who had stepped in front of me.

"I—I must be seeing things... It's just a dog; it doesn't have anyone in its party who can use support magic...," said an onlooker.

"Maybe it's not what it looks like?"

"Is that dog super strong?"

"Urgh... S-say whatever you want; this is all your fault!" shouted the man before shifting his attention to me.

But as soon as he tried to go around Cion and attack me, Cion reacted quickly and put herself between me and the man to cover me.

```
◆Current Status◆
> Arihito activated Defense Support 1 ⟶ Target:
                                            Cion
> Cion activated Covering ⟶ Target: Arihito
> Jack's attack hit Cion
No damage
> Jack's karma increased
> Cion's karma decreased
```

"Agh... I didn't do nothin'! He just jumped in front of me all of a sudden!" cried the man in a panic. Cion wasn't hurt, but since she jumped in front of me, she ended up taking the man's attack. Even with no damage, the man's karma went up when he tried to attack...which meant that we could return a single attack. Cion slowly turned to stare at the man, who seemed to misinterpret the gaze as a threat and gripped his knife tighter.

"—Get him, Cion!" I shouted.

```
◆Current Status◆
> Cion activated Tail Counter ⟶ Hit Jack
Knockback
11 support damage
> Jack was knocked unconscious
```

"Gah?!"

It happened in the blink of an eye. Cion swung her large, fluffy tail at the speed of lightning, smacking the man right in the side of the head, the impact enough to send the man flying. The man landed headfirst with a crash in a garbage can on the side of the street and lay there immobile. That was finally enough to draw over some armored guards. The karma should've been evened out with that, but the guards mercilessly picked up the garbage can the man was in and carried it away.

"…Waaaahhh…!!" Plum came rushing toward me, wailing.

"I'm s-so glad…you guys are okay…" Eyck himself was doing everything he could to hold back his tears, delighted to see us unharmed.

"You were brave, Eyck," I told him. "You're a good big brother… You did great."

"Gh…gah…waaaaaaahh!"

He must have been on the edge of breakdown, because the moment I patted his head, he burst into tears and wrapped his arms around my legs. No surprise, considering they were so young and had just been through something scary.

"…Geez, Atobe. You're lucky that dog is strong. You shouldn't be so reckless," chided Igarashi. We usually met up nearby, so she must have heard the ruckus and come over. Sounded like she saw Cion and I fight together, too.

"She's such a brave, strong dog. She helped me pluck up a bit of courage, too," I replied. Cion was still monitoring the area as she tried to continue to protect us. I thought about all the people who'd just watched the situation unfold and hadn't tried to step in and help, but in the end, them not getting involved meant that fewer people were hurt. The man named Jack just panicked, not knowing what to do—I guess scammers weren't the most levelheaded bunch.

"*Hic*... You were so cool, big bro..."

I was kinda relieved that Plum called me *big bro* as opposed to *mister*, even though it meant Eyck and I shared the same title.

The two seemed to understand somehow that I had helped Cion out. They didn't know that I'd done it with my rearguard skills; all they knew was that I'd protected them somehow.

"Thank you. I'll tell Mommy that you saved us."

"Just tell her Cion protected you. Don't worry about the rest," I replied. I didn't want them to worry about the possibility that the man would come back for revenge. Even better, hopefully the man would just forget everything that happened. Hey, totally plausible, since Cion's Tail Counter knocked him out completely.

Once Eyck and Plum had finally dried their tears, Cion came over and sat down in front of me.

"…Awoo."

"…Wh-what's up? That was a cute bark for such a big dog," I said.

"I think he likes you. Dogs act really submissive toward people they approve of," said Igarashi.

"He says he wants you to pet him. Cion begs people he likes to give him pats," added Plum.

"You wanna pet him, too, miss? Cion's a good boy; he won't mind," offered Eyck. The excitement on Igarashi's face was plain as day, so even the kids noticed. She looked at me as if to ask if it really was all right, and I replied with a smile and a nod.

"…He's so fluffy. It makes me think of the doggy my parents had… I wonder how he's doing now," she cooed, stroking Cion's fur with hands that seemed accustomed to petting dogs. Cion seemed to enjoy it, but he also looked at me like he was hoping I'd pet him, too.

*Even at almost six feet tall, he's still got those puppy-dog eyes… He may be big, but he seems to like being pampered.*

"Ah… K-Kyouka! What are you doing, getting distracted by a dog? Weren't you going to go meet up with Arihito?" asked Elitia suddenly.

"Ellie, Arihito's right here," said Suzuna.

"Hey-o, Arihito! Wooooow, look at this giant pupper! He's so big that it's a bit scary… But I still kinda want to stick my face in his fluff!" exclaimed Misaki. Both she and Suzuna also seemed to like dogs, since they both started to pet Cion with Eyck and Plum's permission. Theresia held back, hiding behind me for a bit, but Cion was so well-behaved that she eventually gathered her courage and reached a hand out to pat him on the head.

"......"

"Oh, good, you're not totally terrified by dogs, then," I said to her. However, it didn't seem like she'd completely overcome her fears; Theresia went back to hiding behind me after petting Cion for a moment. Eyck and Plum smiled in amusement, their tears from a moment before now a thing of the past.

"Right... Shall we take the children home?" I said.

"You think that'll be okay?" asked Igarashi.

"Yaaay! Big sis is coming along, too!" cried Plum.

"Wh-what the heck? She seems to really like me all of a sudden," said Igarashi, confused as Plum clung to her. I suddenly remembered something Falma had said as I watched the two of them.

"Falma said something once about how she admired Valkyries... Maybe Plum feels the same," I said.

"Big sis is so cool! I wanna be a big, strong woman someday!" exclaimed Plum.

"...You don't want to be a Swordswoman? Maybe I just don't come off as mature enough," said Elitia enviously.

"Ellie, don't get yourself down," Suzuna consoled her. "You're an amazing Swordswoman." At level 9, Elitia was very easily the strongest person in our party, but she was still as sensitive as you would expect from someone her age.

*Anyway... Incredible that Cion is so skilled. A guard dog, huh...*

Cion was still in my party. I decided to return her once we got to Falma's house. I looked at her as she walked by my side, and I had to admit, I really wanted a dog like her.

# Part III: Parents and Children

When we arrived at Falma's shop, Eyck and Plum rushed into their mother's arms as she came out to meet us.

"Goodness… What happened, you two?" she asked.

"Um, ummm… A bad man tried to be mean to Cion, but that guy saved us!" said Eyck excitedly. As she crouched down to talk to him, her apron stretched across her ample chest. Obviously, a mother is gonna dote on her child, but I had to avert my eyes for a little bit.

"Mr. Atobe, thank you so much. I'm the one who should be protecting the children, but you went to such trouble…," Falma started.

"It's all right. I'm just glad I happened to be passing by at the time. I couldn't let someone steal a kid's allowance."

"Thank you, Mr. Atobe! I have a present for you!" said Plum as she tried to give me a piece of candy she had clutched in her tiny hand. I wasn't sure if I should accept it, but Igarashi pulled a bit of candy from her pouch and handed it to Plum in exchange.

"Are you sure? Thank you, big sis!" said Plum.

"I like sweet things, too. I hope you like this one." Igarashi bent down to stroke Plum's hair. The street Falma's shop was on was peaceful, and everyone seemed to be smiling.

"People shouldn't be doing such awful things in town where they can rack up karma… But I suppose there are a few who will find some sort of loophole," said Falma.

"Cion was trying to protect Eyck and Plum when she ran into that poor excuse for a man. She really is a brave dog," I said.

"...Woof!" She seemed to recognize she was being praised. Falma's eyes grew large at the sight.

"My... Has Cion grown fond of someone else? Silver hounds aren't supposed to open up to anyone but their master, but it seems like she likes you, Mr. Atobe."

"'Cause Cion knows he protected us," said Eyck.

"Mr. Atobe's so cool! Just being with him, it's like there's some sorta magic that—"

"P-Plum, shhh. Can we keep that our little secret?" interrupted Igarashi.

"Why?" asked Plum.

"Arihito gets embarrassed reeeally easily. If you compliment him, he blushes and runs away," Misaki hastily explained.

"Really? Okeydoke, I'll keep it a secret!" I mean, I understood why Plum wanted to mention my role as a rearguard, and I didn't think word would get out even if she did say it. But whatever.

Cion had likely become so attached to me because I'd supported her. Looks like I'd proved that support increased Trust Levels even while outside the labyrinth, even though my license only showed that the fight between us and Jack had happened.

"I'm so very sorry; the children just get so curious about everything," said Falma.

"No need to apologize," I replied. "Actually, Falma, I was wondering if you might know of a place where I could meet a guard dog like Cion."

"Have you taken a liking to Cion as well? Ha-ha... And you—Ms. Igarashi, was it? You seem to love dogs yourself," said Falma.

"Yes, I used to have a dog... Atobe, are you thinking of getting a dog like Cion?"

"Whoa, are you getting a dog just for Kyouka?" asked Misaki.

"Oh... C-congratulations. I can tell that you two have been really close since before you met us if you're thinking of owning a dog together," said Suzuna.

"N-no, it's not like that. Igarashi was my manager before, so I'm just like her employee." I tried to explain things, but that only seemed to anger Igarashi. She had said before that it was almost like she'd become the employee now, so maybe I should have respected that? I still didn't understand women.

"And I thought that we'd started to build a more trusting relationship now that we're in a party... I guess nothing's really changed from before we were reincarnated, if you still feel that way," said Igarashi.

"Th-that's not true. We're a party; we work together, and I can rely on you and..."

"Ha-ha... Mr. Atobe, you do seem to be such a serious soul," chuckled Falma, stroking her children's heads. "From where I stand, it looks like the entire party has a strong bond, including Ms. Igarashi. Sometimes, I wish I could experience adventures with such friends... Although, I'm quite content with my current life."

While she was talking, Cion seemed to react to something in

the shop's entrance. What came out was a silver hound that was significantly bigger than Cion.

"Falma, you have two dogs?"

"Yes, this is Cion's mom. Cion's only two years old, and look at how big she is," replied Falma. The mom dog had a scar over one eye and gave off an impression you would expect from the massive war dogs of old, but when she saw Cion, she went over to her and started licking her and cleaning her fur.

"She was away for a little while helping the Guild and just came home today."

"Did she? I imagine it must be comforting to have two strong dogs in your home," I commented.

"Indeed it is. I don't think it's particularly unsafe here, but there's always someone with ill intentions... Oh, Cion...!" Cion had left her mom to walk over to me and stare at me. It looked like she was waiting for some sort of command...but she wasn't my dog, so I couldn't really order her around.

"Mr. Atobe, if you like, would you want to try taking Cion with you the next time you go on a seeking expedition?" offered Falma.

"Ah... Would that be all right? She would certainly help us out a lot..."

"Cion's father also works as a guard dog. I think Cion gets bored being stuck in town all the time, so I'd love for her to be able to experience seeking at least once... She's never been attached to anyone but us, so I had been planning to let her go with Eyck when she's old enough to seek. But Cion's gotten quite attached to you, too, so if it wouldn't be too much trouble..."

If Cion came along with us, the party's defense would become even stronger, since she could use Covering. I did feel a little uncomfortable using Falma's dog as a shield...but we shouldn't encounter too many difficult battles if it was only labyrinths in District Eight.

"What do you think? If you're not comfortable doing it...," started Falma.

"No, I'm actually worried about the opposite. Cion would help us so much... Would you like to come seek with us?" I asked Cion, holding out my hand. She lifted one heavy paw to shake, trying not to scratch me with her nails. Her paw pads were surprisingly squishy.

*That means Theresia will have to be around her. But I think I can use my skills to make Trust Levels increase even for relationships that wouldn't normally improve. Since neither of them can talk, it'll depend on how we do things, but here's hoping they'll get along eventually.*

"Would you mind petting Cion? She loves it," said Falma.

"Yeah, sure... Do you like this?" I said as I stroked Cion's head. She started to move and then flopped on the ground, rolling over to show her fluffy belly.

"She looks so blissed out... Arihito, you sure you weren't a dog breeder or something in your past life?" asked Misaki.

"You're right... She's so cute. A gentle giant," said Suzuna.

"See, Atobe, you don't have to be so intimidated by her," added Igarashi.

"It's been a long time since I've petted a dog... I think I'm getting used to it, though. What's wrong, Elitia?" Elitia was sneaking glances in our direction every so often. She hesitated for a moment before deciding to speak.

"...Can I pet him, too?" she asked.

"Of course. Theresia, you wanna try petting him again?" Theresia would have to get used to Cion, too, if Cion was going to join our party. She seemed to understand that, so she came over with Elitia, and they both reached out to touch Cion's soft belly.

"......"

"Cion seems to like that," commented Falma. "She isn't wary around demi-humans, so you have nothing to worry about." Theresia nodded back. Elitia was silently absorbed in stroking Cion's tummy—it looked like my party had a lot of animal lovers..

## Part IV: The Dissection Center

Falma invited us to stay for dinner, but since I still wanted to make it to the Dissection Center in time, unfortunately, I had to decline. I decided I should try to take her up on the offer some other time while we were still in District Eight.

"Ah, Mr. Arihito. You've got quite a few companions with you," noted Rikerton when we walked in.

"Yeah, I'm lucky that I keep finding new friends. Seeking is going well, too."

"Just a short while ago, I received a delivery of materials from your storage unit. The joint dissection of Juggernaut is also complete, so I can give you the report for that and let Melissa dissect the new materials."

Just then, Melissa came out from the back of the shop dressed casually in a shirt and shorts with a yet-unsoiled apron over her clothes.

"...The Carriers just delivered your monsters—Gaze Hounds and a Plane Eater. Can I dissect them?" she asked.

"Yes please. Sorry I didn't get anything rarer," I replied.

"They're rare enough. Be better if they were Named, but Plane Eaters aren't common." She walked over to a table that had the monsters laid out on top, tied a rope around the Plane Eater's foot, and hoisted it up.

"...It's fresh, since you caught it today," she said, licking her lips in a way that was almost inappropriately seductive for a girl her age, and picked up a butcher's knife.

"—Hah!"

She made one swing. Just with that, the Plane Eater's body was sliced open. It was followed with a series of small, fast strokes, and the parts—the materials from the Plane Eater—started to fall onto the table. There was less blood flying about than I would have expected. I felt like I was watching a master of their craft.

"I guess people do really eat chameleon meat, too...?"

"It's considered one of the finest meats of all the monsters in the Field of Dawn. Some of it is used in cuisine... You almost never see a Named one captured, but the meat on those is on par with the finest cut of beef on the market. The stronger the monster, the tastier its meat," explained Rikerton.

"R-really...? But I bet no one would eat Juggernaut meat, though, right?" I asked.

"We don't, no, but its large hunks of meat can be used as bait to distract dragon-type monsters. Different breeds have different eating habits, but the dragons in the Sleeping Marshes prey on anything. Even a level-three party can just about take down one if they prepare large amounts of bait to lure it in."

Monster meat could be used as bait to lure other monsters... I guess even the labyrinths had their own food chain. Now I understood why Cotton Balls were so hostile toward us: We preyed on them.

"When you say *just about*, you mean some parties lose, right? I wonder what happens to them...," said Misaki.

"Eighty percent of novice Seekers remain in District Eight after one year. Fifteen percent never make it back from an expedition," replied Rikerton. "That percentage decreases the higher you go in the districts. Even if they aren't completely annihilated, promising Seekers dying or coming back as demi-humans are an everyday occurrence. So very unfortunate..." He closed his eyes for a moment, almost as if in prayer, but once he opened his eyes again, he'd returned to a gentle smile. "Although, I have heard there's a way to return demi-humans to their previous form. I believe the labyrinths hold the hopes left behind by the Seekers."

"I believe the same. I decided I would do everything it took to return her to her human self when she joined my party," I said. Rikerton looked at Theresia, who didn't seem to understand why she was being stared at. However, she returned his gaze, and he suddenly looked very serious.

"I may have worded things as if it had nothing to do with me, but in reality, I have been searching for a way to return a demi-human to their previous state for a very long time."

"Rikerton... What do you...?" I asked.

"My wife lost her life in the labyrinth once. She came back as a demi-human."

He had told me that he'd gone on adventures with his wife when they were young.

Yet, I hadn't seen a sign of his wife... And this was why.

"My wife died in a labyrinth in District Seven. She was discovered a month later by a search party, having turned into a demi-human. She was pregnant with Melissa at the time. I only realized after living with my wife as a demi-human for three months."

"...That must have been so hard. And your wife...?" I said.

"She's traveling with an acquaintance's party. She has to travel with skilled Seekers and climb the ranks in order to find a way to return to being human. She's become an even better fighter after turning into a demi-human. I'd just hold her back."

"So that's why you've been raising Melissa apart from your wife...," I said, and Rikerton nodded. Melissa didn't seem to notice our conversation. She had sliced open the Plane Eater's abdomen and was retrieving something shiny from inside.

"Melissa's never had much interest in things most kids like. The only thing she's ever shown a passion for was my job—dissecting monsters. She must have been born with the talent, since her skills have already surpassed mine. Every once in a while, we'll go in the labyrinth to keep our levels up. It's a bit embarrassing to admit, but she ends up protecting me instead of the other way around."

Children could inherit skills, so Melissa had inherited Rikerton's skills and developed them while she was still a child.

"The thing is, lately, I've been thinking that it's about time Melissa starts thinking about becoming independent. I think it's a waste of her youth for her to sit here helping me out with the shop, just waiting for the occasional rare monster to come in... How about you, Mr. Arihito? How do you feel about adolescence?"

"Uh... W-well, I can't say I had much of an adolescence, I guess, but I suppose I did do some things when I was young."

"Arihito, were you ever a troublemaker?" asked Misaki. "You sometimes get suuuper intense, like when we're all in a tight spot."

"I...guess he does. But I think it's just because he has a strong heart...," amended Suzuna.

"He's just really brave. It doesn't even have anything to do with his level... He's just a gutsy type of person," said Elitia.

"That's true, but I also feel like he's just old for his age... Sometimes, he's practically like a big brother to me," said Igarashi.

"R-really...?" I'd never led an incredible life like everyone seemed to think of me. I worked a few different part-time jobs and got some life experience, before I decided to put everything I had into studying to live a decent life. People had always told me that

I was pretty down-to-earth, so I guess that was just part of my personality.

"Um… Rikerton, it sounds like you want Melissa to be able to make the most of her adolescence, yes?" asked Igarashi, her cheeks turning a little pink from saying this all out loud.

"I do," he replied, looking at Melissa. "Though, I bet if I try to act like her dad, she'll tell me I'm being overbearing."

"…No I wouldn't," said Melissa.

"Ah… Melissa, you heard that? Sorry, did we distract you?" asked Rikerton. Melissa had come over to us carrying what looked like a magic stone she'd gotten from the Plane Eater. Her eyes made her look like she was half-asleep, but there was a shine in them as she looked at the stone that revealed a fascination for monster parts.

"The Plane Eater had a camouflage stone. You can blend into surroundings if you equip it. A great find," she commented.

"Wow… That's amazing," I said.

"Blending into your surroundings, huh. That sounds like active camouflage. I remember that from before I was reincarnated," said Rikerton. So apparently, Rikerton was a first-generation reincarnate. Melissa, as a second-generation, didn't seem to recognize the phrase *active camouflage*, because she just looked confused. "Ah, don't worry about it. I think a fellow man like Mr. Arihito will know what I'm talking about. Active camouflage is something of a man's fantasy."

"Ha-ha, you're right. But if I just blatantly equip it…," I started.

"What are you talking about, Atobe? Of course you're going to use it. As our rearguard, you can't have too many ways of keeping enemies off our tail," said Igarashi.

"Even if you do use it in battle, you can't go crazy with it. The stone gives the skill Active Stealth, but it consumes a lot of magic," explained Melissa.

In other words, constantly blending into the background would rapidly drain your magic. On the other hand, you could essentially turn invisible by expending this energy... But I wasn't the only one who could benefit from avoiding enemies' attacks or disappearing, so I decided to think more about who to give the camouflage stone to.

"Well, no waaay Arihito would use it for something pervy," joked Misaki.

"...A-Arihito would never do anything like that. Honestly, Misaki...," groaned Suzuna.

"...Besides, we're in no position to talk where that's concerned. Or did you already forget, Misaki?" asked Elitia.

"Erk... Look, I—I have no idea what you're talking about! Everyone was just doing this and that while Arihito was fast asleep..."

"Uh... Misaki, what are you talking about?" I asked on a whim, but everyone looked like they'd been struck by a bolt of lightning. It seemed to imply I'd heard something I shouldn't have... Were they saying that everyone did something to me while I was sleeping? I looked at Igarashi. She wasn't normally one to get flustered, but she certainly was now. She looked at all the others as if begging them to help her, but they all avoided her gaze. She seemed to realize there was no escaping, so she cleared her throat and tried to regain control of her facial expressions. I was actually a tiny bit disappointed that, because she wasn't wearing that knit sweater anymore, her chest didn't get pushed up in the same way when she crossed her arms.

"D-don't jump to conclusions, Atobe. You were sleeping, and your blanket fell off. We just put it back on you. Nothing else happened."

"Y-yeah. You wouldn't think we'd do something weird to you, would you?" said Misaki with a light touch to my upper arm. I started to wonder if they'd casually touched me like that... No, that was absurd.

"Did I look stupid while I was sleeping? That's the only thing I wouldn't want."

"Uh, um... You were sleeping peacefully. You didn't look stupid, and you don't really seem to toss and turn a lot...," said Suzuna.

"T-totally. You sleep like a log, and you're suuuper quiet. Not like my dad, who snores like a freight train," continued Misaki. Actually, along with Misaki, Suzuna had let something slip, but I didn't dare point it out. They saw how I slept, which meant it was a fact that, at the very least, they had all been watching me.

"A-anyway... Back to Melissa. Would you perhaps like to join us on a seeking expedition?" I asked.

"Sure. If someone could take me along when they need a

Dissector from time to time," she said. She had been listening closely to the whole conversation I had with Rikerton. If she was on board with the idea, then I didn't think Rikerton needed to worry about her not wanting to do as he suggested.

"Oooh… Looks like I just stumbled across someone who could be a vanguard for the second party I'm in charge of!" said Misaki.

"Misaki, you can't just randomly assign people like that. Depending on how strong Melissa is, we could just add her to the first party. Swap you out for her," I said.

"Heeey! Although, actually, I've been thinking it's about time I take a break. I can warm the bench for you guys! Seeeriously, seeking's just stress on top of stress on top of stress. I think I'm aging twice as fast as normal."

"Oh, s-stop it with the superstitious talk, would you? …But… You know, if we keep seeking, one day, we might find something that restores youth," said Igarashi. She seemed interested in the possibility. It did seem feasible that there was something like that, but I wondered. I had the impression that anything could happen in the Labyrinth Country.

"I've heard rumors that certain monster meats have anti-aging effects," said Elitia. "Obviously, it'd be too easy if it were your normal monster, and I guess it doesn't do anything if you're under a certain age anyway."

"So there really is something… Good news for you, Igarashi."

"Hmph… You don't have to act like I need it because I'm the oldest girl in the group!"

"Arihito, what age for a girl is a complete no-go for you?" asked Misaki.

"Um... I've never really thought about it, I guess. I suppose the most important thing is if you mesh well with someone... Wait, what am I saying?!" The way I phrased it almost made me sound like I was admitting that I'd never actually dated a girl. Thankfully, the party didn't pick up on that and just took my words at face value.

"I get the impression that you always have good relationships, Mr. Arihito," added Rikerton. "You already... Oops, I think I might be overstepping my bounds here."

"Rikerton, you make it sound like... We're just—" Igarashi tried to say something but ended up fumbling for words.

"Anyway, let's talk about the materials," interrupted Rikerton. "I'll go through the uses for each one. There were seven Gaze Hounds, and we found two gaze stones on them. You can attach them to a weapon to enable a special Stun attack, or you can use them on armor to improve its capabilities."

"Those sound good. I'll have to think about whose equipment I want them added to, though," I replied.

"Understood. The fur can be used for mops and such—what would you like done with them? They do have a slight flame resistance, so they could be made into defensive equipment..."

Apparently, Gaze Hound fur had flame resistance, but their pelts were quite heavy and weak to lightning-based attacks. I decided not to use them and instead sold them.

The gaze stones were tiny, ebony-colored magic stones that formed in the Gaze Hounds' eyes and could be easily added to a weapon.

"I'd also like to use this ore and rune to improve our equipment, if possible," I added.

"Ah, it would be best for you to visit a smith, then. But this rune... Normally, they're made by compressing multiple magic stones, but surprisingly, this one appears to be naturally occurring," observed Rikerton with curiosity as he looked at the character that appeared in the middle of the stone. It seemed he'd seen runes before. "...The ring I gave my wife had a natural rune in it as well. Here in the Labyrinth Country, they're also used as high-class gemstones. Take good care of it."

"Thanks for the advice." I decided to take the materials to a smith instead of having them do the modifications here in the Dissection Center. I'd do that tomorrow morning. Now we needed to talk about the Plane Eater materials.

"Plane Eater meat is in high demand, so I can offer you fifty gold pieces to purchase the meat alone. Otherwise, I could process the meat into jerky or other long-lasting foodstuffs," continued Rikerton.

"We'll sell half and process the other half, if that's all right," I said.

"Of course. We have one skin from the Plane Eater, which can be made into one piece of armor."

"Okay. Could I have you work it into Theresia's equipment? She would find it the best to use."

"All right, shall I make some gloves, then? I'll need some time to work on it, but they should be ready tomorrow."

"Please," I responded. We didn't return with many materials this time, so we were able to settle things quickly. Or so I thought.

"Right, next, we will discuss the materials from Juggernaut. I can offer you three thousand five hundred gold if you sell all but a portion. That's the amount the Guild set," continued Rikerton.

"I don't have anywhere to put that much. Could I use that for future work with you?"

"That's perfectly fine. I arranged for the parts that could be used as weapons to be sent here... But it will take some time until they're delivered from where Juggernaut was dissected. I believe it should arrive tomorrow."

"Thank you for taking care of that."

I didn't expect we'd be able to suddenly get something as powerful as some physical attack-immune armor, but I was excited at the prospect of getting a weapon made from Juggernaut. I didn't mind at all about having to pay. If we could dissect, then we could keep all the profits to ourselves, but that'd take our own time and effort anyway.

"...Can I join you tomorrow?" Melissa asked me.

"Yeah, I'll come meet you. We'll probably go into a labyrinth, so make sure you're ready."

"Okay. Nice to meet you all... I'm Melissa. I can perform autopsies and dissections." She timidly bowed to the rest of the party, although the butcher's knife still in hand made her seem a little menacing. Regardless, we were able to add one of the jobs that I'd been hoping for: a Dissector.

I wondered what kind of skills Melissa could use for seeking and in battle. She had long, wavy silvery hair and well-proportioned features, making her look like a porcelain doll. She suddenly realized she still had the bare butcher's knife, so she placed it in its case and smiled.

## Part V: Room Assignments

Our new lodgings were in a place called the Lady Ollerus Mansion. As the name implied, it was a house built by a female adventurer for her to spend her retirement years in. Lady Ollerus lost her husband and all her companions in an infamous labyrinth in District Four known as the Corridor of Failure. She continued to seek in the labyrinths until she was elderly in hopes of having her revenge and didn't retire until she was so covered in injuries that she could no longer walk.

A maid named Millais came out to greet us when we arrived, and she told us a lot as she showed us to our room. As we were climbing the stairs to the second floor, she stopped us on the landing, where there hung a beautiful shield, and told us its story almost like she was our tour guide.

"This is the shield that Lady Ollerus used. It is known as the Kite Shield of the Queen's Knight +8. Very few people are capable of using it due to its heft, but it is a very strong shield and also has value as a piece of art," explained Millais. The shield was so big that it was more than large enough to cover an entire adult's body. Apparently, Lady Ollerus was a vanguard, even though she was a woman.

"What was Lady Ollerus's job?" asked Igarashi.

"She was not a reincarnate but rather from a clan who worked as guards for the royal family. Her job was Royal Order Knight," replied Millais.

"I didn't know there was a job like that... I was thinking she would be a Shield Knight or something," said Igarashi. I had imagined the same thing as her. But even though she was a Royal Order Knight, her party had been stopped in its tracks in District Four. And then there's the royalty of the Labyrinth Country. They were one of the forces in this country other than the reincarnates. Someday, we'd probably run into them... Though, that was a long way down the line.

"Is *maid* a job?" I asked.

"Yes, it is," Millais replied briskly. "Most of us change jobs to become Maids, but there are those who selected Maid as their job when they were reincarnated. There are quite a few skills that are useful during seeking, and there is a surprisingly wide range of equipment to choose from. There are, however, some skills that you can only use when you are wearing a Maid uniform." She was mild-mannered, her soft brown hair pulled back in a loose braid. But the way she spoke gave me the impression she was a force to be reckoned with.

"Did you also seek in the past?" I asked Millais.

"I still do occasionally, though I have never left District Eight. I sometimes seek with my coworkers or people living in the mansion who have done a lot for me."

So there were those kinds of Seekers out there, too. I'd learned from the people I'd met that, other than retirees, there were essentially two roles in the Labyrinth Country: Seekers and Seeker support.

The mansion was separated into two wings that branched off from the entrance hall. Our room was on the second floor of the right wing. Millais unlocked the door to our room, provided me with a key, and then showed us into the suite.

"I made the beds in advance—will six be enough?" she asked.

"Ah, yes, it will. Although, it'd be nice if I could have a separate room, since I'm the only man."

"Oh… I do apologize. I failed to take that into consideration… I prepared beds in three of the rooms, two beds to each. I will set up a bed in the unused room," said Millais in a fluster as she headed toward the bedroom. Supposedly, she would take pillows and sheets there for me, though I felt bad for making her do the extra work.

"Arihito, it's not a big deal if we're just sleeping, right?" said Misaki.

"Uh… I guess, and it's more work for Millais… Sorry, Millais, please don't worry about what I said. The rooms are fine as they are."

"As you wish. I will bring your dinner up to your room at dinnertime. If you need absolutely anything, please just ring that bell to call me. I will be able to hear it no matter where I am." Millais bowed once and left the suite.

Misaki waved as she left, then grabbed a memo pad and pen that was provided and started writing something.

"…? Misaki, what are you writing?" I asked.

"In times like this, we need the fairest way of deciding, riiight? Ta-daaa, time for a lottery!"

"H-hey... Don't draw a heart around my name!" I protested.

"Why nooot? No matter how you look at it, you're basically the prize." I wondered if I should just take that as innocent affection... But then I saw the amusement on Misaki's face, and I had a feeling she was messing with me.

"All right, I guess everyone else should write their own name... There," said Suzuna.

"Hey, Kyouka, no peeking! I know you wanna share a room with Arihito, but so does everyone else," chided Misaki.

"......"

Theresia was the person who reacted the most obviously to Misaki's remarks; her lizard mask began to gradually turn red. We played rock, paper, scissors to decide who would pull names, and the five girls carefully shuffled up the names. In the end, it turned out I would be sharing a room with Suzuna, though I felt weird saying that she'd "won."

"Suzu, you sure that sharing a room with Arihito won't make you too nervous to sleep?" asked Misaki. "Wanna switch with me?"

"N-no... I'll be fine. Arihito, I want to be of more help to everyone as a rearguard, so would you mind if I asked for your advice later?"

"If you say so, Suzuna... We can trust you to be a gentleman, right, Atobe?" said Igarashi.

"Igarashi... Don't look at me like that." No one seemed too

upset about the room assignment results, since we did it by lottery, but Igarashi did warn me… It wasn't without reason, since men in our previous world did tend to prefer young girls. I probably couldn't convince them that wasn't the case with me, but I wanted to at least prove I was closer to a toothless wolf…or a sheep even.

"…Since we'll be staying in this suite for more than one night, I think it would be a good idea if we rotate. I also would like to get Arihito's advice on something," proposed Elitia. We decided to go with Elitia's suggestion that we only use three of the four rooms in the suite and then swap who sleeps where every night.

"Thank you for agreeing to help me tonight, Arihito," said Suzuna.

"Oh, no problem… What's wrong, Theresia?" I asked.

"……"

Theresia was staring at us and seemed to be thinking something as she sat on the couch in the living room.

"Oh… Theresia, don't worry about it. I'm used to your lizard mask by now… Though, I guess it might surprise me if you pop up in the middle of the night," said Igarashi.

"I'm totally fine with it, tooo!" added Misaki. "Actually, since you're all smooth and cool to the touch, I think I'd like to share a bed with you when it gets too hot to sleep in the summer… Hey, don't gooo! Running away just makes me wanna chase you!" Theresia must have been picturing Misaki using her as a body pillow, and she attempted to protect herself from such a fate. I was suddenly curious if the Labyrinth Country had all four seasons or not, but before I could ask Elitia, Igarashi saw something in the middle of the room.

"Hmm... Atobe, do you think this thing is an air conditioner?"

It was a rounded object made of dark metal that had a blue button and a red button, which looked like magic stones. Elitia seemed to know how to operate it and pressed the blue button, and cool air started to flow out from the vent-like holes on the surface.

"Once you get above a certain rank, most of the housing has magic-operated temperature control apparatuses. You have to charge this filler stone here with magic in order for it to work... We have to limit our use, since we don't have a magic user in our group," explained Elitia.

It took time to recover magic. You couldn't recover all the magic you used during a day of seeking unless you spent a night sleeping in good accommodation. There was no way our party had all the jobs and skills that we'd need. It wasn't a season that we would need to use air-conditioning, but we'd need to find a way to solve our lack of magic once we were in the middle of a sweltering summer.

## Part VI: Skill Levels

After finalizing room assignments, we decided to get changed, then hold a party meeting until it was time for dinner. Everyone's level went up, so I wanted to double-check their skills. Everyone brought their license and flipped to the skills page. There were different reactions to what each person saw, but even Elitia's eyes shone with excitement when she saw her new skills... Though, I couldn't say that her expression was entirely happy. There was a lot of risk with any of her Cursed Blade skills.

*I'll start with my skills... Whoa, I finally got it!*

```
◆Acquired Skills◆
Defense Support 1
Attack Support 1
Recovery Support 1
Morale Support 1
Hawk Eyes
Rear Stance


◆Available Skills◆
    Level 2 Skills
  Attack Support 2: Adds your weapon's attack
                    onto the attacks of party
                    members in front. Skills
                    of duplicate types do not
                    stack.
 Defense Support 2: Creates a defensive barrier
                    equal in strength to your
                    defensive capabilities for
                    party members in front.
                    Skills of duplicate types
                    do not stack.


    Level 1 Skills
  Magic Support 1: Increases magic consumption
                   and spell strength by 50
                   percent for party members
                   in front.
```

```
Evasion Support 1:  Occasionally activates
                    Auto-Dodge for party members
                    in front.
       Rear View:  Spends 5 magic points to
                    expand your vision to cover
                    your rear for a set period
                    of time.
   Outside Assist:  Spends 5 magic points to
                    designate a target outside
                    your party to support.
        Backdraft:  Automatically counters when
                    attacked from behind.
Remaining Skill Points: 3
```

I was finally able to start taking the second step up in the support-type skills. As far as I could see, the amount of support given would change depending on my own abilities.

*Since it says* your weapon's attack, *there's a chance that it'll add attributes and special effects from whatever weapon I have equipped. It'd be worth using instead of Attack Support 1 if my damage exceeds eleven.*

If these skills overwrote my existing ones, I wouldn't be able to use Attack Support 1 and Defense Support 1 anymore. And if my attack or defense was below 11 points, then my support capabilities would be temporarily reduced. But since my damage increased as we grew stronger, it would be a bigger increase to add my attack than to add the set 11 damage. The current number of attacks our entire party could do in one go was near 20, making an 80-point difference in damage between the current 11 x 20 and the potential, let's say, 15 x 20.

I wasn't sure if it was too early to take them... And both Attack Support 2 and Defense Support 2 were equally important.

"Atobe, would you mind taking a look at my skills? I was hoping you could help me choose which to take...," said Igarashi.

"Sorry, I got lost in thought for a moment there. Sure, I can take a look. Elitia, so skills level up, too?"

"You can acquire level-two skills now? Congratulations, but keep in mind that the number of skill points necessary to acquire a skill is the same as the skill's level," she said. That made sense. I wondered if the number of skill points you got per level increased, since we'd be using more skill points now. If so, we could even get four or five points per level.

If I assumed that the more skill points a skill required, the stronger it was, then it would be safe to take Attack Support 2. On the other hand, the support wouldn't be useful at all if we increased the number of attacks that had a certain attribute, but that attribute wasn't effective at all... But then I realized something.

*...Right... The set damage is effective, but if we could Poison the enemy...!*

If we could somehow make it possible to use status effects other than Poison, then the whole party could inflict status effects on the enemy regardless of their own equipment.

The other one I was interested in was Magic Support 1, but that would likely be most useful when we added a magic-using job to the party. Its effects overlapped with magic recovery, too, so there were a lot of instances where it would be useful. The only thing it'd be really applicable to right now, though, was Igarashi's Thunderbolt, so we didn't need it at the moment.

Outside Assist seemed like it could be an interesting skill based on how it was used. Then again, Evasion Support 1 seemed good, but our current defenses were fairly strong, so I decided to hold off on that one.

"Sorry to keep you waiting, Igarashi."

"It's okay. So these are the skills I can take..." She was wearing her knit sweater and skirt, so she looked just like she did when we'd been reincarnated. Maybe they weren't used to the feel of the clothes in the Labyrinth Country, because both Misaki and Suzuna had also changed into the clothes they'd been wearing when they reincarnated.


◆Acquired Skills◆
Double Attack
Thunderbolt
Mirage Step
Decoy


◆Available Skills◆
Piercing Strike 1: A portion of your attack penetrates the target's defense when you're equipped with a spear.

Force Target: Draws enemies' attacks to a specified target.

Mist of Bravery: Nulls party members' Fear status.

```
Freezing Thorns:  Freezes opponent's
                  legs and slows their
                  movement.
Snow Country Skin: Grants immunity
                  to Frozen status
                  and increases
                  attractiveness.
Bulletproof 1:    Enemy long-ranged
                  attacks are slightly
                  less likely to hit.
Remaining Skill Points: 2
```

"Piercing Strike looks good, doesn't it? I also think Force Target would be useful in a lot of different situations," I offered. "The main strategy would be combining it with Decoy."

"Yeah... That's true. You probably don't think that Snow Country Skin is necessary...," said Igarashi.

"Hey, why do you get a skill that makes you prettier?! That's so coool! I want something like that," said Misaki.

"I don't think you can change jobs from Gambler to Valkyrie. You could possibly change from Shrine Maiden to Valkyrie, though," said Elitia. Misaki slumped her shoulders in disappointment.

"Snow Country Skin... What a lovely name...," said Suzuna. She also seemed interested, but since she and Misaki were the youngest in the group, their youthful skin already looked glowing and supple.

Elitia's skin was also soft and fair since she was from northern Europe, but she had dark circles underneath her eyes. Perhaps she was often tired from wielding the cursed blade. I used to have the worst bags under my eyes from work before, but my face had gotten a lot livelier since reincarnating. I'm sure it helped that seeking was such good exercise, and I didn't have much stress these days.

"Right... I don't think Piercing Strike is absolutely necessary since you have my support damage, so how about you try taking Snow Country Skin?" I suggested.

"Huh? ...Are you sure? I shouldn't take it just for my own benefit..."

"If I thought something else was absolutely necessary for seeking, then I'd ask you to take it. I do want you to take Force Target, but there's nothing else that I think we absolutely need right now... I don't think it's right to ask you not to take a skill that you really want to take," I explained.

"...It'll be really useful if we run into an enemy that inflicts the Frozen status. Um... All right, I'll take Force Target and Snow Country Skin, then," said Igarashi, using her license to acquire the skills while everyone watched. And then: "...Did anything change? I knew it. It's not the kind of change that's super obvious."

"Uh, I mean... You sorta look overall more like a Valkyrie or something...?" said Misaki.

"Yeah... You still look like yourself, but you seem to have more of a presence," I said.

"You're just trying to make me feel better. I knew it was stupid to think it'd just make me prettier... Guess that taught me a lesson."

"Why don't you look for yourself? I think it's best if you see it with your own eyes," suggested Elitia, and Igarashi went doubtfully to the dressing room.

"...It makes me think of a Valkyrie standing on a battlefield, snow gently falling around her. That's the kind of impression that I get from Snow Country Skin," said Suzuna. I agreed—Igarashi was already a beautiful woman, so the skill made her feel even more like a real Valkyrie or added an allure only warrior women had.

Igarashi came back looking disappointed, but from where I was sitting, her skin did look like it'd gotten brighter and clearer.

"It really hasn't changed much at all... What do you think, Atobe?"

"Uh, um... I think maybe there wasn't much of a change, since you were already so beautiful."

"Well, I appreciate you trying to make me feel better, but it's not as big a change as I was hoping for. I'll just have to hope the Frozen prevention is good... From now on, I'm letting you choose all my skills, Atobe." The skill was effective, yet she was unable to see it herself. Maybe changes in attractiveness were something only those around you could see. The one effect she did seem happy with was the immunity to Frozen, and its usefulness would become apparent when we needed it.

According to the explanation for Force Target, it might be possible for Igarashi to force attacks on an enemy, which seemed incredibly powerful, but maybe she didn't receive a skill that useful at only level 3. We needed to test it on some weak enemies... Though, I felt bad watching my friends beat up a poor little Cotton Ball.

"...Arihito, I'm sure you're not excited about looking at the skills for my job, but...could you take a look later if you don't mind?" asked Elitia.

"I'm absolutely excited! I bet I'll be blown away if I look at your skills."

"R-really...? I mean, if you're not opposed, then I'd like you to know my skills since you're the leader. I'm a little tired now, though, so I think I'm going to go nap for a bit."

"Okay, I'll wake you up when it's dinnertime. Sleep well, Ellie," said Suzuna. Elitia said good-bye and waved before heading to her room. The room assignments were me and Suzuna, Igarashi and Theresia, and Misaki and Elitia.

"Aren't you getting tired, too, Arihito? I can get your advice another day if you are, you know," said Misaki.

"I'm going to go over my skills tonight with Arihito, so you could talk with him now," suggested Suzuna.

"You sure? What skills do you think would be good?" Misaki asked me.

"All right... It's easier if you sit next to me. Well, maybe not that close."

"Ooh, you're blushing. I mean, there is an age difference between us, but it's not like you're twice as old as me. So does this mean you actually see me like that?" said Misaki.

"You say I'm not twice as old, but a five- or ten-year difference is still a pretty big one..."

"Whaaat? But age doesn't matter since we were reincarnated," protested Misaki.

"M-Misaki... You need to respect Arihito's feelings. We're still like children to him...," said Suzuna, though that's not really what I meant. I was actually just kind of happy that Misaki didn't see me as an old fart.

"Misaki, I know you're the age where you're interested in that kind of thing, but I think it's wrong of you to tease a genuinely honest person like Atobe."

"I wasn't thinking of anything bad; I was just trying to say that he didn't need to be so worried about being close to me like that. Don't you get it?" said Misaki.

"Uh... M-Misaki, even Theresia is staring at you," said Suzuna.

"......"

Theresia was still sitting at the table and staring at Misaki. Her gaze felt somehow intense, so Misaki scooted over to put an appropriate distance between us.

"Um, anyway, so these are my skiiills," said Misaki.

"Look at you separating yourself properly. You know, it's good to know how to read the room," noted Igarashi.

"Kyouka, you're acting like you can have everything for yourself just because you got prettier," said Misaki.

"Wha—?! I am not! Atobe, I'm going to go have a look at the mansion's courtyard. You take care of the kids here."

"O-okay... Have fun," I said, and she stood from her seat and left. The heels of her boots clicked, and there was something bewitching about her figure as she walked away. Maybe it was because she took Snow Country Skin.

"...She is sooo gorgeous. How about you just tell her straight out, Arihito?" said Misaki.

"Even if I did tell her directly...she was known for being a beauty in our old company, too, so she was the most popular among the guys at work. I was her direct subordinate, though, so I never thought about anything romantic between us..." Well, I had, but only in the very beginning. I had thought that being an employee of a beautiful woman, something might just happen... but now I knew I was just being an idiot for thinking that.

"Arihito, this might be a little too pushy of me, but I think you should go with Kyouka. There are other parties staying in this mansion, and I think she needs a man to escort her," said Suzuna.

"Do you really think so?" I asked.

"Of course she does! Beautiful girls like her are always getting hit on when they don't want it. She's probably safe in the mansion, but what if a mysterious burglar breaks in or something?" said Misaki.

"M-Misaki... Why would you say that? What if someone really comes...?" said Suzuna.

Misaki, Suzuna, and even Theresia seemed to want me to go after Igarashi for some reason. I guess if they felt that strongly about it, I'd go, though I had no idea how to tell her *I came to escort you.*

## Part VII: A Happy Home

Igarashi had said she was going to go look at the courtyard in the mansion, so I headed in that direction but was stopped by a man

I didn't know when I'd walked down the stairs into the entrance hall. He was young, maybe even my age, with short, blond hair and a pair of goggles on his head. He was wearing the highest quality clothing that I'd seen available in the clothes shops around here. Based on his outfit and the fact that he was in the mansion, I guessed he was probably one of the other residents.

"Hey, nice to meet you. My name's Georg. I'm the leader of one of the parties staying here. Are you with the party that just moved in?" he asked.

"Yes, my name is Arihito Atobe. Pleasure to meet you; we'll be staying here for a little while, I imagine."

"Atobe, huh? Never seen you before. My party was ranked number one in District Eight, but then our rank dropped to number two out of the blue. I was wondering what kind of rising star had suddenly appeared; I really wanted to talk to you."

"We somehow managed to get more contribution points than I expected, putting us in first place for the time being. Much of it was down to good luck." Luck actually played a huge role in helping us beat Named Monster after Named Monster. We never would have found the giant warrior if it weren't for Misaki's and Suzuna's skills, and luck was still on our side when it came to actually defeating it.

"Pretty humble for a guy who's just scaled his way up the ranks. By the way, no need to be so formal with me. Looks like we're around the same age," said Georg.

"If you say so. One thing from me, then... Calling me *Atobe* sounds a bit stiff."

Georg grinned. He seemed to agree.

"Arihito, then. I suppose your party's got some really powerful people in it."

"Most of us are actually newbies, but we do have one level-nine member. She's definitely pulled the party up." Georg seemed really interested when I said level 9. I got the sense that he was a good guy; he wasn't even jealous of me for having outranked him.

"A level that high—you're not talking about Elitia Centrale, are you?" asked Georg. "I heard she came down to District Eight. I'm surprised you even wanted her in your party."

"We both happened to be in the labyrinth, and there was an opportunity to work together. Hope you don't buy into any of the nasty rumors going around about her. She's a very honest person and a good friend of ours."

"Of course. I'll let my party know, too... My party's name is Polaris. What's yours?"

I hadn't actually thought about it. I didn't realize it wasn't just Elitia's former party, the White Night Brigade, but each party that had their own name.

"I actually didn't know it was normal to give your party a name. I'll have to talk to my party about it later."

Georg patted me on the shoulder with a grin. I wondered if he'd been injured in one of the labyrinths since he had what looked like a bandage over his nose. He had a similar build as me and gave off the impression of being a frank and honest guy. Seeing as his party had been first in District Eight until recently, I could safely assume he was a fairly strong person.

"By the way… I saw this gorgeous girl walk by a minute ago. She in your party?" he asked.

"Oh yeah. That's Kyouka. I guess it's not only Japanese people who think she's pretty."

"A beauty like that's got to be a handful. In any case, what d'you say I show you a good place to have some fun as a token of our budding friendship? I'm sure you've made plenty of money to spend on that kinda thing, right?"

"Fun, huh… You've got places like that in the Labyrinth Country, too?" I asked. Georg didn't say anything, but he just grinned in confirmation.

I was once invited a long time ago by some friends at my part-time job to a place like that, but I was saving up money at the time to get my certification, so I didn't go. Not that I wasn't interested in Georg's offer, but I was sure the party wouldn't react well if they found out. It could break down all the trust I'd built with them so far.

"Hey, only if you're in the mood. If that mood happens to strike you, let me know. Like I said, I know a good place," repeated Georg.

"Uh, yeah… If I get the chance." It might be normal for Seekers in the Labyrinth Country to go together to the red-light district… If that was the case, I might someday end up going, but as of right now, it would be difficult to make it work. Actually, it was pretty much out of the question.

"Atobe, you know that guy? The two of you were chatting like old friends." Igarashi suddenly spoke up.

"Erk… I-Igarashi. How long have you been listening?"

"I just got here, so I didn't hear what you were talking about.

I don't really want to look around on my own, so would you mind coming with me?"

Georg picked up on the situation, flashed me a thumbs-up that only I could see, and then left the mansion.

"Atobe, I thought you were supposed to be talking with everyone else about their skills? You can't just wander off, you know. You need to make sure you check them all over," said Igarashi. She seemed happy for some reason. Maybe she was trying to imply that she was glad I followed her... That thought put me on edge.

"I decided to take a break for today and continue discussing skills another time," I replied.

"Oh... Well, I guess you'll talk with Suzuna later tonight."

"I don't think we'll stay up too late; we'll just be going over the most important stuff."

In reality, I wasn't sure what else I could talk to Suzuna about besides skills. I hoped there wouldn't be too much of a generation gap between us that we couldn't chat.

"Where in the mansion have you looked so far, Igarashi?"

"Just around out front a bit. Next, I was thinking of taking that exit to check out the courtyard."

"All right, sounds good. Let's go."

I walked next to Igarashi, who was in her old clothes from before she reincarnated. We passed a Maid who smiled at the sight of the two of us. I think she might have misunderstood, but Igarashi didn't seem to notice at all.

"The carpet in this hallway is so beautiful. Reminds me of a Persian rug. Are you interested in that sort of thing at all, Atobe?"

"Yeah, a little bit. We've started to make some money, so someday, I'd like to buy a permanent home for us, and we can decorate it however we like."

"...When we do, can we get a pet? I promise I'll do all the work to take care of it."

"Of course. We'll get your favorite kind of animal."

It was much easier to talk with Igarashi than I ever thought it could be in our old world. As I thought about how easily she ran from hot to cold, I decided that times like these were also quite nice.

The dinner provided to us consisted of a white sauce–topped rice pilaf–type dish with crab, made using a Bubble Crab monster that lived in the marshes, and a seafood soup with Mud Shrimp.

"I would've thought that the crab would absorb some unpleasant mud flavors since it lives in the marsh, but it's been prepped well," I said.

"Mm, you're right. I've never had seasonings like this, but it's really quite nice," added Igarashi.

The soft crab meat and plentiful cream sauce worked very well with the rice, which had been cooked with seasonings and spices. The food we ate before in the tavern was nice enough, but it was a more rustic cooking style. What the mansion offered was much more elegant. This style seemed to suit Igarashi's tastes, because she was in a great mood. Suzuna didn't seem picky about her food, but Misaki didn't seem to be a huge fan of shrimp and so pushed her soup bowl toward Theresia, who was sitting next to her and munching away at her meal like always.

"Misaki, you'll never grow if you're so picky with your food," scolded Elitia.

"Whaaat? But I'm already taller than you!" retorted Misaki.

"Urgh... My height varies from day to day. Today's just one of my bad days!" replied Elitia. Meanwhile, she was picking out all of the fresh herbs in her soup—it looked like she didn't really like them. She also didn't seem to like some vegetables, because she'd very carefully picked out all the bell pepper–looking things from her salad.

"Ellie, do you not like vegetables? I'll eat them if you won't," said Suzuna.

"Uh... No, it's okay. I was planning on eating them all in one go afterward."

"You'll be less stressed if you only eat food you like. All sorts of different things will give you the nutrition you need."

"...O-okay... Would you mind eating half of them, then?" said Elitia, a little embarrassed, perhaps because she'd just been reprimanding Misaki for the same thing, and took advantage of Suzuna's kind nature. Suzuna couldn't finish her pilaf, so she passed it over to Theresia. Demi-humans really could eat a lot—or perhaps that was just something particular to Theresia.

"...Mm..."

Mealtimes were some of the few instances Theresia, who was mute, made a sound that was as close to a voice as she probably could. Everyone noticed and was paying close attention to her in their surprise.

"Arihito, can Theresia communicate through writing?" wondered Elitia.

"I don't think so. She can read and listen to people and understand the words, but she can't express herself through words."

"...I want to hear Theresia's voice. It's not like I can hear the voice of her soul with my skills," said Suzuna. Even if Suzuna could use Spirit Detection to read Theresia's emotions, it wouldn't be the same as hearing it in her own voice.

"......"

Theresia looked at the food, then looked at Suzuna. After a moment, she gave a nod.

"Ah... Theresia, are you saying the food is good? I think so, too," replied Suzuna.

"......"

If she could express her intentions, then even the strange-looking lizard mask wasn't a hindrance to her communication. I was sure it wasn't just me who felt that way.

"Oh right. Arihito, there's a bathroom in the suite—do you wanna take a bath first?" asked Misaki.

"I can take one after everyone else. There's nothing wrong with being the first to take a bath, but when I lived alone, I'd just take a quick shower in the morning anyway."

"I'd probably do the same if I lived alone, since I always get light-headed taking hot baths. Suzu's pretty good at not doing that, though," said Misaki.

Misaki and Suzuna had been good enough friends that they were going on a ski trip together, so they probably took shared baths. It must have been nice to take a nice soak with your friends.

"Theresia, since we're sharing a room, should we take a bath together? It'll take a lot of time if all six of us go in separately," suggested Igarashi.

"……"

"T-Theresia, you should go with her, since she's offering anyway," I urged, but she didn't respond. I was nervous that she was about to shake her head, but she gave a tiny nod instead. I might have just been seeing things, but she looked a little sad. She was starting to eat more slowly, and even her lizard mask looked somehow upset. I wasn't the only one who thought this, because Igarashi seemed concerned as she talked to her.

"Theresia, would you prefer to take a bath alone? That's fine, too," she guessed.

"……"

"That's not it, then… Do you want to take a bath with someone other than me?" Suddenly, Theresia shot a glance in my direction. The eyes of her mask locked onto mine and didn't look away.

"He's always helping you out… Right, is that what you're saying? I know you don't mean anything by it, but I feel like washing a man's back is just a liiittle too forward," said Misaki.

"…I won't stop you if Arihito says it's all right," added Elitia.

"W-well… Theresia's the one who wants to do it," argued Suzuna. Theresia was starting to turn red now that everyone's attention was focused on her. Igarashi started to blush, too— It'd bring things full circle if I joined in.

"…I'll be all alone if you two take a bath together…," said Igarashi.

"Huh? …Is that what you were worried about?" I asked.

"O-obviously, I'm not exactly comfortable with a man and a woman taking a bath together, but Theresia seems sad. If she likes you that much, there's really nothing I can do about it..."

The red in Theresia's face started to slowly fade, and then she stared at Igarashi. Whatever emotions were behind her face were the subtle ones of a girl's heart, and I just could not read them at all.

"Oh... I know! Theresia, wait for a moment. If I can get a bathing suit or something like that, then there won't be anything strange if you two do bathe together," suggested Igarashi.

"If we do that, too, then we can all take a bath together! And I'd get to play with Arihito in the bath—although I guess that'd be a little awkward. Even I have a sense of shame, believe it or not," said Misaki. I actually thought it was quite normal to find bathing together awkward. I found it refreshing to hear Misaki say she was embarrassed by something, though, since she normally just said and did whatever she liked... Was it rude to think that?

"...I suppose I shouldn't mention that we have swimsuit-like equipment, huh?" I said.

"B-body armor doesn't count as swimwear! Besides, even if we did get a bathing suit, I feel like taking a bath together is a whole separate issue. You should make note of that, Arihito," said Elitia.

"Y-yeah. I mean, we don't have to go through all the trouble so we can take a bath together...," I replied.

"Well, it's a problem because Theresia's sad. You don't have the right to refuse, Atobe."

Igarashi had way too much faith in the bathing suits. It didn't really manner if she was in one or naked... It would work only to my benefit, even if I could technically see more in one than the other.

Anyway, we split into three groups for the day and decided that I would take my bath last, alone, and that way, I could take my time testing out the tub in the royal suite.

## Part VIII: Night Consultation

This world had a variety of different bath styles. This royal suite had a standalone bathtub instead of one built into the room. There was a shower made by storing hot water in a barrel and turning a tap on to let it out. The water was lukewarm, but that was better than if it were too hot. It was more convenient than what we had in the previous suite, so I was perfectly happy.

*I can't help feeling the technology here is a little hit-or-miss even though there're so many reincarnates... It wouldn't be impossible to implement science and technology if a reincarnate did come along with the necessary skills, though.*

I lay soaking in the tub with my thoughts. Being last meant I could stay as long as I wanted without having to worry about anyone getting in after me. I eventually got out and decided to leave the cleaning for the Maid tomorrow. The Maids had skills that made cleaning easier, so I imagined it wouldn't be too much of an inconvenience for them.

I wasn't normally the kind of person to take long baths, so I didn't spend a whole lot of time soaking. Theresia had come out flushed red from her bath. I had felt bad for forgetting to tell Igarashi that Theresia wasn't good with the heat. Thankfully, Igarashi had noticed quickly and splashed cool water on her to bring her temperature down.

Perhaps she wouldn't get overheated as much once we turned her back into a human. Or perhaps her demi-human characteristics would remain to a degree. Either way, I was eager to find out how to get her back to her original form as quickly as possible.

*If we go to the cathedral in District Four, we will find how to turn a demi-human back into a human...theoretically. Lady Ollerus, who built this mansion, and her party were forced to retire at a labyrinth in District Four. Exactly what kind of labyrinth is this Corridor of Failure that it could destroy a party who could use a shield that amazing...?*

I wiped down my body and dried my hair as much as possible. I assumed I'd have to dry by hand, but there was actually a heat-blast shell present, which was a conch-like thing that blew warm air out of a hole. It wasn't incredibly hot, but it could be used as a dryer.

They had been able to recreate a certain amount of modern appliances through the use of magic stones. This, too, was probably made by reincarnates who wanted a blow-dryer. I couldn't be more grateful to the people who'd developed the black sphere, the "temperature control ball," in the living room.

I went into the living room and stood nonchalantly behind Theresia while I chatted with Misaki, who didn't seem tired at all. Standing there let me heal Theresia's vitality; she lost a little bit when she got overheated. Temperature changes were a literal threat to life for a lizardman.

Theresia seemed to be feeling better, then went into the bedroom that Igarashi was in so that it was just me and Misaki in the living room.

"Phewww… We had a lot going on today, seriously. I still feel so worked up; I don't think I can sleep!" said Misaki. It was she who led us to enter the hidden fourth floor of the Field of Dawn, defeat the Named Monster, and meet Ariadne… A lot did happen today. I felt like I needed to carefully take note of it all in my brain.

"Ellie's already in bed. I'll probably sleep fine. If not, I might go bug Suzu," continued Misaki. Suzuna's Purification spell calmed people down, so it would probably help her fall asleep. Even with me nearby, they'd probably be fine sleeping as two friends sharing a bed.

"Tomorrow, I'll…be staying behind, won't I?" asked Misaki.

"We'll be at eight people with you, Melissa, and Cion, so you could still come," I said. "I'd just be worried about you being the only person still at level two—your vitality will be lower."

"Then I won't do anything in battle. Could Melissa and I just follow behind? Like…a detached squad or something."

Apparently, that was an option, too. My support worked as long as I was behind that person, so if the rear squad was engaged in battle, I could support them just by turning around. It would depend on how strong Melissa was, but it seemed like it would be a good idea to put some close-combat members in the back as well.

"Even if I join, the only thing I can do is increase your luck... So I guess if you want me to, I will. I don't even have any other useful sorts of skills," said Misaki, her expression upset as she pulled her license from her pajama pocket and showed me.

◆Acquired Skills◆

Increased Drop Rate: Slightly increases enemies' rare item drop rate.

Child of Luck: Slightly increases probability of finding a Chest after battle.

◆Available Skills◆

Dice Trick: Guarantees a designated number from a dice roll.

Russian Roulette 1: Chooses a random target among both allies and enemies and halves their vitality.

Poker Face: Renders facial expressions unreadable.

Lucky Guess 1: Allows you to vaguely sense which action will lead to good results.

Coin Toss: Increases luck if the coin lands on the face chosen by an ally.

Remaining Skill Points: 2

*These available skills would be great in a casino... Though, I bet if there were a "dealer" job, their skills would be able to nullify these.*

Russian Roulette 1 would probably not end up hitting an ally very often since the Gambler's luck was good, but the risk was just too great. Lucky Guess 1 didn't have any drawbacks. Misaki had already taken the skills that were obviously beneficial. We'd already been blessed thanks to her Increased Drop Rate and Child of Luck.

"Lucky Guess 1 looks good, but I don't think it's something you need to take immediately. How about you wait a level and see what skills you get then?" I suggested.

"Yeah, I was thinking the same thing. I want to really take advantage of my luck-improving skills. Make it so I can just walk around and find a giant pot of gold sitting on the ground," she said.

"I dunno about a pot of gold, but you do have skills that can help you get stuff. It's really neat to see everyone's different skills."

"Ha-ha! Well, I'm glad you have fun with it. All right, I think I'm off to my room. Niiight!"

"Good night."

Hopefully, Misaki could acquire some skills that were useful for battle, but it seemed like Gambler was a job specialized in support skills related to luck and had a positive effect on the party. Thinking about it that way, it was pretty similar to my job.

I went back to my room and saw Suzuna with her bedside lamp on, sitting on her bed and looking at her license.

"You must be tired, Suzuna," I said.

"Just a little. Would you mind taking a quick look at my skills?" she replied.

"Of course. Were you looking at them just now?"

"Yeah. I was trying to figure out which ones would be good to take, but I'm really not sure."

I stood next to Suzuna, and she showed me her license before looking up at me and smiling.

"Um, you don't have to stand. You can sit if you like. I'm the one asking you for help anyway," she said.

"Oh, thanks." I sat on her bed next to her. She handed me her license, which was currently open to her skills page.

◆Acquired Skills◆
Auto-Hit
Purification
Exorcism 1
Spirit Detection 1


◆Available Skills◆
Archery Master 1: Increases damage from shooting a bow using proper archery techniques.

Exorcism Arrow: Adds Holy attribute to arrows when using a bow.

Cleansing: Adds Holy attribute to whoever is in a body of water with you.

Medium: Allows a nearby spirit to inhabit your body to enable conversation.

Prayer: Party's success rate increases slightly.

```
Salt Laying: Places salt around a
               set area to prevent
               monsters from
               approaching.
Remaining Skill Points: 2
```

"Ah, right… I remember you have both your Shrine Maiden skills and archery skills."

"Archery Master seems good, and Medium is a skill that I always wanted before I was reincarnated but never would have been able to do… I sort of want to know what it'd be like."

"The skill explanation mentions *spirits*, so I guess that means they really do exist here. Can you detect them, Suzuna? Is that something you can sense with Spirit Detection?"

"Yes. It was like that in the labyrinth last time… There were the spirits of Seekers who died in there before they accomplished their goal."

If we could listen to the regrets of the people who died there… maybe we could learn some secrets about the labyrinth. Then we could get a different perspective from other Seekers and learn more about this place.

Archery Master 1 could be good, but I thought it was better to focus on increasing the number of attacks instead of the strength of each attack. Shooting two arrows at once or some sort of scatter shot weren't normal archery skills, but it was entirely possible they existed here.

"All right. Since you want it, too, I think you should take Medium. Cleansing could be useful if we go into a labyrinth where the Holy attribute is really effective, but I don't think it's something you need to take right now."

"Understood. Thank you, Arihito."

"I think Archery Master is also a strong skill, but it's not necessary at the moment since you're in a party with me. The more important thing is increasing the number of attacks."

"I'd get really strong if I got a skill that let me shoot multiple arrows at once."

"I was thinking the same thing. I think we will be a very powerful party if we can get defensive skills in place, too, and not just offensive ones."

We didn't talk about skills as long as I'd anticipated. We ended the conversation when Suzuna stopped being so worried about her skills. Well, everyone else was probably already asleep; we should get some rest, too.

"Right... We'll take care of some errands tomorrow and then take the day off," I said.

"Okay. Good night, Arihito." I went to my own bed, lay down on my back, closed my eyes, and tried to sleep.

I lay like that for a little while, but then I heard Suzuna moving in her bed.

"...Arihito, could we talk a little?"

"Hmm? Yeah, I don't mind. Ask whatever you like."

"Thank you. I'm not sure I can just ask this, but I thought since it was just the two of us... I just sort of wanted to know..."

"I don't mind. I don't really have anything to hide."

"...I was wondering if you could tell me about what you were like before coming to the Labyrinth Country— Actually, no, just about yourself in general..."

She sounded really nervous, even though there wasn't anything to be so hesitant about. I tried to decide what I should tell her, then ended up giving her a brief overview. I explained that I was an orphan with no close family and spoke about my time at work. After listening to me talk about my previous life, Suzuna then told me about how she went to an all-girls school and how she and Misaki had been together up until middle school, but that they'd gone to different high schools.

"A high school sophomore... I hate to say this, but you had practically your whole life ahead of you," I said.

"I actually don't think being reincarnated has been that bad. I was afraid at first, but sometimes, things happen, and you can't stop them. That's what I was thinking when I joined Ellie."

She'd kept her cool even though she'd just lost her life and was able to decide that going with Elitia was a good option. It seemed like everyone was trying to make their own path after being reincarnated, instead of just going with the flow. Well, Misaki did start off on a dangerous path, though.

"But then I met you, and I realized something—I didn't want to just go with the flow. I also wanted to make my own path and not just give in," said Suzuna.

"Not give in, huh... I've only managed to keep it together when things got rough because you're all here. I'm able to keep going down my own path because everyone else is headed in the same direction."

"…That's why everyone relies on you so easily. Because that's the kind of person you are. I think it's really amazing."

"Y-you do…? Suzuna, you sure you're not just overestimating me? I'm really nothing special." Suzuna was staring at me intently. She realized she was leaning forward and clamped her hand over her mouth before rolling over until her back was facing me.

"…Please forget what I just said. I already know—I know I'm pushy and overbearing."

"There's nothing wrong with being open about how you feel. I'm not, so I've always admired those who are."

Suzuna didn't say anything for a little while. She carefully smoothed her glossy black hair, which had gotten messed up when she rolled over, then turned over on her back and glanced sideways at me.

"…Arihito, are you saying you're not honest? I'm not sure that's true."

"W-well… You'll probably be creeped out when I tell you this, but when I got on that bus, I thought, *Wow, that girl's super pretty*. Then you caught my attention again at the Guild after we were reincarnated."

"R-really? …I noticed you on the bus, too, but I thought you looked really tired… S-sorry…"

"You don't need to apologize. I *was* really tired. I was actually hoping to take a break while skiing, but I doubt it would have gone that well. I mean, I like to ski, but I'm pretty bad at it."

Suzuna laughed. Thankfully, the mood had lightened.

"If we go to a labyrinth where there's snow and it's hard to get around, I'll teach you how to ski," she offered.

"It'd be fun if there really was a labyrinth like that... Actually, I'd be willing to bet there is. You can teach me then."

"Yes... Good night, Arihito."

Suzuna turned her back to me again. I stared at her back for some reason, but my eyelids started feeling heavy, and I was soon drifting off into sleep.

*I feel like I'm...forgetting something... Must be imagining things...*

I thought I saw a faint light in the dark room, but I had fallen asleep before I could really think about what it was. That night, I had a dream that someone came and slept in my bed with me. When I woke up the next morning, Suzuna had vanished from her bed. She was already dressed and up, waiting in the living room, but she mumbled and shrugged me off without giving a clear answer when I asked her why she'd gotten up so early.

# CHAPTER 2

# What Emerges from the Labyrinth

## Part I: Stampede

Once everyone had woken up, we rang the bell to call Millais and ask her to bring us breakfast. It featured eggs from a bird-type monster called a Sweet Bird and was topped with smoked meat from the same monster. Both were quite nice, and everyone in the party enjoyed the food. It came with a salad made from stalks of a plant-type monster called a Goblin Bush, which had a flavor and texture similar to watercress. The salad was topped with a sweet and tangy fruit-based dressing, which also wasn't bad. Apparently, the root of the Goblin Bush looked like a strange, little goblin face, but it was similar to a turnip and tasted quite nice, though we weren't served it this time.

We finished breakfast and got ready to head out. Millais and the other Maids were all lined up in the entrance hall to bid us farewell, making me feel like the master of the house.

"See you later," I said to them.

"Might I ask when you are thinking of returning? A general guess is perfectly fine," asked Millais.

"Uh, we'll probably be back around six tonight," I replied.

"Thank you. I will have dinner ready around then. Have a wonderful day."

""""Have a wonderful day!""""" chimed the remaining ten Maids in an impressive chorus. It made me think of the one time I'd gone to a maid café just to see what it was like...though these Maids seemed way more professional.

Before we took the rune and ores to a smith, we decided to first make a stop at the Guild. When we arrived, we saw a leaflet with something written in red pinned up to the notice board. A bunch of Seekers were crowded around reading it.

"If we don't do something about the stampede, then monsters'll just start coming out of the labyrinth, right?" one remarked.

"The location's not great... The Sleeping Marshes. Guess everyone's been avoiding it," said another.

I squeezed my way through until I was close enough to read the notice.

Due to the drastic decrease in the number of monsters defeated in the Sleeping Marshes, a Stampede Alert has been issued. We request the assistance of all Seekers level 3 and higher. Rewards and contribution points will be tripled until the Stampede Alert is lifted.

District Eight Guild General Manager

*   *   *

*Louisa…must have a lot on her plate.*

I wanted to help out as much as I could since the Guild had put out this notice. Our test was tomorrow, so there wouldn't be a problem if we went to the Sleeping Marshes today.

"What should we do, Arihito?" asked Elitia. The rest of the party didn't seem to know much about stampedes, so I wanted to check with Elitia that I was understanding it correctly.

"Elitia, what exactly happens during a stampede?" I asked.

"Labyrinth monsters are living creatures and reproduce as such, but they also *spawn* in order to maintain the conditions inside the labyrinths. Conversely, when there are too many monsters in a labyrinth, those monsters are forcefully ejected via the labyrinth's first floor entrance. A 'stampede' occurs when there is an abnormally large number of monsters."

While the entrances to the labyrinths may look like simple stairs, I was aware that you were actually teleported part way down the stairs. Apparently, the monsters could also come out the same way.

"Saying it like that makes it sound like a labyrinth itself is some sort of living thing… Like it has a mind of its own," said Igarashi. I remembered Ariadne, the 117th Hidden God. If she was the 117th, that meant there were over a hundred of these Hidden Gods.

*…A hidden floor completely different from the previous floors—the obvious conclusion would be that the Hidden God sleeping there was closely related to the labyrinth. Like a representative*

*of the labyrinth's will, maybe... Although, Ariadne didn't do any-*
*thing to imply that.*

But if there happened to be a Hidden God in a secret floor of every labyrinth, if we could find Hidden Gods other than Ariadne, we could possibly get some clues as to what exactly the labyrinths were in the first place.

"Good morning, Mr. Atobe. I do apologize for the fuss around here," said Louisa.

"Oh, good morning, Louisa. It looks like things are in pretty dire straits at the moment. Would it be all right if we help to hold back the stampede as well?"

Louisa opened her eyes wide. I seemed to surprise her a lot, even though I thought it was a perfectly normal suggestion.

"I appreciate your consideration. Your party is currently my... No, the entire District Eight Guild's most powerful party. We would greatly appreciate your assistance."

"Louisa... You don't need to be so hesitant to ask for help. It's normal for us to help each other out in times of need, isn't it?" I saw her wipe a tear from her eyes with a handkerchief. Apparently, the situation was that bad. The Guild employees most likely had a significant amount of extra work and pressure on them when stampedes occurred.

There wasn't much they could do about the fact that people avoided the labyrinths that had a lot of monsters, which could inflict dangerous status ailments, and instead went to the safer labyrinths, which were easier to advance in. There were most likely a lot of people who stayed in the easy and scenic Field of Dawn even after they got fairly strong. That's probably what I would have done had I not found so many companions.

"All right then, I will update you on the current situation. Please come into this room…," said Louisa as she started to show us to a meeting room—but that's when it happened.

"—Monsters! There are monsters in the city! Call the guards!"

"There's too many of them! All Seekers, get in the building now— Gaaah!"

A strange, inhuman something was flying outside the Guild entrance, attacking people. The Seekers had no way to defend against the attacks from above, instead getting brutally injured before scrambling into the Guild and collapsing. Louisa ran over to them, calling out bravely while she checked them over.

"We need a Healer immediately! Everyone, please remain calm—the guards will be here any moment!"

"Louisa, it's no good! The guards are deployed at front lines across the city. It'll be some time until they make it here!" replied one of Louisa's junior Guild workers.

"No… Then, wh-what can we do…?" asked Louisa, her voice shaky. I placed a hand on her shoulder to try and calm her. "Mr. Atobe… I am so sorry; a Guild employee like me should not lose their head so easily…"

"We'll fight, too. We've got some experience fighting flying monsters, so leave it to us… Everyone, are you ready?" I asked, turning back to see that the entire party had already drawn their weapons. I didn't know what it was like outside, but the ruckus made it sound like there could be ten or even twenty enemies.

"Suzuna, sorry to ask all of a sudden, but take the Salt Laying skill. Louisa, do you have salt? If you do, we can keep them from attacking the Guild," I said. There were a lot of level-1 and level-2 Seekers in here who didn't even have any equipment. If we could establish this as a safe haven, then we could go out to fight without worrying about the people here.

"Salt... Yes, I'll go get some. Mr. Atobe, please, the town...," said Louisa.

"We'll protect it no matter what," I replied. There were people in District Eight who had helped me so much. The only reason I'd been able to live as a Seeker was because Louisa had given me those Mercenary Tickets. Everyone here had been kind to me.

"Arihito, I have the salt!" Suzuna called out.

"Good! First, Elitia, push back the enemies coming this way! Then we'll rush out together!" I ordered.

"All right. Kyouka, Theresia, follow behind me!" said Elitia.

"We're on it! Misaki, you follow carefully once we've gone outside!" shouted Igarashi.

"Y-yeah... I'll follow as cautiously as I can!" Misaki yelled back.

Elitia made up our advance guard and leaped out the door. The monster trying to make its way in was strange: It was covered entirely in tentacles.

*First, let's test whether I can still use Attack Support 1 even though I took Attack Support 2... Activate Attack Support 1...!*

"—Haaaah!"

"KIIII!"

Elitia ran out, sliding her sword from its sheath and lashing out with a Slash Ripper in the process. The ball of tentacles came flying down, and surprisingly, a gigantic maw opened from where it was hidden by the tentacles. Sticky saliva splattered out as it tried to gulp Elitia down, and—

```
◆Current Status◆
> ELITIA used SLASH RIPPER  ⟶  Hit FLYING DOOM
11 support damage
> 1 FLYING DOOM defeated
```

—the monster was sliced in half with one strike. The two halves still had momentum from when it had tried to swoop down and eat Elitia, so it continued on its trajectory and crashed through the door into the building, causing the young Seekers to screech in fear. I looked at the monster halves on the ground. Its upper and lower jaws were lined with sharp teeth and covered in green blood. No wonder nobody wanted to enter the Sleeping Marshes if it had monsters like this in it.

I'd just used Attack Support 1, but I wanted to test out how effective Attack Support 2 was. But right now, we needed to focus on eliminating monsters, not experimenting with my skills.

"Good. Everyone, stay inside! There will be less damage and injury if you leave things to the more experienced Seekers!" called Elitia. As a level-9 Seeker, her commands held some weight. The Seekers followed her orders, since there were none there above level 3.

We exited the Guild, and Suzuna used Salt Laying around the entrance and windows. Before long, more Flying Dooms appeared in the sky above the nearby buildings and started hurtling down when they saw us. I fired a long-range shot from my ebony sling at one that was coming after me, but the one hit didn't have enough power to bring it down—!

"Ack!"

"Atobe, watch out!"

"—!"

Igarashi interrupted the Flying Doom's path with her cross spear, and Theresia blasted it away with a Wind Slash.

"—Suzuna, Misaki! Step in front of me, even if it's just half a step, then continue the attack!" I ordered.

"Got it, Arihito! Hah!"

"Eat my dice—!"

Suzuna's arrow and Misaki's die struck the Flying Doom that had bounced off a wall and was now coming again for another attack. With the twenty-two support damage, they were able to finish it off, even though they weren't as strong as Elitia.

"They're just flying all over the place... Arihito, we need to help the support people and Seekers who can't protect themselves," said Elitia.

"Yeah, I know. These monsters are the ones that came out of the labyrinth because of the stampede... Which means they'll be coming from the entrance to the Sleeping Marshes. The guards will most likely head there, so let's cover a different area."

""""Right!"""""

The sky was full of these flying monsters all across District

Eight. There were at least a couple dozen Flying Dooms, with a bigger, vibrant one mixed in—likely a Named Monster, which we'd need to do something about.

Suzuna would continue to lay salt to create safe havens as we kept saving the residents of the city and defeating monsters. It was the start of a surprisingly chaotic day.

## Part II: A Flurry of Wings

We finished our first fight after leaving the Guild, and Elitia showed us that our license would display the monsters' locations when they were in the city. In the labyrinth, you couldn't tell where a monster was unless it was within your detection range. There weren't any people other than the party members displayed on the license, perhaps to maintain privacy.

About fifty monsters had entered the city as a result of the stampede. Half of those were gathered around the Named Monster. The blip indicating the Named Monster was pulsing, making it look ominous even on the license.

I realized something looking at the map: There were a number of monsters circling around Falma's shop.

*We need to clear out the closer areas first. There's a lot around the Mercenary Office in the east, too... But would they be able to send the mercenaries out to fight...?*

There were sure to be other Seekers who were level 3 or higher and had gone outside to fight, but the enemy was moving erratically, making it impossible to join up with them and work together. Some places ended up locked in a stalemate. The monsters were flying relatively high, out of range for magic and your average ranged weapon, so there was no way to shoot them down.

*We could lie in wait for them to come down. That'd be tough work, but our only other option would be to wait for them to come attack us... No, hang on... There's that skill...*

I could theoretically use Rear Stance on the Flying Dooms in the sky, but it would essentially be a suicide attack. No, I was actually thinking of Auto-Hit, which would make it so that the arrow would hit no matter what, even if the enemy were out of the bow's range. The problem with that, though, was that Suzuna's magic was going down every time she used Salt Laying, even if it was only a small amount. I'd asked her to regularly throw salt to create a larger area that the monsters couldn't enter, so it wasn't ideal to use up even more of her magic... Which left us with one option.

"Elitia, could you lure the enemy down for us?" I asked.

"Not a problem! I probably can't take that vividly colored one down in one hit, but the rest of 'em are all mine!"

"All right... Igarashi, use Force Target on Elitia!"

"Understood... Brave spirit of the warrior, draw the enemy's wrath... *Force Target*!"

◆Current Status◆
> Kyouka activated Force Target ──→ Target: Elitia
> 3 Flying Dooms and 1 Demi-Harpy switched targets
  to Elitia

*A Demi-Harpy... So those are mixed in, too. I wonder what kind of attacks they have...?*

"Guys, we've got a new enemy coming! Keep your guard up!" I shouted instinctively.

◆Current Status◆
> Arihito activated Morale Support 1 ──→ 6 party
  members' morale increased by 11

Just then, I realized something: It was less than twenty-four hours since the party had used their Morale Discharge. Morale Support shouldn't have had an effect, but everyone's morale still went up.

*So after one night... No. Did staying in the nice lodging improve morale? Will we be able to get the party's morale to one hundred before we fight the Named Monster?*

If a person's morale reached one hundred, they could use a powerful set skill called a Morale Discharge. Whether or not we had that final trick up our sleeves could greatly influence the outcome of the battle.

Flying Dooms weren't too much to handle so long as you were capable of catching and landing an attack on a flying enemy. Even a level-3 party could defeat one. I imagined that Named Monster wasn't as strong as some monsters we'd fought so far, but even if it were a bit of an overkill, I wanted to try and activate Igarashi's Morale Discharge, Soul Mirage, which would give each of the party a duplicate of themselves in the form of a mirage warrior and double the number of our attacks. That was much better than risking a long battle that someone could get injured in.

Force Target was working on the monsters flying above the Chest Cracker shop; the Flying Dooms started to come down one after another into a street a short way from the shop.

"Makes no difference how many of you there are... You're too slow!" shouted Elitia, easily evading the tentacle-ball tackles without using any skills to improve her speed. Twice, three times she dodged, then Igarashi and Theresia leaped forward to attack the one that had ricocheted off the ground after Elitia dodged it.

*I'll use Attack Support 1 again... I should focus on using the stable extra damage for now!*

"Here I go! *Double Attack!*"

"—!"

The Flying Doom was pierced by dazzlingly fast strikes from Igarashi's cross spear. Suzuna's arrow then struck the monster, finishing it off. The effect of Force Target was still active, wrapping Elitia in a yellow light that seemed to scream caution and pulled in the remaining two monsters. Elitia evaded their attacks, and one bounced from the ground to the wall before coming down to try and swallow Elitia whole, but she readied her sword and slashed out with a killing blow.

"—Fall to your death!" she screamed, even more forcefully than usual, attacking twice even though she was in such close proximity to the two incoming creatures.

◆Current Status◆
> ELITIA activated RISING BOLT
> Stage 1 hit FLYING DOOM A
11 support damage
> Stage 2 hit FLYING DOOM B
11 support damage
> 2 FLYING DOOMS defeated

*What a terrifying skill—multiple attacks on an upward swing... Wait, there's still the Demi-Harpy... Where the hell is it...?*

A chill ran up my spine— That couldn't mean anything good. Right as the feeling struck me, I heard a song. I couldn't understand any of the words, but I could feel my consciousness slipping the moment it reached my ears.

◆Current Status◆
> DEMI-HARPY activated LULLABY
> ELITIA, KYOUKA, SUZUNA, and MISAKI fell asleep

"Ah... Atobe..."

"This...song..."

"Arihito..."

"Agh... Get it together, guys! You'll die if you fall asleep here!" I shouted. I was being completely serious. If we couldn't locate the Demi-Harpy, it would use Lullaby on the rest of us, and we would never wake again.

*These things are really dangerous if they can put us to sleep... I can't believe this... If I don't do something...*

"—SKREEEEEE!"

◆Current Status◆
> Demi-Harpy activated Call Reinforcements
> 2 Sweet Birds were summoned

It summoned other monsters with its birdlike call. My slumbering friends would be hurt if I didn't act!

*Can Theresia and I handle this alone...? Even if I back her up, things will get bad if we're surrounded... Dammit, this wouldn't have happened if I'd gotten stronger...*

I heard the sound of flapping wings—bird-type monsters—from far away. Two of them appeared from the sky and saw us, then circled above us before bursting into song.

◆Current Status◆
> 2 Sweet Birds activated Flurry of Wings
> Attack and defense of winged monsters
  temporarily increased

*For these foes to buff their own abilities... They're way different from the monsters we've fought so far!*

I needed a way to wake my sleeping allies—if only I had a support skill that removed status ailments. I'd known that was a weak spot in our defenses, but I hadn't found a way to fix it yet. Being put to sleep would directly result in death here. We needed to find a way to defend against all status ailments that prevented action—before we encountered them.

"KAAAAAW!"

The two Sweet Birds swooped down to attack. They were covered in bright green feathers with a blazing red cockscomb on their head—but the comb pointed forward like a spear...! To make things worse, the two birds weren't going after me or Theresia, but rather Elitia, who still had Force Target on her.

The only way I could protect her at this distance was if I used Rear Stance to teleport and used my own body as a shield. But if I did that, then I'd—

*...Even if I'm left with a single vitality point...that's better than letting Elitia die!*

Theresia used Accel Dash, but she wouldn't make it to Elitia in time. I activated Rear Stance and tried to be her shield.

The moment after I teleported, I heard the roaring of wind as I watched the two birds dive down. I prayed they would leave me with at least one vitality point and threw myself over Elitia, and then—

"Awooo—!"

◆Current Status◆
> ARIHITO activated REAR STANCE ⟶ Target: ELITIA
> CION activated COVERING ⟶ Target: ARIHITO

*—Cion!*

The massive dog shot out like a bolt of lightning and placed himself between me and the enemies. Cion got the defense boost from my Defense Support 1 and took the attack of the two Sweet Birds, and then—

"Awooo!"

◆Current Status◆
> Cɪᴏɴ activated Tᴀɪʟ Cᴏᴜɴᴛᴇʀ ⟶ Hit Sᴡᴇᴇᴛ Bɪʀᴅ A
11 support damage
> 1 Sᴡᴇᴇᴛ Bɪʀᴅ defeated

A one-hit KO, but there was still one more Sweet Bird. It had bounced off the defensive wall from my Defense Support 1, strengthened by Cion's own defense, and was now flapping awkwardly in the sky as it tried to pull back.

It was then that another massive form leaped from the street that the Chest Cracker was on.

"Grraaaaw!"

I couldn't believe that beastly howl came from a dog. Cion's mother leaped at the remaining Sweet Bird, knocking it dead with a single swipe of her massive forepaw.

*Incredible... That mom dog has got to be a pretty high level.*

"Mr. Atobe, are you all right?!"

It was Falma. Of course—with the two silver hounds, she wasn't in much danger at all... Actually, that wasn't true.

*If the Demi-Harpy gets them with its status effects, even Cion and her mom... I have to do it, then!*

"Falma, please look after my friends! I'm going to finish the last monster!" I shouted.

"Ah... Mr. Atobe, where is the last monster?!" I didn't know the answer. Most likely, it was hidden somewhere on a rooftop. I'd just have to risk using that skill in order to find and capture it instantly!

*Even if I can't see it, as long as it's in battle with me... Please let it work!*

◆Current Status◆
> Arihito activated Rear Stance ⟶ Target:
                                    Demi-Harpy

My senses stopped working for a moment, and then the next moment, I found myself behind a young girl who had wings instead of arms.

"KAAW?!"

It was on top of the roof. I didn't bother to secure my footing; I just used everything I had to grapple the Demi-Harpy.

"—Cion! Or mom dog even! Catch us, please!" I shouted.

"Woof!"

"KAAAW!!"

Since I wasn't capable of close combat, the only real option I had was to pin the Demi-Harpy's wings and jump from the roof. As I plunged down with the Demi-Harpy, Cion leaped from a window ledge on the building, catching us perfectly on her broad, fluffy back.

"Oof!"

We landed, and the impact threw me off Cion's back. I was pretty roughed up from the fall, but I'd managed to hold on to the Demi-Harpy.

"Well, now... So cute, yet such a giant pain... Nasty little miss monster," Falma said.

"Cheep...cheep...," it replied. It'd suddenly become quite cooperative, for good reason. It was surrounded by Falma, Cion, mom dog, and Theresia with her short sword drawn. And Cion's mom was growling in anger at the Demi-Harpy because Cion had been attacked.

"Grrrrrr!"

She opened her jaw threateningly, wide enough that she could easily swallow the Demi-Harpy whole. Even I thought the sight was scary. The Demi-Harpy must have actually thought mom dog was going to eat her and so stopped struggling. Actually, she seemed to completely lose consciousness out of sheer terror.

"Well, we somehow managed to make it out of that... Uh, T-Theresia?" I said. She was still cautious about the Demi-Harpy possibly waking up, but she moved behind me and wrapped her arms around me. She was shaking. Maybe I made her worry when I jumped off the building.

"I'm all right; Cion caught me. I'm sorry I scared you. I couldn't think of any other options. The only way to beat it was to grapple it from behind."

"......"

Theresia silently shook her head. Maybe she was saying I didn't need to apologize.

"Mr. Atobe, there's a stampede, isn't there? That's why there are monsters in the city," said Falma.

"Yes. This Demi-Harpy sings a song that puts people to sleep. It's dangerous if you don't have anything that prevents you from falling asleep, so you should hide in your shop until it's over. We'll make it so that no monsters come into this neighborhood."

"I have a few accessories in the shop that protect against Sleep inflicted by monsters' attacks. I purchased them for the store when multiples were found in chests that I opened..."

"Huh? ...Really?!"

"Normally, I'd supply them to a specialty shop, but please take them. I think they're needed now. I'll go to the nearby Pharmacist to get some medicine that will wake your allies up. Astarte, please carry everyone back to the shop."

We'd need to gather ourselves and prepare for the fight against the Named Monster and its group of monsters. Theresia and I worked together to place our still-sleeping companions and the unconscious Demi-Harpy atop Astarte—Cion's mom. I was uncomfortable killing the Demi-Harpy because she looked so much like a human... This wasn't really the place to be so kind, but it wasn't a threat as long as we could keep it from singing. My party faced annihilation thanks to this small Demi-Harpy, and I was now very well aware of the dangers of status ailments. I needed to take them as seriously as possible to make sure no one got hurt because of them.

Theresia followed close behind me the entire way. She still seemed worried about me. I wanted to avoid any crazy suicide attacks in the future so that I didn't make her worry more.

# Part III: Battle Interception

We carried our companions into the Chest Cracker shop, and Eyck and Plum came up from the stairs. They'd probably been hiding just in case.

"Welcome back, Mommy! ...Huh? Everyone's asleep," said Eyck.

"You okay, Arihito? You got a scrape here. I'll give it a bandage," Plum said to me.

"Oh, thank you. It's not that bad, though."

"I can't believe you would do something so dangerous... You are braver than I had thought, Mr. Atobe," praised Falma. It didn't seem all that extreme from my perspective. I was only able to do it because Cion and the others were there. It's not like I would've done something that reckless without thinking.

"Mommy, can I give Arihito medicine?" asked Plum.

"Ah, don't; potions are too valuable for that...," I refused.

"Oh, no, there are things called healing herbs that are used to make potions," said Falma. "If you dry them and grind them into a powder, you can use those alone to heal minor injuries. The biggest problem is they don't taste very nice."

"Oh, I see. Even so, if they're used as ingredients for potions, they must be valuable...," I started to say, but Falma put a finger to her lips, like she wanted to keep that part her little secret.

"The Guild provides a number of different medicines to the

city people in a medicine kit to keep in their homes. Some people do sell the contents for money, but we haven't used ours... Please let us help you, especially considering the situation outside." Falma brought me the healing herbs on a piece of paper, along with a glass of water. She warned me they didn't taste good, so I braced myself for the worst, but it was sort of like herbal medicine. It was almost spicy, but the taste wasn't really that terrible.

*Oh... My vitality recovered. They were just minor wounds, but I feel better now that I can actually see them heal.*

"Ah-ha-ha, you made a funny face when you took it," Plum observed.

"The worse it tastes, the better it works, you know," said Eyck.

The two seemed to have taken a liking to me, and they were both watching as I swallowed the medicine. I couldn't ask for Astarte's help in the coming battle since Falma and the kids would need her protection, but I was hoping I could ask them if I could take Cion along.

Theresia and Falma were working together to give the rest of the party some pills. Falma came back to where I was once she was done and seemed able to guess what I wanted to ask based on my expression alone.

"Cion is still in your party. She thinks of you as a companion, which is why she was the first to notice that your party had come near," she said.

"Oh... I'm sorry; I forgot to return her to your house's party," I said.

"No need to apologize. I'm the one who asked you to take Cion along with you. Actually, I think it's quite wonderful that she protected you. Astarte is obviously brave, but Cion's grown up to be quite the courageous guard dog as well," said Falma as she petted Cion's head. Even though Cion was sitting, her head was as high as a grown adult's, so she had to lower it so Falma could reach.

"…Then, I hope you don't mind if he helps us again. I would ask her to use Covering while I support her to increase her defense, but…I feel really bad using your beloved dog as a shield."

"Silver hounds are regularly used as vanguards. They're bigger than humans and have high vitality… So please don't worry. Please feel free to put her in whichever position you think would best benefit your party," said Falma.

I really felt like Falma herself was quite courageous. She might have retired from seeking, but she would need to go into the labyrinth every once in a while to maintain her level and skills, so she probably had plenty of battle experience.

"Mmm… Where am I…?" murmured Elitia.

"Is this Falma's shop…? S-sorry, it looks like we've caused you some trouble…," said Igarashi. Misaki and Suzuna also started to open their eyes shortly after.

"Ah… Arihito, watch out! That weird song—!" cried Misaki.

"The monster… Did you defeat it, Arihito?" asked Suzuna.

"Luckily, Theresia and I weren't put to sleep. Cion and her mom helped out, so we somehow managed to defeat them… We actually captured one, too." I explained about the dangers of Lullaby, and everyone looked warily at the Demi-Harpy. Apparently, many monsters became quite cooperative if you took away their sense of sight, so we'd blindfolded and gagged her and tied her wings to her feet... She'd be dangerous if we hadn't, but I felt bad for her, so we didn't bind her up any more than that.

"Mommy, is this feathery girl a monster?" asked Plum.

"Yes. I think it's safe now, but don't get too close to her. Mr. Atobe, since you captured her alive, do you intend to hand her over to the Monster Ranch?" asked Falma.

"Monster Ranch...?" I asked back.

"It's a place that cares for and trains monsters to become allies of Seekers. It's like a storage facility that houses the monsters until you use a specialized summoning stone to call them to help you," explained Elitia. I hadn't considered capturing monsters until now, but if it was like she said, it would be possible to get monsters to help us out... Monsters with special attacks would be particularly useful.

I decided to try putting the Demi-Harpy into the Monster Ranch, partially so I could learn how the ranch worked. Also, the thought of her being dissected was just a little too grotesque for me to think about.

"By the way, what do other Seekers do when they beat a Demi-Harpy?" I asked.

"While there are many humanoid monsters like orcs that attack and prey on humans, Demi-Harpies just disturb humans, allowing other monsters to prey on them," said Falma. "The Demi-Harpies themselves don't eat meat. Because of that, Seekers don't see them as an actual enemy. Many capture them, take feathers, clip their nails, then release them." That part of the conversation was probably disturbing enough for the children, so Falma leaned in to me and spoke low for the next part. "Some people don't like to engage in battle with them because of how they look, but it is standard practice to kill them as soon as they're seen, since Lullaby is such a dangerous skill."

So there was the option of sending monsters to the Monster Ranch if I had a hard time bringing myself to kill them because of their appearance. Then, when we needed more strength, I could summon them to increase the skills available to us... I decided to think about whether or not I could fight alongside a monster whenever I came up against something in the future.

"Please keep in mind that only a portion of monsters can become allies with humans, since the majority can't communicate with us," explained Falma. "It would be best to consider those tentacle monsters in the sky untrainable, for example. Even though there may be people with the necessary skills to accomplish that."

"Right, I see... Thank you very much for the information. Now, you mentioned some sleep prevention equipment...," I said.

"Yes, that would be these accessories. I have earrings, bracelets, and necklaces. Thankfully, accessories that protect against Sleep 1 are fairly common, so I have enough for the whole party."

*Sleep 1*—that meant there were attacks that had even more powerful sleep effects, and we weren't set for sleep protection from here on out. I filed that information away in my mind, but this should be plenty for now.

I was considering the possibility that the Named Flying Doom was also capable of inflicting status ailments, so I wanted to ask Falma if she had anything else.

"Sorry to ask for more, Falma, but do you have anything that protects against other status ailments?"

"Let's see… This headband protects against Confusion. Would you like to use this as well?"

"Could we borrow it just in case? I don't know what the enemy will come at us with, so I'd rather have the insurance."

"That's a good mind-set to have. Please take it, then."

"I think you should wear it, Arihito, since you're the leader. I want to make sure you have a strong defense since we take our orders from you," said Elitia, and I accepted the headband and put it on as she suggested. It had a metal plate on it to protect my forehead, so I felt more protected after securing it in such a way that it wouldn't slide around.

"All right… Let's keep an eye out for any other Demi-Harpies and go beat that Named Monster," I said.

"I wish you all luck. Are you certain you don't want to take Astarte with you?" asked Falma.

"There's always a chance something might happen here, so I think it's best if she stays with you. There are other Seekers and mercenaries outside," I replied. "We'll definitely be able to push back these monsters if we meet up with some of them."

"Good luck, Arihito!" said Eyck.

"Be careful! Don't get hurt!" yelled Plum.

We headed back outside, encouraged by the children—only for the Flying Dooms circling in the sky to notice us and start heading our way, one after another.

"—Let's keep moving as we defeat these ones! Don't do anything reckless!" I ordered. I couldn't forget to activate Morale Support. Elitia and Cion made up the front line of our party, reducing the number of enemies coming at us. Any that made it through the front two were forced back by Theresia and Igarashi, and then me, Suzuna, and Misaki would attack with our long-range weapons.

"Boooowwow!"

"You're pretty capable... Good girl. Let's do this!" said Elitia as she ran alongside Cion. The mob of Flying Dooms coming at us from high in the sky weren't going to be any match for my party.

We fought our way through a number of small encounters and were able to reduce the total number of monsters by a fair amount. There weren't any more small groups of Flying Dooms left, leaving just the large mass with the Named one. I'd been regularly using Morale Support, building up everyone's morale, but something happened when we got near the square in front of the entrance to the Field of Dawn.

"Ribault! ...Madoka!" I shouted. Ribault spent his time rescuing Seekers who'd gotten themselves in trouble in the Field of Dawn, the labyrinth where most newbie Seekers started out. He'd helped me out a few times as well, and now he was up against the monsters in the city. And then there was the weapons seller, Madoka, hiding in the shadows of one of the buildings.

"Arihito, don't come any closer! The monster— The monster's song...!" warned Madoka.

"Take cover! It'll attack the second it sees you... Agh!" shouted Ribault, holding a shield up as a laser-like beam of heat shot at him.

◆Monsters Encountered◆
★Death from Above
Level 5
In Combat
Dropped Loot: ???
18 Flying Dooms
Dropped Loot: ???
2 Demi-Harpies
Dropped Loot: ???
3 Sweet Birds
Dropped Loot: ???

Based on the Named Flying Doom's actual name, it would be coming at us with every intent of annihilating us. It had also solved one major weakness of the Flying Doom, which was that it had no long-range attacks. Instead, it was breaking the trend by having a high-firepower attack.

"Gah... Agh..."

"Ribault, pull back!" I shouted.

"R-right... Thanks..."

Ribault was carrying a kite shield he'd borrowed from one of his party members and had rushed out to draw the enemies' attacks. Unfortunately, the shield wasn't enough to completely block the attacks, and Ribault's vitality was getting whittled down.

In the middle of the square were a number of injured demi-human mercenaries and Seekers. Some had taken direct hits from the laser, suffering horrendous burns all over their bodies. They still seemed alive...but we couldn't waste a single moment. If we didn't defeat these monsters soon, people would die.

"—Look out!" I shouted as my heart skipped a beat. Madoka had been hiding by a building after her stall had been burned down, but she was now leaping out from cover. She was trying to protect one of the fallen Seekers that a Flying Doom was swooping down to attack.

"Cion!" I cried.

"—Woof!"

Cion followed my command and used Covering to guard Madoka. With my Defense Support 1, a Flying Doom's tackle at least would be reduced to zero damage.

"Get back into cover by the building!" I shouted. "Elitia, can you draw that thing's fire to yourself?"

"I can dodge it if I use Sonic Raid... Okay, Arihito! I can draw it with Force Target and then finish it off when it comes down to attack!"

"All right... Everyone, be careful of that laser fire! I don't know if my Defense Support will be able to deflect it!"

The Death from Above was flying slowly around in the sky,

seeking its next target. But like Elitia said, the moment that thing came down, we wouldn't be letting it fly up again.

## Part IV: Protection

Cion used Tail Counter, her big fluffy tail whipping out to knock back the Flying Doom, then she and Madoka ran into cover by one of the buildings. But we weren't out of the woods just yet.

"Ribault, get out of here! You'll die if you take any more damage!" I shouted.

"Like hell I will... You're the ones who should run! That thing's got its sights on me; I can take at least one more shot! You run. I'll follow after!" he yelled back.

"But, Mr. Ribault, you're not even a Shield Knight— What are you saying?!" called Misaki.

"You're right; I'm a Lumberjack! And that's why I'm not about to leave without cutting this thing down!"

I understood Ribault's insistence, but I simply didn't see a need for him to risk his life here... Although, I empathized with the guy. Ribault was not the kind of person to go quietly when face-to-face with a monster.

"—Elitia, can you dodge that laser?!" I shouted.

"I got this! Let me help you in your time of need! ...Kyouka, use Force Target on me!" replied Elitia.

"No, I'm going, too! There's no way you can handle that many!" said Igarashi.

"Igarashi... I'll back you up! Just make sure you dodge that laser!"

""Understood!""

The two rushed out, and we could suddenly hear the song of the harpies that were hiding on the roofs of the buildings surrounding the square, almost like they'd been lying in wait for us.

*If those monsters use Lullaby now, Ribault and his party will... Wait, no... Oh, if the Demi-Harpy isn't essentially right overhead, then they'll be outside of Lullaby's range. If the Demi-Harpies just come this way...!*

But the Demi-Harpies weren't going to be so kind as to take to the skies and show themselves without getting ready first. The three Sweet Birds responded to the harpies' song, using their own Flurry of Wings to enhance all their abilities. Two of the Sweet Birds came our way, the last heading toward Ribault, who couldn't see it coming because the shield was limiting his field of vision. Elitia saw it approaching and went to cover him.

Fights were breaking out across the square, and I was at my limit trying to take in everything and issue orders. The moment I thought that, my field of vision seemed to expand, so much so that I seemed to even be taking in the sky.

◆Current Status◆
> ARIHITO activated HAWK EYES ⟶ Increased
  ability to monitor the situation

I suddenly realized I was looking at the Death from Above almost like it was right in front of me. It had a cooldown period after it shot off its laser. Its entire body glowed white from the heat. After that, its brightly colored, spherical, tentacle-covered body faded to a red-hot color... But considering there were only about fifteen seconds before it could shoot again, we couldn't waste any time. I also realized it could use Self-Destruct if its vitality was low, which meant we needed to give it everything we had when it got down to half its vitality, in an attempt to kill it in one shot.

"Theresia, push back just one of the birds! We'll take care of the other one!" I ordered.

"—!"

Theresia used Wind Slash, separating the two Sweet Birds and knocking one back. The other one flew toward us rearguards, but an arrow, a die, and a slingshot bullet mercilessly pierced its head. The three of us long-range attackers were just about able to take down the bird by working together.

Theresia waited until the last second before the other bird's counterattack to use Accel Dash and dodge. It wasn't able to slow its flight and ended up crashing to the ground. Only I would be able to follow up with an attack; Suzuna wouldn't have an arrow ready, and Misaki wasn't yet used to preparing ranged attacks that quickly!

But at that very moment, something came flying from behind me—a metal ball attached to a long chain. It was a direct hit on the

Sweet Bird and bought enough time for Suzuna and Misaki to add in their attacks.

Behind the Sweet Birds came the Demi-Harpies, even though their Sweet Bird cover had been destroyed. They assumed they could still win if they could just put us to sleep.

"Dumb move. We're pretty good at staying awake!" I shouted at them.

"—Cheep?!"

◆Current Status◆
> Demi-Harpies activated Lullaby
> No effect on Arihito's party as they are all immune

It appeared they hadn't considered their song wouldn't be effective, because both of the young-girl-looking Demi-Harpies seemed shocked. By then, we had all had time to get ready for our next attack.

"Everyone, fire!"

"Dice Attack!"

"—Hyaa!"

"—!"

My slingshot and Misaki's die hit one of the Demi-Harpies. It took an extra eleven support damage and lost its balance, making it stall in midair and crash clumsily to the ground. Suzuna's arrow pierced the other's wing, tearing off feathers. It fell and tried to get control of its flight again, but in that moment, Theresia leaped toward it and launched a Wind Slash. Forced off-balance, it used the last of its strength in one more vain flap of its wings but gave in, falling slowly to the ground.

That got rid of some of the more dangerous enemies here, but we needed to capture the unconscious Demi-Harpies. Afterward, we retreated to the cover of the buildings, where we saw the person who'd helped us out earlier with their chain flail.

"Leila... Good, you're all right," I said.

That person was Leila, the assistant manager of the Mercenary Office. She gave the impression that she was fairly strong, but her red hair was in disarray, sticking to her skin from sweat, her leather armor broken in several places.

"You all right, Arihito?" she asked. She'd come from behind us, but now I could see her eyepatch was torn. Below it, I could see her eye... It didn't look injured, but there was no life in it, like when you looked into a blind one.

"Leila, your eye...," I said.

"Oh, this... A long time ago, I fought a monster that steals your senses. I took an attack on my sight, and it was lost. I can still fight a bit, though, since I have the other one."

"All right, want to fight together, then? Do you have any skills to help with evasion? If you don't, then right now... Igarashi!" I shouted when I looked over and saw the attack.

"It's all right, Atobe! I can do this three... No, four more times!"

◆Current Status◆

> ★Death from Above activated Brilliant Flame
> Kyouka activated Mirage Step ⟶ Dodged Brilliant Flame

In a flash, the Death from Above's whole body was cloaked in brilliant light, which then gathered into a single point. The next moment, it shot out a beam of flame toward Igarashi, but she created a mirage of herself and dodged the attack. With her entire focus set on evading, she was unable to attack the Flying Doom that followed as well. She couldn't use Double Attack, nor could she knock back the monsters coming for her. She knew the risks she faced if she didn't defeat her enemy with a single hit.

Before the Flying Doom that'd attack Igarashi could return to the sky, Suzuna let loose an arrow, and Misaki took a gamble and threw one of her metal dice at it, doing at least some damage... But without the vanguard's attacks, there was no way we could take down a monster in one go, and so we couldn't reduce the enemies' numbers.

"If they all came at us at once, I could just take them all out in one go... This is so frustrating!" shouted Elitia, dropping them one by one as they took turns coming down. A Slash Ripper or Rising Bolt was a one-hit KO for these things, but it'd be far more effective to reduce their numbers if she could get a large number of them to gather in range of Blossom Blade. Instead, they were coming down in alternating twos and threes to attack. It was almost like they were aware and cautious of area attacks.

"Miss, I can lure them down—," started Ribault.

"I'm fine—you just run! What do you think your party will do if you die here?!" shouted back Elitia.

"Hmph... All right. I'll leave it to you, then... Haaaaaaah!"

Ribault was determined. He sprinted toward the buildings on

the other side of the square where his companions were hiding, picking up one of the fallen on his way, the whole time with the massively heavy shield on his back.

"Hurry! We'll lure the enemy!" shouted Elitia.

"—One more hit! I can take one more hit... Haaaaah!"

Cion was guarding Madoka. If I had Cion cover Ribault instead, she could take serious injury if my Defense Support didn't completely ward against the laser. My mind was racing. There were nine Flying Dooms left; the Named one was uninjured... And then I realized something.

*Death from Above hasn't used its laser... Has it run out of magic? Or is it aiming for something else—?*

As a mere ball of brightly colored tentacles, this monster was incapable of facial expressions...but I could've sworn it smiled. The remaining Flying Dooms went after Igarashi and Elitia, and Death from Above went for Ribault and the collapsed magic user he was carrying.

◆Current Status◆
> ★Death from Above activated Swallow Whole

*Crap—it's going after Ribault!*

Ribault was running with the shield on his back, which blocked his view of the sky. The beast's mouth was massive enough to consume a person in one bite, and it was flying down with intent to kill.

The name *Death from Above* didn't just refer to the laser

beam it shot from the air. It literally came from the heavens to kill. I'd been using Morale Support as I called out to everyone on the battlefield, but their morale was still only at ninety-nine. I just needed to pull off one more Morale Support. I could use Rear Stance on Ribault to go behind him, but then I'd just be eaten. Elitia had to use Blossom Blade to kill five of the Flying Dooms. Igarashi was forced to dodge. No one would make it to him in time.

But I wanted to save him. I couldn't let someone like him die, someone who was so aware that he couldn't win yet refused to back down. What could I do? If I was going to save him—I'd have to risk it all on one option. There was Ariadne, the being who'd given us her protection. If anyone could do it, it was a Hidden God!

"Ariadne, protect the person I'm going to support!" I said. My license responded to me, showing the page I wanted before I could even swipe my finger. I could only support those in my party...and Ariadne's protection was likely the same. But I did have one skill available that let me ignore that rule: Outside Assist. I hadn't thought I could help other parties, but this skill solved everything.

"Ribault, I'll back you up!"

"Arihito—?!"

◆Current Status◆
> Arihito activated Outside Assist
> Arihito activated Defense Support 1 ⟶ Target: Ribault

"GWOOOOOOOHH!"

Death from Above hurtled down to consume Ribault. I could tell that Defense Support 1 wouldn't be enough to defend against that attack. That mass, that speed—it was like a meteorite crashing to Earth and bringing death with it.

Would my prayers go unanswered? My throat was sore from shouting. No matter how much I yelled, I couldn't make them reach her ears.

*Can I do this...? Can I protect someone who's spent his whole life putting others first...?!*

I was filled with regret and anger, but the scene in front of me started to change, as if trying to rewrite those emotions. The area around Ribault as I supported him seemed to...*twist*. I heard her voice in my mind. Before, it had been mechanical and self-deprecating, but now, it was filled with fire.

*"I, Ariadne, grant my devotee and his allies my protection!"*

◆Current Status◆
> Arihito requested temporary support from Ariadne ⟶ Target: Ribault
> Ariadne activated Guard Arm
> ★Death from Above's Swallow Whole was ineffective

If his defenses failed, Ribault would be swallowed whole with his shield—but that didn't happen.

"What...is that...?" he stammered.

Put quite simply, it was a massive arm. It was like the hand of a giant, stopping Death from Above in its tracks despite it being so much bigger than Ribault. It crackled and shot sparks of electricity as it wrestled with the brightly colored beast. It was the hand of some mechanical person, appearing out of thin air to protect Ribault. I had heard Ariadne's voice, and then that huge arm appeared. That meant Ribault was being saved by a *Hidden God's protection*...and confirmed that the Hidden Gods were extraordinarily powerful beings.

"Wh-what the hell...? There's a hand comin' out of thin air...," said Ribault.

"Ribault... Oh, thank goodness... You idiot! Were you trying to get yourself eaten alive?!" shouted Misaki.

"Shit... You're not a regular guy, are you? ...Arihito, what the hell can't you do...?" said Ribault.

The Named Monster landed for a moment, but we weren't going to let it fly away again. I ordered Cion to cover Igarashi to buy us enough time for her, Theresia, and Misaki to use their Morale Discharge.

"Let's finish this here... Morale Discharge, Soul Mirage!"

"—!"

"Let's go! Morale Discharge, Fortune Roll!"

◆Current Status◆

> Kyouka activated Soul Mirage ⟶ All party members gained a Mirage Warrior

> Theresia activated Triple Steal ⟶ All party members received Triple Steal effects

> Misaki activated Fortune Roll ⟶ Next action will succeed automatically

"Scatter like flower petals! *Blossom Blade!*" cried Elitia.

The gigantic hand had flung back Death from Above, and Elitia dashed toward it, raining blows on it along with her mirage warrior. Stealing was successful on the first hit thanks to Fortune Roll, then the attacks piled up with the set damage. Between her and the mirage warrior, they landed a total of twenty-four attacks, shooting past three hundred total damage. Death from Above was a lower level than the Giant Eagle-Headed Warrior had been. The attacks cut down its vitality, and it was unable to float anymore. It crashed to the ground, motionless.

Suzuna, Cion, Leila, and I combined our attacks to go after the Flying Dooms that had encircled Igarashi. With the additional mirage warrior attacks, cleaning up the rest of them wasn't an incredibly difficult task. I realized how much of a help it was to have a duplicate of Cion.

◆Current Status◆
> 1 ★Death from Above defeated
> 4 Flying Dooms defeated

There were no more monsters left. By the time we'd all caught our breaths, the mirage warriors disappeared, too. I checked the map on my license and saw no remaining monsters displayed.

"Is it…over? Seriously, only you guys could have pulled that off…," marveled Ribault.

"Yes, it's all over… We managed to beat it somehow. But we're not done just yet."

The people who'd collapsed needed first aid; some of them had severe burns from the laser beam. We were happy to have won but put off any celebrations for the moment to begin helping the injured. The guards eventually arrived and started to lug off the injured to the Healers.

I went over to Ribault and his party of three others. He raised a hand and smiled as he saw me come over.

"We practically just met, and you're already the one saving me. You're something else," he said.

"Look who's talking… I'm just glad you're all right," I replied. He grinned, then looked at his friends. There was a heavy-set man who had lent Ribault the shield and a girl with a bow who seemed fine, but the magic user was unconscious. The person he'd saved was one of his friends.

"We dragged you into our mess… Sorry. And thank you," said Ribault apologetically.

"You don't need to thank me; we all fought together to protect the city. But couldn't you have hidden in the labyrinth?" I asked. One of Ribault's companions explained that when there was a stampede, you couldn't enter the labyrinths until all the monsters had been defeated, though they didn't know the reason why. It would've been a huge miscalculation on our part had we hidden in the labyrinth, unaware of this. I made sure to remember that tidbit and turned to help out the rescue squads, when…

"Melissa… And Rikerton!"

"Thank you for protecting the city, Mr. Arihito. We were only able to defeat some of the monsters that appeared near the shop;

we couldn't get near the big one... You really are quite strong," noted Rikerton.

"...Can I dissect the Named Monster? And the others, too?" asked Melissa.

"Yes please," I replied.

Melissa was covered in what looked like Flying Doom blood and was holding her butcher's knife. That meant they were at least strong enough to take on a Flying Doom between the two of them.

I was happy to know some of the people I knew were safe, but the damage to the city seemed quite extensive. I looked around at the square and building walls, which were covered in scorch marks and holes from the monsters' collisions, and wondered if there was any way we could help out with rebuilding.

## Part V: After the Battle

According to Leila, the monsters that appeared because of the stampede had rampaged around, attacking the city's residents and destroying buildings. When Leila and her coworkers got word, they tried to mobilize the mercenaries but were attacked before they could get everyone ready. They were unlucky in that the monsters were flying right above and started attacking the moment they saw the mercenaries leaving the office, damaging the office in the process as well.

The mercenaries had been taken to the Healers by the guards and were receiving medical treatment. Luckily, the one mercenary who'd taken a direct hit from the laser possessed a skill that improved their flame resistance, so they'd managed to escape with their life.

"No doubt we would've seen fatalities had the battle lasted even a little longer... I can't quite say everyone's doing fine, but we managed to make it through, and it's all thanks to you and your party, Arihito," said Leila. "As witness to your bravery, I intend to report your accomplishments to the Guild."

"No, that's not neces—," I started.

"Don't be so modest," she interrupted. "Having seen it in person, I have no doubt of your courage and your party's abilities." She'd already thought highly of me for adding Theresia to the party, and it seemed now her opinion was even higher.

"And that strange skill you used when you saved Ribault... Arihito, can you summon?" she asked.

"Summon...? Oh, I mean, I guess it's similar. Just think of it as a defense-type skill," I replied.

"Hmm... All right. Guess that's one of your party's secrets. I did see something similar once in a different district when I was still seeking..."

So there really were other adherents to the Hidden Gods... Either that or what she saw was some type of actual summoning magic. Although, I didn't think it'd be possible to summon just a hand like that to defend against an attack with the Summoning Stones that were used to call for actual living monsters.

"Leila, what you once saw summoned before... Was it like a giant, but only a part of it?" I asked.

"No, someone called forth a mud golem and used it as a shield. Golems can shape-shift, so it would be possible for it to change its whole body into one giant hand."

"Ah... I see. Thanks for letting me know." So it was something different. Finding a Hidden God wouldn't be quite that easy, nor would they be hiding in plain sight. Even though I'd requested Ariadne's protection in front of everyone, I doubted people would be able to realize it was connected to the Hidden Gods. Even Ribault and his friends probably assumed I was just using a skill called Guard Arm.

*That said, I'm not sure a human would be capable of using a defensive skill like that... Although, I'd like to believe my Defense Support skill is sort of headed in that direction...*

Carriers were called over to the site where we asked them to take care of the monsters we'd defeated. This time, we should let Rikerton handle everything. Melissa had already brought a cart over, and Rikerton was helping her take Death from Above back to the shop. I'd feel better if everything was all in the same place.

"Right, I'm gonna go check on the mercenaries. I also need to think about what we're gonna do about rebuilding the office... Wonder if we'll be able to rent a different building for a bit," pondered Leila.

"Let me know if there's any way I can help. You've done a lot for me; I want to pay you back if I can," I said. She didn't reply right away but just stared at me for a moment. She normally looked like a powerful and brave Amazon, but there was something different now with her red hair sticking up as she rubbed her ear... She was a battle-hardened warrior carrying a heavy chain flail, but I think she might have been a bit bashful then.

"...Do the people you fight with always feel this safe? It's almost like being hugged and protected from behind...," she admitted.

"Uh, um... I-I'm not really sure...," I stammered. She had moved in front of me after that first attack with her flail, so perhaps the Outside Assist skill let me support her as well... I wondered if Attack Support 1 felt like that, too.

"Hmm... Never mind. It's just my imagination. Forget I said anything. I'm gonna head out now," she said.

"A-all right... Take care, Leila." She shot me an awkward smile, took a cord that she had on hand to fix her eyepatch, and then walked off. She was probably embarrassed since she'd let me see her sheepishness, which was very unlike her.

I cast a glance across the square and noticed that Madoka was with the rest of the party. I went over to them, and she trotted away from the group to meet me.

"Arihito, thank you for saving me... If your party hadn't come, I'm not sure what would have happened to me...," she said shakily, her face pale. It was normal to be afraid after having a group of monsters that big come and attack you. Her stall, which she sold beginner weapons from, hadn't taken a direct hit, but the laser had scattered and broken a lot of her goods.

"It's really unfortunate what happened to the equipment. Will you still have enough to supply the new Seekers?" I asked.

"W-well… I can't say anything for sure without checking what exactly was lost…"

When we'd opened the Black Box, we ended up getting a lot of weapons that didn't have any pluses, but they were plenty strong enough for the beginners. There were limits to what job could equip which type of equipment, and apparently, there was even strong equipment that you couldn't use unless you were a high enough level… I hadn't come across anything that I couldn't equip yet. I was concerned, though, thinking that Madoka could get pulled into things if a stampede ever happened again like this.

"I know you provide weapons for beginners here, which is important work… But, Madoka, would you like to join our party exclusively and work as a Merchant? I mean, if you're in some sort of organization, I obviously won't tell you to leave that…," I said.

"Hmm… A-are you sure? I'm still only level two…"

"I'm only level two, too, Madoka. How 'bout we level up together?" suggested Misaki.

"Misaki…," said Madoka.

"I mean, that's just because I want more party members at my level! Suzu's one level higher and already doing tons of stuff. I shoulda gone with kendo or something…"

"I'm still trying to catch up to Arihito and everyone else," added Suzuna. "Madoka, why don't you try working with us? I'm sure you'll enjoy your time with Arihito." Madoka already seemed convinced, and the two girls were basically just adding on more reasons she should come. Madoka started to weep, perhaps finally feeling safe enough that she could, and Igarashi handed her a handkerchief for her to dry her eyes.

"To tell the truth, I was really thinking how much I wanted to level up and learn new skills. But...there were so many of those monsters, and I've never even gone to the end of the beginner labyrinth. I thought I was totally useless... So...," started Madoka.

"Don't give up. A party's all about helping each other out, and any job is an asset at higher levels. I wouldn't be able to do anything if I were alone," I said.

"...But you're so much stronger and more capable than me, Arihito. You didn't even seem scared when you saw all those monsters."

"Yeah, he does remain surprisingly calm. But that's why I think it's a good thing for you to join us. We might be all girls, but Atobe doesn't do anything weird," said Igarashi.

*On the contrary, I'm starting to suspect they all did something weird to me in the middle of the night that one time... Not that there's any real way of confirming it, since it'd blow up in my face if I were wrong and it was just a weird dream.*

Perhaps someday, I'd find an item that would let me video record while I was sleeping. Like...a record stone. *Hey, this is the Labyrinth Country—anything's possible.*

"U-um... Then...if you don't mind, I'd like to join your party," said Madoka.

"Of course. Thanks for joining. We might ask for your help as a Merchant, but we'll look for ways to help you gain levels, too. The more skills you have, the better you'll be able to assist us."

"Yes, thank you so very much!" said Madoka, the little Merchant girl with her turban. I'd met her right after coming to the Labyrinth Country, and now we were in the same party. I thought it'd be a good idea to add more people who could do things in town, not just people who were good in a fight.

"All right, now that you're convinced, I'd like to make a report. Arihito, I was able to steal this earlier," said Elitia, handing over the dropped loot she got from Death from Above. It was a rose-colored rock, most likely a magic stone. I had some Novice Appraisal Scrolls from when Falma opened that Black Box for us, so I used one here. According to the scroll, this was a confusion stone.

*Magic stones often reflect the special attacks of the monsters that have them. In other words, Death from Above had some special skill that inflicted Confusion... I wonder if it just doesn't use it that often, and that's why we were able to defeat it before it did. Anyway, we were lucky.*

Confusion made it so that the affected person chose their target randomly, regardless of whether that target was an ally or an enemy. It was similar to when Elitia was under the effects of Berserk, but it'd be a horrendous situation if more than one of the party was Confused. There'd be no way we could avoid taking friendly fire.

But if you equipped your weapon with a confusion stone, you'd be able to use a hypnosis-type skill. Magic stones could be removed after they'd been put into a weapon, and you could even equip more than one, so I'd get two status ailments I could inflict if I had both the confusion stone and poison crystal on my slingshot.

I took a look at the Demi-Harpies, hoping they had something like a sleep stone, but I didn't see any magic stone-like objects on their foreheads. Oh well—we could still have them trained and work together with them, so we'd be able to take advantage of their Lullaby on the battlefield if we summoned them. Also, neither Theresia nor Elitia had acquired new skills this time around, so we could at least use that to our advantage during the test.

"It looks like all the injured have been safely moved. Shall we go back to the Guild for a bit?" suggested Elitia.

"Yeah, let's do that," I replied. "We need to let Louisa know everything's all right."

Once we were back at the Guild, we saw Louisa running about checking on the amount of damage received with the other Guild workers. She ran over to us the moment she noticed we'd arrived and then bowed her head deeply. She was showing us that both the Guild workers and the other Seekers were grateful for us going out and fighting the monsters.

When Louisa finally lifted her head, she didn't have her usual lovely smile; her expression was cool and tense.

"Mr. Atobe, you and your party have saved District Eight from danger. This may be overly forward of me, but as a representative of the Guild and as your caseworker, I wish to express our incredible gratitude… Thank you so much."

"Things won't be easy after all this, but I'm glad we were able to make it through," I replied. "I hope all the injured make a speedy recovery."

"Yes… Thank you for your kind words." Tears welled up in her eyes now that she didn't need to remain on alert. We were able to get rid of the stress and pressure she must have been under as the person responsible for handling the stampede. My friends were relieved, as was I.

The party went over to Louisa to cheer her up, except for Theresia, who stood next to me. Perhaps she didn't join the circle around Louisa because of the lizard mask she wore. Her mouth didn't show any expression, but the lizard mask eyes were looking at me. She also seemed relieved— But she was shaking slightly, maybe from the memory of the moment when I jumped off the building with the Demi-Harpy.

"We all need to get stronger so that we can keep battles under control. Me, you, everyone," I said.

"……"

Theresia nodded and brought a hand to her chest, like she was trying to say that she wanted to draw out more of her own strength.

# Part VI: Skipping a Grade

The damages in District Eight totaled approximately thirty destroyed buildings. Forty-six people suffered injuries, two of whom were severely wounded.

It wasn't uncommon for stampedes to result in fatalities. Novices avoided the Sleeping Marshes, which was prone to monster swarms, so higher-level Seekers were regularly asked to clear it out as a preventative measure. This time, however, the labyrinth reached high alert much more quickly than normal, resulting in the events leading to the damages.

The guards didn't enter the labyrinth and cull monsters because their priority lay in maintaining the city's peace. They needed to be able to mobilize immediately if someone's karma went up, yet their numbers weren't very high, and neither were their levels. The District Eight garrison commander was level 5, and most Seekers within the district were only just below that.

That was one reason why it was so hard to gain levels…supposedly. But my party kept running into Named Monsters, which was how we leveled up faster than anyone would have thought possible. Elitia obviously wasn't going to gain another level yet, but I looked at my license and saw that five of her experience bubbles were full. She could potentially gain another level if we defeated two more level-5 Named Monsters. We also hadn't had any experience-point penalties since we'd been seeking without rest. I needed to figure out how much it went down if we did take a break.

The others waited outside for me again while I did my leader duties of reporting to Louisa about the battle.

"Right, please allow me to view your license… Ah, of course…," said Louisa.

```
◆Expedition Results◆
> Suppressed stampede from a 1-★ labyrinth:
  1,000 points
> ARIHITO grew to level 5: 50 points
> THERESIA grew to level 5: 50 points
> KYOUKA grew to level 4: 40 points
> SUZUNA grew to level 4: 40 points
> CION grew to level 4: 40 points
> MISAKI grew to level 3: 20 points
> Defeated 32 FLYING DOOMS: 480 points
> Defeated 5 SWEET BIRDS: 80 points
> Defeated 3 DEMI-HARPIES: 240 points
> Defeated 1 bounty ★DEATH FROM ABOVE: 1,600
  points
> Party members' Trust Levels increased: 300
  points
> Rescued a total of 32 people: 960 points
> Rescued RIBAULT: 100 points
> Rescued MADOKA: 100 points
Seeker Contribution: 5,100 points
District Eight Career Contribution Ranking: 1
District Seven Contribution Ranking: 332
```

Louisa checked the numbers using her monocle and let out an admiring sigh. We'd run around town, defeating every monster we came across, but we received far more contribution points from quelling the stampede, defeating Death from Above, and saving the injured than we did from all the other monsters combined.

"Louisa, what do you mean by *of course*?" I asked.

"Since you earned so many contribution points in such a short time, the Guild has already put you into the District Seven ranking, without you having to take the test. Congratulations, you will be able to use the mid-tier lodging in District Seven right from the beginning."

"Middle-class housing... Does that mean we'll be able to rent a house?"

"Yes, it'll be a town house. There are quite a few, though, who prefer communal living and instead choose to live in an apartment."

"To each their own."

We'd be renting for the time being, and we'd be able to rest fine as long as the property was nice, but we'd eventually need to think about finding a place in one of the districts to make our permanent base.

"Actually, I'm a little sad about not having to take the test," I admitted. "There's a party called Polaris staying in the same building as us, and they're already waiting for their exam. I was kind of hoping we could take it together."

"Polaris... Oh! If you're talking about who I think you are, they left this morning for the Shrieking Wood to take their test," said Louisa.

"That explains why I didn't see them around town. Does the test sometimes take a few days to complete?"

"Yes. Starting in District Seven, you'll need to set up camp within the labyrinth, so the test doubles as practice for that. Monsters occasionally attack during the night, and the test will include how to deal with such situations."

"That would be good practice. I'll have to double-check with my party, but would it be possible for us to still take the test tomorrow?"

"Yes, I will prepare the test if you like. Now then, I have a meeting to attend concerning the city's recovery efforts, so if you would please excuse me."

"Rebuilding will take a lot of money, I imagine. If it's too much, then maybe I can help—"

"No, that won't be necessary. The residents of the city prepare funds for cases like this, so it's a general rule that no one person should pay out of pocket for repairs. I do appreciate the thought, though."

"Oh, all right... I feel better, then. The Mercenary Office had been mostly destroyed, so I thought it would be hard to rebuild, and then there's the other buildings that were damaged when we were fighting."

"Even so, the damages were relatively small. There have been times when a type of monster that goes around destroying everything in its path appears, resulting in extensive damages to both the city and its residents... We need to make sure to keep stampede risks low at all times in order to prevent something like that happening."

I'd felt like Louisa was slowly starting to let loose around me, but her formality in answering my questions gave me the impression that she felt personally responsible for what happened in the stampede.

"We also felt that these particular monsters were dangerous, so I understand why people tend to avoid that labyrinth. Is there some way to seal whatever the source of the monsters is away?" I asked.

"Well... There are certain conditions that lead to monster spawning, and if we come to understand those conditions, we can keep them from appearing. Monster Researchers have only published information on a select number of monsters; the vast majority of the information is generally unknown."

"Which means you can only respond when things get more dangerous. Please let us know if you do hear anything. If we have a good countermeasure, then we should be able to cut the monsters' numbers down efficiently."

"Once a stampede occurs, it's days before another one can happen as long as there's a swift response. That's why I want to rework the monster culling schedule so that we can prevent it from happening again."

There were likely other labyrinths in other districts like the Sleeping Marshes that people just avoided, making the risk of stampede greater for those labyrinths. The Guild Saviors or the guards probably had to deal with those.

Scariest of all would be if a stampede originated from a labyrinth in the higher districts. That was because even though people were trying, they couldn't manage to keep the monster numbers down. If District Eight could end up taking this much damage, that kind of stampede could lead to extensive damages from just one small mistake.

I suppose another Seeker duty was to venture into the labyrinths that were suited to their strength in order to defeat monsters and prevent stampedes from happening in the districts. But not everyone worked hard or continued to fight and risk their lives.

"...Are you perhaps starting to get the sense that the labyrinths are quite a hassle?" asked Louisa.

"I do, to be perfectly honest. They're burdensome and mysterious, and if you're not careful, a stampede can happen. It makes me wonder why in the world there are so many of them concentrated in this country... And that's part of the reason why I plan to keep climbing the ranks, so I can learn about these things."

"Mr. Atobe..."

"Ah... S-sorry, I didn't mean to put on airs. It's just that I don't mind doing what I need to do as a Seeker. A part of that is because I have so many friends supporting me."

"No... I think it's a wonderful goal. I'm impressed. I want to do everything I can as your caseworker to help. I hope you'll continue to help me do that."

"I'm the one who should be asking for your help."

We stood and shook hands. I remembered I'd been so nervous the first time I met this beautiful woman; I couldn't believe I'd gotten to a point where I could be this calm with her... Perhaps I'd grown a little since coming to the Labyrinth Country.

## Part VII: The Merchants Guild

Once I finished reporting to Louisa, I stopped at the nearby Healer clinic to check on how Ribault and his party were doing. Apparently, their magic user wouldn't wake up for a few days, but their condition was stable.

"Thanks for comin' all this way to see us. You must be tired yourself," said Ribault.

"Yeah, I'm always a bit worn down after a fight, but it's not too much of a load on me since I have the party," I replied.

"You really are somethin' else. It's only been four days since you started, and lookit how you've built a name for yourself since. I bet you won't even spend much time in this district. I'm glad I got the chance to meet a rookie like yourself. You oughta come visit District Eight every once in a while; I'll get lonely otherwise." Ribault had met his fair share of rookies—and seen plenty of them off, too. It was nothing short of an honor to know I'd left that much of an impression on him.

"Thank you, Arihito. It's because of you that our friends are all still here," remarked Ribault's companion with the shield.

"We owe Ribault a lot. He saved us when we were seeking in one of the beginner labyrinths…," said the woman with the bow.

"All the more reason you should keep going into the labyrinths, find incredible weapons, and aim for the top," added Ribault. "That's why you're such a marvel to us. We're just gonna do what we can. This might sound overly dramatic, but I want you to fulfill our dream."

"...All right. I'll go as far as I can. But honestly, I believe you're capable of rekindling that dream whenever you want," I replied. They could pass on their work of looking after the junior Seekers to someone else and go back to seeking. That was an option that any party was free to choose.

"...Yeah. You're right... What am I talking about? Like we've given up. Arihito, you're just too...," said Ribault.

"I still wanna go toe to toe with some strong foe I've never seen before. I know that sounds weird coming from the guy who lent his only shield to Ribault, but...," said the man.

"I was so scared; I couldn't do anything to that super-brightly colored thing. But to give in would just shatter my very core... So I'm going to keep trying—do everything I can," vowed the archer.

"I get anxious before every fight, too, but I have my friends with me. They're the reason I just about manage to not run away and get something done," I said. If we ever met a challenge we couldn't overcome, we'd work together, or someone in the party would get a new skill, and we'd find a way to get over it.

Rearguard was a job that could cover all sorts of support, so I sometimes felt like there was no limit to what my skills could do, but they also worked together with my party's skills, and that'd helped us on many occasions.

Ribault and his party seemed to have a new gleam in their

eyes, a renewed ambition for seeking. I felt we could likely run into each other someday in another district. That was one thing to look forward to as I continued my life here in the Labyrinth Country, since there were only so many parties among all the ones in the Labyrinth Country that we'd make a connection with.

I left Ribault and his party and headed back toward the square in front of the Guild. Cion came to meet me, too, and he'd brought Falma and Astarte with him.

"Oh… Well done today, Mr. Atobe. I'd like to thank you as one of the city's residents for saving the city," said Falma.

"Well, I'm a resident myself. I like to see the city peaceful as well," I replied. Falma smiled elegantly, then looked at Cion, who was sitting down while Igarashi petted his head.

"I got a real understanding of how Cion feels after everything that happened today. Mr. Atobe… If it's not too much trouble, would you please take Cion with you? As a member of your party."

"Huh? …B-but she's so fluffy and huge and cute—are you sure you won't mind us taking her?" asked Igarashi.

"…Woof!" barked Cion.

I didn't understand why Igarashi was so flustered by the idea; I would've thought she'd be ecstatic to have Cion as a party member. Cion had saved us with her Covering skill so many times, and I was sure she'd be a great asset to us. Theresia no longer seemed afraid of her, and if she could work as a vanguard with Elitia, our party would become even more impenetrable.

"Thank you, Falma. If you insist, then we'll be happy to borrow her... Or do you mean you'd allow us to officially add her to our party?" I asked.

"Yes, gladly. It would make her very happy, too... See, look at her tail go!" Cion was still sitting, but her fluffy tail was wagging back and forth—a gentle wagging, not like when she used Tail Counter.

"Astarte, if Cion goes with Mr. Atobe, she'll come back an even stronger guard dog. You don't need to worry," Falma reassured Astarte, who quietly returned her gaze before going over to Cion and beginning to clean the fur behind her daughter's ear. Once she finished, Cion pushed her head into her mom's fuzzy chest for a moment, then separated. Astarte narrowed her eyes, then came over in front of me and lay on the ground.

"She's saying, 'Please take care of her.' Would you please pet Astarte? It would let her know you understand," explained Falma.

"Of course... I'll make sure Cion comes home safe. I know you might miss her, so we'll come back to visit regularly," I said and rubbed Astarte's head. She closed her eyes, either in a show of obedience or perhaps a sign that she trusted me.

"By the way, Falma, what level is Astarte?" I asked.

"She is level thirteen. She normally assists the Guild by going into the more difficult labyrinths in some of the higher districts." Astarte was far stronger than Elitia, who was currently at level 9. Plus, I got the impression that she could single-handedly keep the peace in District Eight, but I suppose the strong had to handle things that only the strong could.

"I wonder if Cion will get that big when she's level thirteen...," said Igarashi.

"Ha-ha-ha! If level had anything to do with size, then Ellie'd be much bigger than she is!" laughed Misaki.

"Hmph... I-I'm not short; I'm perfectly average for my age!" retorted Elitia.

Falma smiled again as she listened to them joke. She also seemed a little sad to see Cion go as she scratched the dog's neck when she went over to her master.

Madoka had to take down her normal stall in the square in front of the Field of Dawn because of the rebuilding work going on, so I rented another storage unit, and we put her goods in there while she continued her Merchant work. She was shocked at how extravagant the Lady Ollerus Mansion was, but we sat down in the lounge so she could tell us what she was capable of as a Merchant. Everyone in the party was there as well, so she introduced herself, and we had some tea while we talked.

She wasn't wearing the turban she normally had on, so we could see her black hair was in a sort of messy bob. Everyone who normally wore headgear had also taken their respective equipment off, and their hair was disheveled in the same way. I guess that was one drawback to headgear.

"Arihito has already introduced me to everyone, but I'd like to take a moment to reintroduce myself. My name is Madoka Shinonogi." Everyone gave their names in return. Since Cion couldn't enter the mansion, she was instead staying in the doghouse reserved for guard dogs. There were apparently some rentals that allowed animals, though.

"I selected Merchant as my job, and I am a member of the Merchants Guild. I can use my license to contact other shops within District Eight that are also members of the Merchants Guild. I can also use it to search for whatever specialized equipment you need or workshops that can handle processing various materials, as well as contact them to confirm the schedule and status of any jobs they are working on."

"That's...an advantage specific to Merchants, right?" I asked.

"It'll be nice, since it means we won't have to go around to each and every shop looking for something."

"I'd like to find somewhere to attach a rune myself... But would you be able to get quotes for it using that?"

"Yes, though it does take some time to get a response. But I can get quotes from multiple different craftspeople," Madoka replied. From her little explanation alone, it sounded almost like Merchants had the job-specific advantage of online shopping privileges. Whether or not a party had one with them could change a lot.

"I can also contact Melissa's shop, so I can get reports on the materials from the monsters you defeated earlier or ask them to process some of them without having to go in person. However, I would require the party leader's approval. So, Arihito, could you please press this button on the license screen?" she asked.

"Hmm... Like this? Whoa, that *is* useful," I said.

◆Dissection Center Report—Mr. Arihito Atobe◆
> 32 FLYING DOOMS: No usable materials
> 2 VITALITY ABSORB STONES discovered while
  dissecting the FLYING DOOMS
> 5 SWEET BIRDS: Materials usable for meat,
  modifying weapons or armor
> 1 ★DEATH FROM ABOVE: Skin usable for modifying
  armor
> 1 RED CHEST discovered while dissecting
  ★DEATH FROM ABOVE

I hadn't expected that the Flying Dooms, which were just balls of tentacles, would really be usable for much, and it looked like I was right. The fact that they couldn't even be used for food meant they were likely as disgusting to eat as they were to look at. Even so, we killed so many that they found two vitality absorb stones. Based on the name, I guessed they let you steal a small amount of vitality when you attack. The Sweet Birds' feathers could apparently be used to make arrows, so I asked for them to be used to modify Suzuna's. The down could be used to make a hat, so I asked them to go ahead and do that, too.

They were able to remove Death from Above's tentacles and then skin it, which could be used to make armor. They also found a red treasure chest, though it wouldn't have as much in it as the Black Box did. Even so, there was something fascinating about treasure chests, so I was really looking forward to opening it.

"...The armor you can make from that Named Monster sort of feels rubbery, and it tends to fit very close to the body...," said Elitia.

"Wh-why are you looking at me? ...Do you want me to wear it? I think my Ladies' Armor is perfectly fine as is. You're the one who suggested it," responded Igarashi.

"Yes, I do think your armor can be used for a while longer, but it's not often you can make armor from a Named Monster, so I think someone should wear it. How about you, Theresia?" proposed Elitia.

"......"

Theresia just looked at me since she didn't seem to know what kind of equipment it was. What would it be like if she upgraded from her current body armor to rubber armor...? She wouldn't look like a lizardman from the neck down anymore.

"Well, let's decide once we know its characteristics. We'll ask them to make the armor, though, since we have the chance," I said.

"All right, I will place the order, then. Which blacksmith would you like to use?" said Madoka. Louisa would probably be able to recommend a good place if I asked, but for the moment, I just took a look at the list of available blacksmiths.

"...This one's the highest level. The same as Falma—level seven," I said.

"That means even the support people are more powerful than us Seekers...," observed Igarashi.

"Craftsperson levels range from one to seven, so not all of them are strong. Their level goes up naturally as they improve their skills," explained Madoka.

"Okay, then we'll go with this person... Yikes, look at that waiting list! I mean, I guess that makes sense," I said.

"A two-week waiting list means you'll be waiting quite a while, even if there are some cancellations ahead of you. What would you like to do?" Madoka asked me.

"Right, I think we need to find someone to introduce us to a place. Maybe I'll ask Millais, the Maid, after this."

It was early afternoon by the time we finished, so we decided we'd all go about our own business until dinnertime. I elected to take a short nap, then go try to find information on a blacksmith.

## Part VIII: Self-Improvement

I woke from my short nap and went out into the living room to find Theresia waiting outside my door.

"Were you there the whole time? You can relax, too, you know," I said, but she shook her head and stared at me. Was she saying she was waiting for me to wake up?

Theresia's magic was down a little bit, whereas Igarashi was quite tired because she'd used her skills to their limits. It'd be great if we had a way to immediately restore magic, but it was hard to get our hands on potions right now. The best thing was just some good, quality sleep.

I went to the living room and saw Elitia and some of the others talking. Suzuna noticed me and stood up as she tried to say hello, but I stopped her.

"No, don't bother getting up. I'm going out soon anyway. Is

there anything you guys want me to pick up while I'm out?" I asked.

"Urgh, I sooo wish we had convenience stores!" lamented Misaki. "But I guess things here can't be that simple."

"Everything we need for daily life is provided in the royal suite anyway. I think they refill it every day, too," said Suzuna. I'd forgotten how women had more necessities than men did. But I guess the problem had solved itself just by us upgrading to better lodging.

"If there's anything you need, please let me know. I can always get it for you," said Madoka.

"Oh right, everyone can use a hundred gold pieces as their allowance. We still have over ten thousand after that, so if there's anything expensive you think we need, let us know, and we'll decide as a party if we should buy it," I said. We'd received 9,500 gold from the bounty on Juggernaut and from selling its materials, then we got another 1,600 for the bounty on Death from Above. That alone put us over ten thousand. I didn't want us to be strapped for cash when we needed to make a large purchase. I had been thinking of putting half our income in a party fund and dividing the rest between the members, but I wanted to be careful with our money so it was there when we needed it.

"Wow... I bet your party is the richest in District Eight," marveled Madoka.

"Maybe for District Eight, but we'll see how it is in District Seven. We should get a little more from that red chest, but we won't know exactly how much until we open it," I said.

"We get a discount when we buy stuff because Madoka's in our party. And we can sell things for a little higher than normal. We'll make a tonnn of cash off whatever we don't need!" said Misaki.

Not that it would matter for dirt-cheap items, like the newbie equipment that we got from the Black Box, but even a 1 percent increase would make a significant difference for the more expensive items. We'd be dealing with other Merchants, too, so it'd probably be best not to try and negotiate every single time. We should reserve that for the most important transactions.

"Arihito, would you like to take a look at everyone's skills? I think you got more skills, too," suggested Elitia.

"Oh, you can do mine later. Too much work for Arihito if we aaall ask him at the same time," said Misaki.

"Weren't you talking about chatting with him after dinner?" said Suzuna.

I didn't actually mind looking at them all at once, but I wanted to make sure I thought through the decisions properly, so each person would take some time. Speaking of, Madoka was in the party now, so I'd be in my own room tonight. Well, I was the only man, so that made the most sense anyway.

"Uh, ummm… You and Kyouka are really close, aren't you? If you're a couple, then… I-I'm sorry, it's too soon for me to ask about that," said Madoka.

"N-no, it's okay. Um… Actually, Igarashi used to be my boss. We were always together for work."

"Oh really… That's so nice that a man and a woman can get so close through work."

"Awww, Madoka, you little lamb... You're just too pure...," Misaki commented. She probably had her own assumptions about our relationship. Really, though, there was nothing more between us than what I just said.

Igarashi came out of her room while we were talking. Elitia saw her and called over to her.

"Oh, Kyouka. Is something wrong? You should rest more if you're not feeling well."

"N-no, it's not that. I just got the feeling you guys were talking about me."

"We were discussing how you and Arihito get along so well. I've never really interacted much with men, so I guess I just felt a little...jealous," Madoka admitted.

"Uh... *Cough, cough.* Atobe, is that what you guys were talking about? L-like, when you say *get along*, then sure, like as a team... And I guess if I'm honest, Atobe's become, like, someone I can really rely on..."

I felt like if I responded with *Is that really how you see me?* then the others might have made this out to be more than it was. In reality, there was never anything remotely romantic between us. The closest thing was that time she accidentally bought hot coffee instead of iced and gave it to me to finish after she took one sip. I remembered how she'd make me come into work on my days off. I'd get there, and she'd be all pumped and ready to go. No one was better suited to that work than she was.

"The fact that you formed a party together and it's going so well means you must have always matched each other well," said Madoka.

"...W-well, I guess it's not too late to change things. But we never would've gotten any work done if we didn't mesh," added Igarashi.

"That is true. Though, I thought you would've been angry if I said it," I agreed.

"Awww, there's something sorta bittersweet about you two. Like, one step from an office romance, but at the same time, so close that you've gotten used to being coworkers. You see that aaall the time in TV shows," Misaki remarked.

"That only happens in TV... I'd never get any romantic ideas about a boss of mine. I'd feel bad for Igarashi..."

"And I'm your subordinate now anyway, so you don't have to feel 'sorry' for me anymore."

"Uh, well... Um...," I stammered, scratching my cheek as I tried to think of what to say, but everyone just gave me an exasperated smile. I'd always thought of Igarashi as the kind of person who'd blow up at the littlest thing. It was refreshing to see her respond with such maturity and grace.

"...Phew, sorry. I just woke up; I think I'm still a little tired," said Igarashi.

"You won't completely recover unless you sleep a whole night, even in a nice place like this... I've actually gotten tired, too...," said Elitia.

"You sleeepy, Ellie? Suzu, wanna take a nap?" suggested Misaki.

"Yeah, my magic's a little low, too... *Yaawn*...," said Suzuna.

Misaki wasn't tired since she didn't have any skills yet that required magic, but Suzuna had used a lot for Auto-Hit and Salt Laying. Even so, Misaki apparently wanted to join in on naptime. She, Suzuna, and Elitia all left, leaving me in the living room with just Igarashi and Theresia. Apparently, Madoka used magic when she placed long-distance orders through her license. I checked everyone's magic on my license and saw that hers had gone down by about a quarter.

"Igarashi, I'm just killing time now that I'm awake. You can take it easy for a little longer. I think I'm going to go out with Theresia for a bit."

"Oh, okay… Hey, do you want some tea before you go? Although, I guess the Maid would make it for you."

"Most likely, but I feel bad calling them for every little thing. I can make the tea."

"No, you sit down. You're the leader, and that's a lot of work." Igarashi went around behind me and placed her hands on my shoulders. Her touch seemed natural, and her gentle tone sounded nice, both easily putting me in a good mood.

"W-well…then. Since I'm your replacement Maid…," she said.

"Uh… Igarashi?"

"I—I would like to offer my apologies… I still haven't made up for everything I made you do at work."

"It's fine; I'm really over it—"

"I won't feel right if I don't. You can laugh; just let me do something for you."

"A-all right. By *do something*, do you mean make tea?"

This conversation was taking a bit to get anywhere. Theresia had been staring at us for a while, and Igarashi must have felt embarrassed because she was slowly getting redder and redder. Even her ears were bright red now.

Actually, I was a little off. I never could have guessed what Igarashi was actually so embarrassed about until I heard her utter the next few words:

"...I—I will be back shortly with your tea, m-master."

"...Um, uh, a-all right! I'll w-wait here!"

I was a bit slow on the uptake. This wasn't the kind of service I'd expect from Igarashi— Sure, apologies were one thing, but I couldn't believe she'd act like a Maid while she went to make me tea. I'd be entirely unable to resist if she started teasing me that I didn't get Maids like this every day.

"Good, you seemed to enjoy that. You'll have to tell me what you like later, when we have time," she said and headed toward the kitchen. I stared after her, utterly dumbfounded, trying to figure out who this charming woman was. The change I'd seen in her was so huge that it left me wondering if I even knew her.

*Some might say she's acting coy, but I'm a simple man. I'm just going to enjoy it.* I realized Theresia was staring at me, so I adjusted my tie nervously, even though it wasn't really crooked.

"Theresia, it's not what you think...," I told her. "I know you're probably a bit tired, but d'you want to go take a walk with me?"

"......"

She nodded, but I felt like there was something else she wanted to say.

"What's wrong? ...Oh right, should we choose your skills

now?" She nodded again; looks like I guessed right somehow. She gained a level, so there should be more skills she could take. I wanted to take a look at the new skills while we had time.

I pulled out my license and turned the display to show Theresia's skills. She didn't have her own license since she was a mercenary before. Instead, her skills showed up on my license.

```
◆Mercenary Skills Display: THERESIA◆
Lizard Skin 1
Accel Dash
Scout Range Extension 1
Lookout 1
Silent Step


◆Available Skills◆
    Level 2 Skills
        Shadow Step: Evades attack and leaves
                     an afterimage of yourself,
                     confusing the enemy.

              Hide: Renders you unnoticeable
                    unless hit by an enemy's
                    attack. (Prerequisite:
                    Silent Step)

   Sleight of Hand 2: Undoes medium to difficult
                      locks and traps.
                      (Prerequisite: Sleight
                      of Hand 1)


    Level 1 Skills
       Double Throw: Throws two throwing weapons
                     at once.

       Sneak Attack: Attack damage is doubled
                     when attacking an enemy
                     unaware of your presence.
```

```
    Pickpocket 1:  Steals a specified item
                   from target without their
                   knowledge.
     Escapology:   Escapes even when
                   restrained.
Sleight of Hand 1: Undoes simple locks and
                   traps.
Remaining Skill Points: 7
```

"You got both attack skills and support skills... Hmm, Double Throw seems good."

"......"

Both Double Throw and Sneak Attack looked useful, so I decided to take those. Then we could take Shadow Step so she could get away after using a Sneak Attack... But if we were going to take those, then I'd want to take Hide, which could clearly be used in conjunction with Sneak Attack. Now that Sleight of Hand 2 was available, the other option was to take that and Sleight of Hand 1.

"Theresia, could I ask you to be in charge of undoing locks and traps?"

"......"

She seemed most interested in the battle-related skills, but I told her I was thinking of taking three in that area already, and she nodded. *We'll think about Hide again after the next level she gains.*

"We'll need to get you some throwing weapons for Double Throw. I want you to keep the short sword for melee fighting, so it'll have to be something that's not too heavy for you to walk around with."

"......"

If we got some throwing knives, she'd run out after a couple of throws, but Misaki was using her metal dice as practically one-use weapons, and I was having a hard time thinking of anything else. We could strengthen the weapon with magic stones and runes if it was something that came back to her, which would give us more to work with when trying to increase the damage she could do in one go.

"All right, I'm up next..." I changed the display on my license to my skills. I felt like it was a bit unfair if I could look at Theresia's skills, but I didn't show her mine, so I decided to let her take a look. The moment I saw the skills, my eyes opened wide in surprise—there were a number of skills that I'd been hoping for.

◆Acquired Skills◆
Defense Support 1
Attack Support 1
Attack Support 2
Recovery Support 1
Morale Support 1
Hawk Eyes
Outside Assist
Rear Stance


◆Available Skills◆
    Level 2 Skills
    Defense Support 2: Creates a defensive barrier equal in strength to your defensive capabilities for party members in front. Skills of duplicate types do not stack.

| Rearguard General: | Improves abilities based on the number of party members in front. |
|---|---|

**Level 1 Skills**

| Cooperation Support 1: | Activates a front-line ally's combined skill. |
|---|---|
| Magic Support 1: | Increases magic consumption and spell strength by 50 percent for party members in front. |
| Evasion Support 1: | Occasionally activates Auto-Dodge for party members in front. |
| Summon Support 1: | Summons a nearby party for rear support. |
| Charge Assist 1: | Gives a portion of your magic to an ally in front. |
| Rear View: | Spends 5 magic points to expand your vision to cover your rear for a set period of time. |
| Backdraft: | Automatically counters when attacked from behind. |

Remaining Skill Points: 3

"......"

Theresia silently pointed to Rearguard General. The rearguard force was often used as the tail of the army during retreats. They'd handle any enemy attacks, and it was a position that often resulted in death. This skill actually resolved one of the major weaknesses of the rearguard job, which was that I was unable to support myself. Obviously, I could use it as the original meaning intended and improve my own abilities such as defense so that I could protect the others while they retreated, though I'd have to see how much it improved my defense before deciding whether or not that was a valid tactic.

Theresia seemed to be suggesting I should take skills that helped me protect myself. She kept her finger firmly on Rearguard General, not moving it a single inch.

"Like always, I just don't have enough skill points... Anyway, for now, I'll take Charge Assist just in case. As for Rearguard General..." There were a lot of skills I wanted more than that—Cooperation Support 1, for example. Used properly, that could bring up the entire party's attack.

"......"

"You really think I should take it...?"

Theresia answered with an emphatic nod. I thought how upset she would be if I took a different skill. She was trying so hard to express herself, even though she couldn't do it through words, so I couldn't very well ignore her completely.

"...Okay. I don't think it's a rearguard's duty to put themselves first, but I do want to acquire it sometime."

Theresia silently pulled her finger back and placed her hands on her knees, and her lizard mask started to turn bright red. I could tell that she was finally catching on that she'd gone out of her way to give me her opinion on my skills.

"To be honest, I've been wanting a skill that strengthens me. This one doesn't do anything if I don't have any allies, but it does mean I'll get stronger just by you and the others being in front of me."

"You have a skill like that...? Your job really does get stronger when you're in the back," said Igarashi as she placed a teacup in front of me. Theresia wasn't good with hot things, so Igarashi had brought her cool tea that'd been brewed earlier.

"Oh yeah, I want to try a skill I just took. Could you stand in front of me with your back toward me?" I asked Igarashi.

"Uh, sure... Like this?"

*Give some magic to Igarashi... Charge Assist!*

"Ah!"

Magic left my body and combined with Igarashi's magic to increase it. My magic went down by about a tenth, but Igarashi recovered twice as much as that. Maybe I just had more total magic than her since I was a higher level, but it looked like the amount she recovered was more than what I spent.

"Oh... I felt a bit sluggish, but now I'm not quite as tired. Was that another one of your skills?"

"Yeah. I use my magic to recharge a vanguard's magic. I can recharge your magic if you don't have enough magic to use Mirage Step."

"Erk... That's what was on your mind when you picked that skill? Am I too reckless...?"

"I took it because evasion is important. Also, I'm just glad you're feeling better now."

Igarashi looked like she was going to say something but couldn't get the words out and instead just went to sit down opposite us.

"...With a guy like him in our party, we'll have to give this our all, right, Theresia? He's not gonna make it easy to repay him for everything," she said.

"......"

"Huh...? You agree, Theresia? Hang on, is Igarashi just that much better at communicating with you...?"

I was shocked. Theresia looked back at me and shared a nod with Igarashi. Guess this was one of those things where you needed to be a woman to understand. It made me a bit jealous, but I was happy to see how comfortable the two seemed to be with each other.

# CHAPTER 3

# The Different Parties

## Part I: The Runemaker

I rested in the room for a little while, then Theresia accompanied me when I went to visit Millais's room.

"Excuse me, do you have a moment? I was hoping to ask you something," I said.

"Of course. I am happy to answer if I can. If I am unable to answer, then I can ask my coworkers as well," replied Millais, sitting at a fancy table with carved wooden legs along with two other Maids. The furniture in the Maids' waiting room wasn't any less extravagant than the furniture in the rest of the mansion.

"Would you happen to know a skilled blacksmith? I was hoping to go to one as soon as possible."

"I do know of a very skilled blacksmith; they normally handle repairs to our knives and such. If you like, I can show you the location on your license's map?"

"Yes please." I took out my license and displayed the map of

District Eight. Millais stood next to me and looked down at my license while she pointed to a spot near the top of the display.

"If you head west down this road from the central square, you'll find the workshop near the district boundary here," she explained.

"District boundary... Is that the wall here?" I asked.

"Yes. The Labyrinth Country is almost entirely encircled by the city walls, and then each of the districts is divided with these walls, which are the district boundaries. It starts with District One at the top and then continues clockwise to District Two and so on, so in the east, you will find the district boundary dividing this district from District One. The wall is thicker, and the security more severe than for the wall in the west."

"I assume that even if you could use your skills to get past the wall, they'd remove you immediately if you weren't supposed to be there."

"I believe so, yes. I have heard that it is impossible to use teleportation-type magic to move past the wall if you don't follow the proper procedures. The actual district boundary does stop at a certain height, but you will be returned to your original location if you try to find a way over the wall."

There was the system that transported you to the chest-opening rooms, so the Labyrinth Country did use teleportation in a variety of different ways. You could say that the Labyrinth Country wouldn't be what it was today if it didn't have teleportation.

Even if District One and Eight were divided by a wall, people would be able to get over the walls and go to the other district using various skills if there wasn't some sort of ceiling blocking entry on the whole thing. Even if they didn't have the skills to fly, they could theoretically use magic to scale the vertical wall. But anyway, I now knew, thanks to Millais, that it wasn't possible to jump the walls like that. I bet you probably couldn't dig under them, either.

Still, everything had its flaws. There were always exceptions to the rules—me, for instance—which probably meant there were other people with unknown jobs and skills they could use to beat the system. They could go to the higher districts to try out the stronger but more profitable labyrinths if they had strong skills that let them do so despite being at a low level. Personally, I thought it was better to steadily increase my level and keep moving, but you couldn't pass your rivals by if you played it too safe.

*If someone has a strong job and is a high level…was this really a place where they would linger around? Those Seekers rarely come to the lower districts, probably because the competition is so fierce in the higher ones.*

Elitia's appearance in District Eight was such a strange sight that it caused a bit of an uproar. Maybe there wasn't much a Seeker could gain from going to a low district after having climbed their way to the higher ones. Elitia had joined our party and done some incredible things in battle but still only gained one level.

"Mr. Atobe, if you like, I can show you to the workshop?" offered Millais.

"Oh, no, thank you… I should be fine. You already told us how to get there. What's the name of the place?"

"It is called the Mistral Forge. The blacksmith there is nicknamed the Armored Smith since they are always wearing full plate armor. You may be surprised when you first see them, but the Mistral Forge's blacksmith is a very kind individual. I hope you won't be frightened."

Rikerton and Melissa were pretty strange themselves. I was starting to feel like all craftspeople here were eccentrics. Actually, no, I shouldn't assume this blacksmith was an oddball just because they wore armor all the time.

I thanked Millais, and we left the mansion. Theresia lagged behind me for a little while, but she seemed to realize she was falling behind and so caught up until she was walking by my side.

"......"

"Watch your step; they're still repairing the city. We should also keep an eye out for what's overhead, too," I cautioned. There were people around who seemed to have architecture-related skills, because they were working on repairing the places that had been damaged by the monsters' attacks. At this rate, it'd only take a few more days for the city to return to its normal state.

We arrived at the location indicated on the map and saw a stone building with a sign out front that read MISTRAL FORGE. Most of the city's buildings were built so close that there wasn't much space between them, but perhaps because this was a forge, which would use fire, there were canals running on either side of the building.

I rang the doorbell and heard the heavy *clank, clank* of metal shoes coming our way. The door opened, and I was faced with a figure who was slightly larger than me and entirely encased in plate mail.

*"Hmm, you're not the appointment I was waiting for. My name is Steiner. I'm the blacksmith in this here forge. What can I do for you today?"* said the suit of armor. The voice didn't come from inside the armor, though; I could hear it as if it were spoken directly into my head. It sounded throaty, not at all deep and booming like I'd expect from armor so massive, and I had trouble identifying if the speaker was male or female.

*"Ah, you must be surprised by the sight of me,"* continued Steiner. *"Please pay no mind. Equipment enhanced with magic stones is a necessity to protect from the heat of the forge and to avoid damage to the eyes."*

"Right...," I replied. I had heard that when using the old *tatara* furnaces, the workers had to constantly observe the light of the fire that heated the iron, and many of them lost sight in one of their eyes in their old age. I guess it was plausible that full body armor would help against that. If it had some heat protection modification, then it wouldn't be nearly as uncomfortable as it looked.

"......"

"Hmm? ...What's wrong, Theresia?" I asked. She seemed on guard, wary of something in the shop behind Steiner. Maybe there was someone else in back.

*"Your companion is a lizardman... It seems you have no prejudices against demi-humans, sir. Is that correct?"*

"Yes, Theresia is a good friend of mine," I replied without

hesitation. Theresia looked at me, clenching her fist to her chest. I wished I could tell her somehow that I really meant it.

*"That is wonderful. It is one of my desires that there be more people who interact with demi-humans without prejudice. Sir, may I ask your name?"*

"Oh, right. Sorry for not introducing myself. I'm Arihito Atobe."

*"Thank you, Mr. Atobe. And welcome again to Mistral Forge. Please come this way."* Steiner opened the door wide and beckoned for us to enter. Immediately inside was a room for customers to wait in while the work was being done. Steiner suddenly asked me a question as they showed us into the forge.

*"By the way, what sort of work have you come for today?"*

"I was hoping to have some weapons strengthened with magic stones and ores. I'd also like to have a rune placed in a rune slot..."

"Aha... A rune!" came another voice. A small girl appeared from back in the forge. She wore a robe with a hood pulled up, which made her look like a magic user. I somehow felt like she was different from a normal human. Her hair was a pale yellow, and her eyes were the deep green of forest trees.

"Oh, darn it. I just jumped out, didn't I? And Steiner was supposed to be the one in charge of dealing with customers," she said.

"N-nice to meet you... Um, Steiner, may I ask who this little girl is?"

"I am not a *'little girl'*! Believe it or not, I'm actually your elder. You don't seem to have anything against nonhumans, so I suppose I can give it to you straight. I, Ceres Mistral, am the proprietor of

Mistral Forge!" The girl threw her hood back to reveal her pointed ears. They were like elf ears.

"Your ears… Oh, you must be a race native to this world," I said.

"Indeed. Most reincarnates call us *elves*, but we're called *jades* because of the color of our eyes," she explained.

"Jades… All right."

"We are able to work in jobs that reincarnates are not able to choose. In my case, that would be Runemaker," Ceres went on. "And this is a set of armor that works using runes. Golem makers are also capable of rendering nonliving objects animate, but what's different here is that Steiner is their own being."

"*I am strong, as my looks may imply, so I am responsible for the smithing work. My master oversees all rune work,*" said Steiner. They didn't seem to mind that Ceres had just revealed their identity. If Steiner was closer to something like living armor than an iron golem, maybe that meant their armor was empty inside?

"Oh, as a side note, there *is* something inside Steiner's armor. Wouldn't want you to get the wrong idea and think you could mess with 'em because there's nothing in there," said Ceres.

"*Um… N-no, Master, there really isn't anything inside. I am nothing more than moving armor.*" Their conversation just made me all the more curious about what was in there. Were they like a doll given life with runes? Either way, Steiner didn't seem to want to reveal it, so I shouldn't push it.

## Part II: Black Magical Slingshot

Ceres came up to me and smiled happily as she looked back and forth between me and Theresia. She seemed friendly, but her features were just a little too perfect, and it made me feel nervous as she stared at us.

"This human's especially fascinating. It's one thing to hire a demi-human mercenary, but you don't see many people willing to just go for a stroll around town with one... And she seems quite attached to you. She's stood where she can protect you ever since I came out," said Ceres.

"......"

"Theresia, you don't need to be wary of Ceres... Or actually, maybe you should be. It's probably normal to assume there's something behind someone who uses animate armor to run a blacksmith shop."

"Precisely— Wait, what am I saying? I wouldn't reveal myself so easily if I had something to hide. I only decided to tell you who I am 'cause you piqued my interest. How could you be so cold?!" Ceres grumbled as she stroked her braided, flaxen-colored hair, looking nothing like a blacksmith and everything like a little girl.

"*Sir, it is incredibly rare for my master to show herself. I understand why you might have your suspicions, but I ask that you put your trust in her. I promise you will get more than your money's worth if you do.*" Steiner clapped a fist to their chest like a knight would. It looked a bit like a salute.

"No, I don't actually think you're suspicious," I said. "I just sort of wondered whether it was okay for you to tell me your secrets... Are you sure you can trust me, considering we just met?"

"I wouldn't quite call them *secrets*. To put it plainly, I quite like you. You have no problems letting yourself be seen walking around the city with a demi-human, and the two of you quite obviously care for each other. You don't seem to understand how rare it is to see something like that," explained Ceres.

"It's never really bothered me that Theresia's a demi-human. I'm not just satisfied with how she is right now; I want to help her return to her original form."

"...*That is quite incredible. Master, this person...*," said Steiner.

"Hmph. That is not an easy road you walk, but should your intentions be true, then I will be happy to assist where I can. What work would you like us to do for you?"

I showed Ceres and Steiner the ores, magic stones, and rune I had with me.

"Yes, two elmina iron, a poison crystal, two gaze stones, a confusion stone... And this rune—it's a magia rune," observed Ceres.

"Magia... What does that do if you apply it to a weapon?" I asked.

"You will be able to change your weapon's attack from a physical attack to a magical one. It is useful against monsters who, for example, respond with horrific counterattacks when hit with a physical attack, but you can also increase its capabilities by combining it with other runes. Though, you would need a weapon with at least two rune slots for that," explained Ceres.

You could draw out the runes' true power when enhancing weapons if you combined multiple runes. Anyway, for now, I'd just have her put the magia rune on my slingshot. Igarashi's armor and weapon each had one rune slot, so I'd like to eventually fill those up, too.

"I have this ebony slingshot—could you place the rune in this?"

"Yes, if you wish. I can also add up to three magic stones, so shall I go ahead and do that as well? The abnormal status effects will work regardless of whether you're using physical or magical attacks."

"Yes please. What can the elmina iron be used for?"

"Reinforcing armor. It could be used for strengthening weapons also, but elmina iron's greatest strengths are in its durability and light weight."

"I see... But I didn't bring my companions' armor with me. What should I do?"

"You can really only ask the Carriers to bring it here for you. If you are the party leader, you can display your allies' equipment on your license. You select which you'd like to be modified, and we will handle the rest."

"Thank you. Is there anything from this list that you think would benefit most from the reinforcement?"

"Let's see... These two will see the greatest increase in defensive power if you reinforce their armor."

Igarashi's armor and Theresia's armor were already fairly strong, so they wouldn't see much of an increase, but Misaki and Suzuna would see a significant improvement if we modified theirs. They were going to add a chest guard to Suzuna's upper body armor, which would make it easier for her to shoot her bow, and I asked them to modify Misaki's while they were at it. Both would become +1 armor, their defense would increase, and they would become lightweight.

"We will work on your weapon until the armor is delivered," said Steiner.

"Yes, first, I will place the rune in the rune slot. When you wish it to be removed, don't try to force it out yourself. Leave it to the experts. Those strong enough to get their hands on something like this don't usually stay long in this district," noted Ceres.

"I'd like to bring my equipment here as much as possible. One of my companions is a Merchant, which I believe will allow us to place orders remotely," I said.

"Happy to hear it. Well then, feel free to call us when you find yourself with another valuable rune. It'll be safer that way," said Ceres with a smile, but her face turned serious as she took my weapon and started to place the rune in it.

"Words of power, become one with this object... Enchant Rune!"

◆Current Status◆
> Ceres activated Enchant Rune ⟶ Success
> Ebony Slingshot transformed into Black Magical Slingshot

"Whoa... That's completely different from when magic stones are added...," I said.

"Looks like it went well... It's said that weapons change their very nature when runes are added. It is a different process from adding magic stones at the most basic level," explained Ceres.

*"Next, I will embed the magic stones into the handle. Quite useful to be able to use three status effect attacks,"* said Steiner, activating a skill called Insert Magic Stone and embedding the stones into the slingshot with a dexterity I wouldn't have expected from looking at them. The process added pluses to it, so it became a Black Magical Slingshot +3. It looked like it was significantly more powerful than before, but the actual damage it did hadn't really increased that much.

With this, though, everyone would be able to attack with status ailments if I used Attack Support 2. I wanted to test out exactly what effect it would have during our next seek. The purple stone was poison, the pink was confusion, and the black was gaze, otherwise known as a Stun effect.

"You should transfer over the rune when you find a more powerful weapon. Magia runes are not that uncommon, but there's usually only about one found every three months in Districts Eight and Seven. Even if you tried to compress magic stones to make one, it'd take a decent amount of time and luck to do it," said Ceres.

"Thank you for the information. We still have one more gaze stone... Theresia, which would you prefer: to defend against Stun or to inflict Stun?"

"……"

Theresia held up her short sword to say she would like to add the Stun effect to her weapon.

*"I'm happy for you, Theresia. It'd be a shame for you to come all this way with your master and not receive any presents,"* observed Steiner.

"Ngh..."

Theresia seemed surprised and shook her head vigorously. She was being really hesitant in accepting a present. I did understand why she might, but her reaction was a bit over the top.

"......!"

"Y-yeah, I get it. You're saying that strengthening your equipment isn't really a present, right?" I vocalized.

"......"

I had been trying to support her, but she just seemed upset. Guess she really did want a present and just panicked because she felt bad about accepting.

"Don't be ridiculous! A present is a present, no matter what form it comes in. You should graciously accept," urged Ceres.

"......"

Theresia had turned red again, but when she got the modified short sword back, she traced over the magic stone in the hilt with her finger. The action almost seemed loving, but maybe that was just projection on my part.

"I think she's saying she'll treasure it. Arihito, I do think I like the two of you. Watching you express yourselves to each other shows me that the world isn't just full of hopeless things," said Ceres.

*"It's been a long time since Master has taken a liking to a human. She always lets me deal with the customers, but now she is so talkative...,"* added Steiner.

"I talk more when I'm in a good mood. Well then, we will have the rest of the equipment delivered to your residence when it has been finished. Where would that be—? Ah, of course, the highest-ranking lodging in the district," said Ceres admiringly as I wrote down the Lady Ollerus Mansion's address. She really did look so innocent that I just wanted to ask...but it could come off as rude, so I'd need to be careful how I worded my question.

"Um, Ceres...," I started.

"I'll be a hundred and fifteen years old this year, though I stopped aging at fifteen. Or was it before that...? The longer I live, the fuzzier my memories get," she said.

"A hundred... So does that mean you're basically immortal?"

"Time flows for every race. Simply by living, the fusion between a being's soul and its body weakens over time until the soul separates and is reborn in a new body. The cycle merely takes longer with my race than others."

When I was reincarnated, it had seemed like my body and appearance hadn't changed, but I had felt much more full of life, like I had actually been reborn. Perhaps that was because my soul had moved to a new body. The Labyrinth Country had proved that souls really do exist, which meant it wasn't over when you died; you still got more chances.

"I have heard that the highest-ranking Seekers in the Labyrinth Country can even choose their reincarnation. I've also heard there's a limit of a thousand years of cumulative life, though. Which means it's not only my species that is long-lived. Any race can do it, if they are prepared to fight for it," said Ceres.

"That's amazing... Ceres, can you live for hundreds of years?" I asked.

"Hmm, I wonder. It would mean looking like this at one hundred and fifty, then dying of old age while still being young. I'd like to have a family before that, though... Mm?" Theresia stood in front of me with her two arms spread wide to each side— Was she protecting me? In any case, I didn't think that's what Ceres was getting at.

"Ha-ha... Don't worry; no matter how much I said I like him, I wouldn't think of that after just one day. Besides, I doubt Arihito could think of me as a woman with this girlish body."

"Uh, um... I'm not really sure how to respond to that...," I said.

"See, he sees me as just a child... But it's surprisingly fun to tease young men like this." She covered her mouth with her sleeve as she laughed, which was somehow both childish and flirtatious... Something that came with her kind of longevity, I guess.

The doorbell rang just then, and Steiner went to answer it. Somehow, the equipment had already arrived for modification. It had both Suzuna's and Misaki's upper body armor.

"...It's all women's armor. Arihito, there's nothing wrong with recruiting allies who suit your preferences, but you need to show self-restraint so that you don't injure your hips. A Seeker needs their hips!" cried Ceres.

"Look, even I thought it was weird my entire party is female, but it wasn't an intentional choice... Right, Theresia?"

"......"

"That face says you're annoyed by how much of a womanizer

your master is, yes?" Ceres asked Theresia. "If it makes you so frustrated, you should just lock your master down by getting it on with him. Men turn to putty if you do that, or so I've heard."

"Ngh..."

I had no idea what Ceres was talking about, but Theresia suddenly turned bright red and walked out of the shop, stopping outside the door to stare back at me.

"*This is one area in which Master has some issues, but I hope you'll be open-minded enough to work with us again. I'll provide a discount for any troubles caused,*" said Steiner with a tap on their chest plate. I didn't think my relationship with Theresia had been seriously damaged, but it was true that Theresia was acting incredibly awkward.

### Part III: The Swordswoman's Tears

I thanked Ceres and Steiner once the modifications were done and headed back to the Lady Ollerus Mansion with Theresia. Just then, I overheard a conversation taking place:

"...Hey, you hear that Polaris is taking the promotion exam now?"

"Word has it that not many people are gonna pass 'cause there'll be a Named Monster in the Shrieking Wood. Think they'll be okay?"

"They're at the top of District Eight. No way they can just skip the test. Wonder if we'll make it to the top someday..."

Georg, the leader of Polaris, had known they'd fallen from first place in the ranking because it showed on his license, but it sounded like the other Seekers didn't know we had stolen the top spot.

"Has it seriously been ten years since I got reincarnated? Man, time flies. Maybe it's time I give up on climbing the ranks and instead try to find a nice girl to settle down with."

"We gotta work at it some more first. Income and quality of life's so much better in the higher districts. Even the top of District Eight's like a totally different world from what we've got."

I'd jumped from lodging to lodging in a short span of time, so I could sympathize. Though, I'd been lucky to get a nice enough place to sleep right from the beginning. Anyway, more important than that, one thing I noticed was that a Named Monster had appeared in the labyrinth that Polaris was taking their test in. Without any specific information about what kind of monster this was, I had no details to go on. I wondered if the Seekers that came up against it were killed or if they had to just run away.

Juggernaut was a similar case of an absurdly strong specimen that seemed to have gone through a sudden mutation of some sort. But Polaris had been the top-ranked party in District Eight, and they had confidence in their abilities. It'd hurt their pride if we suddenly barged in.

"……"

"Oh, sorry… I was just worried about something," I said, realizing I'd stopped walking, and Theresia was looking at me in concern.

There were a lot of times when someone lost their life to a monster, and that was it: There was no saving them. People who ended up as a demi-human in the Mercenary Office lost their ability to live their life as they saw fit. You couldn't really say that everything was fine as long as they were alive. I couldn't help feeling angry and powerless when I imagined the first time Theresia died, even though I didn't really know what happened.

It was arrogant to think I could save all Seekers, and I wasn't going to allow myself to think that way. But at the very least, I wanted to save the ones I knew. I couldn't really see what good it'd do for me to be safe and succeed in life if I couldn't even accomplish that much.

Georg from Polaris was a good guy. I couldn't help myself from wanting to see the people I met in the Labyrinth Country survive.

"...Okay, sorry, Theresia. I'd wanted to prepare for the test tomorrow and then rest, but plans have changed. We'll go home and then go to the labyrinth, and we'll just take the people who seem up to it. I don't want anyone to feel like they're obligated to come along."

"......"

Theresia nodded. Then she thought for a moment before taking my hand and squeezing it. Her hand looked like she was wearing fingerless, scaly gloves, but it wasn't a piece of equipment—it was a part of her body since she was a lizardman. Between the scales, though, was her pale skin, which had a human warmth.

"...Oh, and another thing. When we get back, we'll ask Madoka if she can get you some throwing weapons. Otherwise, you won't be able to use your new skill, right?"

"……"

"Um… Are you okay with your hand like that? You're not embarrassed?"

"…!"

I must have seemed worried, because I think she was squeezing my hand to reassure me, but she hadn't let go, which was starting to get embarrasing.

She yanked her hand away, then turned her back to me, pressing her hands to her lizard mask. I could tell she was blushing even from behind. She shyly turned back to face me, and I tried my hardest to flash her a reassuring smile. Her face grew visibly less red, even if only just barely.

*…I think she might've just been the type who blushed easily. I got that sense from the beginning that she was pretty sincere.*

I really had no idea what kind of person the human Theresia had been. If she hadn't changed just because she wasn't able to talk, then her personality probably wouldn't have changed when she became a demi-human. Not that it mattered whether she stayed the same Theresia or there was a big change when she turned back into a human. I'd be fine with either.

"……"

"Hey, looks like you've calmed down a bit. All right, let's go."

Theresia nodded. She walked alongside me, her steps making no sound. There weren't many people who seemed surprised to see us walking together, maybe because they'd all seen the two of us so many times before.

We returned home and told Madoka we wanted some throwing knives. She suggested a small dirk, explaining that small knives would probably be the best option. Apparently, weapons for the robber-type jobs were in high demand, so it would be difficult to get a large number of them, but we were able to buy six knives for ten silver. I wanted to buy an even number, since they were for her to use with Double Throw.

Video games never really seemed to be concerned with the weight of throwing knives, but similar to bullets, the weight of metal knives was not insignificant. We also bought a belt with a holder for the knives. Theresia quickly tried it on to see how it felt. Misaki's and Suzuna's modified armor had also arrived, so the two of them put it on with Madoka's help.

Millais must have seen us arrive, because she brought some tea up. Elitia and Theresia were taking a rest. Igarashi was still sleeping, but she would probably wake up soon. Melissa had apparently taken a liking to Cion, because she'd come over from the Dissection Center and was playing with her in the garden. She always seemed a bit eccentric considering how obsessed she was with dissecting monsters, but I'd never met an animal lover who was a bad person. Maybe I was just biased.

"Soon, it'll be more efficient for us to seek in District Seven than here in District Eight. I think we're moving up at just the right time," said Elitia.

"And thinking of your friend, we want to move up as fast as we can... Though, it still looks like it'll take some time," I said.

"...The Guild still hasn't received any word that the Shining Simian Lord my previous party fought has been defeated," continued Elitia. "That monster is known to capture the humans it defeats and enslave them... Many Seekers have fallen into its clutches."

"Simian... So it's a monkey monster?" I asked.

Enslaving people was something only a creature with a fairly high intelligence could accomplish. Among all the monsters we'd fought so far, even the bipedal orcs, I hadn't really felt any significant intelligence from them. But in the future, we might encounter monsters that were capable of strategic thought.

Demi-Harpies, for example, could annihilate a group of Seekers by coordinating their attacks. Speaking of which, those three Demi-Harpies I'd defeated were still at the Monster Ranch. I'd have to stop by so that we could use their Lullaby in battle.

"...But if it enslaves them...that means it sees some value in keeping the people that it defeated alive. That means your friend probably isn't dead," I said to Elitia. That's why she was trying to make it back to the place where she had lost her friend, but just because they were living, it didn't mean we'd be able to easily save them. Elitia looked down, squeezing and pulling her golden pigtails in clenched fists in front of her chest.

"...I'll never forgive that foul beast... I swear... I'm gonna kill that thing... How dare it...!"

"Elitia...!"

The cursed sword Elitia wielded was partly to blame for the

dramatic shift in her personality during battle, but there was another reason, and that was pure rage. For her to harbor this much hatred toward the monster meant she probably saw it terrorizing her friend. Her face was twisted with anger, but Suzuna had come back into the room and wrapped her arms around her from behind in a hug.

"...It must hurt so much to think about. But it's going to be okay. Everything will be okay...," Suzuna consoled her.

"...Ah...," uttered Elitia as Suzuna unclenched Elitia's fists on her own hair, lifting one finger at a time. Misaki watched them sadly, then tried to smooth Elitia's hair with her hands, stroking it back to its normal straightness.

"...You do that, and you'll accidentally perm your pigtails. I mean, that's probably cute, too, buuut I think you look better with your silky-smooth hair, y'know. Right, Arihito?" said Misaki.

"Yeah. I'm not sure how to put this, but...I worry that if you let your anger get the best of you, you'll do something reckless. You need to take care of yourself first and foremost—mind, body, all of it."

"You shouldn't try to harm yourself... If you're hurting, you can mess with my hair instead," offered Suzuna as she held out her black tresses. Elitia put her hand on Suzuna's, and her shoulders started to shake, tears streaming from her eyes.

"Ugh... Guh... Th-thank...you... I'm s-such a child...and so weak... I couldn't save my friend... I just ran... I couldn't do anything...," she said between sobs.

"...Even so, you decided to go back and save this friend of yours.

You're doing what you can," I reassured her. "You've decided you're going back no matter what, even though this monster is so powerful that not even the high-ranking Seekers can take it on. We've only been able to get this far because you've been with us. I say we show this monkey just how strong humans can be."

"...That monster's really tough... It eats the men... And the women..."

"It's awful that so many people have been defeated and eaten by this thing. But if we're careful enough, we can beat it. We'll do it safely, take it seriously, and get out with as few injuries as possible. The way I see it, that's the shortest route... But I guess I sound a bit full of myself, telling that to someone so much more experienced, like you."

Elitia rubbed her red eyes and looked at me. There was no blame in those eyes; she just looked at me like she was clinging to me, asking me to help her with her body language. She was a level-9 Swordswoman. She'd seen the fiercest battles and come out on the other side, so it wasn't surprising she would feel such desperation when she came against an enemy that she had no chance of winning against on her own, one that she couldn't save her friend from.

There's no way we could win as we were. If everyone got to level 10, or if we tried to fight it with more than one party, maybe. It was better to have more allies. The people from District Eight aiming for the top like us, or those already fighting in the higher districts... There was nothing in the rules saying we couldn't gather them for a big fight against a boss.

"Suzu's hugs are really calming, but in times like these, you want an adult's broad-mindedness, riiight? Oh, don't just stand there all indifferent, Arihito! Go!" said Misaki.

"N-no, I'm not... Igarashi's way more tolerant than me."

"Huh... Wh-what? Tolerant...? What are you talking about?" asked Igarashi, who had finally woken up. Igarashi noticed how red Elitia's eyes were when Elitia turned around. She shot me a look, one that didn't imply I'd made her cry, but more along the lines of *What's going on?*

"...Um... I'm not really following all this, but you shouldn't blame yourself, Ellie. If you're feeling bad, you should talk to Kyouka. She may be a lower level, but she has more life experience."

"...Thanks. I'll do that."

"Huh? ...Wait, what? What's going on all of a sudden? What should I do...?" said Igarashi.

"Give her a hug; that's the best thing for Ellie right now. Even Arihito agrees," urged Misaki.

"Uh, really...? You sure you want a hug from me...?" said Igarashi, but she obeyed and leaned over to hug Elitia where she sat. She was wearing her favorite knit sweater as loungewear, pressing her ample chest against Elitia. If Igarashi were a dental hygienist, I'd probably go to get my teeth cleaned all the time even if I didn't really need it.

"...Th-thanks... Um, I'm getting kind of hot, so can you let go now?" said Elitia.

"R-really? Well, you seem like you're back to your usual self, so that's good," replied Igarashi, and Elitia stood up. I thought it'd be good for Elitia to take a bit of a rest, but instead, she came over to me and handed me her license that displayed her skills.

"...Are you sure?" I asked.

"It doesn't matter what my level is or how much experience I have; I'm still a member of your party. Treat me the same as everyone else," she said.

"Oh... All right. With skills, I might ask you to take certain ones, but in general, you should focus on what you want."

"Okay. But I want to take your opinions into consideration as much as possible," she replied. She looked almost afraid of what was displayed on her license. Was that how incredible the skills associated with the Cursed Blade were?

◆Acquired Skills◆
Double Slash
Slash Ripper
Rising Bolt
Blade Ronde
Blossom Blade
Armor Break
Parry
Slice 1
Counter Slice 1
Air Raid
Sonic Raid
Secrets of the Sword 2
▶Berserk

◆Available Skills◆

Level 3 Skills

▶ Bloody Roar: Can only be used while in Berserk mode. Unleashes an attack whose damage is increased based on the amount of blood you have lost.

Red Eye: Can only be used while in Berserk mode. Activates Red Eye status, greatly increasing attack and mobility. Consumes magic while in use.

Level 2 Skills

✕ Cross Slash: Unleashes a powerful attack using weapons equipped in both hands. (Prerequisite: Dual Wield)

✕ Dual Wield: Attack strength is not reduced even when equipped with a weapon in your nondominant hand.

✕ Hit and Away: Increases evasion when hit with a counterattack. Boosts accuracy of indirect attacks against foes.

Level 1 Skills

✕ Pierce 1: Attacks pierce straight through target when using a thrusting-type sword.

| | | |
|---|---|---|
| ✕ Weapon Break: | Targets the opponent's weapon to reduce its durability while equipped with certain types of swords. | |
| ✕ Maintenance: | Allows you to know in advance when equipment will break and perform emergency repairs if you have the proper tools. | |
| ✕ Feats of War: | Increases experience points and dropped loot rate when you defeat the enemy's leader. | |

Remaining Skill Points: 3

Some of these I'd seen her use before while others were new to me. I could look at the details of the skills she'd already taken, but first, I wanted to make sure I understood the information this display was giving me. The ones with the ✕ were probably Swordswoman skills that she couldn't select now that she'd become a Cursed Blade.

*...Some of the Cursed Blade skills like Berserk have this ▶ symbol, which I'm guessing indicates some sort of inherent risk. And Bloody Roar, huh... We won't know its drawbacks until we select it.*

Even so, Elitia'd already taken one of those skills with the ▶ symbol: Berserk. *I wonder why?*

"Secrets of the Sword 2 unleashes the hidden strengths of a sword... When I had to draw out this sword's power, it made me automatically acquire the Berserk skill," explained Elitia. So

Berserk was a skill that the Scarlet Emperor forced on her, and there was no way for the person to get away from the curse. On the other hand, I felt like Red Eye was probably a Cursed Blade skill, but it didn't have the ▶.

"Is Blossom Blade a skill you've acquired since you became a Cursed Blade?" I asked Elitia.

"Yeah. It needed four skill points, but I chose to take it myself. The Brigade members praised it as the power of a cursed sword... They just chose to ignore the Berserk part of it."

"...Even though they knew they'd be at risk if they went along with you into battle?"

"Yeah... I was part of their 'experiment.' The Brigade believed they would scale the Labyrinth Country's top ranks if they could harness the power of cursed weapons without the risks. They said that I gave in to Berserk because of my own psychological weakness, and that I might be able to overcome it if I grew stronger... But..."

*That possibility is what eats away at Elitia's psyche. It pains her to know that she might hurt one of her friends.*

"...As far as I can tell, Red Eye probably doesn't have any curse risks. Blossom Blade doesn't have that symbol next to it, so I think it's safe to assume Red Eye is no different. But there are a lot of other interesting skills, too. Should we hold on to skill points for you to use when you return to a Swordswoman?" I asked.

"...No. I'll take Red Eye. At the end of the day, I want to help the party however I can."

"All right."

"Although... The first time I use it, please make sure you're not close to me."

Everyone nodded in response. Elitia then took Red Eye of her own volition.

"...I really should have chosen this skill, Hit and Away, before I was cursed... Then I could've earned Suzuna experience points more efficiently."

Hit and Away would've boosted Suzuna's accuracy with a bow and arrow so she could have landed the killing blow. Suzuna could have grown much more quickly even if it had just been the two of them.

One plus side was that once she took a skill, she could always use it. That meant if she returned to a Swordswoman, we could assume she'd probably still be able to use Blossom Blade.

"All righty, now that you're done talking with Ellie about her skills, it's me and Suzu's tuuurn!" exclaimed Misaki.

"I haven't gone yet, either. Should we just do the three of us in one go?" Igarashi suggested.

"All right, we'll get it out of the way... There's something I wanna run by everyone, too. Today's a rest day, so I want you all to choose for yourselves what to do next," I said.

I told them I wanted to go into the Shrieking Wood after this. I explained why, and none of them said they would be staying behind. I double-checked whether or not Morale Support was working now that we were done resting, and we decided to choose our skills, then go try out a new labyrinth.

## Part IV: Skill Selection

Igarashi showed me her license first. I tried to get up, but she insisted, flustered, that I stay sitting and came over to me.

"You're always on the go. You don't have to keep fussing over me like that," she said.

"She's right; you can just sit there and not move a muscle. We'll even feed you. Oh, and if you want, we can all take a nap together, tooo!" suggested Misaki.

"…You sure that's not just something only *you* want to do?" asked Igarashi.

"Ha-ha…"

She didn't deny it, and based on her strained smile, I got the impression she was worried about Polaris as well. We didn't have time to waste.

"Seriously… Kids these days. I can't tell if you're being serious," said Igarashi.

"Um, but weren't you gonna do something, too? Like, as a way to say thanks for everything," teased Misaki.

"Hey, hey—I'm the one Igarashi's supposed to get mad at, so quit pushing it—"

"…Um, I—I mean, she's right," admitted Igarashi. "You let me take a nice long rest, and I'm grateful…for, like, everything…"

"Uh…"

She then went around behind me. I had no idea what she was

going to do as she placed her hands gently on my shoulders. I practically jumped when she started massaging them.

"Y-you don't need to be so surprised. I just thought your shoulders looked tense… You're probably on edge all the time because you're always surrounded by girls," she reasoned.

"N-no… I wouldn't say I'm on edge…" Igarashi wasn't exactly amazing at giving massages, but her technique was effective. She had a gentle touch, and before I knew it, I started to feel a little strange.

"…You're more relaxed than I thought. It doesn't hurt to get a massage when you're not tense?"

"N-no… It feels fine."

"Good. Next, you'll feel a light tapping. How's that?"

"Uh… Yeah, that works better. Thank you…"

The vibrations from the tapping felt good in a different way. It reminded me of the salons that would give you a massage after cutting your hair. But the fact that Igarashi was trying to relax me was starting to show in her physical affection, and I could see Misaki and Suzuna were starting to feel uncomfortable.

"I'm happy you're feeling relaxed, Arihito. I'll have to think of something I can do for you…," said Suzuna.

"Suzu's good at massages, too," Misaki volunteered. "Apparently, she used to do it for her grandma and grandpa… And the one time she did it to me was really nice."

"R-really? …I mean, you all help me out, too, so there's no need to spoil me like this…," I said.

"...Is this spoiling? It feels weird when you put it like that... But I've already started, so I'll only stop when you're happy," said Igarashi.

*...There's something kinda pillowy... Oh, sh-she's really getting in there... Is this really okay...?*

Igarashi started using her elbow to tap my shoulders, which, for some reason, brought her closer to me than when she was using her hands.

"...Uh, um... Kyouka... That's sort of...," stammered Suzuna.

"Shhh, Suzu. Don't say anything," hushed Misaki. "But whoa, Kyouka's—! Must feel nice to have that as a neck pillow."

"Neck pillow? I didn't hear the first part, but that really brings me back," said Igarashi.

I used to use a neck pillow all the time, but they were never this soft. She was pressed up against me so I could even feel the texture of the lace on her bra. Igarashi was calm the whole time, so she probably hadn't noticed what she was doing.

"I've gotta do this side, too. Otherwise, your balance will be off."

*Maybe she doesn't have a problem with pressing up like that, since it's a massage?* That thought made it even worse for me, so I tried to meditate, trying to make my mind go blank. As the soft pressure moved from the left to the right, I couldn't stop my mind from drifting: *Guess I really do like 'em bigger.*

"...Just having big ones is all men need to feel happy," observed Suzuna.

"Even me and Suzu combined couldn't compete with Kyouka;

no waaay!" added Misaki. "What'd you eat to get like that, seeeeri-ously?! Must've been tons of milk, I bet."

I had the feeling that drinking milk to make them bigger was an old wives' tale. Apparently, drinking too much soy milk wasn't good for you, either, so it was probably best to just leave things to nature.

"Kyouka, what're your favorite drinks?" asked Misaki.

"I'd like some black tea right about now. It's nice and refresh-ing with a little bit of juice in it... But there's no black tea here, is there?"

"Ha-ha... Ummm, I'll go ask if they have anything like it. You can talk about skills while I'm gone. Don't make out or anything," said Misaki.

"M-Misaki! ...Sorry, I think I'll go, too," offered Suzuna as she stood up suddenly and followed Misaki out. We were left in a bit of an awkward silence, and I decided to actually follow Misaki's suggestion.

"We're not making out or anything. Seriously, that girl...," I said.

"...Are your shoulders less tense now? Or should I keep going?" asked Igarashi.

"Uh... No thank you; they're pretty relaxed now. It's weird if you keep standing; sit down."

"O-oh, okay. Um, here..."

At my suggestion, she came over to the chair next to me and hesitantly took a seat. She opened the skills page on her license and held it out to me.

◆Acquired Skills◆
Double Attack
Thunderbolt
Mirage Step
Decoy
Force Target
Snow Country Skin


◆Available Skills◆
   Level 2 Skills
      Wolf Pack: Boosts abilities the
                 more guard dogs are in
                 your party.
   Spinning Spear: Increases damage when
                 attacking by spinning
                 your spear.


   Level 1 Skills
      Ether Ice: Installs Ether with Ice
                 attribute.
   Dance of the Slight chance of
Warrior Maiden 1: canceling an attack
                 from an enemy of the
                 opposite sex.
Piercing Strike 1: A portion of your attack
                 penetrates the target's
                 defense when you're equipped
                 with a spear.
  Mist of Bravery: Nulls party members' Fear
                 status.
  Freezing Thorns: Freezes opponent's
                 legs and slows their
                 movement.

Bulletproof 1: Enemy long-ranged attacks are
slightly less likely to hit.
Remaining Skill Points: 3

"It looks like the Valkyrie job can choose from at least three main roles," I said.

"There's so many things I can do that I can't decide which would be the best...and there's no way to practice the skills so you can use them properly in battle," stated Igarashi.

"Yeah. There may be some skills you can use in combination with your other skills. Like, could you use Spinning Spear with Double Attack..."

"I want to test that as well, but the level-two skills need two skills points..." While she was talking, her eyes were glued on one particular skill, Wolf Pack, which wasn't at all surprising considering her love of dogs. That skill would probably have the most noticeable effect when you put as many guard dogs in the party as possible. It did seem that my skills were the only ones that let me see the values in number; all the others seemed to be very vague about the amounts.

"All right, how about you take Wolf Pack and one other skill?"

"Uh... Are you sure? We only have Cion right now, so it probably won't make that big a difference."

"Even if it's a small amount, it's a constant improvement to your abilities, so I think it'll be effective. I also just think the skill really suits you."

"...Th-thanks. How about Ether Ice? I think it'd be useful if I choose skills that no one else can do."

"I don't think you should take that right now. The Ether skills summon an ether, which is like an object that responds to attacks with a certain attribute," interjected Elitia. I thought she was going to go rest, but she'd come back to give us some advice. Misaki and Suzuna came back then as well and gave us the herbal tea they brought back.

"We definitely think you should go for Dance of the Warrior Maiden 1. More girl power, then," said Misaki.

"You think…? I wonder what kind of dance it is… Do Valkyries dance?" asked Igarashi.

"It's not that weird; you have Mirage Step. Dances are made up of steps," I said. If monsters had genders, too, then it would be interesting to be able to catch a strong male enemy off guard.

"Were you in a dance club before, Kyouka?" asked Suzuna.

"Yeah, my first year in high school… But I changed to a different club in my second year, so I wasn't in it very long." Everyone seemed to guess why Igarashi changed clubs. I did, too, but I kind of wished I could have seen her in her dance club.

"What d'you think, Atobe? Is it better to save the points? I also wanted to take Piercing Strike sometime."

"Yeah… How about we save one point for now, then," I suggested.

"All right, I'll take Wolf Pack… Oh. Wow, I just felt like some strength flowed into me." Apparently, at this level, the amount it went up with just one guard dog in the party was large enough for her to feel it. If that was the case, then taking Wolf Pack was the right decision.

"I'm neeext! I didn't take any skills at level two, so I have tooons of skill points," said Misaki.

◆Acquired Skills◆

Increased Drop Rate: Slightly increases enemies' rare item drop rate.

Child of Luck: Slightly increases probability of finding a Chest after battle.

◆Available Skills◆

Lucky Seven 1: Achieves good results when you roll two dice with a total value of 7.

Magic Number 1: Each party member is given a random number. The individual with the winning number can force one person to follow a single command.

Dice Trick: Guarantees a designated number from a dice roll.

Russian Roulette 1: Chooses a random target among both allies and enemies and halves their vitality.

Poker Face: Renders facial expressions unreadable.

Lucky Guess 1: Allows you to vaguely sense which action will lead to good results.

Coin Toss: Increases luck if the coin lands on the face chosen by an ally.

Bad Luck: Slightly reduces enemies' luck.

Remaining Skill Points: 4

*Ack... Risky skills galore!*

"Ha-ha! Seeee, there's tons of exciting-looking skills. Like this Magic—"

"W-wait a minute," I interrupted Misaki. "Don't you think this Lucky Seven is a good idea? You're always rolling two dice anyway," I said.

"I guess... And if I use it with Dice Trick, then I could guarantee a seven every time."

"Even if a skill doesn't explicitly say it used magic, it can still wear you down. And there's usually a cooldown period before you can cast it again, so you wouldn't be able to keep using the skill back-to-back," explained Elitia. She was still able to give us relevant advice even without viewing Misaki's license.

"Atobe, what's wrong? You don't look so hot..."

The Magic Number skill was basically the same thing as Truth or Dare. Nothing good would come from that skill if Misaki acquired it.

"Right, how about I take the first three and then Bad Luck?" suggested Misaki. "I wanna help you guys out somehow."

"...F-fine, but...make sure you only use this second skill when it's appropriate," I added.

"It'll toootally be useful! I can't believe there's all these fun skills to pick from! I'm sooo glad I wrote down Gambler for my job!"

"You seem like you're really enjoying yourself, Misaki... I'm glad you got some good skills," said Suzuna.

"Thanks, Suzu! Get excited, 'cause I'm sure these skills will help you out, too!"

*Well, I suppose Misaki's a good girl at heart... No harm done as long as she doesn't abuse Magic Number.*

I'd have to keep an eye on Misaki to make sure she didn't start causing trouble. She wasn't necessarily going to use it for something like Truth or Dare, so I couldn't claim it was an entirely problematic skill.

Last up was Suzuna. She came over to sit next to me and showed me her license. Unlike Misaki, whose skills had the potential to cause so much trouble, Suzuna's new skills were very reassuring.

## Part V: The Monster Ranch

Suzuna came to sit next to me, and the rest of the party went to the other rooms for a moment to get ready for the next expedition. Maybe they felt like they weren't going to gain anything from observing us. There were even more skills on Suzuna's license that really suited a Shrine Maiden. In the Labyrinth Country, the job was obviously geared toward support.

```
◆Acquired Skills◆
Auto-Hit
Purification
Salt Laying
Medium
Exorcism 1
Spirit Detection 1
```

◆Available Skills◆

| | |
|---|---|
| High-Angle Shot: | Fires an arrow upward to strike the enemy at the end of the arrow's arched trajectory. |
| Archery Master 1: | Increases damage from shooting a bow using proper archery techniques. |
| Exorcism Arrow: | Adds Holy attribute to arrows when using a bow. |
| Cleansing: | Adds Holy attribute to whoever is in a body of water with you. |
| Prayer: | Party's success rate increases slightly. |
| Handwash: | Purifies water scooped with your hands. |
| Wash Away: | Uses water to null a portion of abnormal status effects. (Prerequisite: Purification) |

Remaining Skill Points: 2

"Handwash... I wonder if that's anything like when you wash your hands before entering a shrine," I said.

"I think it is. Incredible that this lets you purify water just by scooping it up... It's like magic," replied Suzuna.

"I don't think this is what it's intended for, but it could be really useful in making sure we have water to drink. But High-Angle Shot seems powerful, too... I'm not sure what to go with."

We could take something now, but they all seemed like they had their uses. It might be better to take them when we needed them, like we did with Salt Laying. I decided we'd hold off for the time being and pick the skills we needed when we knew what we should take.

*It'd be best if we could take all our skills, but that won't be possible unless we get fewer new skills as our levels increase. Elitia hadn't been aware of any other method for obtaining skill points, so at the very least, I can assume that if a way exists, it's as unknown by the general populace as the Hidden Gods are.*

"Atobe, we're ready," announced Igarashi.

"We just finished looking at skills, too. I'll go get changed," I said.

"Check it out, Suzu! I got the chest part reinforced, so now it's more like Kyouka's and Elitia's armor!" exclaimed Misaki.

"Gamblers can only equip light armor, so don't do anything reckless just because your armor is stronger. There's a limit to the amount I can cover for you," warned Elitia.

"Yuuup, I'll be careful!"

Elitia was trying to tell Misaki what was best for her, but Misaki didn't seem to understand the danger she might get herself in... I was a little worried.

"You sure you'll be all right...? You can't tap out now that you've come this far," I said.

"Hee-hee... I just wanna be with you, Arihito, so I'm gonna keep working as hard as I can," replied Misaki. I couldn't tell if she was being sincere, but no one teased her for it, and she started to blush.

"......"

"Mm? ...Theresia, do you mean you feel the same way?" I asked.

"Us too. I imagine it'll be necessary for us to be put on the bench sometimes, but we'd rather fight together than be left behind," said Igarashi.

As you might expect from someone who chose Valkyrie, Igarashi had fought some incredibly powerful enemies so far without ever getting scared. I sort of understood why she could learn the skill Mist of Bravery, which got rid of her allies' Fear. Perhaps Valkyries were resistant to Fear? If there really were secret abilities, it meant that every job in the Labyrinth Country had incredible hidden potential.

Our current party had seven members as well as Cion, our guard dog. I had Madoka and Melissa make our second party and wait in town. As the leader, I could manage up to sixteen parties, so the other two still appeared on my license. However, as a two-star Seeker, I was limited to two parties for the time being.

Melissa had a butcher's knife equipped, which was apparently quite a powerful close-combat weapon. I wanted to see it in action, but I'd have to wait on that.

"Arihito, everyone, I pray for your success in the upcoming expedition," said Madoka.

"...Take me along the next time you get the chance. I want to do some on-site dissection, too," added Melissa.

She and Madoka had decided to stay behind. Apparently, they

would be working in the small workshop that was in the courtyard of the mansion.

"If you nab a rare monster, bring it back right away," said Melissa.

"Will do. And give our regards to Rikerton," I replied, and the two saw us off as we headed toward the Monster Ranch.

We needed to teleport to the Monster Ranch the same way we did for the storage units. We walked from the mansion for about five minutes, then came across a sign that said RANCH INFORMATION OFFICE. The building looked too small to fit all of us comfortably, so I went in alone, and the rest finished getting ready to go into the Shrieking Wood. We'd meet back up afterward.

"Hello, my name is Atobe," I called, knocking on the door. A moment later, a white-haired but healthy-seeming elderly man came to the door. He had on a cap and protective leathers and sported a thick beard.

"Welcome, Mr. Atobe. I am the Manager of the Seventeenth Monster Ranch, William Christensen. Have you come to register the Demi-Harpies you sent earlier for summoning?" he asked.

"Yes. If possible, I'd like to register them immediately. Will that take a while?"

"That will depend on whether or not the Demi-Harpies are already obedient to you. You can summon them whenever you like as long as they have equipment that will respond to the summoning stones. My granddaughter can explain the details further; she's in the ranch at the moment. This way, please." He guided me down the stairs where, as I suspected, we came upon a teleportation door, though this one seemed to have only one possible destination.

"Due to the nature of the Labyrinth Country's Monster Ranches, we are required to care for and manage the lives of the monsters left in our care. The first week of care is free, but there is a fee after that," explained William.

"All right. Does the fee vary depending on the monster?" I asked.

"It does, yes. The large monsters require larger spaces, and we have to provide appropriate feed. If males and females are kept in the same area, the monster numbers may increase, which would also require an appropriately large space. There aren't many who capture monsters in District Eight, so our ranch here always has space available."

"That's good to know, as long as you're not feeling overwhelmed by the monsters I leave in your care." William seemed happy, in a way, to hear it. I wondered why, but he started explaining.

"Whenever there's a fee involved, there are those who decide they wish to dispose of or free the monsters we have in our care. There's nothing to gain from paying for the care of a monster that can't help you in battle. Anyway, when that happens, we Zoologists take in the monsters in order to study them. I prefer to study live monsters wherever possible to learn about their biology. That was actually the reason I requested approval to open this Monster Ranch." ·

"Huh, really?"

"There are so few people who select jobs when they reincarnate that allow them to speak with monsters, and then it's even rarer for there to be people who are suited to the Monster Tamer job. My granddaughter is one. She used to be affiliated with a Seeker party and would bring back monsters for me."

"Your granddaughter was a Seeker? And you...?"

"Yes. I had quite an embarrassing record in the end, but I spent many a day and night in the labyrinth. It was all spent studying monsters in their natural habitat, though," said William with a sheepish smile. I was interested in learning about monsters, too, but our chat was coming to an end, and he indicated I should touch the teleportation door.

"Oh, William. I've thought about it a little, and I'd like to have all three of the Demi-Harpies I captured stay here for summoning. I imagine they'd get lonely if I kept only one," I said.

"Ah... I think the girls will be happy to hear that. They seemed on edge, since they weren't certain what would become of them," he replied, making it sound like it was possible to communicate with the monsters. I'd have to ask his granddaughter as well, since she was a Monster Tamer.

The door opened, and I was instantly teleported upon passing through. In front of me now was a calm ranch spreading as far as I could see. I'd gotten used to dramatic changes of scenery when teleporting, and I thought this ranch looked almost exactly how I expected... But I looked up at the sky, and something just felt wrong. It looked like a blue sky stretched above us, but it felt like it was just an illusion. I was able to see it thanks to my Hawk Eyes. The grass that spread to the horizon was also a trick of the eye; it stopped eventually. What that meant was that this space was really a rectangular "room" in much the same way as our storage units were.

*I guess that's to be expected... If this were an open-air-type labyrinth, monsters would be coming out of nowhere. This is just a man-made space somewhere in the Labyrinth Country that was made to look like a field.*

William must have put his own money into making this or modified an existing facility. Either way, the feeling of the dirt below my feet felt real, and the air that filled my lungs was cleaner than that in the city, which made it feel all the more realistic.

I saw some cow-like animals enclosed in a fence—maybe they were the Marsh Oxen I'd heard about before. Feeding the cows was a young girl wearing a cap with cow-like horns sprouting from it. She was wearing leathers similar to William's, but no matter what I did, I couldn't keep my eyes from resting in a certain place.

*A cow tail...? Some sort of decoration, maybe?*

The girl noticed me and came over. She jumped the fence and gave me a bow. I bowed back, and her face split into a kind, gentle smile.

"Welcome. My name's Millith; I'm the caretaker here at the ranch," she said.

"Hello, I'm Atobe. I came to, um...register the Demi-Harpies for...um, summoning."

"Oh, they're playing in the woods over there. Please wait a moment; it's feeding time for these guys here."

The reason I suddenly stumbled over my words was that I was shocked by her huge breasts, which bounced up and down with the slightest movement. She looked exactly like those anime girls that were based on cows. I couldn't very well point out how funny it was that a cow girl would be taking care of cows, but that's really the only way I could describe the situation. I berated myself for thinking such stupid thoughts and stared at the blue sky to get it out of my head.

"Sorry for the wait. I was just feeding the last one when you came. Let's go then," said Millith, setting down the bucket that had the feed in it and leading me toward the Demi-Harpies. As I followed her, I suddenly realized something: Her tail was swishing back and forth.

"Oh, sorry, did I hit you?" she said as I stared.

"N-no... I was just thinking that it almost looks like you've got a tail."

"Oh, Gramps didn't tell you? My dad's a human, but my mom's a monster called a Minotaur."

"...What?"

So the tail wasn't a moving accessory. I'd just assumed something like that existed, since there were so many magical tools here... But this was totally beyond what I could have imagined.

"My dad's a Monster Tamer. He and my mom were seeking companions. And then... Well, stuff happened, and I was born."

"I—I see... Sorry, I'm just surprised."

"I think it's pretty incredible, too. But female Minotaurs aren't like male Minotaurs in that they're not really that much like cows. That's why I'm not super, super monstery... Oh, I'm sorry. Are you uncomfortable around people with horns?"

I had thought she was wearing a hat with horns on it, but the horns were as real as her tail. Those and her breasts were probably characteristics of a Minotaur, but otherwise, she was completely human-looking.

"One of my friends is a lizardman. So I don't have anything against demi-humans or half-monster half-humans, either," I replied.

"Oh... That's good. Gee, a lizardman friend..."

We reached the woods while we were talking. Millith took out a flute and blew on it, and the Demi-Harpies that had been sitting in the trees came flying in our direction.

"......"

The Demi-Harpies looked frightened when they saw me. The one who'd been intimidated by Cion's mom had gone completely pale and started to shake... I guess she was still afraid she might be eaten.

"Oh... I'm sorry, it seems they're still afraid from when you fought," said Millith.

"I was pretty rough with them... It was wrong to scare them into being obedient. It's my fault."

"When humanoid monsters are captured, they're often put into circus-like shows, or people just strip the parts off them that can be used as materials. I think that's what they're afraid of."

I had thought they'd need to be trained and tamed so I could summon them...but thinking about it that way, I realized the only goal there was to use them. If possible, I wanted them to help us voluntarily. I couldn't really tell them we'd take time to build a trusting relationship, but I could try to tell them how I felt.

I gathered my thoughts and stepped up in front of the Demi-Harpies. They seemed afraid and eyed me timidly.

"You three gave us a hard fight. In the beginning, I thought our only choice was to kill you. And maybe it's just my arrogance, but I won't kill or do terrible things to monsters that are similar to humans. I promise you this: Even if I stop needing to summon you and I end the summoning contract, I will set you free, back to where you came from."

Each of the Demi-Harpies had individuality in their appearances. The first one I fought, the one I'd jumped off the roof with, felt like the middle sister, if I thought about the three as sisters.

"...Do you understand what I said?" I asked, and the oldest-sister-looking one responded for the group with a nod. She had an indescribable allure. Her long, brown hair covered one eye and only one of her breasts. It was obviously normal for monsters to be naked, so neither she nor Millith seemed to care that one was visible, but it just seemed a little strange to me. The second oldest had hair just long enough to brush her shoulders, with an innocent, childlike face, and she was a little smaller overall than the oldest. The youngest looked like a ten-year-old girl—I decided I couldn't stare at them even though they were monsters, so I needed to take care when sizing her up.

"You can let me know if you have any other requests. I don't want to say it's in exchange for that, but I hope you will help me sometimes," I said.

The middle sister wrapped the youngest in her shaking wings, but they seemed to listen to what I had to say because the eldest stepped up toward me, pressed one hand to her chest hesitantly, and nodded.

"Good... Right, then we have a deal. I'll mostly have you use Lullaby when I summon you. You should probably do regular voice training," I said.

"..."

""...!"""

The eldest nodded, and the other two looked surprised, but then all three bowed their heads to me.

Looking at them, I suddenly realized something. They couldn't speak, but that didn't mean they were incapable of expressing themselves. And they were called *Demi-Harpies*.

*Is it possible...that these girls are demi-humans?*

"Oh, how nice. Do you understand what voice training is? It's singing practice, but don't put me to sleep! All right, next is equipping them with an accessory that will respond to your summoning stone. Which would you like to go with, Mr. Atobe?" asked Millith. The choices were earrings, necklaces, bracelets, or anklets... I thought it might be better to have the three choose their preferred accessory. They probably had their own preferences, and it was always good to let them choose that.

I asked them to choose one, and the eldest picked a pair of earrings, the middle one took a bracelet, and the youngest selected an anklet. All of them were made of a silver metal, and the bracelets and anklets had leather on the inside where they contacted skin.

"This is the summoning stone. Here's some earrings you can use with it, or a bracelet...," said Millith. The summoning stone wasn't very big, and it was fitted into metal to make a pendant, so I could attach it to myself there. The item information was displayed on my license as the following:

◆Summoning Pendant: Monster Trio◆
> Can summon Demi-Harpy I
> Can summon Demi-Harpy II
> Can summon Demi-Harpy III
> Slightly increases evasion.
> Additional effects available as Trust
  Levels increase with contracted monsters.

*So it even has effects as equipment. I wonder how I can raise their Trust Levels?*

"Ms. Millith, can I ask you something?"

"Oh... Um, you can just call me Millith. Being called *Ms.* makes me feel a little uncomfortable; you don't have to be that formal with me."

"Oh... Right, Millith, then. How can I raise a monster's Trust Level?"

"You can give them presents or work with them for a long time; there's quite a few different ways. Different monsters like different things, so you'll have to observe them to find out what to do."

If that was the case, the first thing I could do was give them some equipment, though I wasn't certain they'd like that. I asked Millith's opinion, telling her that I was hoping I could give them something that covered their chests and she could give them some clothing that they'd be able to wear even though they had wings. I gave her the money for the clothes and left the ranch.

Having done that, I'd be able to use the summoning stone to call them at any time. *With more trump cards, we ought to be able to manage from here on out.* I thought about it as I hurried back to meet with my friends.

# CHAPTER 4

# To Save Those Who Could Be Saved

## Part I: The Shrieking Wood

I came out of the ranch, thanked William for his help, and headed toward the entrance of the Shrieking Wood. There was a plaza in front of the labyrinth entrance, where Seekers were waiting for one another and discussing strategies. The door to the labyrinth was covered in thick ivy vines. The only person I saw there was Louisa, who had come to see us off.

"Should you receive any contribution points from this expedition, you will be officially approved to advance to District Seven," she told me. "As I explained previously, your party can receive approval at any time, regardless of the outcome of the test."

"I understand. We'll come back without letting anything go wrong so we can make sure we keep going up in rank," I replied.

"Please be careful... There is already another group in the middle of their test. I would appreciate it if you could check in with them if you happen to see them. They are skilled themselves, but I am a little concerned, since a Named Monster has appeared in the labyrinth." So even Louisa was concerned about Polaris. I told her that I'd like to look for them in the labyrinth if possible, then the party passed through the ivy-covered door.

The other side was cloaked in fog. Louisa had told us that the fog would thin if we kept moving forward, so we all walked ahead.

"…Since it's a 'forest,' I imagine we won't have a great range of vision. Everyone, stay on guard," I said. In front was Cion, who had keen senses of hearing and smell. Behind her was Elitia and Igarashi, with Theresia behind them, right in the middle of the formation. Behind her was Suzuna and Misaki, and I brought up the rear. Thanks to my Hawk Eyes, I could get a bird's-eye view of our party, so I was still able to see what was happening in the front of the formation even though I was in the back.

"…Arihito, this labyrinth…feels more ominous than the other ones," said Suzuna.

"Yeah, I sort of feel it, too… Like a monster's gonna jump out at any moment," I replied.

"W-well, you could say that about the other ones, too, so stop giving me the heebie-jeebies. I think what Suzuna meant is that it's just more cramped than before," added Misaki.

"R-right… Sorry about that. But we still can't let our guard down," said Suzuna.

Apparently, the test was held in a different labyrinth every time, so it was actually an option to wait until the conditions changed so we wouldn't have to go into this creepy forest. The only problem with that was that one of our goals was to check up on whether or not Polaris was all right, so it wasn't really an option we could consider.

"Eek?!" shrieked Igarashi, who was in the second row on the righthand side.

"Whoa... Igarashi, what happened?"

I looked and saw that her feet had sunk into the grass. She hadn't noticed that there was a pool of still water and stepped in it.

"Geez, that scared me... Sorry for raising my voice."

"That's just the kind of place this is," agreed Elitia as she wiped off Igarashi's feet. "Now that I look more closely, I can see little pools of water all over... We need to be careful not to splatter mud everywhere."

I thought that was awfully considerate of her. At the same time, I was considering how it might mess up our ability to react to danger if we succumbed to Fear in this unknown situation.

"Igarashi, sorry to ask this, but could you use Mist of Bravery? I'd prefer to have a way to null Fear other than to just use battle cries to pump us up."

"Y-yeah... Sure. Right, it's not just monsters that inflict status ailments; there's environments that'll do that, too..."

Just as Igarashi went to activate her license, Cion reacted to something.

"—Bowww!"

"EEK! ...N-no, it's fine. I have this... Mist of Bravery!"

◆Current Status◆
> Kʏᴏᴜᴋᴀ activated Mɪsᴛ ᴏғ Bʀᴀᴠᴇʀʏ

There wasn't a problem with her activating it immediately, since Cion wouldn't react like that to nothing. When Igarashi did activate it, exactly as the skill description implied, a thick steam-like substance wafted from her body and wrapped around the party.

"...Does this skill turn a Valkyrie's sweat into mist...?"

"Ellie, don't say that so seriously! This is, like, magic turned into a physical thing or something like that!" snapped back Igarashi.

"Igarashi, that's not important right now! We've got company!"

"...!"

The next to react was Theresia. We looked at what was coming from the dense forests to our left and were all lost for words.

```
◆Monsters Encountered◆
FEAR TREANT
Level 4
In Combat
Dropped Loot: ???
DIRTY MUSHROOM
Level 2
In Combat
Dropped Loot: ???
DIRTY MUSHROOM
Level 2
In Combat
Dropped Loot: ???
```

These enemies were well suited to a forest labyrinth. One was a tree monster, and the others looked like the kinds of mushrooms that must have been growing on its trunk.

*Level 4... This is probably one of the more difficult labyrinths in District Eight.*

The Fear Treant could move its roots like feet, and in the shadows of the otherwise normal tree, there was a face-like something formed from knots and holes. It had the sort of twisted expression that would make an appearance in a haunted house to scare little kids. But while it might've been able to scare children, there wasn't anyone in the party who'd be afraid of that... Or so I thought.

"—GWWOOOOOOHHH!"

◆Current Status◆
> Fear Treant activated Terror Voice
> Elitia and Misaki were Frightened
> Fear status resisted due to Kyouka's Mist of Bravery

"Hyaaaa—?!"
"Bwah—?!"

Both Elitia and Misaki were inflicted with the Fear status effect by the sudden strange noise the Fear Treant emitted, but Mist of Bravery immediately canceled it out.

*So it can protect against status ailments even though it was activated in advance!*

There wouldn't be any need for it to be a mist-like substance if it was only effective right when it was activated. That meant that Mist of Bravery was the kind of status healer that could be used as protection as well.

"I can't believe I got scared by a tree!" said Elitia angrily as her face turned red. She must have felt embarrassed by getting hit with Fear even though she was at a much higher level than the enemy.

"Eep... That sent a chill down my spine... But I'm all better now thanks to Kyouka's sweat!" said Misaki.

"I told you it's not sweat... Seriously!" snapped Igarashi.

I felt like the Valkyrie job had a lot more secrets than I'd initially thought, but I decided to just put that aside for now. It took a lot to build up someone's perceptions of something, and it wouldn't be easy to get the girls' trust back if I ruined it with one stupid remark. More importantly, though, I really needed to focus on the battle at hand.

"GRRAW, GRAH!"

"Igarashi, Theresia, you two attack the mushroom things!"

"Right!" replied Igarashi.

The Fear Treant's trunk wasn't very thick, but it was easily taller than a grown human. It rushed at Cion, who was practically the same size. The two mushroom things, which were like some fungi with arms and legs, attacked Theresia and Igarashi—taking them on, one-on-one.

"—!!"

"Hyaa!"

"I'll back you up! Let's give it our all!"

```
◆Current Status◆
> THERESIA activated DOUBLE THROW
Threw two small dirks
> Stage 1 hit DIRTY MUSHROOM A
11 support damage
> Stage 2 hit DIRTY MUSHROOM A
11 support damage
```

```
> KYOUKA activated DOUBLE ATTACK
> Stage 1 hit DIRTY MUSHROOM B
11 support damage
> Stage 2 hit DIRTY MUSHROOM B
11 support damage
> ARIHITO activated MORALE SUPPORT 1 ⟶ 6 party
  members' morale increased by 11
```

The two dirks that Theresia threw hit one of the faceless mushroom people in its fat, white stem and poisonous-looking cap. Igarashi's spear landed brilliantly, but—

"—Woof!"

Cion stopped her attack against the Fear Treant to let out a warning bark. Before the thought even crossed my mind, I cautioned Theresia and Igarashi.

"Both of you, pull back!"

```
◆Current Status◆
> DIRTY MUSHROOM activated CONFUSION SPORE to
  counter physical attacks
> THERESIA was CONFUSED
```

"...?!"

The mushroom person that Theresia attacked released a cloud of spores. I should've been wary of that the moment I realized we were up against a mushroom monster. Of course these things would have a special attack that used spores.

"Don't breathe in the spores! Suzuna, try to drop it from a distance!" I ordered.

"Okay...!"

The Dirty Mushroom didn't live to see the second shot. The first arrow tore through its cap, and it collapsed to the ground and lay there, unmoving. But before Suzuna could let loose her second arrow, Theresia moved. Because she was Confused, her target became Igarashi.

"Kyouka, I'll handle it!" said Elitia.

"Ellie!"

"Gah... Arihito, do something while I've got her stopped...!" yelled Elitia as she deflected Theresia's sword with her own. My Defense Support had affected both of them, and with Theresia attacking Elitia in earnest, one of them could get injured if they kept swinging at each other.

*What should I do...? How can I get rid of that status ailment...? Hang on, but first...!*

"Cion, wait!" I shouted.

"—Boww!"

There was a chance that the Dirty Mushroom would counter with its spores if it were hit with a physical attack. Cion was about to strike the remaining one, but I ordered her to hold off so I could use the nonphysical attack that I'd just acquired.

"Arihito?!" cried Misaki worriedly, pausing just before she was about to throw her dice. But I didn't have time to respond at the moment.

I gathered the magic flowing through my body between my thumb and forefinger where it formed into a sphere about the same size as my slingshot bullets. It was a magical bullet. I shot it at the mushroom person that was trying to attack Theresia and Elitia from the side while their swords were locked against each other.

"—Get lost!"

◆Current Status◆
> ARIHITO activated FORCE SHOT ⟶ Hit DIRTY MUSHROOM B
> 1 DIRTY MUSHROOM defeated

*Holy crap... That was more like a laser than a magical bullet...*

I managed to bring down the mushroom without activating its Confusion Spore, like I'd intended. Suzuna turned her second arrow toward the Fear Treant, and Igarashi and Cion pulled back cautiously.

"...HWOOO!!"

The Fear Treant was about to attack. It'd used the Dirty Mushrooms to buy it time so it could prepare a long-range attack. It shook its boughs with a rustle, inflating a huge number of nuts hanging from its branches. I imagined they might explode and it would aim for us with its projectiles. I prepared another magical bullet for my Black Magical Slingshot and activated the black magic stone and its Stun effect before firing at the Fear Treant.

"Ack...!"

"Arihito...!"

I hadn't realized using magic would feel so tiring, but it was great that I could fire two shots. At this speed, the magical bullet could land before the Fear Treant could attack!

*Come on!*

◆Current Status◆
> Arihito activated Force Shot (Stun) ⟶ Hit Fear Treant
> Fear Treant was Stunned
> Fear Treant's action was interrupted

"GWOOO!!" bellowed the Fear Treant as it took the magical bullet in its face, striking it off-balance. Igarashi and Cion saw their opening, but before they could even react accordingly, I was giving Suzuna an order. Theresia and Elitia were still taking swings at each other, splattering water as they moved—which happened to jog my memory.

"Suzuna, use Handwash and Wash Away! Purify the water and then throw it on Theresia!" I shouted.

"A-all right...!"

That was the only possible method our party had of nulling the Confusion status.

"Let's go, Cion! ...Hyaa!" called Igarashi.

"—Woof!!"

"I—I...I'm through with being useless!" shouted Misaki.

◆Current Status◆
> CION activated POWER RUSH ⟶ Hit FEAR TREANT
11 support damage
> KYOUKA activated DOUBLE ATTACK
> Stage 1 hit FEAR TREANT
11 support damage
> Stage 2 hit FEAR TREANT
11 support damage
> MISAKI's attack hit FEAR TREANT
11 support damage

"OOOOAAAGGGHHH... AAAH!!"

The Fear Treant's trunk groaned and creaked with the impact from Cion's tackle. Igarashi's spear and Misaki's die struck the monster next, but it seemed like it had a resistance to physical attacks because it didn't go down even after the volley of blows.

"I've got the water! ...Theresia, please return to your senses!" shouted Suzuna as she scooped water from the ground. The muddy sludge turned clear and sparkled in the light as she did, and then she splashed it onto Theresia.

"......"

◆Current Status◆
> SUZUNA activated HANDWASH
> SUZUNA activated WASH AWAY ⟶ THERESIA's CONFUSED
  status was removed
> FEAR TREANT began charging SEED EXPLOSION

*Going by the name of the attack, it scatters the seeds, then they explode on us... But before that happens—!*

Next to Theresia, who had snapped back to reality, Elitia was activating Sonic Raid. She dashed toward the Fear Treant.

"—Rot in hell!"

```
◆Current Status◆
> ELITIA activated DOUBLE SLASH
> Stage 1 hit FEAR TREANT
11 support damage
> Stage 2 hit FEAR TREANT
11 support damage
> 1 FEAR TREANT defeated
```

Elitia lopped off the armlike branches from the Fear Treant, and its terrifying face faded away. It looked like a normal, nonmoving tree.

"Well, we somehow made it out of that without getting hurt...," said Elitia, wiping the sap from the Scarlet Emperor before sliding it into its sheath. Igarashi was relieved, and Cion was staring at the Fear Treant, perhaps making sure it wouldn't move again, but she eventually seemed satisfied because she turned to me and gave a cute little woof.

### Part II: Hope and Despair

"......"

Theresia was still standing there holding her sword, looking like she was lost in thought about something. She must have felt guilty about turning her sword against her friends, even though it was only because she was under the influence of Confusion.

"Theresia, don't let it bother you. I'm not upset," said Elitia. "These things happen. Just make sure you throw your dirks from as far away as possible next time."

"......"

But Theresia didn't nod back right away. I wasn't sure how to help her in this kind of situation. Even if I tried to say kind things to her, knowing her personality, she'd probably just blame herself even more. While I stood there worriedly thinking, Suzuna went up to Theresia and started toweling off the water that she'd dowsed her in.

"I'm sorry I threw water all over you... Was it cold?"

"......"

Theresia shook her head, and Suzuna smiled, then draped the towel she was using on Theresia's shoulders.

"You should keep it like this for a little bit. You'll get cold if you're wet," said Suzuna.

"Atobe, is that one of Suzuna's abilities? Healing people by pouring water on them?" asked Igarashi.

"It didn't specifically say in the skill description whether it was effective against Confusion or not, so I wasn't certain it would work. It does seem to bring people back to their senses, though," I replied.

"I didn't know what Suzu was up to when she scooped the water from the ground. It was like magic. It was so cooool; I want some magic like that," said Misaki, even though I thought she had plenty of skills that seemed pretty magical. Though, maybe she was just jealous of the mystical sight of it all happening.

"Elitia, was that your first time fighting those mushroom things?" I asked.

"Yeah... It was just luck that I'd never run into them previously. I hadn't entered this labyrinth before I got promoted... There are a lot more annoying monsters here than I'd expected."

In other words, these monsters were probably unique to this labyrinth. I felt like mushrooms grew everywhere, but... Anyway, we had to check for dropped loot first.

"Ah... This fruit on the Fear Treant looks a lot like an apple. What should we do with it, Atobe?" asked Igarashi.

"Should we identify it? I'll use a Novice Appraisal Scroll," I said as I took the apple from her.

◆Apple of Wit◆
> Increases maximum magic capacity when consumed.
> Rare dropped loot from Fear Treants

*Huh! Didn't take long for us to find a rare item. This is definitely one of the benefits of having Misaki around.*

A rare dropped item was hard to come by, so we really hit it big this time. Increased magic was a really useful effect, but who would most benefit from eating it? I was trying to decide, but everyone else was staring at me, curious about the results of the appraisal.

"Apparently, eating this increases your maximum magic. Anyone want it?" I offered.

"You have a skill that lets you share your magic with other people in the party, so I think you ought to eat it," answered Igarashi. "Besides, you seem pretty beat... Those slingshot attacks from before were amazing! It was like a laser beam, or something you'd see in an anime."

"You thought so, too? It actually surprised me... But it consumes a lot of magic, so I can't use it all the time," I said.

"You can use it when we're in a tight spot. You know, I really can rely on you to have our backs," added Elitia, her eyes filled with a natural trust. I felt overwhelmed that someone so powerful could feel they could rely on me, but I was honored.

"......"

"...Theresia?" I said. She still seemed hesitant, but she took out one of the dirks she hadn't used, took the apple from me, and started peeling it.

"Huh? You're really good at peeling apples, Theresia," Misaki observed.

"That's amazing; I could never peel it in one piece," said Suzuna. It wasn't just the two of them—I was surprised, too. She held the dirk perfectly still, rotating the apple to quickly and cleanly peel off the skin. She sliced it in half and removed the core, then cut it into six wedges before handing one to me.

"......"

"Th-thanks... You've got all sorts of surprising talents, Theresia," I said. Part of me couldn't help thinking that this was the fruit from a monster that'd been fighting until just a moment before, but I had to trust the appraisal scroll, so I decided to eat it. I looked at the cut surface and saw a thick syrup, which seemed more yellow than the juices from apples I was familiar with, but—

"Mm... Wow, that's good. Nothing like any apple I've ever tasted ... Mm!" I said. It was crisp in a similar way to an apple, but its flavor was completely different. Apples that weren't carefully bred and cultivated could be quite tart, but that wasn't the case with this at all.

"Watching you eat that really makes me want some apple pie or something," Suzuna remarked.

"Ooooh, that sounds delicious... B-but Theresia? What's wrong? You're turning red," said Misaki.

"Theresia... You're going to make me blush and I'm just watching," added Suzuna. Just after she said that, I noticed that Theresia was holding out another piece of apple for me, this time higher than before.

"Let's hurry ahead, Arihito. Could you finish the apple off?" said Elitia.

"……"

"...Y-yeah, sure. We need to keep moving," I agreed. This wasn't the time or place to sit here deciding how to react, so I let Theresia feed me the apple. It kinda felt like I was part of a petting zoo.

When I finished eating the apple, my license display showed that it had increased my magic.

◆Current Status◆
> Arihito used Apple of Wit
> Arihito's maximum magic increased

My head felt clearer, and power flowed through my body. It had managed to recover the same amount of magic as the incremental change in my maximum magic capacity. I double-checked, and my blue magic bar had returned to one-fifth full.

"......"

"Th-thank you. It was delicious," I said.

"Theresia, do you want to wash your hands? You have apple juice on them," noted Suzuna as she purified some more water. That skill was way more useful than I had expected. She was able to get crystal-clear water even though she scooped it from what was essentially a mud puddle.

"Cion, too... Better than letting her drink from the puddles..."

Suzuna gave Cion some to drink from her hands, since the dog seemed thirsty. Igarashi looked enviously as Cion lapped from Suzuna's hands, but that's something Suzuna got for being a Shrine Maiden who could use Handwash.

We still had the Dirty Mushrooms left to check. We were able to collect a spore sac from the one that hadn't released spores. After appraising the sac, we learned it would burst in order to protect the mushroom, but if you were able to get a whole one, it could be used to make some sort of medicine. Apparently, the sac didn't burst unless the mushroom did it itself when it was in danger, so it was safe enough to carry around with us as it was.

"All right, that's done. Let's get back to the mission at hand," I said, and we fell back into battle formation. There must not have been many Fear Treants or Dirty Mushrooms, because we didn't meet any other enemies for a while. This labyrinth might not be explored that often if the monsters didn't multiply quickly, meaning there was a low risk of a stampede occurring here.

*It also seems like you wouldn't make much money from this labyrinth... Sure, you can find Apples of Wit here, but their rates are low enough that it'd be a waste of time trying to track them down.*

The license did let you reverse-search the monster and current location by using the dropped loot. I'd have to remember which monsters dropped ability-increasing items, for possible future use.

"Cion, don't go so far ahead. It's dangerous," called Elitia. I realized then how far the dog had gone. She'd entered into a thicket just off the side of the path a little way ahead and was now coming back with something in her mouth. It was a pair of goggles.

*These goggles... They're Georg's!*

"Are you saying that the person who dropped these is nearby?" I asked Cion.

"Those goggles... Wasn't that person you were talking to back at the mansion wearing these?" asked Igarashi.

"Oh... Th-they're really scratched up... A-and this...red stuff...," stammered Suzuna.

"Elitia, you shouldn't touch that. It's probably blood," I said.

"...You're right. Whoever wore these was bleeding...and quite a while ago," she replied. There was one possibility I could think of: Georg was injured. Maybe he was attacked by monsters nearby, something happened, and he dropped the goggles.

"Cion, can you follow the scent of the owner of these goggles?" I asked. She seemed to understand what I asked because she started to sniff them, then set off walking again. She sniffed around to confirm the direction before leading us through some trees off the side of the path.

"Be careful up ahead. Cion should be able to detect enemies by scent even if our sight is limited," I warned.

"Got it... Definitely looks like someone's passed through here."

"These tracks seem fresh... But the blood on those goggles..."

The blood on the goggles had completely dried, which meant that some time had passed since Georg was injured.

We came to the center of a dense thicket of trees. Cion found a tree that was larger than the ones surrounding it and went around to the back side. Sitting there was George—he was cradling his head in his hands, his body covered in wounds.

"Georg! Hey, pull it together! We'll get you some help!" I called.

"...I feel like...I've met you before... Oh, in the Lady Ollerus Mansion... H-how've you been...?" he said weakly, his eyes not entirely focused on me. He must have run into something that put him in this state; he barely escaped with his life and made it here. I pulled a potion I'd bought for emergencies out of my bag. In that moment, I didn't even care how valuable potions were; I took the bottle with the red liquid and had Georg drink it. But while it did heal the wounds on his body to an extent, it did nothing for his delirium. Thankfully, because Suzuna was in our party, Georg's condition was improving ever so slightly thanks to her Purification skill. His eyes had been unfocused when we first found him, but after a moment, he finally seemed able to see me clearly. Then he suddenly buried his face in his hands.

"…What happened? Tell me; we can help," I said.

"What…what happened…? I don't even know!!" he shrieked in panic. His physical wounds had been just as bad. He had a gash on his forehead from whatever attack had taken his goggles off.

"Calm down. Your companions from Polaris are still in this labyrinth, right? Did they get captured by monsters, or…?" I asked, waiting for him to calm down. He lowered his hands from his face. He was shaking; his lips trembled as he tried to say something, but no words came out no matter how many times he tried.

"…Don't worry. We came to take the test, too, but we can help your party members on the way. It's okay to ask for help," I said. Georg was so conflicted; he couldn't get the words out. He couldn't easily ask for our help because of his Seeker's pride. But I couldn't just leave him, not in this situation. We couldn't just keep going with our own test, then go home when we passed. I wanted to save whoever could be saved.

"…My friends were…on the second floor of the labyrinth… in the woods, wh-when…something attacked from below…like, some monster vines… I-it…sucked their vitality out…," he finally managed to say.

"All right… They're on the second floor. Georg, you need to get out of here. Thankfully, there aren't many monsters on the first floor. You should be able to get out safe if you focus on escaping," I reasoned.

"…I can't… I can't just run…and leave them…"

"That's not something for the wounded to think about. You need to escape and get help if you can. I know you don't feel good about it, but it's far better than sitting here shaking," said Elitia.

"Ah... Gah... Haah... Aaaaaahhhh!!" screamed Georg, hugging his knees to his chest.

Misaki and Suzuna flinched at his pain-filled shriek. I had no idea how he and his party got separated, but just imagining the possibilities made my heart ache. I'd thought I'd known that the labyrinth was a merciless, perilous place for Seekers, but witnessing the horrific condition Georg was in brought something like anger bubbling up inside me to the surface. It felt like I was on fire, like I needed to do something about it now.

*...I will save all of you. Just stay alive until then!*

"Georg, leave it to Atobe and us. You need to focus on staying alive, do you understand?" Igarashi confirmed.

"...Okay... My friends... Please, save them...," said Georg, a small flicker of understanding returning to his eyes at Igarashi's compassionate words. We could trust him not to do anything desperate now.

I handed Georg his goggles, which he gripped tightly before turning in the direction of the exit and walking away. The potion must've worked, because he seemed steady on his feet. He should be all right.

"From what I could follow, his party was attacked by some sort of vine monster that suddenly appeared from the ground and captured his companions...," summarized Igarashi.

"Georg must have been able to escape immediate danger but wasn't able to get out of the labyrinth. His friends are likely still alive. Let's go," I said.

They'd run into the monster on the second floor. That's likely where the Named Monster was. There was some monster we knew very little about that managed to capture the entire Polaris party in one go. We had to stay on our toes, but we also couldn't waste a single moment in finding and defeating it.

"...Everyone, will you—?" I started.

"Don't bother asking if we're coming with you," interrupted Misaki.

"I'm going with you, Arihito. We move forward as a party. That's how it always is, right?" said Suzuna.

"Same for me. But if some strong monster comes at us and I get injured, don't you dare blame yourself. A party isn't just one person protecting everyone else or one person just being protected, right?" said Igarashi. Her little speech made me realize that while everyone was protecting me, I had started thinking that I was protecting them more with my support skills. And now, too, I'd gotten so arrogant that I thought it was fine to drag everyone else into helping me save Polaris.

"...I'm sorry. I've gotten full of myself. We're only saving them because I want to. It's why I wanted you to come along," I said.

"Of course we're coming along. It's not like you're forcing us to do what you want us to. That's why—," started Elitia.

"Ellie, we'll talk later. Cion's found a monster; it's time to fight!" I interrupted.

"Ah... Right! Kyouka, Theresia, let's go!" called Elitia as she dashed down the path Cion was leading us. It led the opposite direction from where Georg had gone; it seemed to be the path to the second floor, but it was now blocked by a group of Dirty Mushrooms and a Fear Treant.

"Kyouka, use your sweat— Uh, I mean, that nice-smelling stuff!" corrected Misaki.

"It's called *Mist of Bravery*! Get that through your head!" shouted back Igarashi.

We already had a strategy down for these monsters, since we'd fought them before. We used long-range attacks on the Dirty Mushrooms and defended against the Fear Treant's Fear-inducing attacks using Mist of Bravery. Doing that made these monsters no stronger than an average monster of the same level.

## Part III: The Vine Puppeteer

We easily defeated the Fear Treant and three Dirty Mushrooms, then found a wooden chest wrapped in the Fear Treant's roots. It almost looked like part of the Fear Treant's body had morphed into a chest. It was a bit large to carry with us, so we used our storage unit's key to send it there.

"That storage unit key's suuuper useful. Wish it could send a person, though," said Misaki.

"It wouldn't work. You need different types of teleportation magic for transporting nonliving and living things. Even if it did happen to work, there'd probably be an accident," replied Elitia. We could send monster remains to the storage unit, but we couldn't transport them if they were still living. I could assume that moving objects and summoning living things required different kinds of magic.

"Hmm... Isn't it reaaally dangerous to be teleported by a trap, then?" asked Misaki.

"Well... I can't really say no. I haven't heard of it happening in District Eight, but I have heard of people dying when they were teleported by a bad trap in my old district," replied Elitia. Apparently, it was a good thing I decided to prioritize Theresia's Sleight of Hand so she could handle traps. She could potentially even have undone any traps on that chest and opened it... But I decided it was best to leave it to the experts for now and that I would ask Falma for her help.

The monster that defeated Georg's party should be up ahead. I wanted to be able to go into the fight with full morale, so we'd have our Morale Discharges available, but everyone's morale was currently at sixty-six...making it just under thirty minutes since we'd entered the labyrinth.

*The most I can increase morale right now is eleven per use, so using it nine times gets everyone to ninety-nine morale... That's not very efficient. I'd be able to charge everyone up in forty minutes if I could just raise their morale by twelve each time. I really want to find another item like these Chain Gloves that improves the effectiveness of abilities that strengthen my allies.*

They'd have full morale if we waited another twenty minutes, which wasn't that long. But I thought about Georg's condition when we found him and knew we couldn't wait a single second to save his friends.

"All right, let's keep going. I'll try to get everyone's morale charged while we're exploring the second floor... We need to be really careful until then," I said.

"Yeah. Let's go, Cion," said Igarashi, and Cion woofed in response as she took the lead. A thick fog had crept up and was obscuring our vision the same way it had when we first entered. I kept moving forward toward where it was getting ever-so-slightly lighter and tried not to lose sight of Misaki and Suzuna, who were walking right in front of me.

We reached the second floor, and the air felt more oppressive somehow, like it was more humid and heavier.

"Eek...! Th-that scared me. What's that weird sound...?" shrieked Igarashi. There was a cry coming from among the trees that I could really only describe as a strange *kaw, kaw,* like from a bird or some other kind of animal I'd never heard before. I used my Hawk Eyes to look around but didn't see anything nearby. I was certain Georg's party would have passed through here, but there weren't any tracks or signs of them.

"There's kind of a path here... It'd be more difficult to seek as more time passes if we just let it be," noted Elitia as she used her sword to hack through the tall grass in her way. It must have been able to regenerate rapidly, because as soon as she cut it, I could swear I saw it start to grow back. We'd already come up against tree and mushroom monsters, so even the grass here could be an enemy. It wasn't a comforting thought.

"Atobe, can I activate Mist of Bravery just in case? We'll be in trouble if those tree things jump out at us again."

"Go right ahead. It does use a bit of magic, though, so I'll charge you," I replied.

◆Current Status◆
> Kyouka activated Mist of Bravery
> Arihito activated Charge Assist ⟶ Kyouka
  recovered magic

"Ah... But you need magic, too, so don't keep doing that," she said.

"It's because you're in the vanguard. I want to make sure you can use Mirage Step as much as possible," I replied.

"Atobe... Oh, all right. I'll try not to waste it."

Cion came to a stop as we were talking. She'd frozen, her eyes locked on the clearing in the trees ahead of us.

"Woof!"

"...Cion, is something there? Ahead of us?" asked Elitia, who was in the second rank of the formation. Cion just stood there with her ears and tail erect, staring ahead the whole time.

"...Is that...a person...?"

There was a single woman standing in the middle of the grass-filled clearing. Her hair covered her face, so I couldn't make out her expression. Her hair was white, but based on her physical appearance, I estimated she was about the same age as Igarashi, maybe even a little younger.

She started coming toward us. Even though her equipment was broken here and there, she didn't appear to have any major injuries that I could see.

"Are you...a member of Polaris? I'm glad you're all right, but where's the rest of the party?" asked Elitia.

The woman lifted her head so her shoulder-length, white hair fell back from her face, revealing a pale, bloodless visage and a smile as she gazed at us. She looked friendly, but there was something off about her. To put a finer point on things, she seemed lifeless and unnatural.

"My friends are doing well. They're resting just ahead—would you like to come see them?" she asked.

"Oh, I see... That's good," replied Elitia. "I heard you were attacked by a Named Monster, but it looks like you managed to get away."

"Yes, we were in no real danger. My name's Sophie, by the way. It's nice to meet you."

"I'm Elitia, one of our party's vanguards." Even as she conversed with the young woman, Elitia never once let her guard down. I knew that she was ready to draw her sword at any moment. What Georg told us and what this woman was saying didn't match up. And it was weird that she could remain this calm after having been so close to death.

"We ran into Georg on the first floor. He's already left—you should leave, too. We'll help if you need us for anything," I said.

"Leave...? There's no need to rush. Oh, but come to think of it, we have more than enough loot from when we defeated the Named Monster. Would you like some?" she asked with her hands together. So they did defeat the Named Monster. Not entirely out of the ordinary, seeing as they had been the first-ranked party in the district until recently. It was also possible that Georg just ran off for some reason and the danger wasn't as extreme as he'd thought.

*...But her equipment's damaged, and she has no weapon on her...*

Georg hadn't told me what jobs the members of his party had, but the woman was wearing light leather armor, which made me think she was either a Rogue or some sort of agility-based Swordswoman. She did have a sheath at her side, but the weapon that belonged in it wasn't there. The front of her leather armor had a large rip in it, and vines were wrapped around her torso like some sort of emergency measure to cover her body.

"...I know this is a weird thing to ask after you've just gone through a brutal fight, but what kind of enemy was the Named Monster?" I asked, just to double-check. Georg hadn't given us much information on the monster, but if their stories matched, then we probably didn't need to doubt her. He'd said some monster-like vines came from the ground and sucked his allies' vitality.

*...Vines...?*

"—Woof!"

◆Current Status◆
> Cɪᴏɴ activated Sᴇɴsᴇ Dᴀɴɢᴇʀ 1 ⟶ Sensed that
  Sᴏᴘʜɪᴇ is a Pᴜᴘᴘᴇᴛ

"—Guys, get away from her!! Don't let your guard down!" I shouted.

"No way...!"

The woman who'd called herself Sophie hung her head again, but I could see a smile spread across her face, one far more psychotic than she had on before.

"You want to know what kind of monster...? All right, I'll tell you. One that will turn you into nutrients, too!" she cried.

```
◆Monsters Encountered◆
★VINE PUPPETEER
Level 5
In Combat
Dropped Loot: ???
SOPHIE
Level 4
Puppet
Dropped Loot: ???
JAKE
Level 4
Puppet
Dropped Loot: ???
MIHAIL
Level 4
Puppet
Dropped Loot: ???
TYLER
Level 4
Puppet
Dropped Loot: ???
```

Cion had remained wary of the open space in the forest, where dirt in random places now burst up as vines rose violently toward the sky. Elitia gasped as she watched.

"...What on earth...? So Polaris really was—"

All of them except for Georg had been defeated and were now being controlled by the monster. That's the only reasonable conclusion you could make from what was happening.

The rising vines were twined together in some sort of cocoon.

From inside came a number of Seekers, their hair snow-white, their faces lifeless. They must be the rest of Polaris. Their bodies were wrapped in the vines that were probably both sucking their vitality and turning them into puppets.

"I need more nutrients... More, more, more, more, more, I need more...!"

Vines stretched out from Sophie's back, and the ones wrapped around her suddenly spread out to entangle her entire body before blooming with numerous pale blue flowers.

*We might be able to release them from the vines if we defeat the main body... That's what I have to believe. But where is the main body...? How can we draw it out if it's underground?!*

"You'll be my nourishment, too, doggy!"

◆Current Status◆
> JAKE activated POWER STRIKE
> ARIHITO activated DEFENSE SUPPORT 1 ⟶ Target: CION
> CION took 4 damage
> CION activated TAIL COUNTER ⟶ Hit JAKE
11 support damage

"—Awooo!"

"Gaaah!"

At level 4, part of Jake's mace attack made it through Cion's defenses. Cion was also level 4, so I couldn't reduce the damage to nothing even with Defense Support. Cion's counter, though, was far more powerful, tossing Jake backward across the ground. Mihail, who looked like a magic user, and Tyler, who was carrying an ax, had watched the clash unfold before them but didn't flinch at all as they rushed in to attack.

"How dare you attack Cion—!" shouted Igarashi.

"Kyouka, Theresia, wait!" interrupted Elitia. "Arihito, these people are—!"

Could we still save them? Or would they be unable to return to normal after being controlled? But even with Defense Support, this enemy could hurt us, so we couldn't take the time to figure things out.

*Could we get some water and use Suzuna's Wash Away to get rid of the Puppet status? Wait, it's too dangerous to put Suzuna in front of Jake and Tyler. There's got to be a way... Something!*

◆Current Status◆
> Arihito activated Hawk Eyes ⟶ Sensed ★Vine
  Puppeteer's actions

As my mind raced, I suddenly sensed Sophie's next move—or rather, not Sophie, but something behind her. That menacing something was going for Misaki!

"Could you not forget that I'm still here, too?" taunted Sophie.

"Rrgh... Guys, it's coming from below! Jump away!" I shouted, trying to stifle the sense of dread I felt. Everyone followed my order and leaped back, and then the attack came.

◆Current Status◆
> ★Vine Puppeteer activated Vine Puppets

"Eeeeek...!!"

"Misaki!"

She had tried to jump away but had fallen backward instead, and vines exploded from the dirt right in front of her. Suzuna grabbed her and tried to yank her farther from the vines while I loaded a magical bullet into my slingshot and fired.

"Theresia, back me up!" I shouted.

"...!!"

```
◆Current Status◆
> ARIHITO activated FORCE SHOT (STUN) ──→ Hit VINE
  PUPPET E
> VINE PUPPET E was Stunned
> THERESIA activated DOUBLE THROW
> Stage 1 hit VINE PUPPET E
11 support damage
> Stage 2 hit VINE PUPPET E
11 support damage
> 1 VINE PUPPET defeated
> ★VINE PUPPETEER's vitality was reduced
```

I hit the vine monster with a shot from my slingshot, but it didn't faze it. Thanks to Theresia's follow-up attack, though, we were able to bring it down with the support damage. That set damage was really useful. I glanced at my license and noticed that the main body's vitality had also gone down from that.

"Won't you join us...? We'll become something even stronger if you do. Just take my hand... Hee-hee-hee!" the short-haired, freckled boy named Mihail called with an outstretched hand.

"Sorry to burst your bubble... I don't make a habit of accepting invitations from strangers!" replied Igarashi as he frothed at the mouth and unleashed a lightning-type spell. Igarashi dodged using Mirage Step, then flipped her spear around and jabbed him with the blunt end.

"Gah... Hee-hee... C'mon, I like it a bit rougher than that!" he teased.

"Urgh... Damn you...!"

The attack wasn't meant to kill him, since Igarashi had tried to hold back, but Mihail regained his footing almost immediately. The blow should have at least left him in severe pain, but apparently, their sense of pain was gone while they were puppets.

"A woman... A womaaaaan!!" roared Tyler, brandishing his ax and swinging at Elitia.

"Ah!"

She evaded by stepping aside but couldn't counterattack. With her high level, she could have killed him. I wanted to think that it was because he was being controlled, but Tyler's carnal howls and full-out attacks were clearly starting to grate on Elitia's nerves. He was the kind of opponent who could wear someone down psychologically as you faced against him.

*We can't stop them from attacking as long as they're puppets... We can keep attacking it over and over again when it pops out from underground to use Vine Puppet, which should eventually kill the main body... I hope.*

It was a gamble to assume that continually destroying the Vine Puppets would also kill the monster. If we took that gamble, we'd be putting a huge burden on the vanguards' shoulders...with no real end in sight.

"Hee-hee-hee! You're sooo pretty when you dodge like that!!" cackled Mihail.

"Grr... Quit being so gross, asshole!" shouted Igarashi. Her magic was slowly going down as she used Mirage Step. Mihail might not be in his right mind, but forcing her to deal with such bare lust meant more danger for us considering how precise we needed to be. Besides, if I were going to just go out and say it...

"Don't you dare look at my party members like that!" I shouted.

"Huh...? A-Arihito...?" said Misaki.

"Arihito... You're angry... I am, too," said Suzuna. I knew that the Polaris members weren't doing it themselves, but I couldn't stand them looking at my friends like that. I needed to at least shut down Mihail.

"Come forth, Demi-Harpies!"

◆Current Status◆

> Arihito summoned 3 Demi-Harpies

I pulled out the summoning stone pendant I had around my neck to call them forth. When I did, three magic circles formed around me, then burst into three columns of light, the Demi-Harpies appearing inside them.

"... Arihito, what are you—?" asked Elitia, who had the time to glance back. As for Tyler, his own carnal urges were growing more and more apparent to the point that I couldn't even meet his eyes. He'd most likely have some traumatic memories if he remembered all this once he was back to his right mind, but for the moment, I just needed to stop him from doing anything else.

"I'm just gonna have them take a nap... Sing, harpies!"

◆Current Status◆

> Demi-Harpy A activated Lullaby
> Demi-Harpy B and Demi-Harpy C activated Musical Round
> Jake, Mihail, and Tyler were Asleep
> Musical Round continued Lullaby's effects

The Demi-Harpies flapped their wings and took to the air as they began singing. This was the first time I'd seen them use Musical Round, but since they were continuously singing, I decided it was safe to assume that the three sleeping members of Polaris wouldn't be waking up anytime soon.

"I didn't realize we had this option... Arihito, good thinking...," said Elitia.

"Huff, huff... But, Sophie... Why isn't she asleep?" asked Igarashi. Maybe she had sleep-resistant equipment? No, that wasn't it. When Sophie made her attack earlier, my license had displayed that the Vine Puppeteer had activated Vine Puppets. Sophie was further under the Puppeteer's control than the other three.

## Part IV: The Guild Saviors

Sophie looked at me with intense hostility, like she was representing the monster's will.

"How dare you... You're all nothing but trouble," growled

Sophie. "I wanted to get nutrients from Georg, too, but he didn't come back... He must've sent you all here, didn't he? The stuck-up, good-for-nothing Mr. High-and-Mighty is really screwing us over."

"Georg was trying to save you guys!"

"Kyouka, don't let her get you worked up!" said Elitia. "Sophie's under the monster's control right now. If we can just cut those vines wrapped around her, she should come to her—"

"Ha-ha... Ha-ha-ha! What are you talking about? There's nothing more wonderful than becoming nutrients. Come, let us become one! Maybe if I take that man first, you ladies will actually listen to me?" suggested Sophie.

The enemy had its roots stretched throughout the soil and could activate its Vine Puppets anywhere. My mind raced as I tried to think of the best way to deal with it.

"—Atobe!" shouted Igarashi.

◆Current Status◆
> ★Vine Puppeteer activated Full Bloom ⟶ Target: Arihito

Vine Puppets whipped out from the ground all around me, caging me in. I wouldn't be able to escape like this— At least, that's what the enemy thought.

*Perfect... Getting separated from the party had its risks, but that "something" behind Sophie was just starting to catch my eye...!*

When I realized that Sophie was being controlled by the monster, the question became: Where were the vines that wrapped around her body coming from?

The answer: from behind.

◆Current Status◆
> Arihito activated Rear Stance —→ Target: Sophie
> 8 Vine Puppets activated Marionette —→ Target:
                                            None

I activated my skill and teleported behind Sophie. When I appeared behind her, I saw a flower blooming there that was a different color from all the others. This one was white. I couldn't believe that an evil monster could look this pure and delicate.

*So it* was *behind her... If I aim for that...*

I aimed carefully with the magical bullet of my Force Shot and put everything into the shot.

"Take this!"

◆Current Status◆
> Arihito activated Force Shot —→ Hit ★Vine
  Puppeteer
> ★Vine Puppeteer activated Emergency Withdrawal

"—GYEEEEEH!!"

The magical bullet smashed the white flower, scattering petals everywhere. A massive plant erupted from the ground in the center of the clearing— That must be the real Vine Puppeteer. The white flower on Sophie's back withered and fell off, then somehow returned to the main body where it bloomed once again.

But Sophie was still under Puppet status. Looking at her back now, I saw the vines that stretched from her back were still wrapped around her entire body. Her equipment had lost most of its original shape, leaving her near naked.

"Argh... Stupid nutrients... Get off... Get away!"

*Ack... She's really strong!*

I grappled her from behind to stop her from moving, since she was still a puppet. Either it was because she was being controlled by the monster still or she was originally quite strong, but it was really difficult to keep ahold of her as she struggled against me with all her strength.

"Everyone, attack the main body now!" I ordered. Even if they didn't have my rearguard support skills, there was no enemy that wouldn't go down under the full fire of the party, especially with Elitia as our main attacker.

"I'll rip you up from your roots!" shouted Elitia.

"Eek! ...Quit jumping out from underfoot, you cowardly weed!" cried Igarashi.

"...!!"

"Booowwow!"

The four of them attacked with Elitia in the lead: Rising Bolt, Double Attack, Double Throw, Power Rush. Then Suzuna used Auto-Hit and let loose an arrow at the white flower, its weak spot.

"Just a little more...! This should do it!"

Elitia's Rising Bolt connected with her Blossom Blade skill. We needed to end this now; she was trying to chain her attacks together.

"Don't forget that I'm here, too... Lucky Seven!" shouted Misaki, who hadn't joined in the combined assault. She tossed two dice; I couldn't see what the pips were, but Misaki's good luck activated the skill.

◆Current Status◆
> MISAKI activated LUCKY SEVEN ⟶ Success
> ★VINE PUPPETEER's rare item drop rate
  increased

"D-did it work?!" cried Misaki.

"Don't worry; it worked! Fall back!" cried Igarashi.

"Awww... Good luck, you guys! This whole situation is making me wish I chose to be a Cheerleader!" she hollered as she pulled back. At the same time, Elitia was unleashing her Blossom Blade, raining repeated slashes down on the raging plant monster.

"—Die!!"

◆Current Status◆
> ELITIA activated BLOSSOM BLADE
> 12 stages hit ★VINE PUPPETEER

"GYEEEEEHHH!"

Her crimson blade danced through the chain of twelve attacks, carving away at the Vine Puppeteer. At the final push, the nightmarish plant finally stopped moving and sank to the ground in front of us.

◆Current Status◆
> 1 ★VINE PUPPETEER defeated
> SOPHIE, JAKE, MIHAIL, and TYLER were released
  from PUPPET

"Phew…"

"Yikes… That was close. Ack, the vines are dying—!"

The vines wrapped around Sophie started to wither and fall off along with the main body, which meant I couldn't really look directly at her, so I closed my eyes.

"…Nn…"

"Good… It looks like she's going back to her normal self now that we defeated the main body," said Igarashi.

"But what should we do…? We can't really get her help with her looking like this…," I said as I looked around at the forest. Maybe we could cover her with leaves? I decided the others might get mad at me if I suggested that, so I had everyone gather the broken bits of her equipment and try to work something out.

"If we wrap this towel and handkerchief around here, maybe it'll look all right?"

"It'd be really great to have needle and thread for times like this… What about bandages?"

"You mean wrapping her body in bandages? I mean, that's what samurai used to do, I guess…"

"I've done that before, so I'll handle that part."

The four girls debated on the best way to deal with the situation while I had Cion inspect the area, and I checked that the other three were still breathing. They seemed to be weakened, but I didn't think their lives were in any danger.

"……"

"Hmm? …What's wrong?" I asked Theresia as she stood next

to Mihail and stared at me. She clenched her hand into a fist and made a punching motion over him.

"Are you asking if I'm mad at him? I mean, he was under someone else's control... And yeah, I did get angry during the fight, but he wasn't saying those things himself. Just leave him be for now." She lowered her fist and came over to me. Then she just stared at me in silence, like maybe she was trying to say she agreed with me.

"We don't know if he was being honest because he was controlled, or if he isn't the type of think these things normally, but...I guess people as composed as Arihito don't come along very often," said Elitia.

"When you're behind... No, just whenever you're nearby, I feel so much calmer. I know I can't rely on you for every last need, but I really want to be like that...," said Misaki. Everyone must have felt relaxed now that the battle was over, but I still felt uncomfortable with all the compliments, even though they were the same ones they always gave me.

"......"

"Oh, we need to see if it dropped anything... Cion, did you find something?" I asked. She had sat down and was thumping her tail as it wagged.

*...Whoa!*

I went over and saw that a Black Box had fallen from the withered vines.

*It went a long time without being defeated, killing more and more people... So I guess it created a Black Box like Juggernaut did.*

That list of victims ended at Polaris, and my own party was

safe. Cion's back was to me, which activated Recovery Support, so everyone was recovering.

"Atobe, did you find something...? Oh, th-that chest... Is that a Black Box?"

"It was a powerful monster and unconfirmed, so there was always the possibility, but... There's always something exciting happening in this party, isn't there?" said Elitia with a small smile in my direction. I felt the same. These Black Boxes were rare enough to surprise Falma, so it was normal for a long time to pass before you'd see another one. I was happy but surprised as well.

*A Black Box... The one that Juggernaut dropped had the key to the hidden floor. If there's one in this box...*

If this labyrinth had a hidden floor, too, and if we got into it, we might be able to find the parts that Ariadne spoke of, or we could meet another Hidden God.

Once we made sure Polaris was safe, we'd go have this Black Box opened. My heart had been racing since we'd found the unexpected item.

"...Oh, right. They're still flying. Thanks for your help; you can all come down now," I called up to the Demi-Harpies, who were still circling in the sky even though the fight was over. They landed in front of me, and I saw that the previously naked girls were now clothed, so I didn't have to be as careful about where I looked. The smallest and youngest of the three girls did seem quite nervous, since she was hiding behind the middle sister, but she didn't seem outright afraid of me.

"Atobe, have you given them names?" asked Igarashi.

"Uh… I'm terrible at deciding names. How about everyone else thinks of something? Or do you have names already?" I asked, and the eldest sister shook her long, brown hair to say no. Her clothing was a simple poncho-like piece of thin cloth, and it seemed like she wasn't wearing a bra underneath because her chest bounced quite a bit when she did. I really couldn't make reprimand Mihail if I was reacting in the same way. "How about the name *Asuka*? It's written with the kanji for *fly* and *bird*, so I think it fits."

"Asuka… Then, maybe *Yayoi* could work as well, if we're going with historic periods. That said, it's kind of old-fashioned."

"And maybe the third one could be…*Himiko*? Although, only one of them would have a queen's name, then."

And just like that, the Demi-Harpies had names, the group of girls making quick work of it. From eldest to youngest, we had Asuka, then Himiko, then Yayoi. But I felt like a legendary queen's name was most suited to the eldest sister, so maybe we should go with Himiko, Asuka, and Yayoi?

"We'll have you name the next monster, Elitia," I suggested.

"I feel like naming is a big responsibility… But I'll try to think of something if you want me to."

The Demi-Harpies' Lullaby had been incredibly useful, so I wanted to keep an eye out for other monsters who could use special attacks and be recruited.

"Hmm…? What's that…?" I said. I heard the sound of footsteps from a group of people coming from the direction of the first floor. I turned and saw a heavily armored woman with a massive shield leading the group. I'd seen the large symbol emblazoned on the shield before—it was the Guild's mark. The woman had short, smooth hair and wore a headband with a metal plate wrapped around her head. She looked quite a bit younger than me, but I got the impression that she was very experienced.

The group she led was made up of two more women and three men. They wore helmets that covered their faces, so I couldn't make out their expressions. Each had an impressive air, and I could see that my companions were a little shaken by them.

"...Are you members of Polaris?" asked the leader in a soft voice akin to a whisper that didn't match the heavy armor she wore. I suddenly realized who they might be.

"No, we're a different party. We just defeated the monster that attacked Polaris... And you are?" I asked.

"We are the Guild Saviors. We received a request for assistance from the leader of Polaris. We've come in response to that," she explained. The Guild normally monitored anyone who was in the middle of an advancement test. Even so, we'd managed to save Polaris in the time that it took them to receive the report and respond.

"Thank you for assisting us in our duties. You will be provided rescue reparations if you submit a report to the Guild. However, I must ask that you promise not to assist any party who has been defeated in the future," she continued.

"I'm sorry, but...it will all depend on the situation, so I can't make that promise," I replied.

"...I see," she said simply, though I was afraid I'd offended her. "...Every party in the Labyrinth Country is competing against one another. You'd do well to remember that. You should prioritize your own party above all else."

"I'll keep that in mind. Now, the Polaris party members...," I started.

"We will transport them back to town. We've brought the personnel necessary," she replied as two expert-seeming people from her group started casually drawing magic circles on the ground.

*Teleportation magic...* Seeing it like this, I realized just how useful it was. Before long, the members of Polaris were laid on the circles and whisked away.

"We will also teleport you if you're leaving the labyrinth," offered the lead woman.

"Thank you. I forgot to introduce myself earlier. My name's Atobe."

"...Arihito Atobe. That name has gained far more attention than I think you are aware. My name is Seraphina. Seraphina Edelbert," she replied, sticking her massive shield in the ground and taking off her gauntlet before extending her right hand. I took her hand and saw a tiny smile on her face, the first emotion I'd seen on her so far.


My party took up the offer of teleportation and used the circles to leave the labyrinth. It only took a blink of an eye for us to appear in the square outside the entrance to the Shrieking Wood. Seraphina's party must have arranged for the first responders to be there, because they were already carrying away the members of Polaris.

"It's a good thing the Guild Saviors came, right, Arihito?" said Suzuna.

"Yeah, they helped out a lot. I did want to get out of there for a little bit," I replied.

"I can't believe we found a Black Box... I wonder if there's a hidden floor in the Shrieking Wood, too...," said Igarashi, having had the same thought as me. If there was a hidden floor, it was likely that the key to it was in this box.

We'd already made more than enough contribution points to pass the test, so we'd achieved our current goal. We'd go back to the city for a little while and see what was in the Black Box; if there was a key in it, there might be a hidden floor as well...but we wouldn't know if there was until we opened it.

"...Arihito, Black Boxes aren't the sort of thing you go looking for. We don't know if we'll find another one even if we keep hunting Named Monsters," said Elitia. "But if we do happen to find one like this, then we have the right to go to any hidden floor there might be. That's not a chance we can throw away."

"That vine monster didn't seem like a normal Named Monster, either. If they only drop Black Boxes after they've done a lot of damage...then the god that made Ariadne is horrible," noted Igarashi. Juggernaut and the Vine Puppeteer— The one thing they had in common was that they caused a lot of damage before they were eventually taken down.

We got ahold of the Black Box because Georg and his party had been defeated. Thinking of it that way, I couldn't help but feel like the box's entire existence was vile. But that's exactly why we couldn't waste it. We could go up to District Seven and get stronger before coming back, but we could also use whatever we gained from following through with this box's contents to give us an edge in District Seven. Neither option was wrong.

"Arihito, Misaki and I will find the path to the hidden floor," said Suzuna.

"If there's a key in there, that is. But what Ariadne said made it sound like almost every labyrinth has a hidden floor," added Misaki.

We could theoretically go to the bottom floor in every labyrinth; it'd just take time. Even if we did, though, there'd be things we'd never find. Then there was the possibility that the hidden floors had already been found by someone else, so even though we spent the time and effort to get there, it could have been cleaned out. There wouldn't actually be anything to find. Thinking of it that way, we could only aim to find any hidden floors if we happened to find a Black Box in that labyrinth… That'd be a good policy.

"All right, it's decided. First, I'll go report to Louisa. The rest of you can go take a break at the mansion. We'll open the box tomorrow," I announced.

""""Okay!"""" chimed the rest of the members, even Igarashi. I knew she had accepted me as the leader of the party, but it still felt a little strange.

" . . . . . . "

"Huh? ...You wanna come along? No, you can take a break instead; it's fine," I said to Theresia, who stuck close to me. I wondered what was wrong—maybe there was something on her mind?

"...Are you maybe thinking about that Seraphina lady from before?" I asked.

"—?!"

I had said it even though I thought I might be projecting this onto her, but Theresia reacted pretty strongly, her face turning bright red as she pressed her hands to her lizard mask and crouched down.

"The way things were going, it would've been rude not to shake her hand. It's not like I'm interested in her or anything," I continued.

" . . . . . . "

Theresia looked up at me as if to ask if I really meant it. I held my hand out to her and helped her stand up. Her hand was really warm. Being a lizardman, she wasn't good with high temperatures, so I should try to avoid letting her get overheated.

"In any case... Looks like everyone got the wrong idea. How about we go together like always?"

" . . . . . . "

Theresia gained her composure. The red faded from her mask, and she nodded. She walked by my side all the way to the Guild, holding her right hand, the one I'd held, to her chest with her left on top, like she was treasuring it.

## Part V: The Puppeteer's Persistence

Seekers milled about inside the Guild. Theresia and I were basically regulars there by now, so one of Louisa's junior coworkers showed us to one of the inner meeting rooms I'd been in before. Not much time passed before Louisa came in with some tea and looked at the results of our adventure on my license, with her monocle on as always.

"These names… These are members of Polaris. You somehow managed to save them before the Guild Saviors could…," marveled Louisa.

```
◆Expedition Results◆
> Raided Shrieking Wood 1F: 10 points
> Raided Shrieking Wood 2F: 10 points
> Misaki grew to level 4: 40 points
> Defeated 2 Fear Treants: 80 points
> Defeated 5 Dirty Mushrooms: 100 points
> Defeated 1 bounty ★Vine Puppeteer: 1,200 points
> Party members' Trust Levels increased: 300
  points
> Rescued Georg: 100 points
> Rescued Sophie: 100 points
> Rescued Jake: 100 points
> Rescued Mihail: 100 points
> Rescued Tyler: 100 points
> Returned with 1 Black Treasure Chest: 50 points
Seeker Contribution: 2,290 points
District Eight Career Contribution Ranking: 1
District Seven Contribution Ranking: 294
```

"No issues where your contribution points are concerned. Congratulations, Mr. Atobe; your party has received official approval to advance to District Seven. I will record your Pass on your license," said Louisa.

"Pass?" I asked.

"That's correct. You can view it on your license. We simply call the official proof of approval to move to a given district a Pass. If you don't have a Pass and attempt to go into a district without approval, you will be forcibly removed, so please do be careful."

With that function, even if you happened to have a skill that let you get past the walls and go into the higher districts, you wouldn't be able to. It was possible that there were still some loopholes, but I couldn't even think of any at the time. On top of that, your karma would go up if you broke the rules, and I didn't want to be arrested if I could help it.

"You contacted the Guild Saviors earlier, didn't you? We met Seraphina in the labyrinth," I said.

"Yes, they aren't normally dispatched to District Eight labyrinths... But this was a special case. They were mobilized during the stampede and staying in the district anyway."

Apparently, they were normally busy with saving Seekers in the higher districts. If they were that busy, I wasn't likely to meet them again anytime soon.

"I will actually be providing you with a rescue reward. There is a bonus, since you rescued all members of the party... It comes to twelve gold per person rescued, so a total of sixty gold pieces."

"Thank you. Would it be possible for you to put that toward Georg and his party's recovery costs?"

"Are you...positive that's what you want to do? I'm sure they have the savings necessary to pay for their medical treatment."

"I haven't known them very long, but I think of them as friends who live in the same housing. I'd like to help out, even if it's just a little."

Louisa seemed a little confused. Even if someone might think it was hypocritical, I wanted to help Georg. If my party members had been taken under the Vine Puppeteer's control and I had no option but to run, I'm not sure I could bounce back from that easily. And Georg had been terrified and beaten down. Just looking at him, I knew it would be hard for him to go back to seeking like before.

"Are you trying to...help Seekers keep going for as long as they can, even if it might be one or two of them?" asked Louisa.

"I always want that to be the case. And I know there's always competition between us, but I want to help like-minded friends when I can."

"I think that's a wonderful mind-set to have. If only all Seekers felt the same...there would be fewer parties facing death in the labyrinth."

That's not how things were at the moment. If my party was on the brink of destruction, another party passing by might not help us... Though, I couldn't really blame anyone for putting their own survival first. Even so, if there was someone I could save, I wanted to do something and save them. I couldn't change how I felt.

"I'm going to go visit Polaris at the Healers. Louisa, would you like to come out and have some drinks with us once things are ready for us to move to District Seven?"

"I would love to. And until then, I pray for your health and happiness."

Theresia and I headed to the Healer clinic near the Guild and went to the room that Georg and the rest of his party were in. All the men of the party were in the room, and other than Georg, they were all asleep. They had had their vitality sucked out by the Vine Puppeteer, so they were in an extremely weakened state.

"...Arihito, you came," said Georg. He had a bandage wrapped around his head; apparently, not all his wounds were completely healed, but I could barely believe how much life had returned to his eyes from when we'd found him in the labyrinth.

"You look rough. If only we'd...," I started, but Georg held up his hand to stop me before I could say I wished we'd started looking sooner.

"When everyone had been taken by that plant monster, I couldn't leave the second floor for a little while. You'll probably laugh, but...I was so scared that I couldn't even move my legs. The whole time, I could hear Sophie's voice from the forest, as she was being controlled. She kept telling me I should come back and become its nutrients."

"...It was an evil monster. It would've been better if you could've taken your test somewhere else, somewhere that didn't have something like *that*," I offered.

"Yeah. But even if we'd avoided that labyrinth and gone to District Seven, we'd probably encounter another monster like it there. Even if you run from danger, it's running right after you… It just means that we weren't ready to go to District Seven…" He wasn't trying to put himself down; he said it so matter-of-factly. I even saw a hint of a smile on his face. "To tell you the truth, my party was just about to fall apart anyway. We used to have another woman in the party besides Sophie… But she got hurt really bad when we made it to rank one in the district, and she retired from seeking. Mihail and Tyler both had a thing for her. It's pretty stupid, but us four guys kind of got our motivation for seeking out of competing for the two women."

"I see…"

Every party had its own things going on—remove one person, and the entire party's balance could be thrown off… That was probably true about my party as well.

"…Sophie was the first one to become that thing's puppet. The rest of us were hopeless after that. It would've been the end of everything if we let her die."

"But you're all right now. You can get back into it whenever you want. Well, I say that like it'd be simple."

"No… It's all right. I think part of me wants someone to tell me to give it up, but that would hurt, too. It's more help to hear someone tell me to keep at it."

He could always retire from seeking like his one friend and move to the support side. That was an option, but I didn't necessarily think that's what he should do. I couldn't just wish him luck. That wouldn't mean anything. But I didn't want them to end things in this way.

"I don't think you need to blame yourself. There have been many times when I've been scared to death in battle," I said.

"...Even someone like you, who defeated that beast, gets afraid sometimes?" asked Georg.

"Yeah. Not that I can show it in front of my party," I added, and Georg smiled. It was the same friendly smile from the day we'd met in the mansion.

"Arihito, I really can't thank you enough. You came all this way and talked to me... But I was actually hoping to ask you one more favor," he said hesitantly, but he seemed to make up his mind and forced the words from his mouth. "Could you go visit Sophie? I'll let the Healer know you're going."

"...Is something wrong with her?" I'd thought we'd been able to save her. But based on Georg's expression, that was nothing more than my wishful thinking.

"Since you're the one who saved her...maybe you can reach her. If you could do something... Say something to make her respond, anything..."

"Georg..."

I couldn't think of anything else to say to him. What must it feel like to lose to a monster? I still couldn't really understand how he felt.

I wasn't sure that Georg introducing us to the Healers would be enough for them to allow us to visit Sophie, but once they learned we were part of the party that defeated the Vine Puppeteer, they led us to her room. I opened the door and saw Sophie in the bed. She was sitting upright, but her eyes were blank. She didn't react when we went in.

"Seekers don't always recover after monsters seize complete control of their minds. Coming into close contact with the monster's consciousness can be too much for a human," explained the Healer, a woman old enough to be Sophie's mother. Perhaps that was part of why looking at Sophie seemed to pain the Healer that much.

"...I thought if we defeated the monster, she'd be released from that. I guess I was naive," I said, the words catching in my throat. If we'd been able to save her sooner... Though, these terrible things were probably happening all over the Labyrinth Country; I just hadn't seen them yet.

"Is there anything I can actually do?" I asked.

"...There's no proof that it will work, but since it was your party who defeated the monster that controlled her mind, there is a possibility," replied the Healer.

"A possibility... What is it...?"

"There's a chance that she is still being controlled by the monster. Plant monsters sometimes leave behind seeds. Unfortunately, those seeds also have a consciousness. They gather nutrients from their host until they can germinate and accomplish their one goal."

One goal... Hearing it put like that made me think of something. *What do monsters think of the Seekers who defeat them? I doubt they just accept it and move on.*

"There are...risks. It is possible that the seed in Sophie will react if someone who the monster sees as a threat is nearby," continued the Healer.

"And if it...germinates, Sophie will be...?"

"It would be best if we had someone with a skill that could safely extract the seed... But those with medical skills are currently in the higher districts. They don't seem to be responding to our requests for assistance."

"...What will happen to Sophie if she stays like this?"

"The seed will continue to feed off her, putting her life at risk. But if we can force it to germinate quickly, then we may be able to prevent that. There is also a chance we could expel the seed."

The Healer knew it was a gamble, but she'd brought me here anyway...so that Sophie would have even a small chance at survival.

"Okay. Would you be able to leave me alone in the room, then? I imagine there's a chance it won't germinate if there are others around," I said.

"...I'm sorry to ask you to do this. You have already saved her once, and to request that you put yourself in further danger... I hate to ask someone with a bright future ahead of them to put themselves at risk," she said.

"Please don't worry about it. I was the first one to strike the enemy's main body. I think I'm probably the one it's most hostile toward," I replied, remembering the dreadful shriek it made when I used Rear Stance to go behind it and shoot it with my slingshot. I imagined it was probably lying in wait, constantly plotting its revenge on me for that attack.

*...I'd prefer to reduce the risks as much as possible, but I can't abandon Sophie here.*

The Healer left the room, but Theresia remained in place.

"Theresia, I'm guessing the monster won't respond unless I'm the only person here. Go outside for a little bit..."

She shook her head. She knew what was about to start would be dangerous, which was probably why she wasn't willing to leave me. We didn't necessarily need to make the situation perfect for the monster. Obviously, it was better for me to have a friend nearby.

"...Okay. Stay here, Theresia. Can you go get help immediately if anything happens to me?" I asked, and Theresia nodded. I moved closer to Sophie, her hair swaying as her face turned toward me. There was no life in her eyes. Could I really get her back to her old self?

That's when it happened. Sophie shot her hand out and grabbed mine, faster than I could react.

*Ah?!*

Sophie was wearing a simple shirt, and a vine suddenly shot out from her sleeve, wrapping around my hand.

"...Become one... Become one with me," said Sophie through pale, bloodless lips. The next moment, my field of vision became distorted, and I could feel it taking over my mind—

I realized I was kneeling in an inky black space, unable to move a muscle.

*Ack... The vines... Where is this...? Is this some subconscious world...?*

Vines wrapped around my entire body so I couldn't move.

Something white appeared in front of me... It was Sophie, strung up in tendrils just like me.

"Sophie—!"

She didn't respond to my cries. Instead, the ivy stretched around us started to move like some intelligent being, twining together to form a massive bud-like shape in front of me. The bud opened—revealing the same white flower that was on the Vine Puppeteer's main body. From the center of the white flower appeared a single little girl. She was like a flower personified. Flower petal–like shapes draped over part of her figure, and she looked at me with emotionless eyes... There was something so plant-like about her.

"Are you...the real Vine Puppeteer...?" I asked.

"...This version of me was formed when I fused minds with Sophie. I will put you under my control by forcing you to succumb here," said the girl.

"You can speak... I've never met a monster that could speak before."

"Nutrients should be consumed and not heard. I have much to gain from feeding from your mind, so I will let you live a little while. If you do well, I may use you for a long time."

Well, she was quite the cheeky girl... Though she only looked like a ten-year-old girl, she was actually a monster.

"...You hurt me before. More than being carved with a sword or pierced with a spear or shot with an arrow. Your attack hurt the most," she continued.

"Agh!"

The vines wrapped around my body squeezed with incredible force; it was like being choked by a gigantic boa constrictor.

"...Accept my control. Or would you prefer to suffer the pain of having your mind broken? There is no creature I cannot break."

*I knew she'd try to attack my mind right now... Sophie won't be able to recover if I don't release her from this!*

I didn't have my equipment; I didn't have any friends to use support skills on. What could I actually do...? It was stupid to assume I could try and monitor her if I did accept her control—that would be a death sentence.

"...Monsters...really do like to do things the mean way...," I said.

"Humans are no different. There were those who tried to burn me away with the forests I lived in. Do you know what it feels like to be burned alive?"

"...I can only imagine. I wouldn't choose that method."

"...Why are you smiling? You should be aware of what will happen if I break your body. This is not a simple threat."

It made me realize I was smiling. My body was being crushed, and I was gasping painfully for breath, but I wasn't really thinking about crying out.

"Not sure how it looks to say this about myself, but...I'm really bad at giving up...and pretty good at enduring...discomfort," I continued.

"...Fine, then. I will break one of your arms; that will make you regr—," she started to say in response, but she was too slow.

"—!!"

Something flew into my line of sight. It was a naked girl with a lizard tail, parts of her skin covered in scales. She shouldn't have been able to come here, but she'd just cracked a heavy kick into the Vine Puppeteer.

"Gah!"

This world might be in the mind, but the Vine Puppeteer apparently only had the physical strength you might expect from its current form, making her unable to stand her ground against Theresia's attack.

"Theresia... How did...you get here...?" I asked.

"...A soul eroded by the labyrinth... The same as me... I see. You placed me on your own body, then climbed along your symbol's connection...," the Puppeteer pieced together.

Apparently, Theresia had put the Puppeteer's vines on herself to enter this subconscious world. Concealed by her hair, the back of her neck held her "ownership symbol," which had certainly formed some sort of connection between the two of us... She'd used that connection to come here and save me.

"...!"

"Do you intend to resist my control and save the human? What can you do? You aren't even entirely a monster," said the Puppeteer. Theresia's back was to me. In here, it was her psychological state, so she wasn't wearing her characteristic lizard mask. Her black hair fell to the base of her neck. She was protecting me, but I knew she'd likely have her mind stolen from her in this place.

"No one can defeat me when they don't even have a weapon. Your fates were sealed the moment you came to this place,"

taunted the Puppeteer, and a multitude of vines sprouted from the ground. There was nowhere to run to in this dark space... But even so, Theresia stretched out her arms and refused to fall even a step back.

"Get out of my way!" screeched the Puppeteer as the vines lashed out at Theresia. She wouldn't be able to withstand the violent attack... Well, she wouldn't if there hadn't been anything protecting her.

"Theresia, I'll help you!" I shouted.

"...!!"

I was behind her. Even if this were just some subconscious world, I should still be a rearguard as long as I was in that position.

The vine bounced off an invisible wall. My Defense Support probably wouldn't have worked if they had instead tried to bind her. I wasn't sure if that had been part of Theresia's plan, but Theresia had skillfully coerced the Vine Puppeteer into attacking her. That made a single opening for her.

"—Go, Theresia!" I called.

"...Hah...!!"

I could actually hear Theresia breathing for the first time in a while. She unleashed a kick that was strengthened with my Attack Support, adding eleven support damage to her martial arts attack.

"Ack!!"

The Vine Puppeteer was flung backward from the force of the strike. That one hit was strong enough to decide the fight, considering the enemy had assumed we couldn't do any damage to it at all. The vines wrapped around me and Sophie withered and fell to the ground. Theresia walked up to the little, white-haired girl, or what was left of the Vine Puppeteer.

"……"

The Puppeteer shuddered on the ground and moved no more. Her real form, the white flower, had seemed the same in that they were both incredibly weak to direct hits. This was the human form that the Puppeteer had made when it came in contact with Sophie's mind. That might be why it looked like a younger version of Sophie.

I hadn't expected my Attack Support to be this effective. Even if it didn't add damage to magical attacks, apparently, it worked on attacks made by mental manifestations. It was nice to know, though I had no idea if the information would ever be useful again.

Thanks to Theresia, I was able to escape certain death. Even the vines around my arm disappeared. There was a lingering pain, but it wasn't anything serious.

Sophie and the body of the Vine Puppeteer started to glow, then slowly faded and vanished. I could only pray that Sophie would wake up all right. Soon, mine and Theresia's mental bodies started to fade as well.

"…Theresia, thank you for coming to save me. Really…"

Theresia hesitated, then tried to turn back to face me.

"……"

I could see in my fading vision that her lips were moving, trying to say something, but before I could really see her face, I was pulled back to my real body. I opened my eyes, and I was in Sophie's room at the Healer clinic. Theresia's hand came from behind me and was placed on top of Sophie's, which was squeezing mine. Sophie was lying back on the bed, unconscious, so we couldn't confirm whether or not she was back to her normal self.

"…Thank you. I'm sorry I worried you."

Theresia pulled her hand away, then hugged me from behind. I was surprised but felt strangely comfortable, placing my hand on hers as she gripped the front of my shirt. Even if she couldn't say it, I thought she was trying to tell me she was happy that I was all right.

*…Hmm?*

I saw something out of the corner of my eye that hadn't been there before I was pulled into the subconscious world. When I scrutinized it, I saw what looked like a seed had fallen on the bed. Apparently, even though Theresia had defeated it in that mental world, it was still alive. I was going to decide what to do with it. It should be fine for me to do that much. I looked at the powerful enemy, who was now small enough to fit in the palm of my hand, and thought of a few options.

## Part VI: The Merchant and the Dissector

I called in the Healer and told her that Sophie had been freed from the monster's clutches so that she could check how she was doing.

"I can't be certain until she wakes up… But her condition does seem to have improved from before. Now that the monster's seed has been removed, I can see her responding to my skill, which accelerates her own body's healing rate," she said.

"Good... I'm going to take the seed that came out with me. Or would you like to use it for some kind of research?" I asked.

"N-no... Unfortunately, we don't have any facilities here that are capable of researching monsters. It would actually be best if you take it, so that we need not worry about it," she replied.

I wondered if I took it to the Monster Ranch and made a contract with it, would it follow my orders? Having a Named Monster on the team would give us a huge edge in certain situations.

"I won't use this seed for anything bad. I hope you're not concerned about that," I said.

"Of course not. Thank you for taking care of it. Georg is currently sleeping, but would you like to visit him again?"

"No, but could you give him my regards when he wakes?" He'd been in a terrible state before; there was no point in disturbing him for nothing if he was finally getting some rest—even if I did want to tell him right away about Sophie, so he could relax.

"...Mm..."

"Ah... Sophie, are you awake? How do you feel?" asked the Healer.

"Sorry, looks like I've made too much noise. Take care, Sophie...," I said as Theresia and I turned for the door.

"...Wait...," Sophie called out, stopping us. She was lying down, with only her face turned toward us. I could understand why Georg and one of the other men in the party would be interested in gaining her affection. Something about her face made me imagine she was normally a cheerful and lively woman, but now, she looked at me with hazy eyes and spoke in a weak voice.

"...I had a dream... A bad dream... I was tied up in vines...but you..." She had memories of what happened in the subconscious world even though she'd been under the Puppeteer's control. That meant she was probably aware that Theresia and I had saved her.

"...I hope you feel better soon. Everything else can wait until then," I said.

"...Yes... Thank you. Could you tell me your name...?"

"My name's Arihito Atobe. This is Theresia."

Sophie looked at Theresia with her mask on, and she seemed quite surprised, since Theresia hadn't been wearing her mask in the subconscious world.

"...A demi-human curse... If it weren't for that...you'd be really...," said Sophie, but she fell asleep again before she could finish. She was still weakened; she had just been in a temporarily conscious state.

The Healer wiped away a tear that was running down Sophie's cheek and checked her condition. I thanked her again for taking care of Sophie and left the room. I looked at the profile of Theresia's face as we walked down the hallway, side by side. What was Sophie trying to say? The only thing I could imagine was that she was trying to say what she felt when she saw Theresia without her mask.

"......"

"Ah, sorry. You know when you came to save me? I was just thinking about how you didn't have your mask on," I said.

"...?!"

She hadn't realized until now... Perhaps she had been too focused on taking down the Vine Puppeteer.

"......"

"I think Sophie may have seen you, but I was behind you, so unfortunately, I didn't get a good look. Well, I know you wouldn't be able to do anything even if I said I wanted to see your face... But I can't really help being curious." Theresia shook her head. If she was saying that she didn't mind if I saw, then I didn't have to feel bad about being curious. But without the mask, it'd be a real problem if she insisted she wanted to take a bath with me.

"......"

"Ah... T-Theresia, it's okay. I don't have a fever or anything," I stammered. Apparently, I was an open book. I'd have to be more careful of that, because she put her hand to my forehead to check my temperature.

"......"

Theresia insisted that I was warmer than her, but could I really be that hot if she was comparing it to her lizard mask, which tended to run cool...? I looked at her always overly concerned self and couldn't keep myself from smiling. But then I noticed something: She had a small wound on the back of her hand. It was probably a cut from when she stabbed the vine into her own hand in order to save me.

"Theresia, could you walk in front of me for a bit?" I asked.

"......"

Theresia did as I asked, and after a few moments, my Recovery

Support kicked in and healed her wound. I checked her hand, and it was completely gone.

"Good, it's smooth. I would've felt bad if you'd gotten a scar…"

"……"

Theresia shook her head silently. I tried to figure out what she was trying to tell me.

"…I made the mistake of believing that I could protect everyone on my own. Even though my job specifically requires me to have someone in front of me before I can even do anything."

"……"

Theresia started to shake her head but stopped. She stepped in front of me again, then turned back and flexed her arm.

"Do you mean you're stronger when I'm behind you?"

"……"

She nodded back and showed me her now perfectly healed hand. I was still so grateful toward her that the scene of her coming to my rescue kept playing over and over again in my mind. Though, I could never admit that I was captivated by the heroic sight of her kicking an enemy while naked.

We returned to the Lady Ollerus Mansion and went to the small on-site workshop, where we saw Melissa dressed in overalls.

"…Welcome back," she said.

"Thanks. I arranged for some materials to be sent here. I was wondering if I could ask you to process them."

"We got 'em. I brought an ax and saw to the dissection of the Fear Treants. I can dissect the Dirty Mushrooms with a billhook."

She could probably equip all weapons necessary for dissection thanks to her job. But as always, there was something intimidating about seeing the porcelain doll–like girl smiling as she gripped a large knife.

"What can you make from the Fear Treant?" I asked.

"Pretty much any kind of wooden equipment. Or you could sell it for a decent amount. A slingshot made from a Fear Treant will generate a sound with the same effects as Terror Voice."

"That's…creepy. But powerful."

"There's also headgear, which would have the Soundproof 1 effect. Monsters that use sound attacks also have sound resistance."

"Headgear? Could you make one of those for us?"

The remaining wood gave us enough materials to make two or three more pieces of equipment, so later, I'd show the party a list of what could be made and ask if they wanted anything.

While Melissa and I talked, Madoka came over from where she had been sitting in the workshop. I had asked her to look into something for me, and it looked like she'd gotten something.

"Good work today, Arihito. I heard it was another tough expedition," she said.

"I can't say they were uninjured, but all the members of Polaris are going to be all right. I'm just glad we managed to save them," I replied.

"You guys always manage to rescue so many people. You must give so many others courage… I know you give me more courage, like I need to work harder."

"I'm not sure about all that… But I do know that we can keep up the fight thanks to you. Sorry to keep you working even when you're not out seeking with us."

"It's all right... You can ask me anything. I just hope I can be of some assistance to you and your party."

"Thanks—I know you will. So what did you find?" I had asked her to look into the alkaid crystal we'd gotten from Juggernaut but still had no idea what it could be used for. It was a transparent quartz that glowed a faint silver. There was some sort of pattern inside the crystal, which made it look like a rune, but that's where the resemblance ended.

"This is a material that has never been found in District Eight before. There have been similar objects found in the higher districts, but never the exact same item," explained Madoka.

"It's that rare... So what exactly can they be used for?" I asked.

"Well... It's unregistered. There's not a single record of them being used for modifications, and the Merchants Guild has no information regarding what the parties who have one in their possession have actually used them for."

But my license at least told me it was an alkaid crystal, so it didn't seem right that there'd be no information about it anywhere else.

*Which means the license can display information that even the Guild doesn't have access to. That's the only reasonable explanation... So then...who made the licenses?*

I had too many questions running through my mind. The person who gave us the licenses when we reincarnated told us that she normally lived in the Labyrinth Country. If that was true, I wanted to ask her who made the licenses if I ever happened to meet her again. Didn't sound like we could get it out of her very easily, though.

"Well, so the only thing we know about this is its name. I guess even that's a result of sorts," I said.

"I'm sorry I couldn't find what you needed. I really am too low a level..."

"No, it was helpful. You'll be able to do more when you level up, but this is plenty for now."

"...Arihito..." Madoka seemed lost in her thoughts, so I placed a hand on top of the Merchant's turban she wore and patted it gently. She was a little surprised and shyly held her turban in place.

"...Atobe, are you good at patting people?" asked Melissa.

"Uh, I think I'm probably average."

"Hmm. I thought you were good based on how Madoka looks," she said shortly, which made me think she didn't mean anything else by her question. Even Madoka's ears were bright red, and she didn't seem to be able to say anything.

"A-anyway... What can we make from the Dirty Mushrooms?" I asked Melissa.

"The white stalk's edible. Sometimes, you find magic stones inside the caps if you cut them open... The arms and legs are unusable and poisonous, so they get thrown away. Sometimes, there is a section on the inside that is patterned, and that can be used to make medicine."

There were five Dirty Mushrooms, and each one weighed a little over twenty pounds. The stalk could be used as food, so we could sell it for a small price. The total edible portion was about ten pounds, but it wasn't massively valuable. The total of fifty pounds of food between the five mushrooms was only worth fifteen gold pieces.

Other than that, I had Melissa cut open the unbroken caps, and she found a magic stone in the fourth mushroom.

"…A confusion stone. You have one on your sling, but you can compress them if you gather ten," she explained.

"That'll take a while… But maybe we'll get enough someday. Okay, so if there's a central part with a pattern, what kind of medicine can be made?" I asked. Melissa glanced at Madoka, then clamped her hands over Madoka's ears.

"Huh? What? …Why won't you let me listen?" asked Madoka in confusion, but Melissa completely blocked her hearing before looking at me, her cheeks tinged pink as she spoke in a low voice.

"…A tonic. Dad says men will pay a lot of money for it."

"I—I see…," I replied.

I guess that meant it wasn't good for physical or nutritional purposes, but rather…*adult* uses. Even so, there might come a time when it could be helpful for some unexpected use, so I wanted to keep some on hand. I hoped that Melissa didn't jump to conclusions when I asked her to check each one of the Dirty Mushrooms for the pattern.

# CHAPTER 5

# Weapon of the Secret Gods

## Part I: The Worries of a Valkyrie and a Swordswoman

Just one in a hundred Dirty Mushrooms could be used to make the tonic. We only defeated five but managed to find one—probably thanks to Misaki. A pharmacy would be able to provide me a sample once we delivered the materials. Madoka dealt with a pharmacy in town, which meant I'd be able to get the sample as soon as it was finished, but I still couldn't think of a use for it. Perhaps there was a way to use it in combination with something rather than by itself. Either way, it was probably safest to have it stay in storage until I could find some use for it.

"I can't believe the monster was still alive... I'm glad you and Theresia are both safe," said Igarashi when Theresia and I went up to the suite and told everyone what happened.

"It rattled me a little, but we managed to get out of it somehow. Sorry to make everyone worry," I said.

"I imagine it wouldn't have reacted had there been anyone else in the room with Arihito. But it still attacked with Theresia present…," said Elitia, imagining what happened in Sophie's room at the Healer clinic.

The Vine Puppeteer had said Theresia wasn't even *"entirely a monster."* Leila from the Mercenary Office had told us that demi-humans were humans who had lost their lives in the labyrinth and come back changed. I knew it was safe to assume that Seekers who were resurrected as demi-humans gained monster-like characteristics. That might be why the Vine Puppeteer hadn't been wary of Theresia even though she had been in the same room. It was thanks to those characteristics that she could save me from a very dangerous situation. Part of it was that she was a demi-human who could slip into cracks in the monster's defenses, but it was more that Theresia had the courage to jab her own hand with the Puppeteer's vine in order to save me.

She hadn't taken a seat when we came into the room; instead, she was just standing at the edge of the room and looking at me like always, but she came over before I called her and sat at the table with the rest of us.

"Where's Misaki and Suzuna?" I asked.

"Taking a bath. They were pretty dirty from fighting in the mud," said Elitia.

"The tub can fit three at a time, but we didn't want to leave you to come back to an empty suite, so we decided to just wait here chatting," added Igarashi.

"…We were actually talking about you. You always go around with Theresia, but we were thinking it might be nice for you to switch who you take with you every once in a while. I can be your bodyguard, too," said Elitia with crossed arms. Igarashi must not have thought Elitia was going to tell me what they were talking about because she started coughing, the tea she was drinking having gone down the wrong pipe.

"Um, *cough, cough*... I don't really have a problem with staying behind. No need to worry about it. You seem most relaxed when you're with Theresia anyway...," said Igarashi. I was about to say she might be right, but admitting it was embarrassing enough. Even I was starting to feel uncomfortable, which meant Theresia was already turning bright red.

"......"

"...Are you saying we could take turns in a set order?" asked Elitia. "No, that's not it... Oh, do you mean Arihito should tell us who should come along each time?" That did seem to be what Theresia was trying to convey, but she didn't nod in response.

"I think that's what you thought, but you're taking it back. Do you mean that you want to go with Atobe all the time? Geez, Atobe, Theresia has really taken a liking to you... I know that's just how it is, but..."

"Well, I suppose it makes sense, since she even helps him take a bath. If he didn't invite her, she'd just go along anyway," said Elitia.

"......"

*How is she not embarrassed by the whole bath thing...? Well, she does actually look like she's blushing a tiny bit. Is she trying to keep it under control because she knows she won't be able to join me if she gets too red?*

It was quite impressive if that were the case. Though, my conscience kept telling me it wasn't okay for us to take a bath together.

"…Um, so what's for dinner?" I asked.

"Marsh Ox steak. Apparently, you can't normally get it in restaurants in town," said Igarashi.

"I get hungry after a fight; I need to make sure I get enough nutrition. I've been so hungry lately," admitted Elitia a little bashfully. She was still growing anyway. I just wanted everyone to be able to eat good food and be healthy.

"But first… About that bath…," started Igarashi.

"You and Elitia can go next. I'll go last," I said.

"……"

"Uh… N-no, Theresia! Look, men and women generally shouldn't take baths together," explained Igarashi. I waited to see how Theresia would react, but my hopes that she would listen obediently were dashed when she shook her head.

"I want to respect your relationship… But we just wait nervously when you're doing it. Do you understand that?" Igarashi reasoned.

"……"

Theresia gave a tiny nod after a pause. Both Igarashi and Elitia seemed relieved to see that.

"Well then, you can come with us today. Then Atobe can go alone—," started Igarashi, but Theresia's response to the suggestion was fast and very clear. She shook her head side to side, and Igarashi collapsed on the table at a loss.

"Um… Igarashi, does it really bother you that much when Theresia and I take a bath together?" I asked.

"…Uh, I mean… That's not a question I feel equipped to answer."

"W-wait, both of you. I know that we can't force Theresia to act a certain way. That's why I was thinking we could switch places with her so she can understand how we feel, or… I trust Arihito, and I don't think anything inappropriate is happening, but if we could see it with our own eyes, then we can put this whole thing to rest," said Elitia.

"O-okay, if that'll convince you… W-wait, you mean now…?" I said as Elitia stood from her seat and headed toward her room. Before going in, she turned back to say something.

"…Well, Misaki and Suzuna are about to finish their bath."

"E-Ellie, I mean, that's definitely an option and all, but if we're actually gonna do this, I'll need some advance notice—"

"Sure, Arihito might be uncomfortable with three women around…but this is all just to put our minds at ease. Don't get the wrong idea." With that, Elitia dragged me into the room, a flustered Igarashi rushing after her.

"Haah, I feel sooo much better! Arihito, we had such a nice bath," said Misaki.

"…Um, will the rest of you be taking a bath together?" asked Suzuna. "I'm sorry, Arihito. I'm not sure why, but Elitia seems really bothered by the fact that you and Theresia take baths together…"

The party's mental health was an important thing for me as the leader to take care of, and I should have been able to avoid us taking a bath together… But now that things had gotten like this, I needed to prepare myself for the worst.

Bathing clothes were apparently commonly sold in the Labyrinth Country. The public baths in town were like massive pools that could be used by anyone, regardless of gender, so you couldn't go in naked. Instead, people would bathe wearing these bathing clothes. The housing for those at lower ranks didn't have baths in their own facilities, so those people would have to use the public baths, meaning these clothes were actually necessities for anyone who'd just come to the Labyrinth Country. Igarashi hadn't known all that when she'd come across it in the shop during her downtime, but she decided there might be a time she needed it and bought it. On top of that, there were two sets of bathing clothes provided in the royal suite. Perhaps they hadn't expected four people to bathe together, so we were still missing a set for me.

"...I feel like it'd be better if I went and bought one to wear," I said.

"I-it's all right... We're the ones making the fuss; we wouldn't want to make things harder on you," said Igarashi.

"Theresia, let's get going and wash Arihito. How do you normally do it?" asked Elitia.

"......"

Elitia seemed to be convinced that she'd be offered some respite if I would just hurry up and get in the bath. I could understand why, but I still wasn't quite sure why washing myself wasn't an option.

"I-Igarashi. This is really quite strange. Wouldn't this be about when you would say this isn't going to work?" I asked.

"W-well, this is just how it's gotta be! Theresia's been showing you her gratitude, and yet, we haven't done anything... We want to express our thanks, too, y'know."

I had assumed that Igarashi and Elitia had been talking about how concerned they were that I was doing something inappropriate to Theresia…but apparently, I was completely off the mark.

"I've only made it this far with everyone else's help… I don't think we really owe each other anything. I might sound stupid saying this, but we support one another; we're all here for one another," I said, but I wasn't sure I could make it convincing, since I was sitting there covered in nothing but the towel wrapped around my waist. Or so I thought, but both Igarashi and Elitia looked impressed.

"…And that's precisely why everyone's so anxious. Even I'm starting to feel it a little bit," said Elitia.

"Seriously… If I can't even take care of you while you're at home, then I'll never be able to pay you back. You'll keep saving me, and I'll never give back to you," said Igarashi.

"……"

I was at least aware that I couldn't just push away their attempt now that they'd opened up to me this much.

"…I'm…surprised that you would express your gratitude with a bath, but I am really happy," I admitted, knowing that saying that would mean any future expressions of "gratitude" could very well involve them washing my back. The bathing clothes made it so I was only a little uncomfortable with the whole thing, but I didn't feel I could tell them it was out of the question.

"A-all right, then… Let's get started," said Igarashi.

"Let's rinse him first. He's covered in some mud from the labyrinth," continued Elitia.

"……"

Theresia made sure the water in the basin was a suitable temperature, then poured it over my shoulders. She tried to do it gently, but it still splashed on the girls a little. When they started washing me, I suddenly realized one potentially fatal oversight.

*...If they aren't wearing anything underneath the bathing clothes...won't it be bad if they get too wet...?*

"Spread your fingers, Atobe. We have to get in between them properly..."

"...Arihito, what's wrong? You seem really stiff all of a sudden," asked Elitia.

"N-no... Nothing's wrong," I said.

"Ha-ha, you don't have to be so nervous. We're wearing clothes," said Igarashi.

I wondered if bath time would end before the three realized how they looked. This would be safer if we could get them actual bathing suits, so I wanted to buy some if possible... But for the time being, my only option was to keep my mind off it.

## Part II: A Suite for Eight

I meant to get out of the tub and let Igarashi and the others take it easy in the bath, but they didn't take a very long one, instead coming out of the bathroom fairly quickly, all of them bright red.

"Um... Kyouka, can I ask what happened? I mean, I probably

don't need to ask; it was obviously something scandalous," said Misaki.

"What are you talking about? Nothing happened; we were just trying to express our gratitude to Atobe…," said Igarashi, thrown off-balance by Misaki's blunt question. Elitia tried to run off to her room, but Suzuna grabbed her by the sleeve and stopped her.

"Um, we don't doubt what Kyouka said. You should sit down and drink some water. It's important to rehydrate after getting out of a bath," said Suzuna.

"Y-yeah… B-but…I'm not sure we were careful enough. I mean, Arihito didn't do anything wrong; I just can't really relax around him right now. I sort of just want to go to sleep and ground myself," replied Elitia.

"Oh, did you start to feel more and more embarrassed even though you thought it would be all right, since you were wearing clothes? You three are so innocent—not that I can really talk," said Misaki.

"……"

Theresia seemed embarrassed to be called innocent. The three of them were so red that I'd fan them if I had a paper fan with me, but I couldn't honestly say nothing happened. I felt terrible about it, but the girls weren't angry at me when they realized their clothes were getting see-through. And while it made me uncomfortable, they had somehow all decided that it had just been an inevitability. But what I saw was burned into my memory. I had known I'd need the purest of intentions when I let all the girls join my party, but I wasn't living up to that now.

"...Hmm? What's wrong, Suzuna? You're staring at me," I said.

"It's nothing. You should just make sure to drink some water, too..."

"Suzu was saying she wanted to help wash you to say thanks, too. She was sighing the whole time we were waiting," volunteered Misaki.

"H-hey... Why would you say that, Misaki...?" said Suzuna.

"It's not scary to run a red light if we're all doing it together, right? So that's what I'm asking of you," said Misaki.

"Hey, what exactly are you talking about...?" I said, but she didn't explain. She instead just went back into her room. She left Suzuna behind, who—even though she was normally such a calm girl—jumped when I made eye contact with her.

"...I... Um, I want to say thanks to you, too, just like everyone else... I was just thinking how much I really wanted to show my gratitude somehow. N-not that I'm jealous or anything...," she said.

"...You don't need to be so cautious, Suzuna. Arihito understands. I haven't even known him that long, and he let me help wash his back," remarked Elitia.

"Y-yeah... I was a little surprised. But I am the adult in the situation. I shouldn't be so flustered...," I replied.

"You're pretty relaxed about it now... Even though you were the most uncomfortable at first," said Igarashi. She seemed the most embarrassed about the whole wet clothes thing. That was understandable considering the size of her chest. I could just see the way the wet cloth clung to her...but I couldn't let my mind drift any further, lest it show on my face.

"...Does karma not go up for someone you're in a party with?" she asked.

"H-hey, give me a break. I don't want to go to jail," I said.

"It seems that the karma isn't reacting, since both parties are on the same page... But your license is always watching, which is an unsettling feeling. You should be careful," said Elitia, slowly downing a glass of water. Soon, it would be time to wrap up for the day and prepare for tomorrow.

"Now that I think of it, what about Melissa and Madoka? They'll be staying with us starting today, right? Since they're in our party now," continued Elitia.

"Oh... Yeah, that's right. We need to assign rooms," said Igarashi, and I finally had a thought. Where were those two? Just as I was thinking that, there was a knock at the door, followed by a voice.

"Arihito, we're back. It's Madoka and Melissa," came Madoka's voice.

"Oh, welcome back. Let me unlock the door for you," I said, opening the door to let them in. Melissa seemed to have taken a bath earlier somewhere else; perhaps she was being considerate, since she had probably been dissecting earlier. Madoka wasn't wearing the turban she normally had on, so I wondered if she had joined her. Her black, bobbed hair was slightly damp.

"Did you take a bath somewhere else? You can use the one here if you want. It's not a problem," I said.

"Yeah... And thank you. But Melissa wanted to take a bath at home today, so I went along, too. I had some business outside and took Cion along as well," said Madoka.

"I see. Did she go back to the shed out back?"

"…She's a good girl. So strong but listens to everything you tell her," marveled Melissa. She must like dogs as well, because I saw a tiny smile on her face. She was wearing a dress instead of her normal overalls, and her hair, which was usually all over the place, had been neatly brushed. Perhaps Madoka had helped her once they were done with their baths.

"Here's the tonic you requested from the Pharmacist," said Madoka.

"Uh… R-right. That was a lot faster than I expected. Thanks for taking care of that," I replied.

"No need to thank me. It's part of my job. I'm glad I could help out." I wanted to just say thanks and move on, but obviously, Igarashi wasn't going to let this pass without asking about it.

"Tonic? Like, some sort of revitalizing tonic? I guess even the Labyrinth Country has health drinks," she observed.

"They're often made from mushroom-type monsters, but I didn't realize you could make something from Dirty Mushrooms, too. We must have gotten some rare materials because Misaki was with us," said Elitia.

"Some mushrooms are poisonous, but some are really good for you, too. I assume those were the kinds of components used here," added Madoka.

Igarashi would occasionally drink health drinks at work, so she was probably curious that there might be something similar here.

Melissa didn't really say anything. She seemed hesitant to talk about the tonic earlier, which was why I'd been certain it was used for...*that*. But maybe I was wrong.

"If someone's feeling really worn out, they can drink it," I offered.

"Huh? ...You sure? But isn't this valuable...?" asked Igarashi.

"We could hunt Dirty Mushrooms if we really wanted to, so I wouldn't say it's so rare that we could never get our hands on it again. It probably has a strong taste, so I'm a little curious to have someone taste test it," I said.

"Geez, Arihito... But I guess you're right. If it tastes terrible, then we wouldn't be able to make ourselves use it even if we needed to," replied Elitia.

It could be helpful if it could make someone in the party feel less tired after our days of seeking. I thought that would be a better use than if we held on to it forever.

Well, then it would make the most sense if I tested it, but my opinion was that anything we obtained from the labyrinth belonged to the entire party, which meant everyone who wanted to taste it could. It wasn't like I was afraid or anything. "It's a nice amber color and looks like it might taste nice... But I'm not sure about the smell," said Igarashi.

"Sometimes, it's hard to just dive in and try it...," said Elitia.

"Misaki and Suzuna might want to try it, too. We should ask them later. And Theresia looks like she wants to try...right?" asked Igarashi, but Theresia didn't nod. I had no intention of forcing them to drink it if they didn't want to. As it was, everyone was tense, and no one was making the first move.

Later, once everyone had left the living room, I used a Novice Appraisal Scroll just to see what it'd say:

```
◆Dirty Spirit◆
> Gives drinker a set period of increased
  endurance.
> Side effects may occur.
```

*Good thing I didn't drink it... Seems high-risk. What exactly are these "side effects"?*

Since it came from a Dirty Mushroom, I understood why it would have *dirty* in the name, but the fact that it also had *spirit* made me think it was alcohol. If it was made by soaking the colored portion of the inside of the Dirty Mushroom in alcohol in order to draw out the effective components, then it wouldn't be a good idea to let the underage party members try it. I hadn't actually confirmed whether or not the Labyrinth Country had any laws regarding minors, though.

It said it improved *endurance*, which could mean something like stamina, but it would be foolish to try it, considering these unknown side effects. I placed the dirty spirit vial on the shelf in the living room and returned to my room.

"Oh... Arihito, what were the appraisal results?" asked Suzuna when I came in.

"The name makes it sound like it's a type of alcohol. I think it's better if the minors don't drink it."

"I see... So the Labyrinth Country uses alcohol in its medicines as well."

She was sitting on her bed and appeared to have been thinking before I came in. We had decided it was too much hassle to choose rooms using a lottery and change rooms every night, so we were waiting until tomorrow to shuffle around.

"Suzuna, are you sure you're comfortable staying in the same room as me?" I asked.

"Yes, I've been able to get plenty of rest as is. Actually... I was wondering if you were comfortable being in the same room as me... If you were with Misaki, for example, you'd probably have lots of exciting conversations."

"It's better to keep things calmer and more relaxed before you go to sleep. Besides, Misaki just makes fun of me most of the time anyway."

"Ha-ha... She's always like that with people she likes."

You often hear about kids teasing people in order to get their attention, though I couldn't decide if I should be happy or not that Misaki was targeting me.

"Do I make any noise when I'm sleeping? Or do you not know, since you're probably sleeping, too?" I asked.

"You sleep very quietly. I was worried that I breathe loudly or something..."

"You're fine; I didn't hear a thing. Well, hearing a little bit of breathing is fine anyway; it's when people start rolling around and kicking blankets off that it gets annoying."

"Ha-ha… Misaki does that a lot. You should tell her not to sprawl out and stick her tummy out if you end up in the same room as her. She'll listen if you're the one to say it."

What could I actually do if the person I shared a room with was sleeping like that…? Probably just cover them with a blanket. I wasn't the kind to wake up once I'm asleep anyway, though, so I probably wouldn't even notice.

"…Ah, sorry. I can't believe I'd say those things about Misaki when she's not even here… I shouldn't be gossiping," said Suzuna.

"You haven't said anything bad, so it's not a problem. Even if you did—she's a mess when she sleeps—it's not something I couldn't have guessed just by knowing her."

"I don't think she wants you to see her in a poor light, though. She really does respect you…"

"R-really…? Misaki's always so glib, though. I feel like I should take everything she says with a grain of salt."

"Ha-ha… Well, I think she feels better that way, at least for the time being."

Talking like this, I couldn't help feeling amazed that Suzuna was the same age as Misaki. I wasn't nearly as composed as Suzuna when I was her age.

"Arihito, you don't barge into other people's business without reason. I think that's part of the reason everyone feels so comfortable with you."

"I'm honestly just not quick-thinking enough to do that. It's probably because I'm a bit slow."

"Oh... You are aware of that..."

"Hmm? Suzuna, what did you say?"

"Ah, n-nothing. I just always thought that men like you only existed in stories... It's unbelievable...," she said, her cheeks turning red. It'd be easy to misunderstand her right now, but it didn't seem that she meant *unbelievable* in a good way.

"...Oh, s-sorry, I think I said something rude again," she apologized.

"No, you didn't bother me. Anyway, I'm just glad that we can chat like this with each other. I want you to be able to talk to me when... Hmm?" I started but noticed that the small box on Suzuna's bedside table was glowing a dim neon blue. It was her license. It was steadily glowing stronger, then fading, as if trying to notify her of something.

"Arihito... Would you mind taking a look at this?" she asked.

"Yeah, sure...," I said and got out of bed to scrutinize it.

◆Notification◆
> Ariadne requested Suzuna use Medium

"Is this...a message from Ariadne? Is it saying I should use Medium now...?"

"...Licenses don't show everything, but I don't think this is a mistaken notification. It's definitely a request from Ariadne."

We couldn't go so far as to say we could communicate with

Ariadne, who was on the fourth floor of the Field of Dawn, using our licenses, but there must be a reason for her to request Suzuna use Medium. I had no reason to doubt what the license showed, and it wouldn't be a good idea to ignore it if it was urgent.

"Suzuna, I'll be right here with you. Would you mind trying Medium?"

"All right. I think Ariadne definitely has something she wants to tell us." Suzuna nodded resolutely, then knelt on her bed and closed her eyes to concentrate. A mystical light that I could only describe as an aura surrounded her body.

"...Enter this vessel and let the world hear your voice..."

"Whoa...!"

Suzuna recited a short incantation, and her body was encased in a pillar of blue-white light like when she used Moon Reading. One significant difference between this and Moon Reading, though, was that I could sense some presence behind Suzuna for this.

"...Are you the rearguard? I am not yet used to borrowing this Shrine Maiden's sight. My perception is flawed. Please respond if you are the rearguard."

"Yes, it's me, Arihito. Thank you for your help today; you saved us."

Suzuna's hair color and speech patterns had changed to those of Ariadne. I could assume that Ariadne's spirit or something like it had come to reside in Suzuna's body when she used Medium.

There hadn't been any emotions in Ariadne's eyes when we woke her from her sleep at the bottom of the labyrinth. A chill

ran down my spine now as Suzuna's eyes had turned lifeless in the same way.

"Just to check—are you truly Ariadne?"

*"Such proof will appear somewhere on this Shrine Maiden's body. My spirit is capable of intervening through a devotee by using their covenant talisman as my target. My crest will appear here when the Shrine Maiden uses Medium to contact me."*

"Whoa, wait! You don't have to show me! It's Suzuna's body; respect that!"

Ariadne had started to unbutton Suzuna's pajama top. She suddenly undid the buttons over Suzuna's chest, and I could see the area between her breasts. And there really was some sort of glowing symbol there. Ariadne's crest was a geometric design, symmetrical from left to right and about the size of an adult's thumbprint.

*"...Humans feel shame. This Shrine Maiden understands what is happening even while she is a medium. She is thinking, 'Thank you for stopping her.'"*

"All right... We'll just keep this between us, then."

*"Understood. I will rectify my behavior going forward. I am equipped with a learning function, but it is not incredibly advanced. Repeated exposure will form a neural network, which functions similarly to a human's collection of neurons."* What she said didn't fit the medieval level of advancement I'd seen so far in the Labyrinth Country. I could only assume that she had been created from some advanced technology.

I felt quite strange speaking with her, since she was borrowing Suzuna's body and speaking so dispassionately, but while I had felt no emotions from her in the beginning, I was starting to see a flicker of something in her. When I noticed it, I stared into her eyes, but Ariadne looked away.

"...*This must be...embarrassment. Suzuna's emotions run deep, and she has a strong sense of right and wrong. However, when it comes to you...,*" started Ariadne, but she stopped partway through. It looked like Suzuna was strongly resisting. For good reason, too. Nobody wanted to say everything they ever thought.

"*...I have decided that instead of requesting Suzuna to use Medium whenever I please, I will only speak through her when she wishes.*"

"Oh, that's good... And speaking of, what is it you wish to tell us?"

"*Yes. I have come to warn you of the Black Box you recently acquired.*"

Apparently, anything that was displayed on our licenses was conveyed to Ariadne as well. She was referring to the Black Box we found when we defeated the Vine Puppeteer. I had been carrying it around in my leather bag. I took it out and showed it to Ariadne, who nodded in confirmation.

"Are you saying this is dangerous somehow? There's probably a lot of money and equipment in here, but..."

Ariadne shook her head and pointed at the box in my hand. "*Some Black Boxes contain armaments.*"

"Armaments...?"

"*Yes. The proper name is armored attachment. I told you about parts for us Hidden Gods. Originally, those parts were held in Black Boxes. However, the Black Box you received from Juggernaut did not contain any parts for me to use. Instead, it should have contained something in place of a part of my body: a small crystal."*

I realized exactly what she was talking about. I had asked Madoka to investigate it, but we still didn't know much about it. It was the alkaid crystal.

"Do you mean this? We don't really know what it's used for...," I said, showing her the crystal.

*"That is a sacred operation crystal for a sword. It will become functional when you equip an armament,"* explained Ariadne.

"Sacred...operation crystal?"

*"You may think of it as an armament controller. Armaments are parts that Hidden Gods equip... They are sacred artifacts. These sacred artifacts have their own wills; they act of their own volition. In general, they will defend themselves so that they are not obtained by others."*

It was hard to keep up with her explanation because I had to deal with all these new words I'd never heard before... But I'd actually bought a small notebook, which could be used for things like this, so I pulled it out from my bag and wrote down the information that Ariadne gave me.

"So what you're saying is that when we open the Black Box, one of these sentient sacred armaments might come out... And it will attack anybody who's trying to take it. Is that right?" I asked.

*"Correct. There is danger that all who are in the vicinity will become involved in the ensuing battle."* That meant we'd have to ask Falma to get out as soon as she opened the box. It might also be best not to take along Misaki and Suzuna.

*"Steadfast rearguard,"* she continued. *"You who has bound*

*yourself to me. As a person who is under my protection, I wish to propose one way that may help protect you against the attack of the sacred artifact."*

"Do you mean with that mechanical arm…your Guard Arm? Do you believe you can defend against it?" I asked. Ariadne hadn't spoken highly of herself, telling us she had been disposed of. I wanted to believe she could defend against an attack from a sacred artifact that a Hidden God would equip, but I didn't want to ask her to protect us when it would be impossible.

*"If my devotion level is high enough, I should be able to nullify more of the attack's damage using my Guard Arm. I ask for your cooperation to that end."*

"Devotion level… Is that us showing our devotion to you, the Hidden God whose protection we're under?"

*"Indeed. I naturally receive devotion whenever I protect you, but I can also receive it when I improve Trust Levels with you. Devotion levels do not decrease over time, so the protection I can provide becomes stronger the more devotion I receive."*

Ariadne was magnificent when she protected Ribault from Death from Above's attack using her Guard Arm. I was certain my Defense Support couldn't have protected him then, so I knew her Guard Arm was a fairly strong defense as it was. If we could improve that even more, we could prevent even greater amounts of damage. But how could I improve Trust Levels with her? I didn't think my conversational skills were good enough to increase it just by chatting.

"So I can assume that we should be able to defend against the sacred artifact's attack if we increase our Trust Levels."

"...Hence, why I asked this Shrine Maiden to use Medium. Your devotion levels toward me will naturally increase if I do something that you are grateful for. One part of that can be if I have relations with you while in this Shrine Maiden's body..."

"Uh... N-no. There's got to be another way. Suzuna didn't use Medium for you to do that."

"That is the method that requires the least amount of time. It will deepen Trust Levels with you and the Shrine Maiden, and you can marry if a child is born."

"Uh, uhhh..."

I bet Suzuna was resisting as much as she could... She'd probably be disgusted with me forever if I agreed to what Ariadne was suggesting or even hate me. Though, it did make me think of the period in history far removed from our own in which shrine maidens would sleep with men in order to spread the religion. Not that all traveling shrine maidens did that, nor did Suzuna become a Shrine Maiden with that in mind.

"A-anyway... While it might strengthen the party that I am the leader of, that is one thing I can't do."

"...If you agree... No. I will say no more or Medium will be canceled. We shall build mutual trust in a way that the Shrine Maiden approves of."

...Wait. By mutual trust, does she mean I need to increase her Trust Level? In which case...

"Ariadne, how about we try something? Sit with your back facing me."

"Understood... Though, I question the logic in such a request."

"Just wait a minute; it activates every once in a while."

◆Current Status◆

> Arihito's Recovery Support 1 activated →
  Suzuna's vitality was recovered

"...? *This body feels warm, and its healing processes have quickened.
What is the purpose of this healing activity?*" asked Ariadne. Based on
the display, I knew that I activated Recovery Support on Suzuna, but
apparently, that didn't mean Ariadne's Trust Levels would increase.

"I used one of my skills to heal Suzuna because healing builds
trust. Though, I assume your spirit presence here is more similar
to magic?"

"*Yes. The Hidden Gods' spirits are made from magic.*"

"If that's the case...it might take some time, but how about
this?" I held my hand up toward Ariadne's back and hoped I was
right... Hoped that if I recovered her magic instead, that Ariadne's
trust in me would go up.

*I'll give Ariadne a portion of my magic... Charge Assist.*

◆Current Status◆

> Arihito activated Charge Assist → Suzuna
  recovered magic
> Ariadne who is possessing Suzuna recovered
  magic
> Ariadne's Trust Level increased

"*Ah...*"

This time was different; I could see a change in Ariadne. She
was looking back at me, her cheeks slightly flushed.

"...A skill that provides magic. I had not thought of such a direct way of building mutual trust. A portion of my spirit is now formed from your magic," said Ariadne.

"All right, well, if we set aside some time and continue this... It even says on the license that your Trust Levels increased. How much was it?" I asked.

"...As far as I can sense, it was not a large amount, but it did increase. I recommend you repeat that a number of times in order to improve the defense of my Guard Arm." Ariadne looked again over her shoulder at me. She pulled her hair forward, exposing the pale white nape of her neck, which really unsettled me.

What the hell kind of adult am I for having thoughts like this about a high schooler...? I mean, we're not actually doing anything indecent, though. I just need to get rid of the inappropriate thoughts and focus.

"I have a skill that gives magic. If I use that to recover your magic, then the amount I will recover when you use Charge Assist will be increased. You and I can create a perpetual loop using only recovery skills."

"That's incredible... If you can give the magic you recover to the whole party, then we'll be able to fight at full charge forever."

"Unfortunately, I can only provide magic to the person who has entered into a contract with me, which would be y...you..."

"Oh... Sorry, maybe it's best if you don't talk right when I'm about to use Charge Assist."

"...That is not necessary. The Shrine Maiden feels things very strongly. I will reduce sensitivity."

Ariadne had originally asked Suzuna to use Medium so she could warn us... She was a being that protected us, so it didn't seem out of the ordinary, but I was grateful. However, I hadn't yet realized that night what using Suzuna's body to increase Trust Levels with Ariadne would do.

## Part III: Energy Sync

Ariadne was possessing Suzuna's body through Suzuna's Medium skill and returning the magic I charged her with back to me, after which I would use Charge Assist again. Well, that was the plan anyway, but when it got to the point where Ariadne would use her skill to return the magic, I suddenly felt really uncomfortable.

Her skill was called Energy Sync, which sounded like it would even out the magic between the user and the person it was used on. My magic went down when I used Charge Assist, but it refilled Ariadne's magic more than mine went down. The amount I lost would be filled using Energy Sync, and I'd use Charge Assist again. That meant my magic would always return to the amount it was before I used Charge Assist.

This was all in the realm of possibility, but we had to be physically touching for Ariadne to be able to use Energy Sync. It shouldn't have been a problem if I touched her somewhere that wasn't problematic, but when it came down to it, I realized I wasn't comfortable touching her anywhere.

"U-um... Arihito, you can touch me wherever; don't worry about it."

"Whoa...! S-Suzuna? You can talk even though you're using Medium?" I said, quite surprised since just before, it had been Ariadne's monotone voice, but it suddenly changed back to Suzuna's normal voice.

"You seemed so hesitant, so I asked Ariadne to let me switch with her... It feels very strange, though." Suzuna wasn't completely unable to act of her own volition while using Medium, but she seemed uncomfortable because it felt strange having just gotten control of her own body back.

"...You have to give her a lot of magic in order to strengthen... Guard Arm...right?" asked Suzuna.

"Yeah... Apparently, her defensive abilities will improve if we improve Trust Levels between her and I."

"And if you do that, it will be more capable of defending against attacks... We should improve trust between you two as much as possible tonight."

"I'm grateful that you're on board. No, not just me. This is about the whole party."

"Yes, it's for the party... All for one and one for all, right?" said Suzuna, a little jokingly, which was unusual for her. She wanted to protect the party, the same as me, and that mind-set directly influenced the strength of our party's bonds.

Thankfully, there was no animosity between any of the party members; we all got along, but that didn't mean we could forget to be considerate of one another and focus on ourselves instead. That was just how relationships worked. I had to be especially careful, since I was the only man in a group of women.

"…Um. She's going to use Energy Sync soon. Could you touch me somewhere?" asked Suzuna.

"Oh yeah… Where? …I think I'd feel better if you tell me." I knew I shouldn't really be thinking about it this much, but I was worried she might be ticklish or something. I just wanted to be incredibly cautious about it.

"Anywhere on my back is fine. Go on."

"Okay… Is this all right?" I said, placing my hand on her back between her shoulder blades. Suzuna put her hands together like she was praying. She was activating Energy Sync.

◆Current Status◆
> Suzuna activated Ariadne's Energy Sync by proxy
> Arihito's and Suzuna's magic synchronized

"…It's warm. I can tell that my magic flows into you and your magic flows back, leveling out," observed Suzuna.

"If only it could be used with multiple party members. We could recover anyone who was particularly low and even out everyone's magic," I said, and Suzuna switched back to Ariadne so she could speak.

"*It would be possible. As of right now, I can only use skills on you. However, a Hidden God's skills become more powerful when the party becomes stronger. Once your party's level passes a certain point, my skills will advance to their second stage,*" explained Ariadne. If she could come out from the hidden level in the Field of

Dawn, then she could even join the party itself. If that happened, she'd be able to use her skills herself.

"*That would be possible if you gather enough parts for me.*"

"Oh... I guess you can still read my thoughts even though you're just here through Medium."

"*Yes... And no. I am not certain. Humans tend to conceal things when they wish to remain private. I will not reveal any of your thoughts to others.*"

"I appreciate it... I mean, I don't actually mind that you can hear my thoughts; I'm just worried it might annoy you."

"*I wish to further understand human emotions. Relations between men and women would be greatly helpful for deepening my understanding—*"

"L-look, I already told you..."

I wouldn't have been surprised if Suzuna took over at any point now, since she was listening to this conversation as well. The best I could really do was explain to Ariadne that men and women didn't engage in such things without good cause.

There was a limit to devotion levels that Ariadne could have based on the party's level, and it had reached that limit. Every time I used Charge Assist, I felt there was some sort of change in Ariadne's behavior as she looked back at me. She seemed more conscious of the fact that I was touching her.

"Are you all right, Ariadne?" I asked.

"*...I am being influenced by emotions. Perhaps it is an effect of the medium...*"

"Wh-what's wrong? Do you not feel well?"

"*...No. Both my and the Shrine Maiden's vitality are full. There is no issue.*" Ariadne clenched her hand to her chest. She really didn't have any life in her eyes, so I definitely did feel strange when she stared at me. She kept saying she wanted to understand humans, which was probably why my thoughts and emotions were going down a certain path. But what could you really expect from a healthy man? I just hoped she wouldn't judge me too harshly.

"*Devotion levels have reached their maximum. Now I will be able to protect you with Guard Arm. It will be even safer if you have a companion who excels at defense.*"

"I see... Well, right now, Cion, a silver hound, is in charge of our defense. Would a guard dog work?" I asked.

"*I am not specialized in protecting beasts. The most appropriate match would be a humanoid warrior who is equipped with metal armor.*"

If that was the requirement, the people in our party most suited would be Igarashi or Elitia, but Elitia was focused on offense, and it was safest for Igarashi if she could dodge instead of taking the hit.

*Specialized in defense with metal armor... The only person I can think of would be Seraphina, of the Guild Saviors. But she's probably not even in District Eight anymore.*

"All right, I understand. Thank you for everything. I think we'll be needing your help soon, Ariadne."

"*Understood. I...believe it has been good for my circuits...to have a conversation with you...*"

Suzuna's head suddenly hung limply. Perhaps Medium only lasted a set period of time.

"Suzuna, are you okay?" I asked, and she slowly opened her eyes and looked in front of her, where I was. She jumped back a little and covered her mouth with her hands.

"Wh-what happened? I'm sorry, did I surprise you because I was suddenly right in front of you?" I asked.

"...N-no... I was looking out from inside Ariadne... She said she was going to sleep for a little bit...," said Suzuna, touching her ears and brushing the bed. She didn't seem able to calm down. I didn't think it was that she'd suddenly become more aware of the fact that she was alone in a room with me. After a moment, she noticed I was looking at her, and she jumped a little again.

"Um... I'll go get some water or something. You've been concentrating this whole time; you should relax," I said.

"Ah... N-no. I'll go. You can just stay there... B-be back soon." It was strange to see her so flustered when she was normally so calm, though she was still a high schooler, so it wasn't like she'd be calm in every possible situation. I knew that, but...if Misaki saw her now, she'd probably assume the wrong thing. I hoped she'd be able to calm down by morning.

I finally fell asleep sometime after midnight and woke up thirty minutes before breakfast. Everyone was able to order what they wanted, so I had a bacon sandwich made from the meat of a wild boar monster. Even though it was boar, it'd been treated with fruit juice to remove the gamy taste and was really quite tender. It was freshly prepared, and the meat was still juicy.

*Kinda tastes like pig, though...and pig makes me think of ginger pork, but you can't get the flavors right without soy sauce... That's something I'll probably never be able to enjoy again.*

Igarashi chose a grilled fish, which seemed to suit her tastes, because she was really enjoying it.

"Thank goodness they've got fresh fish in the Labyrinth Country," she said.

"Suzu, your mom used to always grill fish in the morning, wouldn't she? My mom also— Hmm? Suzu, what's wrong? You seem out of it," observed Misaki.

"...Sorry, what?" said Suzu vaguely, surprising everyone. I'd thought she'd seemed a little off all morning, but apparently, what we did last night wasn't good for her.

"...Arihito, did you do something dirty to Suzu?" asked Misaki.

"No, I would never! Why would you say that?"

"But Suzuna's so shaken up... You can't blame us for thinking something happened," said Elitia, shocking Madoka, who was joining us for breakfast for the first time while Melissa just steadily ate her chili.

"Um... Has Arihito done anything with any of you...?" asked Madoka.

"N-no way! Atobe's too honest. He'd only do something if he imagines a future with them..."

"Kyouka knows him best, after all. Oh! You know, I never asked him if he's got any ex-girlfriends," said Misaki.

"...I don't...*think* so... But I wonder... He was normally just working with me on his days off, and he rarely slipped out to answer any phone calls...," said Igarashi.

"So you noticed that, too... Were you always paying that much attention to him?" asked Elitia.

"Uh, n-no, I, um ..." Igarashi was at a loss. I wanted to come to her rescue, but I felt it might be stupid to say she didn't really pay that much attention at all. Considering she was so controlling a boss that she'd care whenever I got up from my desk.

"...Anyway. Atobe, what happened with Suzu?"

"Uh... I—I guess you could say we had a late night."

"A late night... So you mean you guys—?"

"Pull it together, Misaki! We'll never hear the rest of the story if you keep cutting him off," snapped Elitia, effectively silencing Misaki. I wanted to get the others' feedback on the situation anyway, so I decided I should just spit it out already.

"Well, I figured I should report it to you anyway, but we had a message from Ariadne last night. Suzuna used her skills and called on Ariadne's spirit so we could speak with her."

"So that's what happened... And what'd she say?" said Igarashi.

"There's a chance that a part of a Hidden God will come out when we open the Black Box, and it'll attack anyone who's trying to obtain it... Which means there's a chance we'll end up in a fight when we have the box opened," I explained, and everyone suddenly looked serious. Even Suzuna, who'd been blank and inattentive a moment before, returned to her normal self.

"In order to defend against that attack, Suzuna helped me to increase Ariadne's devotion levels. But if we're going to play it safe, it'd probably be best to wait on opening the box and level up first," I continued.

"…Yeah. If this part is incredibly powerful…," Elitia started to say.

"But it's one of Ariadne's parts. Isn't it likely that she'd be able to defend against it with her power? I don't think she'd suggest we do something incredibly dangerous," said Igarashi. I honestly agreed with both of them. Should we put off opening the box and avoid all potential risks? Or should we open it, knowing we might get the part along with other magical equipment?

*…We can't risk it, can we? There's no guarantee that Guard Arm will prevent all damage…*

"…I'm going with Arihito. I've already decided that much," said Suzuna.

"Yeah… It's a weighty decision, but I don't think we'll easily lose as long as Arihito is there. It's because of him that we've been able to beat monsters I never thought we could," agreed Elitia.

"……"

Theresia was looking silently at me. I think she was trying to say she would be with me no matter what. Safety was most important, but it didn't feel right to put this off in the name of safety considering there was a high probability we'd get one of Ariadne's parts.

"...I want to open the Black Box. It'll probably be dangerous, but we know that the rewards will likely be high," I reasoned.

"Yeah, I agree. Monsters will be more powerful once we move up to District Seven. It will be safer for us in the future if we can change even one piece of equipment up to something better," said Elitia, nodding without hesitation. She wasn't afraid at all; no, it was because she had faith in the party.

"Atobe, it'd probably be good to make sure we're ready to use our Morale Discharges, right? It'll take time to prepare it, but I think it'll be worth it," said Igarashi.

"That means you'll be telling us *Let's go!* or *Keep it up!* ten times, right? Reminds me of a sports coach. I could be into that," added Misaki.

"Which means we'll get to hear lots of Arihito's voice...," said Suzuna.

"Yeah... That's pretty normal now. Are you sure you're all right, Suzuna?" I asked.

"Yes, I'm fine. Actually, for some reason, I feel I can do more today than usual...," she said. She seemed somehow more alluring than normal... Or she was just giving off that kind of vibe. I looked at my license; there weren't any status ailments at work, but I was already aware that the license didn't always show everything.

*Is it just that...her trust in me increased because I used Charge Assist? If that's the case... I used it quite a lot...*

"Suzu, you seem like a caterpillar who's turned into a butterfly for some reason...," said Misaki.

"I think that sort of thing is normal for her age... Or if Atobe's to blame, then he can explain what exactly happened when it's our turn to share a room."

"N-no, it won't work if it's not Suzuna… I don't mean that in a weird way at all," I said. The only reason we could do our perpetual loop of magic restoration was that Suzuna was acting as Ariadne's medium. If that wasn't it anyway, it was possible that Recovery Support increased trust far too much while we were asleep… If that was the case, then the thing this party needed the most was some sort of skill or something that would keep me from rolling over in my sleep.

## Part IV: The Second Black Box

I considered having Melissa join the party so I could see how strong she was, but she and Madoka were prioritizing their production work.

"…I'll do any modifications. Bring back good materials," said Melissa.

"Make sure you all stay safe…," added Madoka.

"Yep. We'll probably get a large amount of equipment again, so I hope you can help us then," I said to Madoka.

"Of course. I'll use my connections and negotiate to get you the best possible price for them," she replied. The two saw us off as we left the mansion, and the seven of us, including Cion, went to the Chest Cracker shop.

*...Hmm? Is that...?*

We passed near the Guild and saw Louisa speaking with a row of armored individuals. They were the Guild Saviors. Maybe they were saying their good-byes because they were about to leave District Eight.

"...Ah, Mr. Atobe. Perfect timing," said Louisa.

"Hmm... Me?"

"Yes, Seraphina of the Guild Saviors would like to thank you again for saving Polaris yesterday," she explained.

Seraphina turned to face me, her smooth hair pulled up this time. She was as beautiful as before, but I couldn't show that on my face in front of Louisa and everyone else.

"As Louisa explained, I would like to thank you again. I would also like to offer your party a Savior Ticket. While you have this, you can use your license to submit a support request to ask for our help," said Seraphina, holding out a rectangular piece of thin metal with rounded corners. It was made of a light blue metal; I had no idea what kind of material it was.

"A Savior Ticket... This seems valuable...," I said.

"It's made from a metal called crystium. You can think of it as a step up from a Mercenary Ticket. You can't hire any mercenaries that are above level five in this district, and Guild Saviors must be level eight before they can even join the Saviors," explained Seraphina.

Higher than level 8... I was starting to think as she spoke. If we asked someone as strong or stronger than Elitia to front our defenses... Before we went to open the Black Box, I wanted to find someone who could protect us, even if they were only with us for a short time, so that they could defend against the first attack that would come out of the box.

"Seraphina, could I ask you something?" I said.

"Go right ahead. We don't have any current support requests, so we have some time until we'll be returning to headquarters."

"Thank you. As far as I can tell based on your large shield, you act as your party's vanguard, or primary defense, right?"

"My job is Riot Soldier. I was originally part of a squadron that worked to maintain the peace, if that makes sense."

*Riot Soldier... Was she in the military, then?! I knew there were women in the military, so she must have been reincarnated, too...*

"I use this riot shield to defend against and suppress enemy attacks. There are no guns in this world, so I don't have one of those. I use a baton instead, making my job here in the Labyrinth Country focused almost entirely on defense."

Her shield had a small window in it. It was made of a silver metal and polished to a mirror finish. It was the kind of high-quality piece of equipment that you'd never manage to find in District Eight. I also understood why she looked like a knight, since the Labyrinth Country didn't have any modern equipment. Even the baton she carried had a mace-like weight on the end and looked like it could do serious damage.

"Thank you for the information. I need to speak with my party for a moment; could you please wait for me?" I said.

"Sure," she replied, agreeing to hang around a while longer as I went back to my friends, who were waiting behind me.

"Atobe... Are you thinking of using that Savior Ticket to ask her to help us?" asked Igarashi.

"You guessed it. I don't think we'll have a chance like this again, so I really want someone with a high defense to join us for opening the box."

"I wonder how dangerous the first attack will be... I don't think it'd be so powerful that even a Guild Savior can't handle it. It's dangerous to ask Cion to use Covering to take it, since she doesn't even have any equipment," said Elitia as Suzuna stroked Cion, who was sitting obediently next to her. Like she said, Cion might be a guard dog, but I was worried about having her take attacks without having any equipment.

"I haven't seen any defensive equipment more impressive than that anywhere. It looks super sturdy," said Misaki.

"You're right... It's incredible that she can move so quickly with armor that heavy...," said Igarashi.

"......"

Everyone seemed to be in agreement. Even Theresia was looking at Seraphina, but it didn't seem like she was wary of her.

Seraphina was waiting by the wall of the Guild building so as not to get in the way. I went up to her and held out the Savior Ticket she'd only just given me.

"Seraphina, if you have the time, I would like to request you join my party while we open a chest," I said.

"...Are you sure? It's not generally recommended that you allow someone outside of the party to be present when opening a chest. A chest and its contents are the property of the party," she said.

"Well… There's a high probability that an enemy will appear when we open this one. We need to defeat it. I understand that there would be risks in you agreeing to help us in that you'd be faced with an unknown attack, so I understand if you decline," I said, and Seraphina stared at me. Her eyes were so sharp and bright that I had the urge to look away. Her hair color couldn't be natural if she was really a reincarnate. It must have changed to this fantastical color sometime while she was living in the Labyrinth Country.

"If that is the request, you won't need to use the Savior Ticket. One of our duties is to support any particularly promising rookies," said Seraphina. "Chests are rarities, and while it isn't common, it does occasionally happen that a rookie party is completely killed by the traps on a chest. Considering the situation, I would hope to prevent that from happening if at all possible."

"Ah… Thank you so much! But I feel like I have to give you something in return. I don't want to feel like we've gotten some sort of preferential treatment…," I said.

"It wasn't just that you saved Polaris. I heard that you also visited the patients we took to the Healers and returned one to consciousness. I am personally interested in what kind of Seeker you are. Don't worry about compensation."

I didn't want my rearguard skills to become widely known, but I had a hard time believing anyone would choose to come to see us open a chest, knowing it was going to be dangerous, just to use my skills somehow.

"…Lastly, I will abide by your decisions. I wish to work with you for the time being. I won't speak of anything I see during that. You may do with me as you see fit if I break that promise," she continued.

"...All right. Though, you don't need to say it like we'd threaten you," I said.

"Threaten... That was not my intention. I was simply providing a suggestion as to what cost I would be willing to pay to gain your trust."

Ariadne was like that, too; I felt like they didn't treat their own femininity with much regard. It bothered me that I got so thrown off by it. I wished I could just be calm like you'd expect from someone my age.

"...I'm getting the impression that Japanese people don't like inelegant women," observed Seraphina.

"Th-that's not true at all... Also, I wouldn't call you that," I said.

"Hmph... Is that so? ...I'm glad you think that way... In some ways, I think my Guild Savior training was lacking... Ahem." Seraphina seemed genuinely concerned about it, but she saw her squad looking at her, cleared her throat as she got ahold of herself, and went back to her normal demeanor.

"Ms. Seraphina, will you be joining these Seekers? We plan to return this evening. I hope to be on the way by three PM," said one of the women, who appeared to be Seraphina's assistant, carefully interjecting. Seraphina looked up at the clock above the square; it was nine in the morning. There was still plenty of time.

"Um... Would you mind coming along?" I asked.

"I will join you. Everyone else, patrol the area. Respond as necessary to any request from the Guild," ordered Seraphina, and the five men and women who'd been standing at attention the whole time broke into grins. She'd said *patrol*, but maybe in practice, that meant they were allowed to do whatever they wanted. Seraphina was the only one left after her squad saluted and went their own ways.

First things first, I wanted to use Morale Support on Seraphina. It would take time, but having her Morale Discharge or not could be the deciding factor in the battle. The rest of my party came over now that it was official she'd be joining us. Now we needed to introduce everyone.


"Wow, I can't believe you've found a second Black Box already. I was wondering if I'd see you again," said Falma when we arrived.

"I'm sorry to bother you, but I want to ask that you teleport away as soon as you open the box... We might have a fight on our hands," I said. I had thought she'd be surprised to hear it, but she was oddly at ease.

"I will know whether a monster will come out or not when I undo a trap. I will inform you right before I do," she said.

"Understood. I'll leave the rest to you, then."

"As you wish. Eyck, Plum, you two hold down the fort for a bit, okay?"

"All right! Be careful, everyone!" said Eyck.

"I'll wait here with Eyck!" said Plum.

We left the children behind as we descended the stairs that led to the teleportation door. Cion's mom, Astarte, wasn't at home.

Being level 13, she was probably off on some Guild mission in the higher districts.

"...I should tell you that I have a number of skills that allow me to draw the enemy's attention if I'm in the vanguard. I can increase their hostility, or hate if you will, toward me. The one most effective against a lone enemy is Provoke. If successful, the enemy will prioritize me for their attacks," said Seraphina.

"All right. I can support your fight from behind. I can increase your attack and defense, for example...," I said.

"You were increasing my morale before... I've never had my morale reach maximum."

"You probably know that you can use your Morale Discharge when it reaches maximum... But I suppose if you never have, then you might not know what your Morale Discharge does?" I asked, and Seraphina nodded. When I first met her, I'd gotten the impression that she was a very strict and disciplined soldier, but she'd become much more compliant when she joined the party.

"I can't be certain it's combat-oriented, but... It might give us an edge when we're in a pinch. If you use it, it takes a while before you can use it again, so we can't really test it out," I said.

"Since we don't know what will happen, I'll save it as a last resort, as you said. How does that sound?" she asked, but Igarashi seemed bothered by something and jumped into the conversation.

"It's hard to know who you're referring to when you keep just saying *you*. It'd probably be easier to follow if you addressed people by their names."

"Oh… Good point. Uh, you can address me however you like," I said to Seraphina.

"Then, I will call you Mr. Atobe, though I suppose it would be more appropriate to call you *captain* as you are the party leader," replied Seraphina.

"You know, that salute from before was sooo cool. We'll call you Captain Arihito. Oooh man, I wanna be called *captain*, too!" shrieked Misaki.

I wondered how useful Misaki's Gambler skills would be for this fight. There was a possibility she'd be useful, but her defense was so low that I wasn't certain I wanted her to participate.

"Misaki, this fight's going to be really dangerous…," I started.

"Mr. Atobe, please trust in Cion's strength in times like this. I can tell she's becoming stronger, like her mother," said Falma.

"Woof!" barked Cion.

"Whoooa… Falma, could you tell he was about to leave me behind? Can I call you *mom*? You've got a mother's intuition," said Misaki.

"Ha-ha… I'm just perceptive when it comes to these kinds of things," replied Falma as she put a finger to her lips and smiled. It probably wasn't the right time to be thinking this, but she seemed to be getting more flirtatious the longer her husband was away.

The number on the teleportation door this time was twenty-five. Like Falma had explained before, it was a room that no other parties were currently using to open their chests. We opened the door, passed through, and found ourselves in a huge room that looked the same as the one before. Falma stood where she could make a speedy getaway if necessary, and we fell into battle formation.

```
◆Current Party◆
1: Arihito    ※◆$□            Level 5
2: Theresia   Rogue           Level 5
3: Kyouka     Valkyrie        Level 4
4: Elitia     Cursed Blade    Level 9
5: Suzuna     Shrine Maiden   Level 4
6: Misaki     Gambler         Level 4
7: Cion       Silver Hound    Level 4
8: Seraphina  Riot Soldier    Level 11
```

That was our party of eight. Seraphina was level 11. With that giant shield of hers, she was clearly the person with the highest defense in the party. Leading the formation was Seraphina; making up the second rank were Elitia and Igarashi. Behind them were Theresia and Cion, then Suzuna and Misaki. I took up the rear.

"I will begin unlocking it now. Oh... I can't believe I get another chance to open a chest this difficult...," said Falma. She was as attractive as always, but she was fairly far from me, so I didn't get drawn in by her allure. I needed to focus for when the box opened.

Falma held her right hand up to the box, which was in her left, and the three-dimensional magic field unfolded. That was the Dimensional Barrier Lock. It was significantly bigger than the one for the last Black Box—and far more complicated.

*What is this feeling of dread...?*

"It's… Ah, what is this…power…? I need to let it out or the box won't open!"

"This is it, everyone!" I shouted.

Falma's magic was flowing down the paths of the mazelike Dimensional Barrier Lock. In its path was a red light. Her magic had to pass through there, but the light completely blocked the way forward. Which meant that there was no choice but to let her magic run into it. The moment she did…the box opened. The last time, the surface of the box had glowed with blue lines, releasing a flood of light. But with this box, the light that flooded the room was purple. It was so intense that it hurt to keep my eyes open. Falma fell to the ground shaking and stared at the scene in front of her.

"Falma, keep it together! Get out of here; leave it to us!" I shouted.

"Ah!"

Falma pulled herself up and started moving, and the purple light started to fade. As it did, our vision was filled with the sea of gold that had been in the box and was now swallowing the ground. In the air was a single sword. It gave off a purple glow and had a shape similar to a Japanese katana.

*Intelligent Stellar Sword awakens; Self-Defense Mode activated.*

◆Monsters Encountered◆
?Intelligent Weapon
Level 6
Dropped Loot: ???

It wasn't just floating there; it was swaying up and down. Lightning raced out from around the sword, which gave a menacing aura to the blade. Even I, in the far back and before the battle had even started, could only think of death.

"There's a sword…in the Black Box… Is that a katana?"

"Seraphina, I'll lend you my support! Ariadne, give us a hand!" I shouted, and a moment later, the sword floating in the air suddenly came down to attack Seraphina in the front line.

"*I, Ariadne, grant my devotee and his allies my protection!*"

"I'll stop this attack… That's my job…!" cried Seraphina. My Defense Support made an invisible barrier over her shield, and in front of her appeared not one but two mechanical arms to stop the incoming sword. Those two arms were the result of our work on increasing our devotion to Ariadne. It was completely different from the last time she'd helped us—these were evolved Guard Arms.

*Please… If we can't stop this attack, we're done for!*

◆Current Status◆

> ARIHITO activated DEFENSE SUPPORT 1 ⟶ Target: SERAPHINA

> ARIHITO requested temporary support from ARIADNE ⟶ Target: SERAPHINA

> ARIADNE activated TWIN GUARD ARMS

> SERAPHINA activated DEFENSIVE STANCE

> SERAPHINA activated AURA SHIELD

> ?INTELLIGENT WEAPON activated BLADE OF HEAVEN AND EARTH ⟶ Hit SERAPHINA

The sword struck down from above, cloaked in lightning. The Guard Arms stopped the blade with their hands, but even though they stopped it from advancing, the strike unleashed a shock wave that crashed into Seraphina's shield.

"Gah... Argh...!"

◆Current Status◆
> Blade of Heaven and Earth created Aftershock ⟶ Damaged Seraphina
> Seraphina activated Counter ⟶ Skill will activate immediately

*The damage was reduced a lot, but it wasn't eliminated completely... She can't keep doing that forever. Wait, she's not just going to stop the attack...!*

"—Haaaaaah!"

◆Current Status◆
> Seraphina activated Shield Tackle ⟶ Hit
  ?Intelligent Weapon
11 support damage

"It worked... It worked against a metal opponent!" I cried. Seraphina hadn't just defended against the attack—she had pushed back and sent the sword flying, and I saw that the set damage from Attack Support 1 worked as well. She seemed surprised, but I was relieved... It had worked for the Giant Eagle-Headed Warrior, which had been metal, but I hadn't been certain we could hurt a sword.

The sword bounced back, twirled in the air, and righted itself, but it didn't come in immediately for another attack. It waited there, suspended in midair.

"*Pant, pant...* Those mechanical arms just now... What were—?"

"Seraphina, I'll explain later. It's coming again!" I shouted.

"I can dodge. I have to make it easier for her!" said Igarashi.

"Don't push yourself! This enemy's attacks aren't normal!" I called.

Elitia and Igarashi advanced. I knew Elitia could keep up with the sword if she used her skills to speed up. Igarashi could help draw some attacks, since she could use Mirage Step to evade. We needed to end this quickly.

"The damage from my skills is as effective as it has been! Find an opening and attack—," I started.

"—?!"

The sword's next target was Elitia. She reacted immediately, bringing the Scarlet Emperor up to stop the blade.

"Argh!"

Slash, parry, thrust. The sword's attacks came one after another, forcing Elitia to defend, unable to counterattack. Blocking a swing with her sword apparently didn't count as an attack, as there wasn't any set damage from my skills.

*We need to break this up and make an opening... But we can't use projectiles. The only thing that would hit for sure...*

If Auto-Hit always landed, then it would still be able to hit that sword, but there was no way to break into their close combat.

"Ellie, fall back!" called Igarashi.

"Kyouka...!" answered Elitia.

Igarashi's movements were significantly different from before; she was moving much more quickly.

*That's right, her abilities are increased with Wolf Pack... She can probably break into their fight with an attack!*

"Hyaaaa!"

◆Current Status◆
> KYOUKA activated DOUBLE ATTACK
> ?INTELLIGENT WEAPON evaded Stage 1
> Stage 2 hit ?INTELLIGENT WEAPON
11 support damage
> ?INTELLIGENT WEAPON activated COUNTER SLASH
> KYOUKA activated MIRAGE STEP → Evaded COUNTER SLASH

"Gah... I dodged it, but it's so fast!" said Igarashi.

Everyone put some distance between them and the sword for a moment. It wasn't just the physical attacks from the sword that were dangerous—there was also the lightning surrounding it. It would be bad to get too close.

Seraphina adjusted her stance and fell back into battle formation. She had been able to stop the first frightening attack... But the enemy moved too fast, making it difficult to get in any significant amount of damage.

*If we can draw its attention, we can get in Elitia's Blossom Blade and our attacks. We have to stop its movement somehow...*

The floating sword readied itself for another attack. That's when Seraphina activated the skill she'd told me about earlier.

◆Current Status◆
> SERAPHINA activated PROVOKE → ?INTELLIGENT WEAPON'S hostility toward SERAPHINA increased

> Seraphina activated Ready Counter ⟶ Probability
  of counter success increased
> Seraphina activated Immovable Mass ⟶ Knockback
  effects nullified
> Seraphina activated Suppressing March ⟶ ?Intelligent
  Weapon's movement range was impeded

"I won't let it pass me. I'll stop it here in the front!" shouted Seraphina.

"Everyone, Seraphina's going to take the attack like the first time. When she does, concentrate your fire on it! Igarashi, Theresia, Misaki, use your Morale Discharges!"

"Okay! Let's do this, everyone... Soul Mirage!"

"...!"

"Thanks for not forgetting me... Fortune Roll!"

◆Current Status◆
> Kyouka activated Soul Mirage ⟶ All party
  members gained a Mirage Warrior
> Theresia activated Triple Steal ⟶ All party
  members received Triple Steal effects
> Misaki activated Fortune Roll ⟶ Next action
  will succeed automatically

A mirage warrior appeared for each member, and our total number of attacks doubled. Seraphina was surprised but seemed to understand what was going on right after. I was watching the enemy for the moment it started to move... Seraphina would stop the attack, and we'd counter with everything we had. We couldn't miss our chance.

## Part V: Reversal

Eight party members and eight mirage warriors totaled sixteen people. If we all attacked at once, we'd have incredible firepower, even if only the set damage made it through the enemy's defenses.

"I will stop you!" cried Seraphina, having used a skill to instigate the enemy's hostility. Almost as if it were responding to her words, the sword turned its edge toward her and started rotating violently, like the wheel of a speeding car.

"Seraphina, use your mirage warrior! It'll act according to your will!" instructed Igarashi.

"Mirage warrior...? Is this like my clone...? If so..." I realized then that I could've improved our tactical abilities if I'd taken Cooperation Support... But we could win this fight with what we had available now.

◆Current Status◆
> Seraphina activated Aura Shield
> Seraphina's Mirage Warrior activated a halved Aura Shield
> Aura Shield's effects were strengthened

The mirage warrior's skills were half as strong as the original. Even so, it was a significant increase to the strength of the shield of light emanating from Seraphina's riot shield as it joined the light from the mirage warrior's shield.

◆Current Status◆
> ?Intelligent Weapon activated Wheel Slash

"Wha—?!"

It wasn't just a weapon. It was intelligent, and it could use skills. Our skills seemed to ignore the laws of physics, and this sword's skills were, in the same way, far beyond anything we could have imagined.

*Full-body...no, multiple attacks!*

The spinning blade unleashed attack after attack like an automatic rifle, and it wasn't just Seraphina it was aiming for. Elitia and Igarashi were behind her and within the arching path of the blade, but—

"I said I will stop you here!" roared Seraphina.

"Ariadne, help us!" I called.

◆Current Status◆
> Seraphina activated Defense Force
> Seraphina's defense scope widened
> Arihito requested temporary support from Ariadne ⟶ Target: Seraphina
> Ariadne activated Twin Guard Arms
> Arihito activated Defense Support 1 ⟶ Target: Seraphina

> Stage 1 hit Seraphina
No damage
> Stage 2 hit Seraphina
No damage
> Stage 3 hit Seraphina
No damage

```
> Stage 4 hit SERAPHINA
No damage
```

It was like an immobile shield, a wall that no one could pass. The surface area of her shield expanded and defended against each of the attacks from the spinning blade. The two Guard Arms grabbed one each, stopping them in place. Two remaining strikes crashed into Seraphina's shield, but—

"Seraphina!" cried Elitia. The attacks didn't stop at the fourth stage. The final attack landed, and Seraphina shook violently, but she did not fall. She cried out, her hair in disarray.

"I'm not going down! Haaaaah!"

```
◆Current Status◆
> Stage 5 hit SERAPHINA
> SERAPHINA activated FANATIC  ⟶ Abilities improved
> SERAPHINA activated SHIELD SLAM ⟶ Hit ?INTELLIGENT
  WEAPON
11 support damage
> ?INTELLIGENT WEAPON was STUNNED
> SERAPHINA recovered vitality and magic
Failed to steal loot
```

The attack from Seraphina's full-body shield stopped the sword's rotation. Seraphina hadn't missed her opportunity to counterattack in the short moment the sword slowed after finishing its attack. Her body glowed slightly as she recovered the portion of damage she did with the counter.

She made an opening for us. We intentionally staggered our

attacks to hit it with a continuous stream. First up was Elitia, sped up with her Sonic Raid, along with her mirage warrior. Next came Igarashi with her spear, followed by Cion, who was in the third rank.

"—I'll cut you down!"

"Hyaa!"

"Awooo!"

```
◆Current Status◆
> Elitia activated Blossom Blade
> 12 stages hit ?Intelligent Weapon
Additional Mirage Warrior attack
264 support damage
> Kyouka activated Double Attack
> 2 stages hit ?Intelligent Weapon
Additional Mirage Warrior attack
44 support damage
> Cion activated Cross Claw
> 2 stages hit ?Intelligent Weapon
Additional Mirage Warrior attack
44 support damage
> Elitia recovered vitality and magic
Successfully stole loot
> Kyouka recovered vitality and magic
No loot in target's possession to steal
> Cion recovered vitality and magic
No loot in target's possession to steal
```

Raging attacks sent sparks raining from the sword, but it still seemed in good condition despite it all. A membrane-like barrier of light appeared to protect it from the blows. The party carved away at the barrier, but it still held intact. I tried to give the order for the remaining four of us to combine our attacks, but there was a vague sense of unease in the back of my mind.

"Suzuna! Misaki!" I shouted.

""Okay!"" they replied. I could have given the order to Theresia as well, but I expected her to act on her own without it. She hadn't attacked yet, and I couldn't help feeling there was some significant reason behind this choice.

*The three of us will corner it...and push through!*

◆Current Status◆
> Misaki's attack hit ?Intelligent Weapon
Additional Mirage Warrior attack
22 support damage
> Suzuna activated Auto-Hit ⟶ Next two shots
  will automatically hit
> Suzuna's attack hit ?Intelligent Weapon
Additional Mirage Warrior attack
22 support damage
> Misaki recovered vitality and magic
No loot in target's possession to steal
> Suzuna recovered vitality and magic
No loot in target's possession to steal

"I hit it! B-but...it didn't really do much...," said Misaki.

"My arrow didn't land... It only works with your help, Arihito...," added Suzuna.

My Attack Support should be working. If I shot my slingshot, we'd get in one more set of attacks.

*But... What is this terrible feeling...? Wait!*

◆Current Status◆
> ?Intelligent Weapon deployed an emergency
  evasion ⟶ ?Intelligent Weapon recovered from
  its status ailments
> ?Intelligent Weapon activated Birdcage

The sword we'd just been attacking suddenly split into a number of swords and surrounded the entire party.

"Wha—?" I murmured.

"Arihito, run!" cried Elitia. "This thing's attack will—!"

◆Current Status◆
> Arihito activated Hawk Eyes ⟶ Detected real
  ?Intelligent Weapon

There I was in the very back, but even farther behind me, I could feel its fierce aggression. That was the weakness of the rearguard job. I was weak if anything attacked me directly. I'd kept thinking about how I needed to find a way to defend against that possibility.

"Atobe!" called Igarashi. I tried to turn around quickly, but I had no remotely decent way of defending. Could I block with my slingshot and prevent a fatal wound? But its attacks were so powerful that even Seraphina with her special defense skills and Ariadne's help couldn't completely block it.

*But I'd rather die facing it than get stabbed in the back!*

"—Haaaaaaaah!"

I looked over my shoulder, holding my slingshot out behind, trying just to avoid death.

"—!"

Theresia had guessed this might happen. She was the only one close enough to protect me. That's why she didn't attack and instead pulled backward, but—

*Theresia, stay away!*

I wasn't about to let her die a second time. I prayed she wouldn't approach.

◆Current Status◆

> ?Intelligent Weapon activated Meteor Thrust

The back of the sword lowered slightly, almost as if there were a person holding it. The next moment, it thrust forward, and I noticed something. It was slower. It had slowed enough that I could likely twist mostly out of the way.

◆Current Status◆

> Arihito activated Rearguard General ➞ Abilities improved based on current number of party members

"Gah!"

The blade slid by me, cutting shallowly into my torso. It burned like fire, but it missed my heart.

"—!!"

◆Current Status◆

> Arihito evaded

Reduced damage

> Theresia activated Wind Slash

```
Additional MIRAGE WARRIOR attack
> Hit ?INTELLIGENT WEAPON
Knockback
22 support damage
> THERESIA recovered vitality and magic
No loot in target's possession to steal
```

Theresia rushed forward, sped up with Accel Dash, and pushed the sword back. The blast of wind made the sword drop, and I wasn't about to miss my opportunity. I put everything I had left into a shot from my slingshot.

"—Haaaaaah!"

```
◆Current Status◆
> ARIHITO activated FORCE SHOT (STUN)
Additional MIRAGE WARRIOR attack
> Hit ?INTELLIGENT WEAPON
> ARIHITO recovered vitality and magic
No loot in target's possession to steal
> 1 ?INTELLIGENT WEAPON defeated
```

How was I able to make the attack that powerful? The slingshot creaked from the force of my draw. The magical bullet I shot struck the hilt of the sword with a sound like a bullet from a rifle.

"*Pant, pant...* Owww..."

"...!!"

Theresia ran up to me. My hardened leather armor had been like paper to the sword. It was slashed clean open, a single gash visible on my skin below.

"Atobe!" cried Igarashi.

"Arihito, use a potion! Suzuna, can you do some sort of first aid?" said Elitia.

"Yes… I have some handmade bandages… But we should take him to a Healer clinic immediately," replied Suzuna. I was bleeding a fair amount, and it did hurt, but I still felt bad for making everyone worry.

The battle was over; the mirage warriors faded. I looked at the display on my license and double-checked what exactly happened to me. It was Rearguard General. That skill had activated, so I'd been able to keep up with the enemy's moves. And while I couldn't say I'd gotten out of it unscathed, I did get out of it alive.

…*It's all thanks to Theresia. She suggested I take the skill. Without it, I'd be…*

As the skill description had said, *your own abilities improve the more allies you have in front of you.* It's likely that the mirage warriors had been counted, too. Including my own mirage warrior, that'd make me the "rearguard general" of a party of sixteen, and my abilities improved accordingly.

Seraphina had taken a hit as well; there was a scratch on the metal plate of her headband, but I didn't see any open wounds, perhaps because she recovered using the effects of Triple Steal. I had recovered, too, but even though I had, that didn't mean I stopped bleeding immediately. The edges of the wound were starting to slowly heal, and the pain was beginning to subside.

"Incredible… I've never seen a rearguard capable of such damage. I feel like I'm seeing slingshots in a whole new light," said Seraphina.

"I can't always do that much; it really depends on the situation... But that was close. And I'm sorry for asking you to put yourself in so much danger."

Seraphina smiled. It wasn't the kind of face that implied she'd been forced into a risky situation. It was a genuine smile. I'd had the impression she didn't smile often, so it was unexpected, in a good way.

"I should actually thank you for allowing me to participate in such an extraordinary experience. I didn't know that Black Boxes could contain such enemies...," she said.

Cion was wary of the fallen sword. She came over to stand guard against it. I let the others do some first aid on me, then went to examine the sword.

◆?Intelligent Weapon◆
> Self-defense mechanism is dormant

I couldn't learn anything about it without having it appraised—or maybe I could have Ariadne take a look.

*...Dormant... So what happens if it activates? I really don't want to have to fight it again.*

The hilt of the sword fit in my hand, implying that I could, even as a rearguard, equip the weapon. But the slingshot was my primary weapon, so I should probably give it to Ariadne. If this was one of her parts, it might give her back a portion of her power.

I looked around at the pile of treasure that came out of the chest and at my companions, relieved to have finished the fight, and finally realized it was over.

## Part VI: Gathering Clouds

I realized that I was just casually holding the sword. That was careless, considering it could have been cursed. Though, if this was the armament that Ariadne told me about, she probably would have warned me if it were dangerous to carry. There weren't any issues in the end, so it was fine.

"Atobe, your knapsack is glowing...," said Igarashi.

"Hmm... Wh-what?"

I looked at the knapsack I'd thrown aside during the battle and saw that it was emitting a blue light.

"A-Arihito, the sword's glowing, too! You sure it isn't dangerous?" cried Misaki.

"It's not... I don't sense any dangerous spiritual presence. I don't think anything bad will happen," said Suzuna.

"......"

Theresia was incredibly worried, but as Suzuna said, I didn't feel anything ominous or threatening. I looked closely at the sword and noticed a cavity in its hilt. That's where the blue light was originating before it ran down the length of the blade. It almost seemed to pulsate.

*It's blue, or I guess closer to aqua... Kind of like the color of Ariadne's hair... Is this a sign that it's connected to the Hidden Gods?*

Glowing inside my knapsack was the alkaid crystal. Ariadne had said that was a *"sacred operation crystal"* for a sword. This sword was really more of a katana, but I felt safe assuming that they were treated as the same weapon in the Labyrinth Country.

"You think this stone goes in the hole in the hilt...?" asked Igarashi.

"...Careful, Arihito. I trust Suzuna's senses, but we don't know what's going to happen," said Elitia.

"Woof!" barked Cion.

All three of them were watching over me. Even Seraphina seemed uneasy about what might happen—her eyes never left me.

"...Mr. Atobe, are you sure it's all right for me to stay for something so important to your party?" she asked.

"You fought with us; I'm actually grateful that you'd be willing to stay even after the battle is over," I said.

"I—I see... If that's how you feel. I promise this will remain a secret. I am interested in seeing this, as a member of the party," she replied.

The moment I picked up the alkaid crystal, silent, blue sparks began to fly from it, though they didn't hurt to touch.

"Ah... No, it's okay. It's just... I feel like this is a way bigger deal than I'd expected!" I said, placing the alkaid crystal in the recess in the hilt. As I did, blue circuit board–like lines spread across the surface of the sword, and its shape changed. The blade and guard morphed from its current Japanese katana-like shape, greatly transforming its appearance.

◆Current Status◆
> ARIHITO is now the owner of ?INTELLIGENT WEAPON
> ?INTELLIGENT WEAPON's first Inscription is revealed to be MURAKUMO

*My name is Murakumo, the Gathering Clouds. I accept Arihito as my master and hereby fall under the Hidden God Ariadne's jurisdiction.*

"Oh…!"

The voice I heard in my mind was the same mechanical voice I'd heard when the battle started, but this time, I didn't feel any intent to destroy us coming from it. I released the sword, and it floated in midair, stopping where there was nothing.

"…There's a spirit in the sword…which is why it was moving like it was alive…," murmured Suzuna.

I made a guess as to what was really going on. The sword wasn't moving like it was alive. The only time the sword had really moved on its own was when it used the skill that made it spin like a wheel; all other times, it'd moved as if it were being used by a skilled swordsman. That was because of the spirit inside, Murakumo.

That spirit suddenly materialized in front of us. It was a girl, standing there and gripping the sword, looking at us with artificial-seeming eyes. She looked like a younger version of Ariadne wearing very strange clothing, completely different from anything a civilization such as the Labyrinth Country could make. It was a close-fitting bodysuit made of some sort of polymer. It looked mechanical in nature, and she wore some type of headgear with it.

"You…are the consciousness residing in that sword. Have you been hiding your presence until now?" I asked. She replied with nothing more than a slight nod. The voice I'd heard in my mind must belong to her. She likely communicated in a similar fashion to Ariadne, without actually speaking words.

"Woooow, that's so coooool! You look like you could go to outer space with that bodysuit, don't you think?" said Misaki.

"Yeah... Even so, I still can't believe a cute little girl put up such a fearsome fight," marveled Igarashi. Murakumo didn't show any emotions, not even at being called cute.

"She's like a solid projection. We couldn't see her at all earlier...," continued Igarashi, but Murakumo didn't nod. Perhaps she wasn't quite like a projection; it was more likely that she could choose to show or conceal herself, since she was a spirit.

I asked a question to Ariadne in my mind, assuming her answer could reach me here.

"...I am glad your party is unharmed. I am able to confirm that the Stellar Sword has entered my jurisdiction. I only hope that I was able to assist you," came her voice.

You did more than help. The only reason we're alive is because of your protection.

"It was an incredible feeling when I stopped the Stellar Sword's attacks with my hand and realized that we fought together. I am grateful to have met someone like you who would wish to become bound to me." I could hear more emotion in her voice than when we'd met. It was still faint, but it was a significant change from before. I thought that it might have to do with raising our devotion, but even if it didn't, it was a good thing to build a strong and trusting relationship.

"...I have received the confirmation code. I will use Murakumo as one of my parts. You, as Murakumo's owner, can equip the sword, or you can allow someone else in the party to equip it. There are limitations on who can equip it, but you will not find a sword more powerful even once you advance to District Seven."

Oh, right. Since it's your part, don't we need to bring it to you?

"It is within my domain simply by it being in your possession. I can summon Murakumo if necessary. If you discover one more part, my ability to teleport would extend to your entire party. However, there is one drawback in that you would lose your equipment when teleported."

That would still be useful in an emergency... Even better if it could be used in areas where we can't use Return Scrolls.

"Skills used by the Hidden Gods are fundamentally different than the skills that humans use and make into tools. In general, there are no places where a Hidden God cannot teleport."

The more I talked to her, the more I realized how big a deal getting this part of hers was. It really was a good thing we decided to try and open the box.

I finished my conversation with Ariadne and realized that Murakumo was looking at me—and that she was starting to fade.

"My manifestation only lasts for a very short time. Master, you must equip me and carry me with you," she said.

"Ah... Y-you can talk? Okay, so I can just take you along?" I asked.

"Truthfully, I should not speak. A weapon must remain a weapon."

"...Sooo cute... Seriously, don't you guys think she's super adorable?" gushed Misaki.

"Misaki, don't you dare try and hug her," I warned.

"I knooow, but... Something about her just makes my maternal instincts kick in..."

"...She seems even cuter in person," said Suzuna.

The entire party was crowding around Murakumo; everyone was completely comfortable despite the fierce battle we'd just been in. It was good to know that everyone was willing to accept her now that she was an ally of ours. Murakumo eventually disappeared as she said she would and didn't become visible again. The morphed sword changed back to its previous katana shape. I decided to ask Madoka for a special sheath so that I could carry it on my back.

"Woof, woof!"

"Cion... Oh, such a good girl, working so hard without us even having to ask!" cooed Igarashi.

Cion had brought the scattered equipment from the box over to us. There didn't seem to be many magical items, but there were some things that I looked at and thought they would be good. We'd probably be able to swap out a few people's equipment.

We spent the next two hours gathering the money that came out of the Black Box, finding a total of 5,500 gold pieces and another decent amount if we added in the silver and copper coins. There were even some coins I'd never seen mixed in the lot. We also found some equipment that I thought might be the equipment Polaris had dropped. There were a few magic stones of types we'd not yet encountered as well as two runes.

Falma had done so much for us that I gave her usual fee as well as a bonus of one hundred gold coins. I wanted to give her more, but apparently, she had a limit to the amount she could accept.

"There's no such thing as having too much money. There will be situations you will need it when you go up to District Seven, but one hundred gold coins is a huge amount for my little family. I would feel bad accepting any more for simply opening the chest," she explained.

"But it's because you opened such a dangerous chest for us. We really are grateful, Falma," I said.

"No, no. Nothing but incredible things have happened since I met you and your party. I have always wished I could go on adventures like everyone else, but it makes me so happy just to listen to the stories of yours," she said, making everyone feel a little bashful, myself included.

## Part VII: The Gateway

First things first, we called the Carriers to come and take what came out of the Black Box. We waited a little while for the Carriers that Falma called for us. The person who arrived was a man about my age with a friendly disposition. He might have even been Japanese. He looked exactly like a delivery person back on Earth—either he had been wearing that uniform when he reincarnated or he'd had it custom-made. But that wasn't very strange considering I still had the suit I'd been wearing when I reincarnated, and everyone else seemed to treasure their clothes from their life before.

"Hey, how's it goin'? I'm a Carrier from Golden Cat Corp. I've got a request to move unwanted goods from a chest for a Mr. Arihito Atobe. Is that correct?"

"Yes, that's me."

"I keep hearing about you. It was incredible last time. I was here doing the job with some newbies. I'd never seen an orc that ginormous," said the man. Apparently, this Golden Cat Corp. had been in charge of moving Juggernaut. The fact that they could move that mountain of a monster meant they must be transportation professionals.

"So I believe you've already taken anything of value you wish to keep, correct? Is it all just goods you'd like to sell?" he asked.

"No, I'd actually just like to donate the beginner equipment. Selling it won't make much money, and when I think of how it's likely that this equipment was lost by a novice when they were defeated…"

"Yeah… I know what you mean. The Labyrinth Country has its dangers. I can't even say that being a Carrier is safe, but we do have specialized skills, and I have the confidence to go and do my job properly even when there's some danger."

"That is impressive… Does the Golden Cat Corp. operate in District Seven as well?"

"Whoa, you're moving up to District Seven?! Congrats! That's right, Golden Cat's in District Seven as well, but obviously, the people in charge there are a higher level than me."

I told him that I hoped I could continue using their services and took a business card. His name was Naomasa Sakai—his card even had his name written in kanji.

"All righty, we'll start moving things, then. We'll process all damaged coins and deduct our moving fee from that. I assume you'd like the excess delivered to the bank?" asked Mr. Sakai.

"Yes please," I replied, and he straightened the cap he was wearing and descended the stairs with light steps. Behind him followed three people who were probably his workers.

"Mr. Atobe, will you be taking Cion along with you as well?" asked Falma.

"Well, are you sure? She's a great help to us, but she'd be wonderful at defending you and your family as well..."

Falma smiled, walked closer to Eyck and Plum, who had fallen asleep in their chairs waiting for us, and stroked their heads gently.

"They say that you must allow your children to experience the world themselves, without your protection. Astarte became this strong while traveling with my husband. I want to give that same experience to Cion... But if that's too hard to do, then like you say, I would choose to have her stay here with us," said Falma.

"...I think that would be a good option, too, but Cion has helped us so many times. I would like her to seek with us if possible," I replied.

"Thank you. Ha-ha... Even Cion looks happy. She doesn't do that too often, wag her tail like that."

"Woof!" Cion's tail was wagging vigorously back and forth while she sat there. I glanced at Igarashi to see how she was reacting, and she looked completely enamored with Cion.

"Awww, she's just too cute... I wanna squish her! Cion, you're so attached to Atobe... What can I do to make you love me like that?" she lamented.

"...I prefer stuffed animals to real ones," said Elitia.

"What did you just say, Ellie?" asked Igarashi.

"Erk... N-nothing! By the way, what are we going to do now, Arihito? We still have some time until Seraphina has to rejoin the other Guild Saviors."

Seraphina needed to go back before dinner, but we still had a couple hours. What could we really do with the time...? In any case, it was around lunchtime, so I decided we could go have some food.

"Urgh..."

All of a sudden, we all heard a gurgling noise and looked at one another. I was about to suggest to Seraphina we go get food together, when her stomach had let out the loud grumble. She realized she couldn't act like it wasn't her and pressed her hand to her stomach. Her breastplate was quite thick, but it didn't cover her abdomen, so I could see the clothing she wore underneath. Her armor was most likely fashioned to be lightweight, but I'd be willing to bet it was still quite heavy.

"...P-people with heavy armor burn a lot of calories... I usually need to eat at least five times a day. I didn't bring lunch with me this time, so...," she said.

"Do you always make food to bring with you?" asked Igarashi.

"Mm... No, but I do usually cook for myself. I generally cook at least two of my meals a day. My lodging has a very nice kitchen," Seraphina explained. She was speaking in a far more relaxed manner than she had been before; maybe the military air was only for when she was working. "I say *cooking*, but it's really just cutting some crusty rolls and putting vegetables and smoked meat in them. It's nice when I can get my hands on some cheese, too."

"Ooh, sounds delicious. I do like a good raclette, though I'm not a fan of stronger cheeses," said Igarashi.

"I've heard there are some people who can make Japanese food. I'd love to try it sometime...but I bet cooks like that are probably very busy," said Suzuna. She seemed to prefer Japanese food. I was fine with whatever, but I started craving something rich, like junk food, when I started thinking about the set meals from the beef bowl and burger joints I used to frequent.

"Well, how about we enjoy this last meal from District Eight? I'm hoping to move to District Seven tomorrow, so today, we can say our good-byes," I suggested.

"Yeah... We should make sure we don't have any unfinished business here. It'd be nice to say our good-byes to the people who've helped," said Elitia. She'd already made her way up to District Five. I wondered how she went about moving from one to the next. I knew that I was suddenly starting to feel nostalgic about the streets of District Eight, even though it hadn't yet been a week since I was reincarnated.

"Uh, ummm... I don't really mean this in some haughty way.

It doesn't matter where we go, since we'll be together. So we won't be that lonely... Um, oh man, what am I trying to say...?" said Igarashi.

"You're right. Our party will be together wherever we go. We'll never be alone," said Suzuna cheerfully. Misaki didn't even do anything stupid; she just smiled brightly. I decided these two girls, who seemed like polar opposites, got along so well because they understood how the other thought.

"...I would do well to learn from your party's inner relationships. I believe Mr. Atobe is able to maintain equilibrium within the party by not having too deep a relationship with any one member," observed Seraphina.

"Ha-ha, you know, Seraphina, I think that soldier-like tone suits you better," said Misaki.

"I agree. I find I can't get in the right mind-set when the time comes if I act too relaxed all the time," replied Seraphina. In a way, the Seraphina with her rumbling stomach was the most refined Seraphina I'd seen thus far...but that wasn't the face she normally put on; it was a rare occurrence.

"You know, it feels like you're already a member of the party," noted Igarashi.

"I know, right? But there's such a huge gap in levels, and she's a Guild Savior," said Misaki.

"There isn't that much of a difference between Seekers and the Guild Saviors. You can apply as long as your level is high enough, and you can leave the Guild Saviors as long as you provide them with one month's notice. I have been with the Saviors for about two years, but that is fairly uncommon. Usually, there's quite a high turnover," explained Seraphina, getting me interested in learning more about the Guild Savior system. I'd see what else she could tell me during lunch.

We went to one of the cafeterias in town and each ordered whatever we liked. Elitia and I both ordered grilled "Gun Fish"; apparently, that was a monster that was hard even for a level-3 party to take out. It had a barrel-like horn on its head, which it used to shoot pressurized water bullets. Its meat was soft and white with a delicate flavor. There was a higher-level monster in District Seven called the Cannon Fish, which was known as a rearguard killer... I guess I was grateful for the information. Igarashi must have started craving cheese from our conversation earlier, because she ordered pasta with a cheese sauce made from Marsh Ox milk, and Seraphina ordered the same thing. Misaki, Suzuna, and Theresia split a seafood paella, and one of the workers cut up a roast Sweet Bird for Cion so she could eat it more easily.

There were foods made from monsters that we hadn't yet encountered, but that was because they were hunted in one of the three labyrinths in District Eight that we hadn't gone in. Most Seekers only ventured into one or two labyrinths, but even so, they could spend days exploring and never make it to the end. The Guild's policy was to advance any party who went to first place on to the next district, instead of having all Seekers try and seek in every labyrinth.

According to Seraphina, once you advanced to a higher

district, you could request information regarding a labyrinth in a lower district. Though, apparently, dealing in information was an important source of funds for the Guild, so it didn't come cheap.

"The Guild has data repositories in the odd-numbered districts. You can submit requests for information to the librarians, and they will research it for you. I use it when I have the time," explained Seraphina.

"Is that like a library? I don't really like them because I have to stay quiet the whole time, but Suzu can spend hooours there," said Misaki.

"I like to read. I often went to my school's library," added Suzuna. I didn't hate books, either, so I'd like to visit it at least once when we got to District Seven. I was starting to feel excited the more I listened to Seraphina.

"I hope you're finding this information useful, Mr. Atobe," said Seraphina.

"Yeah, I'm really looking forward to going to District Seven now. Oh, by the way, you're level eleven—would that mean that District Four is an appropriate difficulty for you?" I asked.

"Yes. You are about two levels higher than is average for District Eight. Ms. Elitia worked her way up to District Five. Seekers there are normally level eight or nine," replied Seraphina.

"I feel this force when you ready your shield, like no attack could ever make it through, Seraphina. Level eleven... We'd have a pretty amazing party if we ever get that high," said Igarashi.

I thought it'd be nice enough if we could safely make our way to turning Theresia back into a human and rescuing Elitia's friend.

After that, we could live a pretty simple life. We probably had enough funds to live for a few years without working. Not having to work—that would've been the dream to me before I reincarnated, but if we stopped moving, we wouldn't be able to save people like we saved Georg and his party. Maybe it'd be best if we just kept our eyes out for chances to help people while we climbed our way to the top. If we didn't have the strength necessary, we'd just end up getting ourselves killed along with whomever we tried to save. I didn't want to ever lose my drive to become stronger.

"Well, if we ever manage to catch up to you… Actually, we still have that Savior Ticket. Would you fight alongside us again someday?" I asked.

"A-Atobe… We just met her. Don't you think you're getting a little carried away?"

"I-it's quite all right… It's a great compliment to a warrior to want to fight alongside them. I do look forward to the day we meet again, Mr. Atobe, everyone," said Seraphina. I would have been crazy to think she might've joined our party then, but I did imagine a day when she might come and act as our vanguard. Even if she didn't, I had every intention of reaching her level and growing.

Later that day, I reported to Louisa that we opened the second Black Box. She joined us for dinner in the evening, and we all went back to our own homes. Louisa would be moving to District Seven with us to continue as our caseworker, but she still seemed reluctant to part ways with us even though, in the end, she decided not to stay at our place. Everyone needed to pack tonight for the move.

We returned home to find Madoka, who had identified the equipment we'd received from the box. I had been hoping I could upgrade some things, but nothing was much better than what I had, meaning I didn't change anything in the end. We did get a lot of good magic stones, though. Three of them were new—a heat stone, a mole stone, and an explosion stone—giving us even more options for added attributes.

"I've heard a lot of people say they prepare backup sets of equipment as well as equipment that has different magic stones for the different labyrinths they go in," said Madoka.

"Ah, that's a good idea. We'll keep this equipment in the storage unit, then. It might be a good idea to get some shelves in there and organize things. Madoka, do you think you could refit the storage unit? I'll give you a budget for it, and it's not a huge rush; it can wait until after we go to District Seven," I said.

"Y-yes, thank you for trusting me with such an important task." She seemed grateful, but it should be the other way around because it'd be a huge help if she did that for us. I decided I'd like to act as her investor for her to be able to try out things she wanted to do.

Standing nearby and listening to our conversation was Melissa, who looked a bit jealous.

"...Hope I can be helpful soon, too. I haven't done much so far," she said.

"That's not true... It's just that Misaki's skills have turned out to be surprisingly useful, so we haven't had a chance to swap out members," I explained.

"Ah, but you know, I'm just a weak little girl. I'm, like, really burned out after back-to-back days of seeking," said Misaki.

"Yeah... It is tiring. We should think about that actually, starting a rotation so that we don't get too burned out," I suggested.

"Then, I can join you. Dissectors have skills we can only use while seeking. I wanna use those again." Melissa's voice was as flat and emotionless as usual, but I could see a spark of motivation in her eyes. Maybe she had a lot of pent-up energy from being left behind.

*Rikerton and Falma, thank you for trusting me with members of your families. I'll make sure they get home safely. It'll be a long journey, but I hope you won't worry.*

"What's wrong, Atobe? You're awfully quiet," said Igarashi.

"It's nothing. Once we get to District Seven, I was thinking of writing a letter to all the people who helped me out."

"Great, then we can all pitch in on writing letters. Although, I'm sure they'll still help you out even if you move on to the next district," said Igarashi.

"Yeah, I know... Sorry, I'm just getting really sentimental or something all of a sudden. I don't even know what I'm saying; I'm a full-grown man for goodness' sake."

Igarashi just listened without getting exasperated with me. The way she was looking at me with such kind eyes wasn't doing much to stop my meaningless rambling.

"If you're feeling lonely, then you can go sleep in the same bed as Theresia. Or Suzu!" offered Misaki.

"Oh... Well... I'm happy to share a room with Arihito. It might feel weird not to at this point," said Suzuna.

"...Hmm? If you share a room with him, you're not going to... do anything with him, are you? He is a man; I'm not sure you've known each other long enough to share a bed..." I got the feeling that Elitia was hinting at something crass. It even made me not want to clarify what Suzuna was talking about. It's not like I wanted to share beds with anyone, though I guess I wouldn't say I'd never do it... As usual, Theresia was staring at me while I was conflicted with myself.

"......"

"...I—I mean, it's not that unusual for people to take baths together, but sharing a bed is more...," I stammered.

"......"

My attempts to rationalize it broke against her silent judgment, and no one seemed inclined to throw me a lifeline today.

"Today's the last day we stay in this suite... We should consider that," said Igarashi.

"Arihito will be in trouble if we try to stop them from taking a bath together. We'll just wait for our turn," offered Elitia.

"Wh-what's with you guys? ...Is Theresia now Arihito's official Back Washer? How about we pick who goes next by lottery instead?" said Misaki.

"Um... What happens if Melissa or I win? Is it really all right if we take a bath with him?" asked Madoka.

"...Hmm? Sorry, I wasn't listening," said Melissa, only responding when she heard her own name. She had been zoned out, entirely in her own little world. She didn't seem the type to feel embarrassed easily, but I wondered... Or was it rude to think that?

"…Sure you'd be all right getting in with an old fart like me? Theresia, don't pass out from the heat, okay?"

"I don't think you're old enough to be called an old fart yet," said Misaki.

"Exactly… A ten-year age gap is still acceptable," agreed Suzuna.

"…I'm worried about Suzuna. We ought to keep an eye on her. Right, Kyouka?" said Elitia.

"Hmm… Even if Atobe did something, he doesn't seem aware of it, so it's hard to blame him." Even I was a bit worried about Suzuna and her recent absentmindedness, but it wasn't like she was letting her mind get away with her during battle, so I didn't think we needed to do something about it immediately.

"Arihito, you should go warm up," said Suzuna.

"A-all right… I'll be quick, since everyone else has to go, too." Theresia stood from her seat and headed toward the bathroom. She seemed concerned I might try to make a break for it, because she turned back to check I was following. I couldn't keep her waiting, so I tried to show everyone a grin and went to change.

Early next morning, we finished making our preparations, then went to say our good-byes to Millais and the Lady Ollerus Mansion staff that had taken great care of us, even if for such a short time. The Maids of the mansion were lined up in the front garden to see us off. Some of them were even crying. Were they really that happy at our quick climb up the ranks? Or was it a show?

"I hope that you will find time to visit the mansion again; we will always be here if you do," said Millais.

"Yeah, we'll stop by sometime. Thanks for everything, Millais," I replied, shaking her hand and promising we'd be back.

We went to leave the grounds, and in came Georg and his party. They must have just been discharged from the Healers.

"Arihito... Leaving already?" asked Georg. He was there along with Jake, Mihail, Tyler, and even Sophie, who'd previously been controlled by the Vine Puppeteer.

"Yeah. I'm happy we get to say good-bye, though. I asked the Carriers to deliver your equipment for you. You should double-check that it made it to your room," I said.

"You'd even do that for us... Thanks. We owe you our lives. Sophie finally woke up yesterday, and ever since, she's been talking about how she wants to say thank you...," said Georg.

The fragile girl I'd seen lying in the bed with lifeless eyes was gone. Even her pure white hair was starting to turn back to its original color. I never realized recovering could have such an impact on that. It was originally a warm chestnut color, and I was starting to really understand how she had gotten the attention of all the men in her party. She was beautiful and gave off a laid-back vibe. She walked over to me, appearing nervous but trying to express something.

"...Thank you. If you and the demi-human girl hadn't been there, I'd...," she said. She remembered that Theresia and I had entered her subconscious world and fought. I didn't think a *you're welcome* would really cut it here. I tried to decide what to do, then eventually shook her hand like I had done with Millais.

"I'm glad you're feeling better. I'm sure you'll face your share of challenges, but I hope we can help out a little. Don't give up," I said.

"Yeah... We've decided to get back into seeking after taking a short break. We fell in the ranks, so we've got to spread out among a few smaller places to stay now. We have to work our way back up."

"That sounds like a pain, but you were once the highest-ranking party in District Eight. Georg was really upset before, but even he's back to his normal self," I said. His goggles had been repaired, and the cut on his forehead fully healed. He had been bleeding quite a bit, but the wound had started to close the moment he drank the potion, helping him heal it completely in such a short time.

"I'm a bit worried that Named Monster might appear again, but we don't want to quit. We chose the name Polaris to show that we are aiming to be the brightest star in the Labyrinth Country. We could never compete with you guys, though," said Georg.

"That's not true; nobody knows what the future holds," I replied.

"...I'd been under the impression that Japanese office workers were all corporate slaves, but that's not the case. You're more like a samurai. I've always admired samurai and ninjas." He held his hand out for a handshake. When he did, he noticed that I actually did have Murakumo, the katana, on my back and gave a whistle of appreciation. "Whoa, so you really are a ninja. That explains everything."

"Maybe I should've tried writing that job instead. I'd probably be pretty good at it," I said, and Georg's face cracked into a smile at our jokes. He gave me a firm handshake, then their party moved aside to let us pass.

"Arihito, don't you think your party should pick a name? It's easier for word of you to spread if you've got a good name to go by."

"Yeah, we'll think about it. See you around," I replied, and we left the Lady Ollerus Mansion after finishing our good-byes. We walked out onto the street, but Millais and Polaris stood there, watching us go until I couldn't even see the gate when I turned back.

In front of us was the soaring wall on the west side of District Eight that separated it from District Seven. We had to pass through the gate there in order to make our way to District Seven. We did see a few Seekers returning to District Eight from District Seven, but there wasn't a lot of traffic around the gate. We went through the process of confirming our right to move to the next district, then waited in front an iron gate so large that I had to crane my neck up to see the top. The doors slid open to the left and right, and we entered the passageway to District Seven.

That's when I saw her—someone I recognized. She was the one who'd guided us through the tunnel when we'd all been reincarnated and first came to the Labyrinth Country.

"Well, this is quite a shock!" she said to me. "You managed to qualify to move up to District Seven in no time at all. You've got the Labyrinth Country record for fastest advancement." Her purple hair was separated into two braids underneath a hat. She was wearing the same shirt and skirt thing she had before, this time with a jacket on top. I guessed the jacket was a uniform that the people who worked the gate wore, since I'd seen a woman in front of the gate wearing one, too.

"Do you work here?" I asked.

"That's correct. Oh, but don't get to thinking that I'm some mere grunt. I've got a decent amount of clout. I actually asked to be assigned here when I heard you got approval to advance," she replied. She looked at the party with a slight grin before taking my license and doing something to it. Once she finished, the words Cleared for Passage Through District Seven Gateway appeared on my license. It looked like it had space to display more authorizations to pass through other gates when you got approval.

"You should know, though, that District Eight is for the newbies—it's like a training ground the size of a district," she continued. "Just because you've made it to first rank in District Eight doesn't mean you can handle District Se— Oh, goodness. Here I am trying to intimidate you, and you're already flying your way up the rank here, too. These are record-breaking contribution points."

"I believe I'm currently rank two hundred ninety-four. How many Seekers are in District Seven?" I asked.

"Ten thousand. Being rank two hundred ninety-four out of ten thousand means you're already in the top. You'll even be able to use housing that isn't all that different from what you had in District Eight."

What a relief. I'd gotten used to the luxury of the Lady Ollerus

Mansion; it'd be a huge adjustment if we had to live in worse conditions.

"Well... I do wish we could chat more, but we can only keep the gate open for so long," she said.

"Of course. We'll be on our way, then..."

"Indeed. Now, this part is just standard procedure..." A mischievous grin played on her lips, and she lifted her arm like a tour guide to urge us onward as she announced, "Welcome, rookies, to the *real* start of your life in the Labyrinth Country."

# The Dissector and the Merchant:
## ~ Another Form of Auxiliary Support ~

Arihito and the party were off in the Shrieking Wood to take the advancement test and check up on Polaris. As the standby party, Madoka and Melissa stayed at the Lady Ollerus Mansion and waited for their companions' return. Madoka went to the storage unit to do an inventory check, where she realized they'd gotten materials from Death from Above during the stampede.

*This is what Melissa worked on... They said she was going to make it into armor, but it's not finished. I wonder why.*

She decided to ask Arihito about it later, then tidied up the storage unit before returning to the mansion. She went to check out the workshop in the courtyard but didn't see Melissa anywhere. Her favorite butcher's knife was wrapped in a cloth and set on top of the workbench. Madoka thought she probably just stepped out for a bit as she looked around the area again.

The inside of buildings where monsters were processed always smelled faintly of blood, making her uncomfortable. She was starting to feel uneasy for some reason. She thought about the time she first met Arihito in front of the Field of Dawn. There was something about him, and it wasn't just that he was Japanese like her.

It was something about his calm demeanor and relaxed tone that made her feel secure.

*If he were here now... N-no, they'd all think I'm a baby if I said that...*

"...Oh!" came a whisper from behind Madoka.

"Aaaah!" she screeched, leaping in fright.

"...Did I scare you?"

"Oh... M-Melissa, it's you. Don't sneak around like that...," said Madoka, straightening her head wrap as she calmed herself down and turned around. But there was no one there. A chill ran down her spine.

*O-oh no... How can there be a ghost here when it's still so bright out...?*

She didn't really hate horror movies, nor was she the type to be easily frightened, but she was having a hard time maintaining her composure, since she had absolutely no idea what was going on. Her knees gave out from beneath her, and she fell onto her rear.

"...Hmm..."

"M-Melissa...?" she asked as she heard a sound. In front of her appeared the shimmering outline of a person. There was a flash of light, and for an ever so brief moment, she saw Melissa, wearing not a single stitch of clothing. The next moment, she was properly clothed, wearing a bodysuit of some close-fitting material, her pale hair unkempt as usual.

"...Welcome back," said Melissa.

"Oh, y-yes, I just got back... Uh, um, Melissa, were you invisible just now?" asked Madoka.

"Yeah... I was testing a stealth suit equipped with a camouflage stone."

"W-wow... You can make some really incredible equipment, Melissa."

"I can enhance gear with magic stones. I can't add runes, though... Dissectors have a skill called Monster Crafting."

"That's so cool... I've been told that eventually, I'll get skills that let me make things to sell. Though, I don't even know what kind of Merchant I'm best suited for yet."

"...What do you think of the stuff I make? Like, in terms of merchandise."

"I think there's tons of Seekers in District Eight who would really want the equipment you make. The materials from the monsters that Arihito and the others defeat are really valuable, and the work you do with them is so precise. It's incredibly impressive... Can I take a closer look at the suit?"

"...Sure."

Her response was short, and her face hard to read, but Madoka didn't feel like Melissa was against it. She took Melissa's arm, running her hands over the bodysuit to examine it.

"I-it's both smooth and rough, but also cool and warm...," admired Madoka.

"Yeah... It feels weird," replied Melissa. "I think it has a lot of resistances. But there's a problem with the camouflage stone."

"Oh... Sorry, that wouldn't happen to be when you turn back from being invisible, you look like you aren't wearing clothes for a moment?"

Melissa replied with a small nod, then started to undo the fasteners on the front.

*Melissa's skin is so pale that it's almost pure white... She's a bit different from regular people... Like, something feels almost off. Why is that...?*

They were both girls, but Madoka felt awkward enough that her cheeks were blushing bright red, even though Melissa herself didn't seem to care. Her demeanor reminded Madoka of someone else in the party: Theresia. She was a demi-human. She always wore a mask that covered her face except her mouth. Her lips were normally pursed, other than when she was near Arihito.

"...This bodysuit has no lining. If I don't do anything, the camouflage stone makes it blend in with the surroundings. But when it does, there's a moment where you look naked. It's not usable unless I do something. I thought the lizardman girl could use it. She's about the same size as me," explained Melissa.

"Theresia's a demi-human, but that doesn't mean she can't switch out some of her lizardman equipment, right?" said Madoka.

"Yeah. Sometimes, when women become demi-humans, their masks don't cover their whole face. No clue why, though."

Other demi-humans had a masklike piece of equipment that covered their entire face and looked like their particular monster. Madoka started thinking about how when she heard *lizardman*, she thought of a half-person half-lizard creature, but Theresia just looked like a human wearing some lizard equipment.

But what interested her more was something she sensed from Melissa's words. She got the impression that she knew more than the one demi-human—that was the implication behind her words. And her eyes, which normally looked like they were focused on something far in the distance, were different.

Madoka was familiar with those eyes. They were the eyes of a child whose parents rarely came home, both too busy with work—eyes that couldn't hide the loneliness as they were reflected back at her in the bathroom mirror. That's not to say Madoka wasn't loved in her previous life. It'd been about a year since she'd been reincarnated, and when she thought back to her previous life, other than the loneliness, she remembered her parents' kindness and her grandmother's smiling face.

"...Are you crying?" asked Melissa.

"Oh...," said Madoka, realizing that tears were streaming down her face. Melissa wiped the tears away with her right hand as if it were second nature. "S-sorry... I just got lost in thought. What a mess, just crying over nothing. I'm not a child anymore."

"...That's fine. Better to cry if you can. I can't cry."

"Oh... R-really...?" Madoka wasn't sure if she fully understood, but she could tell Melissa was being honest by looking into her eyes.

"What's your name?" asked Melissa.

"Oh, uh... I'm Madoka Shinonogi. In Japan, this is how I would write my name." Madoka pulled up her license and flipped to the free-draw space, where she wrote her name in Japanese with her finger. Melissa responded by writing her own name using the alphabet.

"My dad taught me about this. These are Earth letters, and here's how you write it with Labyrinth Country letters," she said.

"I see…"

"Now I know your name, Madoka. I can engrave it into any equipment I make for you."

"Thank you. I won't lose it as easily if it has my name on it," replied Madoka with a sweet smile. Melissa looked at her and stretched her hand out toward her again, this time to pat her gently on top of her turban.

"…You smiled. I'm glad. It's good to smile," she said.

"Melissa…" Madoka had assumed Melissa didn't have much interest in other people, since her responses were always so indifferent. Her first impression of Melissa must have just been a misunderstanding. Sure, she thought Melissa seemed threatening when she used her huge butcher's knife during dissections, but that could just as easily be passion for her work.

"I'm not very good at smiling, so…I'm jealous of you and Misaki," said Melissa. "And Arihito smiles a lot when everyone's around, too. But sometimes, he looks upset, same as my dad."

"Arihito's always worrying about everyone in the party… That's why he sometimes looks upset or serious."

"Yeah, I agree. He's always been like that, ever since we first met." Madoka couldn't help but smile that she agreed with her.

And that seemed to draw in Melissa. She'd said she wasn't good at smiling, but her expression softened, her narrow eyebrows lifted, and her lips curved ever so slightly. She wasn't completely incapable of smiling. Madoka remembered how the time she spent crying had all but disappeared after she had been reincarnated and worked on the things the Merchants Guild gave her to do. And now that she was in Arihito's party, she thought she would cry over her past memories even less.

*...Mom, Dad, Grandma... Manami and Kurumi... I hope you're all happy and healthy. I'm doing my best here,* she prayed, then beamed.

Melissa didn't say anything. Her small smile had faded, and her expression was back to its normal blank self, but she stroked Madoka's head again like she enjoyed doing it.

"...Cion's nice to pet, but I think you're next best," she said.

"Uh, you think so...? But you shouldn't do it too much. I'm a professional Merchant."

"Yeah... I'm gonna do my best to earn the title of professional Dissector." Melissa stroked Madoka's head once more, then pulled her hand back reluctantly. The subtly sad gesture made Madoka smile. She looked like a cat whose catnip toy had been taken away—which would mean Madoka was the plaything. Something about Melissa's eyes looked a little catlike, hence the connotation.

"That's a relief; I thought you were afraid of me," said Melissa. "I'm not exactly normal..."

"Not...normal?"

"My mom's a werecat—a cat demi-human."

"Oh... S-sorry, but right before you said that, I was actually thinking you seemed a bit like a feline..."

"...That obvious?"

"N-no! I just thought you were cute... Like a kitty."

"Cute... No one's ever called me cute before."

Madoka was confused by Melissa's reaction. Just because she

couldn't express her emotions well didn't mean she lacked emotions. So why—?

*If Arihito can understand Theresia's feelings even though she can't speak...then maybe he can come to understand Melissa better. That'd be nice.*

Her mind was made up, expecting great things from Arihito. She wanted to become closer with Melissa, who had shown her such kindness. She wanted to let the others know what she was really thinking, how gentle a person she really was. That's when Madoka remembered why she was looking for Melissa in the first place.

"Melissa, would you like to talk some more over a cup of tea?"

"...Sure."

And that's how this Dissector and Merchant duo agreed to work together as much as possible going forward while the others were out seeking. They'd found their purpose as the auxiliary support party.

They knew the rest of the party would be in line to take a bath once they got back, so the two went to Melissa's house and used the bath there before going back to the mansion. Afterward, they were relaxing in their shared bedroom when Misaki came in, eager to talk to them, since they were still awake.

"Oh my gosh, today was sooo rough! There was this one party that was being controlled by some vine monster, and their leader wanted us to save them... With everyone's help and my own pitiful contributions, we just managed to pull it off."

"That's amazing, Misaki!" replied Madoka. "Since you're a Gambler, do you throw cards or anything? Sometimes, the Merchants Guild gets metal card weapons in their inventory."

"Wait, so could I, like, throw a card, and it'd go *kapow* and stick into the wall, then I'd be all *I'm off to go get some valuables,* like some phantom thief...? You mean like that?"

"...So cool," said Melissa.

"Hey, Melissa, are you actually a people person? I definitely thought you would think I get too worked up and always say too much, or, like, I get out of control when Suzu's not around."

"That's not true at all. I like talking to you. It gives me a boost," said Madoka.

"Me too," added Melissa. "I don't get to talk much to girls my own age. The louder, the better."

"C-c'mon, you guys... Things weren't all that great for me when I was starting high school," said Misaki. "I was trying to be all blinged out and loud and stuff, but it was all half-baked, and I only had a few close friends. But actually, I always wanted, like, a hundred friends! Anyways, starting today, the three of us are friends!"

"Uh... A-are you sure? I'm younger than you...," replied Madoka.

"...Friends... My first friends. I thought I'd never make any. Dad'll be happy," said Melissa.

"You guuuuys! Easy on the tearjerker reactions! You'll make your mascara run! ...Wait, you're not even wearing any mascara! And here I've got it caked on!"

"Ha-ha... Misaki, you're the one who looks like they're about to cry!" said Madoka.

The girls whittled the hours of the night away, each one of them imagining the party they would become in the days yet ahead of them.

Hello, everyone, Tôwa here. Thank you again to all my readers who have made it from the first volume all the way here. I'm glad we get to meet once more. I wanted to talk briefly about the changes made to the story between this and the web version. In the first volume, I explained how I made Igarashi kinder, which is something that's continued into this volume as well. I also corrected the data displays, which are really important for the seeking expedition scenes, and I tweaked some of the fight scenes that were lacking. I hadn't really touched on Madoka's and Melissa's emotions before and after they joined the party, so I wrote an episode focusing entirely on them. I'd like to keep writing individual stories about each party member whenever possible.

I wanted to express my heartfelt thanks to my lead editor, who has worked so hard on this book, as well as everyone who proofread the manuscript.

To Huuka Kazabana, the illustrator—thank you for your stunning visuals, which have enabled me, the author, to see the world of *The World's Strongest Rearguard* more clearly.

Lastly, as I'm sure some of my readers are aware, this series will be receiving a manga adaptation by Rikizo for ComicWalker's Isekai Comic Corner! It's looking so great that even I can't contain my excitement. Please, please go check it out!

I hope to see you all again in Volume 3.

Tôwa